SUPERPOWER

A NOVEL BY
ROBERT BURGESS

Robert J Burgess

NUAGE PUBLISHING COMPANY
AUSTIN, TEXAS

SUPERPOWER

COPYRIGHT © 2002 BY ROBERT J. BURGESS

All rights reserved.

No part of this publication may be reproduced or transmitted in any form or by any means, electronic or mechanical, including but not limited to photocopy, recording, or any information storage and retrieval system, without permission in writing from the publisher, except by a reviewer who may quote brief passages in a review to be printed in a magazine, newspaper or an Internet Web page or voice transmitted via radio or television.

Requests for permission to make copies of any part of this work should be mailed to the following address:

Permissions Department
NuAge Publishing Company
3319 Far View Drive
Austin, Texas 78730-3300

Or by electronic mail to — nuage@austin.rr.com

First Edition December 2002

ISBN 0-9725971-0-7
Library of Congress Control Number 2002095475

Cover illustration by: Stephen Bright

Printed in the United States of America
at Morgan Printing in Austin, Texas

Superpower is a work of fiction engendered from the author's imagination. It is not intended to depict any person directly or by association. Any resemblance to any person living or dead is purely coincidental.

The activities of the characters in this book, including the underlying conspiracy plot, are also created from the author's imagination and are not intended in any way to state or imply that such activities actually took place or were planned.

Acknowledgements

That this book was completed is the result of the encouragement and assistance received from my friends in Russia, as well as Jack Gilligan, Gina Podhorecka, and my wife Donna, who read through the manuscript so many times she can now recite it from memory.

Thanks also to Donna Van Straten, the only author I know, who helped me find an editor and printer and gave me excellent guidance based on her experience with her first book, *The Littlest Big Kid*, RemArt Publishing.

Special thanks to my editor, Howard Wells, for his patient and valuable guidance as well as his many inspiring comments.

To Harold

and the woman who dedicated her life to him

Dear Reader,

Superpower is my first Novel. Its sole purpose is to entertain you. I came up with the plot and wrote the first quarter of the book. Alex, Jenia, Tanya, Jonah, Solomon, Pavel and Mikhail wrote the rest. All of us are excited to hear your feedback.

The main character is Alexander Golubev, a young Russian lawyer buoyantly floating through life, paper on a puddle, now and then cresting on a ripple. He has a brother in philosophy, Buddy, who you will meet in the Prologue. I like Alex and Buddy. Hopefully, you will too.

Alexander's carefree life is devastated when he is assigned to work with the dynamic Tanya, but he has no choice. If he loses his job, he'll likely lose Jenia, mistress to Pavel, who meets Alex for love sessions when Pavel is not available.

Frustrated by his work with Tanya and playing second fiddle to Pavel, Alex drinks too much and foolishly antagonizes Mikhail, the most powerful businessman in Russia. Mikhail has plans to possess Jenia and become President of Russia. He will kill anyone who gets in his way.

Alex soon realizes that Tanya and Jenia are more than they seem. They move him around like their pawn in a dangerous game of chess, while they share responsibility for protecting him from Mikhail's assassin. Suddenly, Alex finds himself alone and unprotected with the fate of Russia in his hands.

Alex and Buddy say "Hi."

Prologue

Moscow – April 1998

Buddy heard it first. The white Shih Tzu whimpered, jumped from the couch and ran beneath the desk on the other side of the room. The office shook as the threatening growl of engines joined the woof, woof, woof of rotor blades.

The broad-shouldered, bald man with stunningly bushy eyebrows pushed his chair back from his desk, stooped to gather Buddy into the crook of his arm, and carried him to the window. The helicopter, laden with two missiles imprinted with the Russian Federation flag, whipped the early morning snow flurries into a blizzard with its rotating blades.

The office windows flexed in and out distorting the view of the Kremlin on the opposite bank of the Moscow River. The two helicopter pilots wore helmets emblazoned with the hammer and sickle, as in the days before Gorbachev and the bloodless revolution. The pilot raised his hand to salute. The man at the window returned the salute with solemn gravity. Buddy shivered.

The helicopter continued up the river past the gold dome of the partially completed Christ the Savior Cathedral and the noise faded. The man turned his gaze to the Monday morning rush of cars speeding past the Kremlin on the opposite bank. He studied the towers lining the red brick Kremlin wall facing the river. At the far left was the Vodovzvodnoya (water) Tower, one of twenty towers in the Kremlin and one of only five crowned with jade-green spires and five-pointed red stars made of ruby, glass and gold. Each star was decorated by a hammer and sickle and turned slowly, pushed easily in the morning breeze though they each weighed almost a ton. The tower was rebuilt several years after it was blown up by the French as they were retreating from Moscow in 1812.

At the far right the wall turned North toward Red Square and Konstantino-Yeleninskaya (Constantine-Helena) Tower, famous as the gate through which Prince Dmitry Donskoy led his troops into battle against the Tatars in 1380.

Beyond, he saw the bulbous cluster of colorful cupolas that identify St. Basil's Cathedral to the world. It seemed only fitting that St. Basil's was commissioned by Ivan the Terrible to celebrate the capture of the Tatar stronghold in Kazan in 1552.

His thoughts wandered to Minin and Pozharskiy, who shared a monument in the garden in front of the Cathedral. The two men, one a prince and the other a butcher, funded the Russian volunteer army that drove out the invading Poles in 1612.

He put Buddy on the floor, walked back across the varnished wood and sank into his oversized executive chair. From the gold case on his desk he selected an unfiltered cigarette, lit it, and inhaled the warm pungent smoke deep into his lungs. He shut his eyes and shifted back and forth to sink deeper into the soft brown leather.

Mikhail dreamed of ruling Russia. He would replace the red stars on the towers and return the double-headed eagles, the symbol of the autocracy. Never again would Tatars, Poles, French or Germans invade Russia. Never again would the demented Soviets defile his city. Moscow's Russia would be the most powerful country in Europe, maybe the world.

The Opening
Massive Oaks From Tiny Acorns

Gaza, between Beit Hanun and Gaza City – December 1987

It took only a moment, but it seemed like eternity. A large green lorry swung into the wrong lane and slammed into an automobile filled with local Palestinians. Dust exploded upward clouding the air then drifted slowly, silently back onto the parched road. When the air cleared, the heat waves returned radiating off the sand and making the cinderblock houses in the nearby Jabalya refugee camp appear to sway sadly.

Shocked, a small group of Palestinian refugees silently stared at the twisted, shattered bodies lying on the road and the mangled mass in the ditch that was once a car. They squinted to protect themselves from the bright sunlight reflecting off sheared metal and broken glass.

Suddenly, shouting and screaming shattered the stillness, as refugees flowed from shops and side streets. A few rushed forward to help the injured and mark the dead. Like ants others followed. Their feet threw new clouds of choking dust into the hot midday air. Flies buzzed around the bodies on the road.

The twenty-five-year-old Israeli driver, crowned with a New York Yankees baseball cap, stepped onto the road from the dusty but almost new truck. He stepped to the front to inspect the damage and then turned to stare at the carnage. He jumped when the truck's radiator burst with a loud bang. Hissing steam shot from under the crumpled hood with an arrogant call for attention.

The refugees turned. They saw an Israeli, a killer, standing by his weapon, watching but not helping. He opened his mouth to say something, maybe "I'm sorry," but he made no sound. He steadied himself with his hand on the fender, stepped back once, twice, toward the small Israeli military detachment that guarded the camp.

The soldiers chattered into their radiotelephones, while they watched dispassionately but offered no help.

World opinion and the Israeli military police would later conclude that this had been an unfortunate accident. But for these Palestinians it was the last straw. The Israeli's immense truck had attacked their small, defenseless car. Their friends were dead. Israel had murdered them as sure as it had shot them with a gun. It was the final straw; the Palestinians had enough of Israeli oppression and privilege.

The crowd's protest began as soon as the bodies were covered to protect them from the sun, flies and dogs. Frustrated, the crowd mumbled, "Why do we die and the Israeli lives? Why is it always so?"

Their exasperation grew into angry calls for revenge, first against the driver then all Israelis. A few shouted, "Kill him! Kill the Jew!"

Like blood, they oozed forward through the sand pushed by those that followed. Now they chanted, "Kill them all. Kill Israelis. Praise to Allah. There can be no Israel. No more chains. This is our land."

The driver slowly shook his head from side to side. The mob moved toward him angry voices roaring like a hurricane. His eyes widened with alarm and he dropped his hand from the fender. Step by quickening step he backed away from the approaching crowd toward the soldiers and safety. A rock flew by his head. Instinctively, he ducked. Another rock landed near him. He turned, ran. A small rock hit his back.

A few Palestinians then hundreds threw rocks and waved knives in the air. They surged forward, a wave of pent up hatred splashing across the sand toward the retreating driver. The soldiers marched forward to protect their own.

This incident and the dozens of rocks thrown by this small crowd at Jabalya became tens of thousands throughout Gaza and the West Bank.

These spontaneous outbursts, instigated by rumors and incited by Muslim clerics, quickly developed into a well-organized Palestinian rebellion orchestrated by the PLO from its headquarters in Tunis.

The Palestinians were determined to shake off Israeli shackles. Soon bodies of Palestinian men, women and children piled high in the streets. Those left standing raised their arms to God and shouted, "Intifada."

Jerusalem – September 1988
Control the Center, Control the Game

Solomon Bashir scanned the faces of his closest advisors. For fifteen years the Orthodox Rabbi had headed Genesis, the largest and most influential right-wing religious party in Israel. This, his inner circle, was a cross-section of intellectuals from every political and economic sector. A few of them held high-level positions in Labor or Likud, but with a secret allegiance to Genesis.

Solomon stood. Everyone stopped talking. The morning sunshine streamed through a large window behind him. It splashed onto his back and created an explosion of light. The fourteen people sitting along the two sides of the varnished cedar table saw only a haloed black shadow. To Jonah Chizhik, at the table's far end, it looked as if the sun had anointed Solomon.

Solomon spoke, "Good morning, my friends. For a few of you this is a fortieth anniversary. For others, this will be a new beginning."

Forty years ago. Jonah remembered. Solomon had come a long way since 1948 when he and Shamir (Ysernitsky in those days) had led the Stern Gang.

Jonah was only seventeen then, a young man looking for excitement and glory. Solomon arranged for him to accompany Yehoshua Cohen to ambush Count Folke Bernadotte's car. Bernadotte was a United Nations mediator who, according to Solomon, had proposed an Arab administration for Jerusalem. Cohen killed the Count with a burst from his Sten gun. Jonah thought he saw one of the Count's escorts, a French Colonel, Serot, reach under his tunic for a gun. He jammed the muzzle of his gun into the car and killed him. It was a mistake, but how was he to know Serot was a good friend to Israel.

Solomon continued, "I've brought you here today, because Israel needs your help. Unless we take drastic steps, we'll share the land of our fathers with Palestinians who multiply like rabbits. In one hundred years we'll be a footnote in the history books. There will be no Israel."

Serot's murder led to a manhunt for the killer by Ben Gurian's government. Although some members of the Stern Gang wanted to sacrifice him, Jonah avoided arrest.

Solomon raised his arms to his shoulders and spread them wide, his palms facing the audience. "This land was a gift from God through Moses. We are the people chosen by God to worship here. Some of our brothers are willing to give away our land for an unsafe, temporary peace. No bribe of land will change the emotions and hatreds created during four thousand years of strife."

Solomon made arrangements with a Zionist friend in Chicago to provide Jonah a refuge. Through his friend, Solomon financed Jonah as he achieved a doctorate in economics at the University of Chicago.

Solomon put his hands to his heart. "This land is our synagogue. We have enriched our land with the sweat of our fathers, the tears of our mothers, and our own blood. We will fight to keep it for our children."

Solomon kept in touch and never let Jonah forget his destiny was with Israel. He owed Israel and Solomon his loyalty.

Solomon raised his right fist into the air. "We are God's superpower. We are the chosen ones. God's strength will invigorate us. We will live on this land forever."

Jonah had wanted to live in New York forever. He had a good career managing international investment funds. His wife and daughter loved the city and adored him. But a rain slick road upstate changed everything. Jonah was working rather than driving and protecting them. He buried his soul and his American dreams with his wife and daughter and returned home to Israel, to Solomon.

Solomon leaned forward and placed his hands on the table. "Some time ago, I chose you to help me build Genesis into one of the strongest forces in Israel. We have succeeded; our task is clear. I'm asking you to help me save Israel for our children and generations to follow. We need to make Israel a superpower, so strong no nation will dare challenge us."

One of the advisors interrupted. "Islam's armies would win any battle of attrition. With each war, they learn better how to fight us. Conventional weapons can't protect us forever."

A second added, "If we want to avoid using our nuclear weapons, our only solution is a preemptive attack to defeat the Palestinians, wipe them out. We can attack and make it look like they attacked first, like in sixty-seven."

Jonah pulled a cigar case from his suit pocket and withdrew a thick Cuban cigar. He leaned back in his chair, lit the cigar and took a deep draw. As a member of Solomon's inner circle, Jonah knew everyone at the table, except three. One, a black-haired woman in her early twenties sat next to Solomon. Jonah assumed she was one of Solomon's political assistants. The other two were young men, probably in their mid-thirties. He suspected they were active field agents for Genesis.

One of the political members said, "World opinion won't support us if we bomb the Palestinians. Even the United States, our only friend, has turned against us during the Intifada."

Solomon responded. "Our enemies have always surrounded us. We have always stood alone, even through the Holocaust when we paid the price for being Jews. It is our fate."

Another politician added, "We have access to all the military power we need from the United States."

Jonah disagreed. "As long as we depend on the United States, we'll never control our own destiny. We'll be nothing but a vassal of America."

Solomon raised his hand for silence. The background mumblings slowly died. "My friends, the solution to Israel's problem is not military. That is the way of the past; the world has changed. During the Intifada, our use of guns has made us a pariah."

He paused to let the audience absorb his words. Mesmerized, his inner circle watched the sun rise higher in the window. It seemed to rise from Solomon himself.

He continued, "Germany is now one of the most respected countries in the world, along with its partner in crime, Japan." He leaned forward. "Why is this so?"

Jonah answered, "Economic power forgives all sins."

Solomon beamed, "Exactly. We must become an economic power and quickly."

An industrialist member objected, "The Moslem block has oil money to finance weapons. Our economy is a shambles. We have no prospects of becoming a rich economic power."

A financial expert added, "It takes decades, centuries to become an economic power. It's not something you do quickly and you don't do it with less than ten million people. It's an unreachable objective."

Solomon promised, "God will provide a way."

Jonah felt blood rush to his head. He had heard those words before, forty years ago. What was the old man thinking? He glanced at the other members to see their reactions. The smokers nervously patted the ashes from their cigarettes. Others quietly stared at their hands.

Solomon spoke again, disregarding the comments. "Today we begin the process of changing the future. Each of you has a special talent that is necessary for analyzing our problems and finding solutions."

They debated for more than four hours. No one could convince Solomon his goal of making Israel an instant economic power was a pipedream. Some even murmured Solomon was old, out of touch with reality. Others, like Jonah, believed if Solomon invoked God, they would find a way.

It was late in the day when Solomon assigned Jonah to lead the industrialists, economists and finance members in a project to find and propose a solution.

Solomon brought the meeting to a close. "This project is important, maybe more important than the wars in forty-eight, or sixty-seven. I have arranged the funding."

Jonah took another long puff of his cigar. He was ready to repay Solomon for years of support.

Three months later . . .
Jerusalem – December 1988

The secretary opened the door to Solomon's office and motioned for Jonah to enter alone. Jonah walked quietly across the large room and stood in front of the patriarch. Solomon was sitting at a small table staring at a chessboard. He raised his head, and his heavy salt and pepper beard opened to make room for a smile. He rose and held out his hand. "*Shalom*, my friend, my son."

"*Shalom*," said Jonah. He nodded his head toward the chess set. "Are you winning?"

Solomon shrugged his shoulders. "Chess is like life. Often you don't win. You don't lose. You simply play the game to a draw. It's not so bad, is it?"

Jonah responded, "I prefer a winner and a loser, and I think you do too." He grinned, "It's time to begin the new game. I have the plan." He handed a wrapped package to Solomon.

"Tell me what you think," Solomon said as he leaned over and placed the package next to the chess set.

Jonah responded, "If we can pull this off, we've solved many of the problems you mentioned at our September meeting. If we're discovered, we'll destroy our country."

The two men embraced and Solomon returned to his seat. Jonah turned and walked to the door where he stopped, turned and said, "It's bold and it's feasible, but takes advantage of a window opened briefly for us by God. We must move swiftly. I'll be proud to lead it."

Solomon nodded, tore the wrapping from the package, and read the title out loud, "Superpower."

The Response
Queen's Pawn to D5

1

Ten Years Later...
Moscow – Tuesday, March 31, 1998

A cold heavy mist silently cleaned the soot-filled air and deposited black slurry onto the clothing of all who ventured forth. It was too warm for snow and too cold for comfort.

Alexander Ivanovich Golubev peered through the thick gray mist at the six-story powder blue building on the other side of Rochdelskaya ulitsa (Street). Alex liked the white trim, but he detested the large glass entrance door and the gold sign above it that read "Peterson, Hobbs and Dodd." The outside restoration of the historical building was well done, even though it was a mere façade, like so much in Russia since Perestroika. The building's inside was completely redone in a Western motif.

Alex was chilled after his leisurely kilometer stroll from the Krasnopresneskaya Metro Station, but his shivering was more from his nervous anticipation than the weather. He and four others stepped from the curb and began their daily game of chicken against the cars. They raced for the safety of the other side, dodging cars that sometimes changed direction trying to catch them. The final victorious step was a jump to avoid the dirt and water in the gutter.

One of the car dodgers touched Alex on the arm. "I've heard they are going to let some people go. You're in legal. Have you heard anything?"

Alex responded, "I've heard nothing. Believe me, it's probably only a rumor." He grinned to hide his own concern. "Unless, of course, I'm one of those to be fired."

Alex broke away and was almost trampled when he paused to wipe his feet before entering the building. Brown puddles spotted the gray tile reception floor. People raced to catch one of two small elevators, but Alex preferred to take the stairs to his third-floor office. He didn't like the climb, but it was better than being stuffed with a bunch of other faithful into a small, windowless ascending box that dangled from a thin cable.

Alex was an attorney in the administrative department, which employed over 100 people, including lawyers, accountants, bookkeepers, janitors and drivers. Like almost everyone else, except the American and European expatriates, he started at the bottom in ninety-three. A few months ago he had been sitting in an open space surrounded by other employees. But with his promotion to manager in July, he became one of the elite. His office proved it, although it was small by Russian standards. It had a window and only enough room for a desk and a chair.

He dropped his empty leather briefcase on the floor next to his desk and glanced at the clock on the wall. It was nine thirty and for Alex still early. He removed his trench coat and brushed his hands over his brown blazer. It needed pressing, as did his tan slacks, which broke heavily over scuffed shoes. He was pleased, because his blue shirt looked as if he had worn it for the first time today. He buttoned his sport coat to cover the small grease spot on his green tie and ambled to the window.

He peered through the mist at the back of Beliy Dom (the White House), a massive, marble-clad building crowned by a golden clock and the Russian tricolor flag. Not yet twenty years old, it already symbolized major events in Russian history.

Back in ninety-one, Alex was optimistic and naïve and joined the hundred thousand Russians who formed a human barricade around the White House to protect Yeltsin, Rustkoy and Khasbulatov. They forced the KGB, the army and the *putchists* to back down.

So Alex, clothed with a hundred thousand bodies, had helped to make Yeltsin President. For this, Yeltsin rewarded him only two years later by dissolving parliament and instructing the army to fire on the White House.

Thereafter, Alex watched from the distant PHD windows as the same group of Soviet cronies returned to power and continued the now centuries long plundering of the Russian people.

On the fifth floor, PHD's Managing Director, Carl Weber, was sitting at his desk reading his mail. He had a medium-build and was in his late forties. He wore only blue or gray suits, white shirts, and red or blue ties. As he did when he was in the United States Marines thirty years ago, he kept his shoes brightly shined.

Carl had been working since he arrived at seven thirty. He told others he came in early to avoid the traffic. The truth was he did his work between seven thirty and nine in the morning, or after seven at night.

Other than those hours, his day was always full. Beginning at nine, he would meet with his finance director to discuss the unpleasant news that their balance sheet still didn't balance. It never had. Carl had wanted an audit when he took over in ninety-six, but London said the books were too messed up to take the time. He was appalled when he found out that prior to ninety-six the company had posted rubles, dollars and pounds as if they were the same currency. Of course, nothing would balance.

By eleven o'clock, he would finish with the finance director and the parade would start. First one, then another of the American or British expatriate partners would shuffle into his office to whine about a fellow partner or some other childish matter. They were always disagreeable. Most didn't want to be in Russia, and had been sent to this outpost as an alternative to early retirement or as a condition for promotion.

Today, Carl had cancelled all morning appointments and closed his door. He instructed Olga to protect him from the sniveling horde. He finished reading his mail and placed it in his outbox. His desk was clear, except for an inbox, an outbox, a clock, which now read nine fifty, and, in the center, a personnel file labeled "Alexander Golubev."

Carl opened the file and read through the pages, especially the special section provided by Tatyana Gunina, one of his research assistants. He pressed the intercom button. "Please tell Alexander to come to me now, thanks."

He stood, walked to the forty-eight inch round conference table by one of his two windows, dropped the folder on the table and peered out the window. Through the morning mist he could barely see the six-lane-wide Kalinskiy Bridge connecting Novy Arbat with Kutuzovskiy over the still partially frozen Moscow River. He stared at the Russian White House near the Most. "White House," he scoffed, and chuckled.

Alex was staring at the rain rolling down his window, but his mind was still wandering. His thoughts of Yeltsin and the realities of Russia depressed him. He didn't want to be at work today. He wanted to be with Jenia. He imagined she was still sleeping and he wished he were next to her, to look at her, to smell her hair, to touch her, to kiss her.

The phone interrupted his reverie. Alex listened and responded in an irritated voice, "Yes, Olga, I'll come immediately. Does he want me to bring any — yes, yes I'm leaving."

He replaced the receiver with a shaking hand and sat down heavily onto his chair. Carl was going to fire him, he was sure of it. His felt his chest getting tight. It was difficult to breathe. His stomach churned. He scratched the back of his left hand. He saw it now. Carl would be sitting behind his desk and Alex would stand in front with his arms at his side. Carl would say, "I'm sorry Alex, but we must let you go. We have to cut administrative costs. If you go quietly, we will make some nice remarks in your work record and give you a good recommendation letter. If you cause trouble, we'll tell the truth."

Even before this morning, Alex had heard the rumors of a cutback. When the human resource culture consultants arrived, he was sure the cutbacks were imminent. That's how cutbacks are done in some Western companies, first the consultants then the walking papers.

What will Jenia say? She'll have nothing to do with a bum. If I'm fired I'll not get a job with another Western company. God, I can't work for a Russian company. I'll slave all day for a pittance, if I'm paid at all, while the company dies a certain death caused by the mismanagement of political appointees.

I'll beg, promise to work harder, take a cut in pay. I can't lose this job, this office, Jenia. I'll convince Carl I have important business friends and know officials high in the government. He won't fire a person with good contacts. But whom do I know who's important?

He gazed at Jenia's picture on his desk. The picture showed a tall, thin, dark complexioned, black-haired woman standing with a hand on her cocked hip. Her hair was cut short like a man. Her face, accented by a self-assured grin, was tan except for a small white scar on her cheek near her nose. She was wearing shorts and white tennis shoes that accentuated her long, well-shaped legs. The first two buttons of her red short-sleeved blouse were open. In the background were some couples in wedding dress and the Victory Park monument glistening in the sunlight. Across the picture was written, "Love Jenia."

Alex lifted the picture, held it to his heart and leaned back in his chair. He shut his eyes and saw her beginning to stir in her bed. She had great difficulty awakening until she drank her first cup of coffee. Once he tried to make love to her before her coffee, never again.

He opened his eyes and kissed the picture before setting it back next to the only other item on his desk, his computer chess game. He studied the chessboard and moved a black pawn to a different square.

He glanced at the clock, ten-twenty. He stood, reluctantly, and stretched. This is going to be an unpleasant meeting. I shouldn't have delayed so long.

※

The door swung open. Alex stuck his head inside and chirped in his friendliest English, "Good morning sir. Olga said you wanted to see me?" In the background, Olga was still scolding Alex in Russian for keeping her boss waiting.

Carl was sitting at the table and making notes on a pad of paper. He pointed to a chair without looking up. "Take a seat."

Alex sat down, leaned forward and crossed his arms on the table. He read his name on the file tab and nervously rubbed the back of his left hand.

Carl dropped his pencil and looked up at Alex. After a few moments he said, "There are seven financial industrial groups operating in Russia. My research analyst has prepared a dossier on each and the key people who run them. Do you know Tatyana Nikolaevna Gunina?"

Alex was surprised, confused. He thought for a few seconds and Tanya's picture finally formed. "I've seen her around, but I've never been introduced." He didn't volunteer she had a reputation; too serious, pushy, and bitchy.

"Her research revealed that the owners of these groups have been in Zurich at the same time at least twice each year since 1989."

Alex was relieved. He's not going to fire me. Something else is up. He felt confident again, even cocky. "So?"

Carl's face clouded. "It's obvious that something is fishy. According to everything we know these people are at each other's throats when in

Russia. Yet, they vacation together in Switzerland? It seems peculiar to me. I'm convinced there's a conspiracy."

"I don't understand."

"They're colluding on prices, exporting hard currency using unfair transfer pricing, manipulating auctions of companies and other schemes designed to avoid competition, taxes and currency controls."

Carl's financial mumbo-jumbo was boring to Alex. The pressure was off and he was having a hard time keeping Jenia out of his mind. He gazed out the window and saw her face in the mist. He heard, "Alex, Alex." The spell was broken. The face disappeared, and he returned his attention to Carl.

Carl said, "I'd like you to look into this with her. She can fill you in with more details."

Alex considered the prospect. I don't want to work with her. It will be terrible. Wait a minute. I have a higher rank. She'd actually be working for me. I'm a lawyer, a manager with an office. She's only an assistant manager in market research, and no office.

He grinned at Carl and said, "You say she'll be working for me?" Carl made no response. Alex pushed on, "Is she any good?"

Carl beamed and responded, "She told me you're still in the Army, and you paid a bribe in ninety-six to avoid going to Chechnya. You tell me if she's any good."

Alex was stunned and couldn't keep his eyes from showing it. His mouth moved to speak, but he hesitated. He unconsciously scratched his left hand. "Does she . . . does she know about your conspiracy theory?"

"It's her theory."

Alex said, "Why should PHD care? We're a consulting firm. We can consult with conspirators as well, maybe better, than with inexperienced Russian political hacks."

Carl stared at Alex for a few moments then responded, "If there is a conspiracy and we are providing services to the conspirators, when it blows up we'll be painted with the same brush of guilt. We'll no longer have a future in Russia. I want to know if we have any clients or potential clients who are involved in a conspiracy."

Alex shrugged.

Carl said, "Meet with Tanya today and get started. I want you to find out if there's a conspiracy and get some hard evidence to prove it. I don't want to drop a client and lose revenue based on hearsay."

Carl stood. The meeting was over. Alex put his hands on the table and pushed himself up slowly. They shook hands. Carl threw the file onto his desk and led Alex to the door. Carl said, "I'm sure you'll do a great job for me. I have the utmost faith in Tanya's abilities."

Alex winced.

"Your abilities too," Carl added quickly, too quickly.

Alex presented a phony smile to save face. He stepped through the transom and saw Olga glaring at him. He turned back. "I'm sure you're right. If there's a conspiracy, I'll uncover it and prove it." He peeked at Olga to see her reaction. She wasn't impressed.

※

Alex's door burst open and a thin, determined woman with light skin, green eyes and blond hair, marched in. Alex had been concentrating on his chess game and jumped as though hit with an electric prod.

Tanya was prettier than he remembered. She wore a well pressed tan business suit and low-heeled clean brown shoes. Her blouse was cream colored with no frills. Her only jewelry was a wedding ring. Even without makeup, she was attractive. With too much enthusiasm she said, "Ready to get started, huh?"

The way she said "huh" annoyed Alex. So did her entrance. He was surprised a research assistant would barge into the office of her future boss without asking permission. He growled, "You've been hanging around the Americans too long. Do you always charge into somebody's office uninvited?"

His comments had the desired effect. She stopped a few feet from his desk. Her smile disappeared. He snapped, "Well, what do you want?"

He saw her angry scowl, but it disappeared almost as quickly as it showed itself. Composed now, she sat in the chair in front of his desk and announced, "I'm ready to begin." After a pause she added, "I've been ready all day."

She stared at him, waiting. He realized getting the upper hand and controlling her was going to be more difficult than he expected. This one was sharp, like Jenia. Better to let her talk, until he assessed the situation better.

She continued, "I know you talked to Carl today. Why didn't you come to see me?"

His face turned red, his eyes narrowed and his jaw drew tight as he clenched his teeth. Before he could say anything, however, she softened her tone, "Or send for me, huh?"

Her attitude irritated him. He responded, "OK. OK. Yes, I talked to him. But I had things to do before I begin wasting time on your hair-brained theories. If Mr. Weber, Carl as you call him, wants to pay me for wasting my — ."

She jumped from her chair. "I've created a war room in the Annex. Let's go there and I'll fill you in, huh?"

This was getting to be too much for him. He needed a break to think. He was having trouble controlling this situation, and she was giving the orders, pushing him around.

"Go ahead. I'll join you later."

Her face flushed and her smile disappeared. Her fists clenched at her sides and her nostrils flared. She growled. "Listen, huh? I know you think this is a big joke and you don't give a damn. Well, if you're not going to be serious about this, go back to your two-hour lunches and the whores at the Knight Klub."

He was stunned. How could she talk to her boss in this manner? There must be something going on between her and Carl. Could she get me fired? She seems to know a lot about me.

She said, "Maybe I made a mistake. I'll ask Carl — Mr. Weber to find someone else."

Alex was angry but cautious. Maybe I pushed too far. Why lose a job over this trivial project?

He imagined the entry on his work record, "Spends too much time at lunch and drinking. Plays chess all day. No production." I'll be lucky to find another job. No money, no Jenia. Time to retreat and fight another day. He stood slowly and came around his desk. Best to pretend I was only fooling.

He put his hand on her shoulder. "Okay. Let's start over. I don't blame you for being frustrated. Let's get on with it." She glared at his hand. Maybe this was a mistake also. Maybe he shouldn't have touched her. He wondered if she was like those American bitches he'd heard about. He quickly dropped his hand.

She said, "If I'm right, this country and its people are in big trouble." She stared hard into his eyes. He returned her stare. Her gaze moved away. She looked past him to the chess game on his desk. He wondered if she realized no paper or other work was there. She nodded toward the chess set, "Do you ever win?"

He answered, "I get a draw every now and then, but I haven't beaten it yet."

She studied the board. She lifted the white queen and took the pawn he had moved earlier. She grinned, winked and handed him the captured piece. "I beat it all the time." She turned and left his office. Her words trailed back to him, "Sometime, I'll show you the secret."

He stared at the chessboard for a few moments and suddenly realized he was squeezing the pawn. His hand was sweating. He placed the pawn on his desk by the other captured pieces and followed her out the door.

By the time he reached the fifth floor, she was unlocking the door at the end of the hall some thirty meters away. She looked back, hesitated. Alex took his time to catch up; so she entered and let the door close.

When he entered, she was standing between three tables and flipping pages on one of four flip charts. A projector sat on one of the tables pointed at a large screen a few meters away. The Annex War Room was large, too large for the ineffectual heaters situated along one wall, and gloomy as it had only one poorly fitted window and a few bulbs hanging from the three-meter high ceiling.

"Come on. Hurry up," she urged. She motioned to some pages taped on the wall. Each page contained a different title, mostly bank names, and organization charts with company names in each position. He recognized the names in the titles. They were companies owned by the oligarchs, as the press referred to the most powerful businessmen in Russia.

She explained. "I've studied each of these organizations using various sources for my information. Oddly enough, the best sources were from the Internet and Radio Free Europe. As you can see, each group holds investments in different industries. But notice! All have banks."

He examined the charts, but wasn't impressed. "This is nothing new. It's been in the press, although without this much detail."

She removed a small metal pencil from her suit jacket. She pulled and it extended into a pointer. He rolled his eyes, but she was undeterred. She continued, "As you can see, I've focused on seven financial industrial groups — ."

"FIGs," he interrupted more to participate than to contribute.

She stopped, turned and glared like a teacher preparing to scold a boy who was talking out of turn. "Right," she responded. "Russian Jews chair and manage six." She stopped to let him look at the names on the charts. He knew some of them from the press reports and the Knight Klub.

He pretended to be interested, but his mind kept wandering to Jenia. All he saw was her face. He heard the pointer strike a chart and his mind returned to the war room. Still unimpressed, he sneered, "So?"

She inhaled deeply and continued, determined to get him interested. "These 'FIGs,' as you call them, control the key industries in Russia. They began by forming banks. As you know from reading the press, they loaned money to the Russian government, which used shares in major state enterprises as collateral. When the government defaulted on the loans, the FIGs inherited the best of Russia's jewels, steel, oil, and others. Look at these charts — ."

"It's almost five O'clock," he interrupted, "can we call it a day? I'm tired and can't concentrate right now."

She slammed the pointer onto a table. Her look scared him and he wondered if he had gone too far. She growled, "OK. I'm sorry if I've taxed your brain. Go ahead. Go soak it in vodka and watch the teenagers take their clothes off at the Knight Klub."

He kept quiet, even though he realized this outburst was enough to get any subordinate fired. Something bothered him, though. How did she know so much about his personal life? Did she know about Jenia? He stared at her in disbelief. Not to worry, he had won this first round. He had made her lose her composure. He was determined to keep his rather than escalate this confrontation.

She regained her control. Her face softened and she continued in a normal voice, "We started late today. Let's try to start earlier tomorrow. Can we agree on nine o'clock?"

He twisted his face. "There's no need to get huffy and disrespectful. I've some things to do early tomorrow. I'll see you at ten." He turned and marched from the room so she could not see his grin.

She stared after him, retrieved her pointer, slowly pushed it together and put it into her suit-coat pocket. She smiled, turned out the lights, locked the door and walked down the hall to Carl Weber's office.

As usual, Olga was on the telephone. Tanya entered the secretariat, waved and pointed to Carl's closed door. Olga nodded for her to enter.

Carl's face brightened when he saw her. "Well, how did it go?"

"It went fine; about as I expected. I've picked the right person."

He laughed. "Are you sure we're talking about the same Alex?"

She grinned. "Well, he's no researcher or analyst and he's a terrible chess player. But no one else will do; so I'll have to make the best of it." She waved good-bye and closed the door.

2

Moscow – Wednesday, April 1

Tanya's second day with Alex was no more productive than the first. He didn't show up at the War Room until almost eleven, and spent most of his time daydreaming. It was seven in the evening and just beyond dusk by the time she left PHD. When she stepped out of the front door, the wind-whipped cold rain attacked her face. She put an old cotton scarf over her head and tied it under her chin.

The sidewalk was jammed with people slipping and sliding on the snow and ice covered walks. Everyone was in a hurry to get home from work. She moved quickly, weaving among them. In some places, filthy wet cars were parked too far onto the walk leaving only a slippery narrow passage between the front of the cars and the stone buildings. She had to be careful to avoid them to keep her suit clean. She owned only two.

Other than at rush hour, the Russian Metro was a pleasant trip. Deep in the bowels of many Metro stations was an abundance of mosaics, moldings and sculptures surrounded by bronze, mahogany, granite and marble. The trains ran on time all the time.

However, Moscow rush hour was a swarm of people bumping and pushing their way through the foul smells. Summer was the worst. In summer, people wore no coats and the heat and humidity brought out the body odors. In spring everyone wore a jacket or a coat, which reduced the odor.

When she entered the Metro, Tanya smelled the wet wool jackets and coats mixed with stale air. The concrete station entrance was huge. The walls needed paint and the floor was worn and permanently dirty from so many years of use. She saw a large lake of heads emptying into six or seven small streams moving through the turnstiles. A lake formed again at the top of the steep escalator leading to the trains.

She caught the Koltsevaya Line and rode it for two stops to the Park Kultury transfer point. The station was a rushing mass of humanity and noise, as trains roared in and out. A man played an accordion in one of the tunnels connecting the different metro lines. A few old women were begging. Another woman was trying to sell some cute, thin kittens. Tanya transferred to the Kirovsko-Frunzenskaya Line to go the four stops to Universitet.

At Universitet, she left the warm metro station and was met by a mixture of rain and heavy wet snow. The damp cool air created a chill worse than cold. She loved snow in the beginning of winter. Then, snow made Moscow seem so clean, at least for a short time. But by April the winter snow turned to a dirty gray and black slush. She hurried toward the kiosks surrounding the Metro entrance.

"I can't wait for summer," she said to someone standing in line with her.

"*Ja tozhe*, anything is better than this," came the reply.

She was tired and wet, but she stood in line for five minutes to buy bread. At another busy kiosk, with an even longer line, she bought three Sturgeon fillets.

When she turned to leave the kiosk, a drunk bumped into her and almost knocked the packages from her arms. Some of his beer spilled onto her shoe. He excused himself, "*eezvineetye*," with rancid breath but the words were garbled. Before he spilt more beer on her, she jumped away from him and bumped into other people. "*Eezvineetye*."

She dashed along the six-lane Prospekt Vernadskovo toward her flat located in a high-rise apartment building on Krupskoy Street. The slush-covered sidewalks were slippery and cars raced by at over sixty kilometers per hour. She arrived at the corner and joined a group preparing to dodge the cars to reach the other side of the street. The darkness, the wind driven rain and snow, the speeding cars and an obsession to get home were all factors that could end a life quickly on a night like this.

During a small break in the traffic, she hurried with the crowd to the middle island. Tanya quickly glanced both ways and decided it was safe to proceed. She did not see the car approaching without headlights. When she stepped into its path, the car's horn screeched. The driver held the horn down to show his irritation. Without slowing, he veered and missed her by less than a meter. The tires threw black slush onto her suit.

She slipped and fell to one knee. She had water inside her right shoe. Shaken, she stepped out of the road and back onto the center island. Her heart was racing from the near miss. The people around her didn't notice that this young mother was almost killed in front of them.

The crowd surged into the street and she joined them. Her shoe squished as water oozed out of it. In the comfort of the crowd, she made it to the other side and safety.

"Almost home," she sighed relieved. It was a short walk to Building Twenty-three. Like many apartment buildings in Moscow, the entrance facing the street was barricaded to keep out the drunks and homeless. She walked along a small passageway through an archway to the rear of the building. The area was always unlit and she wondered when someone would be waiting in the shadows to rob or attack her. The rear entrance was a steel door, but the lock was broken and the door no longer fit properly. It was a heavy, squeaky irritation and provided no protection from the drunks or homeless.

Inside, the building was filthy and smelled of urine and stale beer. It was dark, because someone had stolen the light bulb months ago. No one replaced it; it would only be stolen again.

Her flat was on the tenth floor. The elevator had been broken since September, and she felt sorry for the old babushkas who had to climb the stairs every day with their bags of food. The climb was no problem for Tanya. She kept herself in excellent shape. Her real job required it. She went up all ten flights in a slow jog.

When she reached her flat she was breathing normally. She unlocked the door and entered. Her nine-year old son Nikolai shouted, "Mama. Mama's home. I'm so hungry." He ran to her and hugged her before she hung her coat on the wooden peg protruding from the wall. She leaned over, kissed the brown hair draping over his forehead and ran her hand affectionately over his head. He stepped back and took the bags.

Her husband Dmitry joined them. He was medium height, thin, about thirty-five. They were married ten years ago when she was twenty-two. She was proud of Dmitry in those days. He was one of the better riders in the Russian show jumping competition. He was also the chief engineer in the Moscow truck factory. Unfortunately, the factory closed because it was no longer competitive in the new economy. It mattered little, since he hadn't been paid for almost a year. Of course, the management was paid and found new jobs in the city government or started their own businesses. Dmitry had no job and few prospects.

He continued to search for employment, but Russian companies had little to offer him. They had little money and had cut back their expenses. To Tanya's consternation, Dmitry continued spending money to ride horses.

Because he didn't speak English or another foreign language, he couldn't get a good job with one of the Western firms. "If only I owned a decent car," he would say, "I could make some money as a gypsy cab driver."

He kissed her on the cheek and hugged her. His beard stubble scratched her skin. She smelled vodka. He had been drinking more lately. He whispered into her ear, "It's so nice to have you home." He turned to Kolya, "give me the bags." He took the bags and walked to the kitchen to inspect the contents.

She made her way toward the bathroom and heard him say, "I'll turn on the stove and heat the water. I'm sure everything will be ready for cooking by the time you've changed your clothes."

※

As he did almost every night between ten and ten thirty, Alex left the Pushkinskaya Metro Station and walked along Tverskaya toward Kozitskiy Pereulok. It was snowing heavier now, a wet heavy snow that clung to everything. He didn't mind spring snows, because the weather was warmer and the snow would soon be gone. He hated the winter cold. Sometimes, he wondered if he was truly Russian.

When he turned the corner on Kozitskiy, he saw the two-story stone building with the familiar sign over the entrance, small blinking white bulbs outlining the English words "Knight Klub." Painted beneath the letters at each end stood two chess-piece knights facing each other. One was black, the other white.

He saw five or six men, some in leather jackets and Levis and others in jogging outfits, standing or pacing near the entrance to the Klub. They were usually there and they all carried or talked on cell phones. The local prostitutes were approaching them to receive their assigned spots along Kozitskiy or Tverskaya.

Large dark Mercedes, Volvos and Audis arrived in front of the Klub. Drivers or bodyguards helped the well-dressed men out of the cars and escorted them to the door. Two scantily clad young women with big phony smiles greeted them. A tall, male bouncer with short hair and a neck that looked like the trunk of an oak tree motioned for most to enter. When Alex approached the entrance, the young women's smiles went from phony to genuine and the bouncer held out a friendly hand.

"*Privyet* Sasha, nice to see you again," growled the bouncer in a low voice.

"Thought I'd do something unusual tonight," Alex responded with a broad grin. The two women giggled and each planted a friendly kiss on his cheek when he hugged them hello. The bouncer turned to check out another man arriving in a large black Mercedes.

An explosion of music and men shouting at dancing girls met Alex, when one of the women opened the door and beckoned him to enter. Inside was one large smoky room with a brightly illuminated square bar in its center. Two dimly lit elevated dance stages were positioned equidistant along the walls on each side. Three doors under dim red lights decorated the wall opposite, but the dim lighting and smoke haze made it almost impossible to see them from the entrance.

Upon entering, ones gaze was quickly drawn to a two meter diameter gold cage that hung from the ceiling to about one meter above the bar. A naked girl, about eighteen, danced inside the cage.

Other than the bar, the rest of the Klub was set up with a chess motif consistent with its name. The floor, tiled to resemble black marble, was garnished with white square tables. Two white and two black chairs wrapped each table. Each chair was emblazoned on the back with a white or black rook, bishop or pawn chess piece. The chairs at the bar were taller and similarly decorated with knights. The stages were elevated about one-half meter and were about nine meters square. The floor of each was carpeted in a black and white grid, and a brass pole stood in the center from the stage to the ceiling. White and black alternating wood knights guarded the four corners. At each stage a girl danced and slowly took off her clothes as men shouted, waved and threw money. Young women dressed in skimpy black or white outfits served drinks.

Alex sighed, relieved. Chess at work and chess at play. He headed for the bar, which was almost full of new Russians and Klub girls who joined them. Drinks for the girls were twenty U.S. dollars a pop. Alex made his way to one of the few empty seats and blew a kiss to Monika dancing in the cage. She waved back to him and shouted above the music, "Hello Alex. Missed you tonight."

Sometimes he would arrive before ten and talk with her for a few minutes before she entered the cage and danced. She was a heavy girl when she started a few months ago, but now she was thin. Except for Sunday and Monday, she would enter the cage at ten and dance until three in the morning. She took a ten-minute break each hour.

The girls who danced in the cage had become famous. The new girls were always chubby or overweight. After about two weeks, the men saw the weight disappearing. After a few months, a much thinner girl would transfer from the cage to one of the four stages and a new, chubby girl would take her place.

The Klub held a special half-price drinks party when transfers were made. The men would cheer and the girl would dance naked on the bar and then provide a special dance at each stage. She would receive a lot of money from the patrons and five hundred U.S. dollars from the Klub.

Music battled to overcome the men who shouted and waved dollars. The bartender wiped the bar in front of Alex. Konstantin was a big man, at least six-feet four inches with large muscular arms that never stopped moving. Some patrons called him the tree. His blond hair was curly and short and his blue eyes twinkled all the time matching his perpetual smile. He had a friendly caring manner and always had a joke to tell. He enjoyed talking with his customers and knew everyone by name. "*Privyet* Sasha. The usual?"

Alex responded, "*Privyet* Kostya. I'm exhausted, rough day, need a drink. Today, I had to work with a woman who almost turned me off of women forever."

Konstantin laughed and passed a glass of vodka to him. "I'd sure like to meet the person who could do that. She must be real bad."

Alex nodded. He pointed toward one of three doors at the back of the room. "Is she?"

Konstantin gave a knowing nod. "*Da*. We've had some turnover of a few girls today and she recently finished interviewing some new dancers. God, I'd love to have her job. I can tell you they'd have to pay dearly if they wanted to become dancers." Both men sighed at the thought.

Alex knew Konstantin was joking. He would never treat one of the girls badly or take advantage of his position. One evening, Alex saw him throw out a drunk who had called Monika a fat pig. It was the only time Alex had seen him angry. He was like an older brother to the girls.

The rest of the men at the bar were talking or cheering for Monika, but Alex kept glancing at the door to Jenia's office. He needed to see her this evening, if only for a few moments. He needed something to take his mind off the ordeal of his day.

He motioned for Konstantin and said, "I need to see her. Do you think I should knock at her door?"

Konstantin acted horrified. "Are you crazy? She'd kill you."

The door to another office swung open and both men saw Pavel Mikhailovich Melninski step into the big room. He closed the door and stood studying the activities. Konstantin waved and Pavel nodded.

Alex had to admit that Pavel had a certain patrician bearing. Like many men in their fifties, he looked successful and confident. Alex took consolation Pavel was developing a paunch and his red hair, some of which had disappeared, was mixed with gray on the sides.

After a few moments, Pavel walked the few meters to Jenia's office and entered without knocking.

Alex lifted his glass and pointed to a dance stage. "If you see Jenia let her know I'm here will you?" Konstantin nodded and waved.

Alex sat a table near one of the stages, took a sip from his drink and waved to the dancer. She threw her top into his lap, leaned forward and pursed her lips to him. He threw her a dollar.

✼

Pavel and the bar noise entered Jenia's office. Eugenia Stanoslavovna Tarelkina sat behind a small French provincial desk at the far end of the room. She was making entries into the account books. She glanced up at him, waved and returned to her task.

In addition to the desk, her office contained two brown leather stuffed chairs positioned along one wall with a small table between them. Pavel crossed the room and sat in one of the chairs. He waited a few minutes then said, "How are the new girls doing?"

She answered, "They're doing fine. I mean, how difficult can it be to entertain drunk men by taking your clothes off?"

"A little testy tonight are we?"

She got up from her desk and came to him. She leaned over, kissed his cheek and sat in the other chair. "Sorry, I didn't mean anything by it. I'm simply in a mood. Maybe the job is getting to me."

Pavel smiled, reached to her and squeezed her hand to let her know she was forgiven. "I understand, probably better than you know." He leaned back and looked at the ceiling. "Funny, isn't it? Take a new job, for instance. For the first year or so, it's exciting. The next few years are full of work, but you don't mind because you're so busy. Eventually, it becomes boring toil."

She pouted and said, "Maybe you're right. It's been five years. I'm getting tired of sniveling, uneducated farm girls and drunken men. I'm weary of buying booze, bribing police, keeping two sets of books, and typing the minutes of your meetings."

He turned his head to look at her and smiled. "Well, my dear, most of that is what comes with managing the Klub. As for typing the minutes, I recall you volunteered."

She got up, kissed him on the forehead and walked back to her desk. As she idly flipped the pages in the book she said, "I'm sorry. I don't know what's wrong with me tonight. I like running the Knight Klub. Besides, Konstantin does all the operations work."

"The minutes don't have to be typed. It worked well enough before."

Her head snapped upward and she took a quick breath. "No. No. I'm happy to type them. I shouldn't have said that. I want to help you and the typed minutes are more professional."

"What's really bothering you. You seem restless, like a caged animal. Is it me? Am I smothering you? You know I want you to be happy."

Jenia closed the book and walked to the door. "Please don't worry love. It's not you. Maybe I'm just hearing the clock ticking. This will pass, I'm sure."

She left the room.

Pavel got out of his chair and walked across the room to the window. He stared at the dull yellow bulbs trying unsuccessfully to light the street. A heavy white snow, almost rain, tumbled past and onto the window. He saw the reflection of his tired, old face.

Hell, how much time can a Polish Jew expect to live in Russia. It's been eight high-pressure years. He remembered his promise to his wife Ivona, "Four years, five at the most."

The reflection showed his head shaking back and forth. Men, he thought, we turn fifty and our minds shut off for some reason. I can't believe I bought this Klub. Jenia's young enough to be my daughter. The work, the power, feeling young, I was too excited to quit.

Now it's toil. What's wrong with me? Even my relationship with Jenia is losing its luster. I don't seem to have the energy anymore. Is it me; or is it Mikhail?

※

Alex was getting bored watching the dancers. He couldn't seem to get out of his depressing funk. Why was I assigned to squander my time on her project? I've got to get control or I'll end up working for Tanya. She should be in the army; she'd be a colonel by now, maybe a general.

Conspiracy? Of course there's a conspiracy. Tanya should come here. Most of the people she has on her list come to meetings here. Pavel must be the leader; it's his Klub. I wonder if I should tell her that? God, no, she'd want to come here with me, embarrass me.

Poor Jenia, maybe I should warn her about them. They're dangerous, probably wouldn't think twice about erasing someone. No, she has Pavel to protect her. Hell, she could have anyone she wanted.

Suddenly, he felt soft hands over his eyes. A sweet familiar voice whispered in his ear, "I should scratch those wandering eyes right out of your head."

He grabbed Jenia's hands and turned around to face her, his face brightening. "Can you sit for a minute?"

She put on an exaggerated long face. "No, I have some paperwork to do. Two girls quit today. Konstantin told me you were here so I came by to say hello and let you know I'll be busy all night."

Alex frowned, kissed her hand and said, "Do you need any help with the interviews? If one of the candidates can't decide, I'd persuade her." He grinned and winked to make sure she knew he was joking. It was best to be careful, her mood could change quickly.

She rubbed her hand through his hair and smiled. "See you on the weekend; Pavel will be with his wife at the dacha. I need some of your therapy." She turned and walked to the girls' dressing room door at the back of the room, turned and waved before entering. He smiled and waved back. His heart sank. He had seen her, but tonight she would be with Pavel and he could do nothing but suffer the thought.

The dancing girl didn't interest him anymore. He returned to the bar to get some conversation.

Konstantin was busy, but tried to stop for a few words whenever he got a chance. Alex sighed, "I feel terrible, lonely. Do you think this booze is getting to me?"

Konstantin put his hand on Alex's shoulder. "Your problem my friend is you live for booze and women, but you can't handle either. You have to learn not to be serious about every affair you have. Be satisfied and enjoy the ride."

"What ride? I've got this great horse, but I seldom ride it. Someone else is in the saddle."

"Come on Alex," he chided, "You knew the situation when you picked the horse. Do you know how many other people would love to be in your shoes . . . or bed?" He laughed at his own comment.

Alex smiled. His spirits improved. "Konstantin, one more please. This is my last for the night." When Konstantin returned with the drink, Alex said in a loud voice so all at the bar heard. "You know, maybe I should find a woman who treats me with respect and loves to have sex with me. Every night she'd prepare a nice meal for me and then we'd go to bed. She'd give me a massage with hot oils and then . . . I'd marry her and we'd live happily ever after."

The men at the bar roared. Konstantin said, "What's wrong with men? In the first place it's unlikely, even in Russia, you'd find such a woman. If you did, you certainly shouldn't marry her. Everything will change when you marry her."

Alex responded, "Do you think so?" Again the men at the bar laughed. They were more interested in this conversation than Monika. She stopped dancing to listen.

Konstantin was grinning broadly. He almost shouted, "Jesus Alex, look at the statistics. Talk to some married men. The next time you think you want to ask a woman to marry you remember this."

He threw his immense muscular frame to the outside of the bar and bent down on one knee in front of Alex. He engulfed Alex's right hand in his left. He placed his own right hand over the top. He said in a loud voice so all could hear above the music, "My dear, I want you to stop being the pleasant sex starved angel you are now. I want to marry you so you can turn into a sexless bitch who spends all my money and makes the rest of my life a living hell."

Alex and the other men at the bar howled. One shouted, "God, I wish I'd talked to Kostya ten years ago." Konstantin rose, bowed, and jumped back behind the bar.

Even Vladimir, a Klub regular called Valodya by his close friends, got in the act. He wore an impeccably clean white sport jacket and a black shirt open almost to the naval. Three large gold chains nestled in the curly black hair on his chest. He was a short, thin mustached man with a dark complexion and a full head of hair tied in a ponytail. He would falsely deny in his effeminate voice he was forty and from the Middle East.

Valodya put his arm around Alex and nodded to a girl at one of the stages. "See that one? She's new tonight. Comes from some farm in the Ukraine. Probably still fresh. Why don't I introduce her to you?"

Alex responded, "You know I can't. I'm smitten and there's nothing I can do about it."

All the men groaned. Konstantin said in a fatherly way, "You poor soul. You'll go the way of all men. It's too late for you. When you have children, warn them before they're too old. You owe it to our sex or we'll continue to march the same path and be slaves forever."

Another patron added, "Willing slaves. Unfortunately, willing slaves."

Alex finished his drink and stood. "Thank you gentlemen. Once you admit to yourself you're lost, it's easier to swallow the pill."

Konstantin shook his hand. Every man at the bar got off his stool, patted Alex on the back and shook his hand. Each of the young girls who were sitting at the bar gave him a kiss on the cheek. "We all love you," one of them said. Monika was grinning from ear to ear. She blew him a kiss and he returned it.

When Alex turned to leave, Konstantin shouted after him, "By the way Sasha, do you know why Valodya wears those heavy chains around his neck?" He pointed at Valodya standing on the other side of the bar.

"No, why?"

"So he knows where to stop shaving." Konstantin giggled and turned to wait on another customer. Vladimir made an obscene gesture at him.

As Alex stepped into the snowy, chilly Moscow night, he admitted to himself his time at the Klub and the few moments he had with Jenia every week or so were the best things in his life. Still, he couldn't help but wonder if anything would ever come of his relationship with Jenia. She was on his mind all the time, when he walked, when he showered, when he worked, when he played chess, even when he slept. She controlled his happiness. Yet, she seemed content to stay Pavel's mistress.

It was still snowing, harder now. When he turned onto Tverskaya Street, he saw a small blond prostitute shivering on the corner. She waved and walked toward him.

"Sasha. I'm so cold. Couldn't you take me home tonight?"

"Lidiya. You look beautiful. I wish I had a million dollars. I'd buy you your own apartment and you'd never be cold again."

"Why can't all men be nice like you?"

"Hey, maybe I could talk to Jenia and get you a job dancing at the Klub?"

"Look at me Sasha! Those girls are beautiful."

"Maybe Konstantin would have something you could do. You could be a bartender or a waitress."

"And how do you think Sergei would react? He can be brutal." She showed him a bruise under her left eye.

"I'm sorry. I wish I could help you." Alex waved to her, "*Spakoynoy nochi*," and walked away.

If I were rich I'd buy a big farm in the south where it's warm all the time. I'd let them all come there to live with me. We'd be happy and I'd marry all of them. Imagine what Konstantin and the men at the bar would think, he chuckled. Imagine what Jenia would do, he grimaced.

3

Moscow – Monday, April 6

Alex was his old self again, revived by a glorious weekend with Jenia. He sat in the War Room drawing black and white squares on a tablet. Tanya would drone on forever on the most boring of subjects. "These charts give the background information about each of the FIG chairmen. Alex? Alex?"

He finished a square and slowly raised his head to look at her. He sighed, "Please, I'm tired. We've been at this for a week and we're still on the background material. None of this makes any sense to me."

She leaned forward and put her hands on the table. Her dark shadow covered his tablet. "Well, if we spent more than a few hours a day on this we'd be much further along by now."

He continued to stare at her analyzing her answer. He resumed his doodling and drew another square. He had created a full chessboard on his pad of paper.

Her shadow moved back away from his tablet. She walked across the room and returned. "Hasn't it sunk in yet? These men are taking over our economy. They're working together. Some of the highest government officials are involved. It may even be the sinister plan of some foreign government."

He raised his head, rolled his eyes and shifted in his chair. "You mean the Jews?"

She ignored the question and threw a black and white picture on top of his tablet. "This one seems to be the most powerful. In 1990 he was a university history professor. Suddenly, in 1991 he has enough money to start a bank. He is Mikhail Kolodkin, the richest businessman in Russia."

Alex barely looked at the picture. Besides, he had seen him many times before at the Klub. He was one of a group that met with Pavel at least monthly. Alex yawned into the back of his hand. She was going over old ground and repetition was not going to convince him.

She saw the yawn and sighed. Her son paid better attention than Alex. Doesn't he know what's going on, she thought? Doesn't he know he's about to become a slave again?

"Once these men control the economy it will be only one small step to control the country. Lenin knew this. His first acts were to get control of the banking and other key infrastructure industries. If we don't stop them now, it will be many more decades before we get another chance, if ever."

She pressed on. "Kolodkin's bank and others owned by this group of FIGs loaned millions under the Loans-For-Shares Program, which itself was created by the government under suspicious circumstances. I think the government defaulted on purpose. As a result, Kolodkin owns a number of large Russian oil companies and refineries. His friends own autos, steel, communications, and who knows what else."

He stared past her; his eyes glazed. If he concentrated, he saw Jenia's face on the wall. He had told her over and over he loved her. She said it wasn't true because he repeated it too many times. She's never said she loves me, but the way she makes love to me she must.

"Alex? ALEX?"

He moved his gaze back to her. She was tight-jawed, like a teacher scolding an inattentive student.

"It was a scam," she shouted.

She lowered her voice again. "It's like the whole scenario was planned out for a movie. This penniless history professor turned into a multi-millionaire overnight. He's now a member of the Duma."

Alex sighed again and wrote, "DUMA," in large letters on his tablet.

✤

The Duma was out of control. Buchovsky threw water on three Duma members, and began a fight in one corner of the room. The speaker banged his gavel again and again screaming for order. Masters-at-arms tried to immobilize Buchovsky to stop him from swinging at those around him. He was spitting at them and cursing.

Suddenly, the double doors in the back of the assembly room swung open and hit the walls with a loud bang. A raspy authoritative voice boomed across the room, "*Yapona mat*! What the hell is going on here?"

Silence. Everyone turned to see whose authoritative voice was heard above the shouting. At the door stood Mikhail Nikolaivich Kolodkin, a tall burly man in his early fifties whose most immediate feature was his bald head. Above his eyes hung thick, tangled salt and pepper eyebrows. He looked angry when he pulled them together, which he was doing now.

His bodyguard, Oleg, stood next to him. Oleg was a huge man who challenged anyone who met his glare. His muscles appeared to leap right through the fabric of his dark blue suit. Together, Oleg and Mikhail slowly moved their gaze left and right across the silent room. No one spoke or even cleared his throat.

Oleg moved first and led Mikhail toward his assigned seat. The members along his path nodded to him. He paraded slowly, regally down the steps. He didn't return their nods. He stared straight ahead, a king among his subjects relishing the rush of power surging through his veins. *My former students and fellow professors at the university are struggling to survive, but I'll soon be President of Russia. This Duma will not soon forget this day.* He stopped at his seat, bowed to the speaker and sat down. Oleg left the Duma.

Buchovsky shouted to the speaker, "Now that the king has arrived and taken his seat, can we return to the debate."

The spell was broken. Members of the Duma laughed and chatted with each other. Mikhail turned to look at Buchovsky, who stuck out his chin and sneered. *What a fool*, thought Mikhail.

He searched the room until he rested his gaze on Zyuganov, who was trying to control his Communist faction. Mikhail respected Zyuganov. Before Yeltsin's revolution Zyuganov was an unquestioning mid-level party member. Like Mikhail, Zyuganov had seized an opportunity. When Yeltsin and his entourage abandoned the party and started the "Market Revolution," Zyuganov filled the void.

Mikhail moved his gaze to the speaker and nodded. The speaker pounded his gavel three times to ensure silence. Mikhail walked to the front of the hall and took a position facing the audience from behind a podium. This was normal for him, comfortable. He had done this many times at the University. He gazed at his Duma audience, but in his mind he saw pimply-faced kids with wide eyes full of fear.

In a bass voice, made raspy by too many cigarettes, he began his new lecture in history. "Our grand experiment lasted seventy years and failed. Only fools would try to continue it." He waited, daring anyone to make a comment, but even the hard liners stayed silent.

He continued. "Some would blame our past leaders who put on the robes of the tyrants they deposed. They sabotaged our dream, but they didn't kill our idea. No, the idea was flawed from the start."

He heard soft murmurings of agreement and disagreement. Zyuganov seemed uncomfortable. Tyulkin, the leader of the Russian Communist Workers' Party, was shifting in his chair, his face turning an angry red. Mikhail glared at Tyulkin and then Zyuganov.

"Man must obey the law of the jungle. This law is simple. The strong flourish; the weak perish."

A few of the hard liners and Communists tried to interrupt. Mikhail frowned at the speaker, whose gavel hammered for silence. Amazing what a little money can achieve, he thought. He listened to the gavel fall again and again.

"The new battleground is economic, not military," he shouted above the murmurings. "The powerful countries today are those nations that have accumulated great wealth and developed modern economies. In those market economies, the weak continue to perish. The strong remain. With each cycle, the chaff is separated from the wheat."

Even Buchovsky was listening intently. Though he and many others despised Mikhail and the businessmen he represented, the word powerful had gotten their attention. All wanted Russia to be a superpower again.

Mikhail leaned forward on the podium and put his mouth closer to the microphone. "We are at war, one no less significant than those with France and Germany. The enemies have changed. The rules have changed. This is an economic war, but as dangerous as one fought with guns and tanks. We need new generals to lead us, men in business suits. Their powerful enterprises will bring us victory."

His speech continued for almost an hour. Twice he shouted down opposition. Many times he glared at his interrupters and they backed down. By the time he approached the end, the Duma was buzzing. Those members who agreed with him argued with those who hated him. Mikhail threw back his shoulders and shouted above the commotion.

"History will show. Those who arrogantly look down their noses at us today will rot from within tomorrow. We are the hungry wolves in their pasture. We will feast on their sated cows. Turn your businessmen loose. We'll lead the attack and the fat cats of Europe and America will litter the battlefield."

Cheers erupted from all of the nationalist factions. Buchovsky's face showed his excitement. He pumped his hand into the air. More cheers followed, this time even the Communists joined in the celebration.

Mikhail slammed his fist on the podium, his eyes glared at them, his eyebrows met above his nose. "If you want a superpower, you must have a market economy. You need generals, me, to lead the way to capitalism."

Many members booed and stood waving their arms for him to leave. Undaunted, he shouted as loud as his raspy voice allowed. "Socialism is dead. Your survival depends on men like me. We will devote our lives to make Russia strong and powerful again."

The Duma erupted. Friend and foe leapt up to cheer or boo. Mikhail waited a few minutes and nodded to the speaker. He slammed the gavel down again and again, trying to achieve order.

In the nationalist faction, a member said to Buchovsky, "Shakespeare had Cassius say of Caesar, 'Why man, he doth bestride this world like a colossus.' He also could have been talking about Mikhail Nikolaivich."

Buchovsky responded, "It is possible my friend, even likely. I fear for the future of Russia if such generals lead us. He is more dangerous to our country than a military general out of control."

Mikhail moved from the podium to the center of the hall and lifted a large package of papers over his head. "I hereby submit new proposals to eliminate taxes at the corporate level and on all capital gains. If you want a superpower, you must pass this bill. Otherwise, the money will fly from Russia as surely as the wind blows across Siberia." He spoke rudely, in a threatening tone, to let them know his plans if they did not pass this bill.

The Duma was now in full disarray. Mikhail swaggered up the steps and out of the assembly hall. He knew this group would never approve his proposed tax bill.

He had accomplished his mission. *I'll pull money out of Russia and place it into foreign accounts. It's their fault, not mine. Russia could be an economic powerhouse. Instead, because of them, Russia will struggle over the next seventy years to avoid the scrap heap of third-world economies.*

The door closed behind him. The loud arguing was replaced by the quiet of the hallway. Oleg led Mikhail to the foyer and out of the building. Guards nodded. He didn't acknowledge them.

Mikhail's dark blue Mercedes forced its way into traffic on Okhotny Ryad. The Gai raised his black and white stick to stop the other cars so the Mercedes could enter. Oleg, who sat in the front seat next to Ivan, made a friendly gesture to the Gai, who saluted back so strongly he knocked snow from his hat and shoulder. Mikhail's driver, Ivan, sounded the warning horn to demand other cars make way.

With its blue light flashing the Mercedes charged across the street and turned past the lime-green Nobility's Assembly Rooms building and proceeded toward Teatralny Proezd (passage). Mikhail was particularly fond of this building, which was constructed in the 1780s. As described by Tolstoy in *War and Peace*, the whole of the aristocratic Moscow would attend balls held there.

The weather was terrible, drizzling snow mixed with freezing rain. The Mercedes skidded as it maneuvered through the heavy traffic. The car sped past the Bolshoi Theater, with its classical white columns and piedmont adorned with four horses driven by Apollo, and the Hotel Metropole with its wrought-iron balconies and famous ceramic mural *The Princess of Dreams* façade.

Mikhail lit a cigarette and took a long drag. *I have the charisma to be President. Why not?* The thought sent a warm rush through his body. *Drugs are for children and fools. Power is for men. In Russia, President is the pinnacle of power like in America. I can be the Bill Clinton of Russia.* The thought made him chuckle.

The car reached Lubyanskaya Ploshchad (square), where Lubyanka, famous as the massive headquarters of the secret police, rises in tiers of caramel-colored stucco from a stone-faced lower story. *All leaders have a secret police,* thought Mikhail; *it is a necessity to maintain power.* The car sped into the square and made a sharp right heading for the Moscow River.

His euphoria was short-lived. *I'm dreaming of President, but I can't even become Chairman of our little group of operatives. In less than eight years I've built an oil empire for Jonah and his investors. I've become the Rockefeller of Russia. Yet, what do I have to show for it but a promised pension? They are throwing me a few Rubles, a pittance compared to the wealth I've created for them.*

I did all the work, but there is no appreciation. I continue to play second violin to Pavel, whose success is mediocre at best and certainly no match for mine. Why does Jonah stick with Pavel, instead of letting me take over and lead the operatives in Russia?

He ground his cigarette butt into the ashtray. *Why does Jenia stick with an aging and overweight Pavel? Is it possible she doesn't know that I want her for myself?*

Mikhail's office was located on an island in the Moscow River on Soliyskaya Naberezhnaya, between the Ministry of Oil and Gas and the Defense Ministry Reception Office. When he walked into the outer office, Galina said, "Sir, Pavel called to cancel his meeting with you at twenty-one hundred."

Not unexpected, he thought. He nodded to her and entered his office without saying a word. He closed the door and searched for the white blur that would be Buddy greeting him with a wagging tail. Nothing.

He opened the door again. "Galina, where's Buddy?"

"Don't you remember sir? You left him at home because you had scheduled a meeting with Pavel tonight. Do you want me to have Ivan get him?"

"No, no it's all right."

Irritated, he shut the door and walked across the room. He had moved into this building recently. Still, he could smell the newly paneled walls and fresh varnish on the floor. He listened to his shoes click across the polished floor until he reached the Persian rug in the middle of the room. From a holder on his desk he pulled out an unfiltered cigarette and put it into his mouth and lit it. He stood looking through the window behind his desk at the building housing the Ministry of Oil and Gas.

Amazing, he thought, eight years ago I was a poor man, happy, with nothing to lose. Now I'm rich and powerful and depressed. I need Buddy to cheer me up. He walked to the two large windows facing St. Basil's Cathedral on the other side of the Moscow River. He moved his gaze to the left from St. Basil's to the Kremlin and felt better.

The ringing of his secure phone interrupted his thoughts. It had to be Jonah. Mikhail, the other business operatives, and the governmental operatives all had separate secure telephones and lines to Jonah. Mikhail returned to his desk and answered the phone.

He heard Jonah's voice, "*Shalom*. I hope everything is going well for you."

Mikhail responded, "Well, it's been very busy. I just returned from giving a speech to the Duma."

"What was it about?"

"I told them they had to eliminate corporate taxes and give more power to successful businessmen instead of politicians. It was a waste of time of course, but it will make good press." There was silence for a few moments and Mikhail asked, "Jonah?"

"I'm here. I need to talk to you about the sale of the Samara refinery. As I recall, the open bidding is next month at the Petroleum Ministry."

"Yes, that's right, almost next door as a matter of fact. It should go for about fifty million U.S. Dollars, but it's probably worth much more. The refining capacity in Russia can't keep up with demand now, and with oil prices so low the demand will only increase. If we play our cards right, we may be able to get it for about forty five."

"That's what I called about. I want to tell you before you hear it at the business operatives meeting on Thursday. I've decided that Pavel will win that bid, not you. I want you to stop bidding at thirty five million."

Mikhail was speechless. He felt the blood rushing through his temples and heard the pounding in his ears. He squeezed the phone receiver so hard he thought it would break. The only response he could muster was, "What? Why?"

"There are a number of reasons, but the main one is I think this will enable us to get the refinery for as little as forty million."

"How do you figure that?"

"You're generally considered the most knowledgeable oil investor in Russia. That refinery would logically fit into your group of investments. It would make you king of oil."

Mikhail interrupted, "You've just made my case."

Jonah seemed to ignore his comment. "If you stop bidding at thirty five, the other Russian investors are going to have second thoughts. In no way are they going to go as much as fifteen million over your top bid. It would be too risky, especially considering you control so much of the crude oil."

Mikhail tried to keep his voice calm. He had visions of Jonah and Pavel sharing drinks and colluding on this plan. He saw them laughing at him. He growled, "The government will never let that refinery sell for forty million dollars. They'll cancel the sale unless it hits at least forty five or maybe even fifty."

"It's been arranged. They will sell at whatever price exists when there are no more bids, even if it is less than forty. Pavel is authorized to go as high as fifty million if necessary."

Mikhail tried again, "What about Shell, Exxon or one of the other major internationals? To them it is worth at least fifty. They'll continue bidding."

"No they won't. Before the bidding, the government will announce that foreign bids are not welcome, for national security reasons. Mikhail, we've thought it through."

Mikhail heard the "we" and almost screamed. He had to stop himself from asking. He wanted to run, punch someone, anything to stop that infernal pounding in his head. He pleaded, "Jonah, this doesn't make sense. Pavel is into steel and communications. I have control of oil, and with this refinery I'll effectively have control of fuel also."

"Mikhail. I think it's perfect. Everyone knows that Pavel isn't into oil. He'll say this is to diversify, but they'll know he doesn't know what he's doing when it comes to buying a refinery. Because you stop at thirty five, everyone will think that Pavel is a fool for bidding to forty." The line was silent, finally Jonah spoke, "Mikhail are you there?"

"Yes."

"Listen to yourself. You keep saying 'I have control of oil. I'll have control of fuel.' Mikhail, it's not important that you have control. What's important is that we have control."

Mikhail knew he had to get off the phone and quickly or he would say something in haste that he instantly regretted. He felt the adrenaline surging into his veins as if from a broken dam.

Jonah's voice came charging into his ear, "Mikhail?"

"Yes, I'm here. I'm dumfounded. This is ridiculous and all for a few million dollars. Everyone will be talking about it. In a few months, Pavel will look like a genius and I'll look like an idiot. That refinery is going to operate at one hundred percent capacity. It's going to generate barrels of profits and cash flow."

"Exactly! Pavel has some losses in his steel and communications businesses. We'll use his losses to offset refinery profits for tax purposes. We won't pay any taxes. I'm sorry if you think this will make you look foolish, but that won't last long. Remember, you're part of a group. You're not alone."

Mikhail tried again. "This is not a good decision. It's based on what you know living in Zurich. I'm on the ground in Russia and I'm giving you my expert opinion you've made a mistake. For example, the Russian tax law doesn't allow for consolidated returns."

"We've taken care of that too. In a few months, you'll see a change in the tax code allowing consolidated returns for certain companies. We have our government operatives and our tax consultants working on the wording right now."

Mikhail couldn't contain himself any longer. "I protest. I'll not do it. It's a bad decision and I'll not go along. Who's the expert, huh?"

Jonah's voice was ominous, "You're an historian; I'm an economist. Don't talk to me about expertise. I have my reasons for the decision, and I've given you some of them."

"What other reasons do you have, since I think the ones you gave me are stupid?"

"You know what you need to know. Stop the bidding at thirty five million. Try to think like a team player. We've done very well so far."

Mikhail snapped, "Yes you have."

Jonah's growled. "With my help and investment you've done pretty well for yourself: a nice life style, some wealth from the profit sharing, and a nice pension waiting for you when this is all over. Why would you risk everything over this small matter?"

Mikhail heard the threat, but he was too enraged to hold back, "Maybe I'll buy it from Pavel, secretly. Do you have a problem with that idea?"

Jonah snapped, "In the first place, Pavel wouldn't sell to you without my approval. Yes, I have a problem with that idea. I've heard reports about your interviews with the press. Now you're talking to the Duma. It's clear that the success I've allowed you to have is going to your head. I want a low profile, not a prima donna who raises suspicions. I don't want any public outcry about monopolies or mafia. You should be out of the limelight working behind the scenes."

After a pause, Jonah shouted over the phone. "Do you understand? Keep your mouth shut, no more politics, follow orders."

A click told Mikhail the conversation was over.

He glared at the telephone, slammed the receiver back onto its base and growled, "How dare the son of a bitch hang up on me?"

He grabbed a crystal figurine from the top of his desk and raised his arm to throw it, but he saw his wedding band. *I'd better be careful with this; Marina gave this figurine to me for our anniversary. She's always asking me if I still have it.*

Gently, he returned the figurine back to the desk and leaned back in his chair. *Why would Jonah do this? Pavel's from Poland, he isn't even Russian. I wonder if Jonah's from Poland also? I'll have to check. Maybe I'm not Jewish enough for them. They think of me as Russian. I know Pavel hates me, the jealous bastard. He's getting in my way.*

Jonah's out of touch. Thursday night I'll make my move. He closed his eyes and saw himself walking arm in arm with Jenia. Then she was walking with Pavel. Mikhail's cheeks were hot. *God damn it Pavel, you're in my way.*

4

Moscow – Thursday, April 9

Alex let the crowd carry him through the narrow turnstiles and out the exit from the warm Oktyabraskaya Metro station into cold rain and snow. The strong wind broke his umbrella and the rain and snow whipped against him. He was drenched before he reached the nearest kiosk.

I'll never make another promise to her, he decided. He had agreed with Tanya he would read a file and prepare his written comments before leaving the office. Unfortunately, he ran into Konstantin for a long lunch and got back to the office after three. Tanya made him keep his promise and he had stayed until eight.

It was dark and, if anything, the rain was worsening. He wanted to stop at a kiosk to buy some food, but the lines were long. The wind was getting colder and gusting more. Rain rolled down the back of his neck. He tightened his trench coat and jogged along Shabolovka Street past the Children's Library toward his flat on Apakova Street.

His flat was a forty-meter studio located on the third floor of a six-story building built in the fifties. It was all he needed. He had only a few pieces of furniture, because he used the apartment only for sleeping.

The flat was comfortable, except in the summer. Then it was stifling, especially in the afternoon and evening. It had no air conditioning and the windows faced west. It was all but impossible to sleep in the summer, when the sun didn't set until midnight.

With great effort, he opened the outer door to his building. He hated climbing stairs, but the elevator was too small and he didn't like small spaces. He was convinced some day the elevator would fall down the shaft from the weight of trash and filth on its roof and floor.

When he reached his flat, he heard the elevator door opening. "*Dobry vyechir* Elzbieta," he managed to gasp. He stood dripping at the top of the stair and shook his head to get rid of the water.

Elzbieta Potocka lived across the hall from Alex. She was a tall Polish woman in her fifties. She had been an Olympic swimmer in her youth and kept herself in good shape. In a heavy Polish accent she said, "Dobry vyechir. How are you this evening?"

He was panting and signaled with his hand for her to wait.

She laughed. "You should get in shape or muster the courage to ride the elevator. You'll probably die trying to climb those stairs. Look how much you are sweating." She laughed at her own joke.

He leaned over and put his hands on his knees. He wanted to tell her he had run all the way from the Metro, but he was still gasping for air.

"You need to get more locks on your door," she continued. "Anyone with a good screwdriver could break into your apartment."

"Hell. Why pick the lock? They can easily smash through this old wood," he gasped anticipating her next comment.

"Why don't you get a steel door like mine?"

It was always the same conversation with Elzbieta and his other two neighbors on the third floor. They were all concerned his wooden door and single lock wouldn't keep out intruders.

Alex nodded his agreement. "What would they take? I don't even have an air conditioner or a television."

Elzbieta smiled and her eyes flashed. "If it gets too hot in your flat or if you would like to watch television — have a nice meal."

He winked. "I'll remember your invitation in the summer when I'm dying in here." They both waved goodbye and entered their apartments.

He entered his flat and flipped the switch that turned on a floor lamp in the far corner. He kicked off his wet shoes at the door and hung his wet trench coat on a wooden hook on the wall. It was almost nine and he was hungry. He crossed the bare wooden floor leaving wet footprints, threw his pants on a chair, and dropped his blazer on the bed. He yanked off his tie and draped it over the broken door of a scratched, dried out wood wardrobe.

He hurried to the dirty gray window, opened it and inhaled deeply. The cool, wet air mixed with exhaust fumes and the roar of car engines rushed into the room. He opened his shirt and stared at his stomach. He pinched it. I'm getting old and soft, he thought.

In the kitchen he squeezed between the table and the sink to reach the half-sized refrigerator. Inside he found a large bottle of cheap wine with a dented screw-on cap. It was almost empty. Sitting next to the wine was a bottle of water. The only potential food was some goulash in a blackened can left over from his feast the evening before. Two nights in a row, how lucky can I be?

He pulled the can from the refrigerator, placed it on a gas burner, turned the burner on high and smiled, satisfied, when the flames crawled up the side of the can. He found a small piece of bread on the counter and placed it next to a large plastic spoon on the table. The table had room for only one chair at each end. Alex sat and waited for the goulash to warm. He studied his watch.

Plenty of time to catch some sleep and shower before I leave for the Klub. He closed his eyes and saw Jenia sitting on the oversized sofa in her living room. She was wearing a nightgown and smiling at him. She held out her arms and motioned for him to join her. He moved closer, closer. His face flushed and he raised his arms to meet her. Suddenly, she turned into Tanya, and she was shaking a finger at him.

A sizzle from the stove and the smell of burning goulash saved him from his nightmare.

※

Konstantin leaned over the bar and spoke directly into Alex's ear, "There's a big meeting tonight. All the money in Russia is assembling in that conference room in the back."

Alex burped stale goulash, grinned and responded, "I don't think these guys keep any of their money in Russia. They're too smart and rich. Only poor dumb bastards like you and me keep our money here. They keep their money in Switzerland or Cyprus."

Konstantin nodded and shouted above the music and bar chatter. "If I had a lot of money I'd keep it on one of those islands in the Caribbean. I'd love to live there. Imagine, rising in the morning and walking twenty meters in deep white sand to a warm blue-green ocean."

Alex glanced toward the doors at the back of the Klub and wondered if Jenia would like to live on one of those islands. "They meet here often, don't they."

"About once a month, but this one is special. I think something bad is happening. Pavel's been stressed."

"Jesus Christ, I'd better get my drinks in early. Fill me up."

Konstantin reached for a bottle of Smirnoff's Vodka. Alex refused to drink any other kind. He poured a double shot for him.

"You're right," Konstantin said, "I'd better get in a few myself. This could be a short evening." He poured half a glass for himself.

He lifted his glass into the air in a salute. "Say, how are you getting along with that woman at work?"

"Don't ask. She has this wild theory that the oligarchs are conspiring to steal the jewels of Russian business."

Konstantin shook his head, leaned over the bar and said in a low conspiratorial voice, "That's a profound statement of the obvious. But she's wrong on one count."

"Oh?"

"They're not stealing the economy. They've stolen it."

Alex decided Tanya picked the wrong man to help her. Konstantin probably knew all the answers to her questions.

Alex nodded toward one of the stages. "I'm going to watch a show. If you see Jenia —."

"Yes, yes, I know."

He moved to a chair at the stage located nearest the office doors in the rear of the room. He could watch the girl dance and see if Jenia came out of her office. He sat down. The girl waved at him and pursed her lips in a kissing motion.

Fifteen minutes later, Jenia came bouncing out of her office full of life and smiling happily. She waved at Alex and came to his table.

He felt a warm glow start in his stomach. "You're the most beautiful woman in this club. Will you dance for me?"

She winked, "I do only private dances, and not here."

"How much?"

She cocked her head, "If you need to ask, you can't afford it."

"I pay with performance beyond the value of gold. You can't put a price on that."

She reached over and rubbed his head with her hand then continued on her way to another part of the Klub. He stared after her, drained his glass of vodka and threw another dollar at the girl dancing on stage.

He wondered why he tortured himself like this. It would be better to wait for her to call him. But he wasn't sure she would. She continued with Pavel. Why? What was it about the old man that kept her with him?

I'm the consolation prize when Pavel's away or unavailable. She doesn't love me. I'm just a puppy to her. I'm someone who's fun to be around, but nothing serious.

Jenia returned to her office. He noticed Pavel's door remained closed. Jesus, I'd love to be a fly on the wall in that room tonight.

※

The conference room was large, about eight by ten meters. The room had two entrances at its ends, one from the bar and the other led to Pavel's office. A cart containing a stainless steel coffee urn and a plate of sweet biscuits stood near the bar entrance. A large rectangular mahogany table in the center of the room had three high-back black leather chairs down each side and one on each end.

Six men sat at the table, two down each side and one on each end. Except for Pavel, who sat at the head of the table, the men were smoking cigarettes. In front of each man were small plates and two glasses, one for water and the other for wine or vodka. Some of the plates were empty except for a crumpled napkin and others held small quarter-cut sandwiches. Ashtrays and bottles of water, wine and vodka were strategically placed on the table.

Yerik and Jermija sat closest to Pavel, while Boris and Anatoliy sat closer to Mikhail, at the other end of the table from Pavel. As had been their custom for the five years they'd been having these meetings, Pavel chaired and took copious notes. For security reasons, at the instruction of Jonah, no one else took notes, and the room was swept monthly for any electronic listening devices. To date, none had been found.

Pavel was tense, more than ever before. He was dizzy from all the smoke. He noticed Mikhail's jaw stretch tight from tension. Both men were expecting something critical to happen tonight. It was obvious from the start some two hours ago that neither Mikhail nor Pavel were in a good mood. The other men spoke carefully to avoid an explosion. Pavel ground his teeth as Mikhail spoke.

"Jonah had a good plan, originally, I don't deny that. But his plan is outdated, didn't go far enough. Sure, we've taken over the oil, auto, steel and metals industries — ."

"And banking. Don't forget about banking," interjected Yerik.

Mikhail glared at Yerik. "Yes, I know that. It's obvious. Banking was the *sine qua non* of the whole plan."

Pavel interrupted. "There were and are many *sine qua nons* in Jonah's plan, not the least of which is our involvement."

Mikhail's face reddened and he pursed his lips before he spoke. "We all know that none of us would be involved if it weren't for the Russian restrictions on foreign ownership of key companies."

Jermija said, "Well, I for one am happy with the plan. It has made me a rich and comfortable man and I didn't have to risk any of my money."

Mikhail snuffed his cigarette hard into an ashtray and lit another. "Okay. You're satisfied to have money to spend, but I'm not comfortable with only money. We are merely Jonah's employees."

Pavel hit his glass repeatedly with his pencil. "Okay, let's get back to business."

Mikhail said, "We were talking about my problems with the plan. We didn't get Gazprom, Unified Electrical Systems or Svyazinvest. So, we haven't any positions in natural gas, electricity or telecommunications. We should have moved sooner and we would be the most powerful force in Russia."

Pavel said, "Those companies are themselves entire industries. There was no way we could have bought control in them. They were too big for the Loans-for-Shares program. Besides, there is no way even this corrupt government would give up control of those industries. There would be another revolution."

Boris raised his hand for attention then said, "Pavel, as far as I know you are the only one of us who has seen the plan. Is there a strategy for getting control or ownership in those companies? I think Mikhail has a point. We're all sailing blind here . . . uninformed employees."

Pavel's gut churned. The meeting was getting out of control and sides were forming. He took a deep breath and said, "Yes, there is a strategy; but it doesn't involve us. Our role was to take over key export companies to generate significant hard currency cash flow and get the money out of Russia. So, we concentrated on oil, automobile, air transport, steel and other metals. Gazprom would be perfect, but it was and is much too large for us given our resources. Electricity and telecommunications do not have exports. Investing in them would be similar to buying Rubles with Dollars, not wise."

Mikhail said, "But the political power that would come from those companies is enormous."

Pavel responded, "I don't want to discuss it anymore. Suffice it to say that there is a plan. It involves Jonah's people in the finance ministry, not us. Let's move on with your report."

Mikhail took a long drag from his cigarette and felt the hot smoke fill his lungs. He held it there for a few moments and let it slowly seep from his nose and mouth. He glared at Pavel. You son of a bitch, how dare you tell me what to do? I'm tired of doing your and Jonah's bidding.

He was aware of the eerie silence anticipating one of the explosions for which he was so famous. Wait, he told himself. Better to wait until the right moment. Better to know who's with you and who'll join Pavel against you. Slowly, Mikhail moved his gaze from one man at the table to the next, like Jonah often did during their meetings in Switzerland. He stopped to glare at each man. He was looking for fear and he found it in every pair of eyes except Pavel's. You're the only one, Mikhail thought. You're in my way.

He knew Boris and Anatoliy sided with him. Yerik and Jermija had always sided with Pavel, but Mikhail saw by their eyes they would follow the power. After all, they are sitting in the room with the next President of Russia. Who in his right mind would openly go against such a man?

He began calmly, deliberately. "I know Jonah has asked you to lead our efforts in Russia. That doesn't justify your purchase of the Samara refinery. It doesn't fit with your investments. The refinery fits perfectly with my oil companies."

Pavel shot back, "You have too many oil related assets. If you take this one too, people are going to ask questions. They'll start making noises about monopolies. Jonah doesn't want that to happen. That's why he assigned the refinery to me."

Mikhail saw Yerik and Jermija tentatively nod their heads. He felt the adrenaline rush through his veins. He wanted to strike out and hit the bastards. Better to hold back a little more. Better to test their mettle.

He took another long drag of his cigarette and let the smoke drift from his mouth. "Jonah doesn't understand the situation. Russians don't worry about such things as monopolies. They expect them after seventy years of state-owned industries. Jonah made his decision based on what you told him and to help you offset your losses, not on real facts."

"I didn't tell Jonah anything. He decided on his own. It's part of his plan to ensure proper diversification. He's spoken about it often."

"That's beside the point. This refinery belongs in my group. It fits with the business model I've built. Jonah's out of touch."

Mikhail spoke for the benefit of Yerik and Jermija. He saw both of them whither. He was ready to move.

Pavel spoke again. "The decision's been made. I intend to buy that refinery. You stay out of the bidding after thirty five million dollars."

"Screw Jonah and screw you Pavel. I'll bid a billion if necessary. I'll have it. You won't."

The room went silent. The two men glared at each other, while the others shifted uncomfortably in their chairs. Mikhail moved his glare to Yerik and Jermija. His look said to choose or face the consequences.

Pavel shot back, "This one is mine. It's been assigned to me. What are you trying to do, rape me?"

This was too much for Mikhail. His face turned red and his lips stretched tightly over his teeth. He growled, "Pavel, you don't know yet how wonderful rape feels."

�֎

Alex didn't usually drink much during his visits to the Klub. He would down a few drinks and then nurse one. Seldom did he have more than four before he went home. Lately, he'd been drinking seven or eight. He figured it was a result of his daily confrontations with Tanya. What a waste of time. Who cares about her theory?

Jenia's door opened and she strolled out toward him carrying a coat over her arm. She bounced over to him with a big smile on her face. He said, "Going with Pavel tonight?"

"Yes, I'm sorry. I'll make it up to you this weekend."

Alex's heart sank. He wanted to say something, but he was sober enough to keep his mouth shut. Instead, he reached for his glass of vodka and chugged it.

She quickly added, "Pavel is leaving town this weekend. We can meet beginning tomorrow night."

Alex wanted to say he was busy, but he knew his face said, "yes, yes, yes." He reached for her hand and kissed it. "I'll see you tomorrow night."

He slurred his words, but she heard him well enough. She placed her warm hand on his shoulder. She had an impish look on her face that made her seem like a teenager, even though she was thirty-five. Abruptly, her face clouded and the smile disappeared.

Alex followed her gaze to the doors in the back of the room. Four men walked out the doors and turned toward the Klub entrance. Pavel, Mikhail, and Oleg came toward Jenia. They were walking stiffly, faces drawn, eyes straight ahead.

Jenia had replaced the cloud with the same phony smile given to customers by the young women at the door. Mikhail nodded and returned her fake smile. "It's so nice to see you out and about. You spend entirely too much time hiding in the back office." He turned to Pavel and pointed to the stage. "Don't you think it would be nice if she would dance for us? Will you dance for us Jenia?"

Her face turned dark for an instant and the smile returned. "Sure, come to see me anytime at the Bolshoi. Pavel, maybe you can arrange a ticket for him? Would you need a ticket for your wife?" The smile left her face and she sneered at him, "Or, would you rather take Oleg?"

Mikhail's smile disappeared quickly and his eyebrows dove together. Pavel, always the gentleman, took her arm and pulled her toward him gently. He said, "Let's go. It's been a bad day."

Alex threw his arms out and laughed. "Hey, I think she's having a great day. Nice comeback Jenia."

Mikhail found a new target for his wrath. "Do I know you?"

Alex defiantly responded, "Yes, I'm the man who was talking with the lady before you old men interrupted."

Oleg stepped forward. "Maybe I should take him outside and have a conversation with him, huh?"

That word again, thought Alex. It made him angry and ready for a fight, even with a huge thug. Even if I lose, a punch or two landed on his ugly face would be worth it. He stood and straightened his wrinkled coat. He stepped forward to meet Oleg.

Fortunately, Konstantin was quick to intercede. He stepped between Alex and Oleg. "Ok, enough of this. Sasha, sit down and enjoy your drink. Mikhail, he's a good customer who's had too much vodka."

Konstantin put his arm around Alex and led him back to his seat. Alex saw Pavel leading Jenia toward the door. She looked back at him. He leaned to follow her.

In a soft whisper Konstantin said, "Sasha, sit down. Please."

Mikhail's face was crimson and his eyes were like two missiles aimed directly at Alex. "You've got a big mouth little man."

Oleg added, "Maybe we'll meet again sometime." He turned and walked with Mikhail toward the door of the Klub.

Alex was relieved. He confronted the large man and didn't get a scratch, thanks to Konstantin. But he wouldn't let Mikhail have the last word. He shouted after them, "Bring your stooge old man."

He felt Konstantin squeeze his shoulder, maybe too hard. "Sasha, shut up." With those words, Konstantin sat down next to him.

The girl had stopped dancing. She gave Alex a "thumbs up."

Konstantin spoke again. "Don't push your luck. He's an important man and a vindictive son-of-a-bitch."

Alex was still sneering in the direction of Mikhail. After Mikhail left the Klub, Alex said, "He isn't going to do anything to me. I'm nobody in his world. He'll forget it by tomorrow."

Konstantin patted him on the shoulder and said, "For your sake, I hope so. Have a drink on me. You're usually so pleasant and happy. What's wrong?"

Valodya, who had been watching the confrontation from the bar, hurried to the table. He sat down with a concerned look on his face and asked, "What happened?"

"Alex pouted and said, "I don't like how he looked at Jenia."

Valodya shook his head. "Alex, get over it. She belongs to Pavel and if he were to disappear Mikhail would step in quickly."

Alex felt sick to his stomach. The thought of Mikhail in bed with Jenia made him ill. He wanted to punch Valodya for even suggesting it. "She would never let that bastard near her," he said.

Valodya pleaded, "Alex, I like you. Quit dreaming about her. She's happy with Pavel. If she's not with Pavel, then Mikhail will take her. He gets everything he wants, even if he has to kill for it. That puts you way down the list, my boy. A pawn can't capture a king you know."

Alex responded, "No . . . but a pawn can take a queen."

※

By the time his driver turned the dark-blue Volvo limousine onto Tverskaya, Pavel's heartbeat had finally returned to normal. Until now, he hadn't realized how tense he had been. He looked at Jenia sitting next to him. Her head was back on the seat and her eyes were closed. He was glad she was finally relaxing. He hadn't seen her so angry or so worried.

As he reflected on the evening, especially the meeting with Mikhail and the others, he was more than ever convinced that it was time to get out of this rat race. He was tired, not just for the moment tired but old tired. He knew now that it had been a mistake to let Jonah convince him to stay on two years ago. His friendship with Jonah had stretched his one-year extension into two. This time it was final; he was retiring as soon as all the proper legal documents were in place.

Jenia stirred. He thought about their relationship; it too had to end. She had been the right person at the right time, but she couldn't help him now. He needed Ivona, and she and Lenya needed him.

With her eyes still closed, Jenia reached out to find his hand, held it and said in a contrite voice, "I'm sorry. I didn't mean to cause a problem. I just can't stand the man, and I could tell he had hurt you tonight."

Pavel smiled and squeezed her hand. "It's okay. No harm was done, although I think your friend Alexander should be careful. Mikhail would not think twice about squashing him."

She turned her head to look at him. "Was it a bad meeting?"

He nodded.

"It's more than just the meeting isn't it? Lately, you've been different, melancholy."

Again he nodded. She leaned to him, put her head on his shoulder and shut her eyes. Pavel put his arm around her and kissed her hair. He felt a tear slowly rolling down his cheek. He whispered, "Thank you for being part of my life. You are a good friend and I love you very much."

She lifted her head and their eyes met. "When are you leaving?"

"I plan to talk with Jonah tomorrow. My game is played; time to let someone else on the board."

"So, Mikhail wins?"

"I hope not. It would be a disaster for our project and for Russia. But it's clear I can no longer control him, or the others. Someone else will have to do that."

"I think Ivona and Leonid deserve your full attention."

He said, "I've already transferred the flat to your — ."

She interrupted, "Don't worry about me. I can take care of myself. I'm more worried about you. Power has its grip on Mikhail, and it can make him do some crazy things."

"I'll be okay."

"Are you still planning to bring your boat down the river Monday and be first again this year?"

"Yes. Everyone is expecting it. I am going to bring Leonid with me, as this will be the last time. What are you going to do?"

She laughed, "I'll be looking for a new boyfriend."

He winked, "I think that will break Alexander's heart."

She punched him in the shoulder. "I wish I hadn't said anything to Mikhail. I had no idea Alex would step in like that. It's so unlike him; he hates violence."

"Tell him to be careful. Oh, by the way, I have two tickets for the football game on Sunday. I think it would be better if my family and I spend a quality weekend discussing our future. Do you want them for you and Alex?"

"Unfortunately, I'll be out of town on Sunday."

5

Moscow – Friday, April 10

God I'm sick, thought Alex. He forced another gulp of bitter black coffee down his throat. He felt as if his head were stuck in a bottle of cotton. He was too dizzy to stand properly.

His day began with four aspirins washed down with two small cartons of orange juice he purchased at the kiosk near the Metro. He hoped the orange juice acid would dissolve the aspirin faster.

I should have taken the aspirin last night and again this morning. What I need is a glass of vodka.

He raised his head and stared at the files strewn across the table in the war room. I can't believe I made it this far, he thought. I can't possibly read all this shit today. My life is a mess. What do I give a damn about a conspiracy in Russia? It would be nice to nail that bastard Mikhail though. What an asshole. If I were rich, I'd have him killed. Who can I hire? He giggled at the foolish thought. I hope Tanya is sick today. I don't think I can take her with this hangover. His hopeful speculating was interrupted by the irritating voice he had come to know so well.

"Have you read any of this material yet, huh?"

He lifted his head and squinted at her. The lights were too bright for him to focus properly. He wanted her to leave him alone. Couldn't she see he was sick? Didn't she have any mercy?

He forced himself to be civil and tried his best to avoid slurring words. "This is financial mumbo jumbo to me. I'm not an accountant, I'm a lawyer."

She sighed. "I think this material raises a lot of financial and legal questions. You're supposed to help me find the answers, huh?"

That word again. It reminded him of Oleg the night before. I must have been nuts to start a fight with that monster. Christ he's a big guy. I hope Jenia appreciated my support. I'll have to keep my eye out for that idiot. Reflecting on his actions and his foolish slurred words of the night before, he was embarrassed.

His head had somehow fallen down to the table again. He forced himself to lift it and answered, "Well, I haven't seen anything illegal. If you think something is illegal, why don't you turn it over to the FSB or the Militia?"

What a great idea he thought to himself. I'd be off the hook. No more files, no more Tanya.

She countered, "They're part of this too. We'd all be killed."

This was more than he could take today. The woman was obsessed with conspiracies. He rolled his eyes (or at least he thought he did) and shook his head back and forth. It hurt terribly but was worth the effect. "Oh, come on. This is going too far. According to you the only people not involved in this conspiracy are Weber, you and I. Quite frankly, I'm not so sure about Weber."

"You think Weber's involved?" She studied him suspiciously, as though he knew something.

"I was joking." He couldn't believe she was naïve enough to take him seriously.

His head was really hurting now. He was afraid he might throw up orange juice all over the files. He grabbed a folder to catch anything that might come shooting out of his mouth. He pretended to read, but his eyes were burning badly.

I need some sleep. I was a fool to put all that acid in my stomach. Next time I'll drink milk.

He leafed through the folder. Maybe she'll leave me alone if I pretend to read this. The words on the page were blurred and made his head hurt all the more. His gambit didn't work.

"Look. Once we get you through the background material, I think you'll understand. Maybe if we work through the weekend, huh?"

Alex was horrified. He interrupted her, "I'm busy this weekend." He knew he looked guilty, and grinned in spite of himself. He couldn't wait for this day to end. He wanted to go home early to sleep before going to Jenia's flat. He imagined her opening the door. She was wearing —.

"Damn it Alex. By the time you get off of your ass, this country will be on its back."

"Why should I care? I was an activist once, like you, gung-ho for the country. 'Step up,' I told myself, 'do your part.' Well, look what that wrought. We risked our lives for Yeltsin. Are we any closer to our dream? The new leaders are the old in different clothes. I risked my life but for nothing gained."

"You were at the White House in ninety-one? So was I."

"Really? I didn't see you there. Of course, with a hundred thousand people, who could find anyone?"

"You wouldn't have recognized me. I looked different then." She had been disguised as a man, even a fake mustache. She wondered what Alex would think if he knew his name and most of the others were probably on file at the, then, KGB."

He said, "I thought for sure I was going to die, but I was ready. Young men do foolish things. I still can't believe they didn't fire, or at least arrest the leaders."

Tanya knew what would have happened if the Colonel was there. He would have fired, without a doubt. Her father had told her many times, "For an honorable person, an oath is sacred. I've taken an oath to protect and serve the Soviet Union. I will honor that oath to my death." But the colonel wasn't there to protect the Soviet Union, or to protect his own family. He was in an unmarked grave somewhere in Afghanistan."

She said, "It's the fate of our country, your country, at stake here. As a Russian, I hoped you'd be more committed."

"Hey, I am committed," he almost shouted.

"Oh?"

"Last night. I had a conversation with your friend Mikhail."

Alex loved it. Her look was worth the headache. She was genuinely impressed.

"Really?"

"Yes. At the Knight Klub. He and his rich friends meet there often. I've been checking the place out for months." He was proud of himself for thinking of this response. It was luck but his efforts at the Knight Klub had paid off handsomely. She was gathering meaningless files, but he was getting close to the conspirators. Now he had even made contact. It was the kind of good luck Jenia brought to him.

He looked for her approval. She was irritated rather than impressed. With her hands on her hips staring at him, she prodded, "And?"

He couldn't resist. "I told the old bastard to stay away from my girl." He laughed out loud. She marched from the room. He had won. He could go home now and get some sleep before meeting with Jenia. *I'll need all the energy I can find.*

※

Mikhail rushed to passport control at Heathrow airport, hurrying ahead of the other passengers on his Moscow flight.

When he came out of customs he saw Marina stretching her neck to find him. She saw him and began jumping and waving. Sometimes her exuberance was embarrassing.

She's fallen behind, he thought. *I've moved on to the next phase and she's contentedly stuck in the past. I'm not the simple professor she knew in our youth. I'm now the richest businessman in Russia and probably the next President of the country. I need someone more challenging, someone young and energetic. She's a nester. Let her nest in London.*

"Hello my dear. I'm happy to see you," he said in his best manner. He kissed her on the cheek.

"Are you here for long?"

"Only the weekend. I have to return Monday morning. At least we'll have some time together."

"That's wonderful. Stephan will be so glad to see you. He wants to know if you are coming to the commencement in June. Aren't you proud of him?"

He smiled at her like a parent would smile at a child. "Yes, I'm proud of him. Of course I'll come. I'm so glad you and he moved to London. The schools are so much better here. It's worth missing you to know you are both doing well. Moscow is so unstable."

"I'm happy you're back," she said. She gave him another hug and kissed him on the lips.

He glanced around the terminal to see if anyone was watching. He didn't like the way she publicly displayed her affections.

The ride home was uneventful. Marina kept chatting about London, Stephan and her mother. He didn't listen. He nodded occasionally and said, "Yes," a few times, but his mind was on Pavel and Jonah.

I should have cancelled this trip. Hell, I'll call Jonah from London. Actually that's better. He smirked and pictured Jonah's face. Jonah hated to talk business over a public line.

"I have to make a business call to Switzerland this afternoon," he said. He exited the car and held the door for her. "Let's have a quick lunch and I'll make my call. After that, the rest of the weekend is reserved for you. No interruptions, I promise."

She squeezed his hand and gushed, "I love you so much."

He didn't respond. He merely smiled, took her hand and escorted her to the house. As soon as they passed through the doorway, he took her in his arms, squeezed her and kissed her lips hard, hungrily. "I want some sport later," he said with a twinkle in his eye.

She led him to the kitchen. He asked, "What do we have to eat? I'm starved."

Mikhail wolfed his food, lit a cigarette and reached for his coffee. Marina didn't smoke, but she knew better than to comment about his habit. "I need to make my call now to catch him before he goes home for the weekend," he said. He rose from his chair and gave her a quick peck on the forehead.

His office was a small room next to the reception (living) room. When he entered, he checked to see whether anything had been changed. Everything was as before, a small desk in front of a window, bookshelves along one wall and an easy chair in a corner. Marina had once moved things around and he suspected she might have opened a desk drawer, although he kept it locked. It was one of the few times he had beaten her.

His mind wandered back to the evening before. Jenia was so fine, young, energetic and sassy. What a spirited specimen. He liked spirit in a woman. It gave him something to break, and he would break her. I'll beat her until she screams for mercy, and I'll kill that bastard Pavel.

He was ready now, pumped up, breathing hard, fast. He reached for the telephone and stabbed his finger onto the keys. One after another he punched them, each punch harder than the last. He heard the ringing. Answer you bastard, answer. I'll kill you too if I have to.

Mikhail heard the familiar click followed by Jonah's voice. "Hello?"

Mikhail almost exploded into the phone. "Hello Jonah; Mikhail; we need to talk, now."

"Why are you calling me at this number. Use the other phone. I'm hanging up."

"Don't do it again. You'll regret it for the rest of your life. Listen to what I have to say."

"Are you drunk? Who do you think you're talking to? I'm not one of your bodyguards. If this is about that asset we discussed Monday, I don't want to hear any more whining from you."

Mikhail said, "You hung up on me too soon. Let me finish." He shouted into the phone, "I intend to finish even if I have to come over there and stand on your chest."

Silence. Mikhail concluded Jonah was so angry he was speechless. He guessed Jonah was crazy with anger or completely confused. Mikhail plowed forward. "I'm not creating problems by taking that refinery. Nobody is going to pay any attention to such a small purchase. I've decided. I will have that refinery and I'll do whatever is necessary to get it."

Jonah responded in a calm voice. "I told you before the decision has been made. You're disobeying a direct order and I don't like it. Don't go against my orders."

The die is cast, Mikhail thought to himself. He snatched a pencil and drew circles on a piece of paper, then spoke again. "I'm the one on the ground in Russia. You're in Zurich. This isn't some game you can play through the mail. I'm in the best position to know what we should do."

He drew a crown on the page and filled it until it was thick with black carbon. Again Jonah spoke calmly. "Mikhail, we have a structure. In our structure you report to me. It's like any corporation. There are bosses and there are employees. You're an employee Mikhail. Do you understand what I said? You're an employee. I can fire you. I call the shots and you follow my orders. That's the way it works in our little structure."

Mikhail drew the outline of another crown and responded, "You can make the Zurich strategy decisions if you like, but I'll make the decisions in Russia." He drew a pyramid on the page and made a circle at its peak. He then drew lines coming out of the circle, a sun emitting rays of light.

Jonah responded, "I received a call from Pavel. You upset him when you got out of hand in front of the others."

Mikhail responded through clenched teeth, "Oh? He didn't tell me he had a problem. I'm disappointed that he would come running to you without discussing the matter with me first." Mikhail continued with his doodling. He drew a dagger on the page.

"It's not possible to discuss these matters over the telephone. There are good reasons for my decisions. I know things you don't know. I know the total strategy not only the strategy in Russia. We have to discuss these matters face to face. Come to Zurich next week and we'll discuss them, after I've had a chance to meet with Pavel."

Mikhail drew blood dripping off of the dagger's point. "I don't need a face to face meeting. If Pavel wants to meet with you instead of me, fine. I'll deal with him when he returns."

He didn't wait for Jonah to respond. He gently placed the receiver into its cradle. He put his hands flat on the desk and counted. One, two, three, four, five, six. Suddenly, he grabbed the telephone and threw it against a wall. It shattered with a loud crash.

He heard Marina shout, "My God, what happened?"

"Give me a moment dear. Then we can spend some time together." He knew he was lying. He had to return to Russia immediately. If he went to Switzerland he would never see the light of day again. Even in Russia he may be in danger. He had to take bold action to show Jonah he wasn't dealing with an employee. Now, I have to kill Pavel. Without him, Jonah has no one to lead the Russian activities but me.

He rose and walked to his easy chair. He sat down and closed his eyes. He was still tense and excited. War is hell, he thought. He let his mind wander to relax it. He saw Jenia dancing on a stage in the Knight Klub. Men were throwing money at her feet and she had tears coming down her cheeks. Then he saw him, the little prick with the big mouth. He was drunk and wearing a wrinkled, dirty suit. He was gathering the money. She took off her clothes and the money fell like rain. The little runt kept harvesting the money and stuffing it into his suit pockets. What a body she had.

"Honey. Marina, come here will you? Marina."

The door opened and she entered.

"Come here," he ordered and got out of his chair.

She said nothing. She was frightened when she saw the phone scattered all over the floor. She stepped over the pieces and came to him. He reached out and put his hands on her shoulders and pushed her down onto her knees.

�֎

The door opened. Alex had been dreaming about this moment for days. What will she be wearing? Will she be in a good mood? How long will it take me to get her into bed?

She was holding a glass of Champagne and wearing a black satin dress cut low. She was smiling and had a twinkle in her eye. "Hello Shurochka," she said seductively. "Come into my parlor." She swung open the door and held out the glass for him.

"You, you look lovely," he stammered. She wrapped her arms around him to give him a tight hug. He smelled the light-vanilla aroma of her Angel perfume, felt her smooth skin against his cheek and her warm breath on his ear.

Their glasses tilted and champagne spilled on his jacket and her dress. "Now you've done it. You've wet your dress. Take it off quickly."

Smiling, she stepped back from him and reached behind her back. Her breasts slowly rose and fell as she swayed from side to side. He reached out and touched the soft satin of her dress. When he heard the zipper moving down her back, he pulled the dress forward and it fell away. She was wearing nothing except black silk stockings and a gold chain around her left ankle.

"Are you hungry?"

"Yes," he gushed and took the hand she offered. She led him past the couch, past the two easy chairs, past the grand piano and through the doorway into her bedroom.

She had strewn flower petals over the bed and on the floor. The bed covers and pillows were laid out to create a large basket. She crawled onto the bed, sat in the basket, pulled her legs apart and placed her knees over the pillows.

"Welcome to the feast," she whispered.

�֎

Tanya stood before the door and fumbled for her keys. After Alex had left, she called home to talk to Dmitry; but Kolya answered the phone. He had been sent home for some disciplinary reason. He told her that papa had left an hour ago. He was crying and afraid; so she told him she would come home immediately.

She opened the door to the flat and stepped inside.

"Kolya? Kolya?" she called. No answer. She placed her bag on the floor and made her way through the flat and into Kolya's room. He was sleeping. "Kolya," she said and then repeated his name, "Kolya."

He opened his eyes and was surprised to see her. Then he began to cry. She saw bruises on his arms and hands.

"Papa spanked me. I'm sorry mama."

She sat on the bed and took him in her arms. Across the room, she saw Dmitry's rider's crop lying on the dresser.

Pointing to the small whip, she said, "Did he spank you with that?"

He nodded.

Blood rushed to her face. Her body tensed.

"Mama. I didn't understand what papa was saying. I told him I was sorry. I told him I'd be a good boy, but he kept spanking me. I'm sorry mama. I won't be bad anymore. It hurt so much."

"It's okay honey. It's not your fault. When he gets home I'll tell him you will be a good boy. He won't spank you again."

"Mama?"

"Yes, honey."

"There was a lady with papa. She stopped him from spanking me. He got mad at her too."

6

Moscow – Saturday, April 11

It was dark outside when Alex awoke. At first he didn't know where he was. Then he saw Jenia lying next to him. He rolled to his side and wrapped his leg and arm over her. He kissed her neck and then her breast. She rolled onto her back and opened her eyes.

"What a wonderful night you gave me. Thank you so much. I think I'm in love with you."

He felt the blood rush to his head. He wanted to hear her say those words for so long, but she never had. She always treated him like a toy. Now she was telling him she loved him. He was sure she meant it.

Many times, too many, he had told her he loved her. She refused to believe it and told him he was merely infatuated with her. She said he would know when he was truly in love. He hadn't understood what she meant, but he hadn't argued. He kept telling her he loved her.

She rolled to her side to face him. She snuggled her head into his chest.

He grinned and said, "I wish we could walk down the street hand in hand. We would kiss in front of all the people and let them know we're in love. I want all the ladies to be jealous."

She made a face and playfully punched him in the chest.

He smelled her. He loved her body odor and put his face against her to take a deep sniff.

Again she hit him, but much lower. She said, "Damn you I'm pouring my heart out to you and you act like a teenage boy."

She kissed him affectionately.

He leaned back to look at her and said, "I'm tired of sharing you with some old man. I ought to kill the bastard. Then you and I would walk hand in hand through the park."

She responded, "More than likely we would never take those walks. I'd simply be your chubby wife sharing a communal flat."

She rose onto her elbow and faced him with a serious look on her face. "I don't think Pavel's going to be around much longer."

My God, what does she mean? Maybe I'll have her to myself. Is she going to dump Pavel? Is he going to dump her?

She continued, "He's on the wrong side of Mikhail; that's hazardous. You should be careful too Sasha."

"Did Pavel tell you this?"

"What Pavel tells me stays with me. I don't tell others what you say to me."

"That would be embarrassing wouldn't it? If you told people what I said, they'd think you're sleeping with a teenager."

With those words he grabbed her and tried to get on top of her. She pushed him over. He rolled back and she reached down between his legs and grabbed him.

"You certainly have a teenager's sex drive," she said as she positioned herself on top of him, kissed him and pushed her tongue into his mouth. He sucked on her lower lip.

I've won, he thought, sex before coffee.

✤

It was four in the morning when Tanya heard the key in the door. Dmitry entered, still drunk. He grinned, squinted and hiccupped, "H... Hello. Are you waiting for your man to come home and take you to bed?"

He stumbled into the room and dropped his coat on the floor. She said nothing. He had vomited on his shirt, and his fly was open. The smell of vodka and urine burned her nose. He reached down and undid his pants with difficulty. They dropped to the floor around his shoes. Somewhere, he had lost his underpants. He tried to walk toward her, but tripped over his pants and fell onto his knees. Then he sank to the floor in a fetal position and passed out.

She stared down at what was once a man with a good heart. He was proud of his son, worked hard, provided food and clothing for his family and always hurried home to Kolya and her. He didn't drink much, at least not often. The new economy, she decided. What has it done to you my love, what has it done to you?

She pulled the riding crop from behind her back and hung it on a coat hook on the wall. She pushed the door shut, gathered his pants, took them into the kitchen and put them in the washing machine. Her hands smelled of urine. To get off his shirt, she had to roll the limp body back and forth on the floor and got vomit all over her hands. After depositing the shirt in the washing machine, she went to the bathroom, ran water into the tub, added some bath gel and returned to the foyer to get Dmitry. Her heart was aching and she was quietly crying. Her world was a mess. His world was a mess. They were dragging Kolya down too.

Tanya was strong for her size. Her training had been intense and she knew how to move dead weight. She managed to get him into the tub and washed him. He had lipstick on various parts of his body. She pulled his unconscious body from the tub, dried it, half carried and half dragged it to the bed, and pulled the covers over him. Then she and went to Kolya's room to sleep next to her son.

"An oath is sacred," she whispered to herself, "for better or for worse."

※

Alex asked Jenia, "I thought we had the whole weekend?"

"We have today and tonight," she answered. "Pavel's wife has gone to Poland and he wants me to meet him at his home tomorrow."

"Wouldn't you rather spend Sunday with me?"

"Of course, but Pavel asked me to sail to Moscow on his yacht Monday morning. He has his heart set on it. He wants his to be the first yacht to come down the river this spring. He's been bragging about it to everybody for weeks. Come on Shurochka, we still have tonight." She stood and walked to his chair and pushed her body against his face.

7

Moscow – Monday, April 13

Pavel stared across the breakfast table at his wife, Ivona. She was a matronly forty-two. She took another sip of her tea, and set her cup down. "Why are you staring at me?"

"I'm thinking how much I love you and how lucky I am you love me."

"That is such a nice thing to say. It's like music to my heart. I do love you so much." She grinned, " Is this a revelation or a confirmation?"

He grinned and responded, "It's a reincarnation. I've neglected you lately with my work and all. I'm glad I've decided to sell everything and get out of this rat race."

"Oh, I'm so happy. I can't wait to move back to Poland."

She reached across the table and took his hand. They stared at each other for a few moments. He spoke first, "I miss the old days when we were poor. Remember living in the small flat in Warsaw?"

"Yes, we were always in each other's arms. Remember? We took a walk in the park every day, even in the winter, to get out of the flat for a short time."

"I miss loving you." He squeezed her hand and saw tears forming in her eyes. "I made the right decision to retire. No more pressure. No more risk of jail. No more Mikhail. I'll turn the assets over to whomever Jonah directs for the promised pension. We'll live out our lives in Warsaw and travel to Israel."

Ivona said, "Are you sure you want to go back to the old days? We're probably remembering only the good. We've forgotten the bad."

"I'm not worried about the bad if I have you in my arms." He meant it. He knew in his heart he meant it. Jenia couldn't help him anymore. Now, he needed Ivona. He had come home to her. The last few days had been wonderful. They sat together, talked about their lives, and made love for the first time in months.

"You know she was only a companion. It wasn't a sexual thing. I thought I needed some young energy to keep from getting old."

She squeezed his hand trying to make him comfortable. "Based on your performance this weekend, it worked."

He blushed. "I'm serious. I never slept with her. She knew so much about me, and what I needed. I enjoyed her companionship and conversation. Now, I need only you, forever."

"I understand," she said.

"I need our past. I need you to comfort me. The stress of this last few years has almost destroyed me; and my refusal to accept my growing old has almost destroyed my relationship with you and Lenya too."

"No dear. I don't think our relationship was ever in danger, maybe from your work, but never from Jenia."

He was surprised she knew it was Jenia. Ivona had always surprised him. "Thank you for loving me so much," he said with tears in his eyes. "I'm sorry we didn't get back to Poland this weekend. Can you come with me to Zurich tomorrow?"

"I'm glad we spent the weekend here, together, with no distractions. Of course I'd love to go with you, but who'd watch Lenya?"

As she spoke his name, nine-year old Lenya came bounding into the breakfast room. "*Dobry utra* Mama, Papa," he gushed and took a seat at the table. "I'm sorry I'm late, but I was looking for my camera and my football patch."

Lenya had a Lokomotive team patch he often stuck to his coat. He frequently went to the games with Pavel, especially if Locomotive was playing Spartak or Dinamo. He often bragged that one of the three would win the European championship in 1998.

"I can still go with you to Moscow today can't I Papa?"

"Yes son, you can come with me. We'll take lots of pictures along the river. We'll be first down the river again. I can add them to my scrap book."

Lenya popped some bread into his mouth and spoke as he chewed. "It's snowing. There's snow on the ground. It'll make for better pictures."

Pavel leaned over the table and kissed Ivona. Then he rose and walked to the window. *I can't wait for this day to be over. I'll meet with everyone but Mikhail. I'll tell them I'm resigning.*

He heard a car arriving at the side of the house. He looked out the window and saw Andrei, one of his bodyguards. He was walking across the lawn toward the river with the pilot and a third man. It was Oleg. Pavel's heart jumped. *What's he doing here?*

The men reached the boat and the pilot began checking the engine. Andrei and Oleg stood on the dock; each put one foot on the boat rail and lit a cigarette. Like Oleg, Andrei was wearing a black leather jacket and jeans. Andrei was well built and athletic, but not in a mean way like Oleg, who stayed in shape to hurt people. *Strange,* thought Pavel, *where is Zenon? He had been Pavel's driver as far back as Poland.*

"They're here," he said to no one in particular.

Ivona joined him at the window and put her arms around him. She whispered, "I'm glad we found each other again. I love you. I've missed you."

He put his arm around her and squeezed. "I'm glad to be back. We'll live out the rest of our lives enjoying each other in quiet solitude. No more work. No more dreams. We'll be together and enjoy each other."

"I'm done Papa," Lenya chirped, "Can we go?"

"Brush your teeth first," Ivona said."

Pavel and Ivona stepped through the door and stood by the back of the house watching the men preparing the boat. It was probably too cold for a boat ride, but he had promised Lenya. Besides, the trip had been planned for weeks. He had a reputation to maintain as the first down the river in the spring. Everyone would ask him if he came down the river in the snow with ice floating all around the boat.

The two bodyguards waved to him impatiently. He saw Oleg look at his watch more than twice in a few minutes.

"Go see what's keeping Lenya will you?" he asked Ivona. She returned to the house.

He walked down the path to Oleg and asked, "What are you doing here?"

"Mikhail wants to talk with you. He said to tell you things got out of hand Thursday. He wants to work with you not against you. I'm to give you a lift to his office. Zenon will meet you there."

Pavel returned to the house feeling uncomfortable. In the entire time he had known Mikhail, the man had never apologized or backed down. There is no way I'm going to get in a car with Oleg. When we get to Moscow I'll take a taxi or the Metro to my office. If Mikhail wants to talk he can come to me.

He watched the snowflakes float onto his shoes and melt. More snowflakes died on the brown grass around his feet. He thought, such a short existence and an anonymous death.

Ivona came back a few minutes later with Lenya. "He's ready," she said handing Pavel his briefcase. The three of them walked slowly down the path toward the boat. Their shoes crunched the gravel beneath the snow and cold wind burned their faces. Pavel smelt the musky morning odor from the River. Ivona squeezed his hand.

Pavel was uncomfortable, almost sick. He wanted to go back inside the house and spend the day, the rest of his life, with Ivona and Lenya. It's too late now. Don't get in the car with Oleg. That's the key. Don't get in his car.

When the family arrived at the dock, both bodyguards threw their cigarettes into the water. Oleg walked to the stern and removed the line. Andrei stepped toward Pavel. "Good morning sir. It's not a good day for a boat ride. You'll surely be the first down the river."

Lenya bragged, "I'm riding with my Papa today. I'm going to take some pictures of the Kremlin from the river."

Oleg suddenly stopped what he was doing and turned to look at them. Pavel looked at Andrei, who avoided his gaze and turned away. Pavel's heart sank. His dreams ended. They were replaced by fear for his son and Ivona. He turned to Lenya, "Not today son. We're running too far behind and we'll have to hurry. You can go the next time."

Lenya's mouth fell open to say something but he stopped. Pavel saw a few tears forming in Lenya's eyes, but Lenya was trying to hold them back. Pavel remembered telling him men don't cry after the age of eight.

Pavel patted Lenya's head and said, "You take care of your mother for me. Promise?"

The boy's chin dropped to his chest and he mumbled, "Yes sir."

Pavel looked from the boy to Ivona. He knew from the tears in her eyes she had seen what he saw and knew what he knew. He wrapped his arms around her. Her whole body shook. She squeezed him goodbye and whispered, "I love you." His heart broke. When he pulled away, he felt like he was cutting off his arms and legs. He stared at her, standing there, so brave, with tears running down her cheeks, her heart breaking.

He whispered, "Goodbye my love."

In the background he heard Lenya talking to Oleg, taunting each other about Lokomotive and Spartak. He walked to his son and took him by the hand back to his mother. He leaned over, kissed his forehead then turned away and walked toward the boat. He heard Lenya say, "Mama, why is Papa crying?"

Pavel walked down the gangplank and onto the boat. He turned and saw his son waving to him. Ivona stood stoic, clutching Lenya as if someone might come along and snatch him from her. Pavel threw his briefcase onto the deck and waved goodbye. The boat pulled into the river and weaved among the chunks of ice as it made its way toward the center. Pavel stared back at them until he no longer saw them. He shut his eyes and focused his thoughts on Ivona and on Lenya. They played football, walked in Warsaw's Waszienki Park, searched in the woods for wild mushrooms, and ate breakfast together. Pavel refused to let them leave his mind. He even imagined Lenya graduating from University. In the background, he heard a helicopter and Oleg shouting something. He paid no attention to anything going on around him. He put his arms around Ivona and put his lips to hers. "Goodbye my love."

※

On the shore, hidden by snow and trees, a camper saw an open walk-around boat with a pilothouse coming down the river. The boat was about ten meters long and three meters wide. It had an inboard motor and was slowly worked its way around chunks of ice in the water. A man dressed in a suit was standing on the main deck leaning on a rail near the middle of the boat. The camper saw the pilot in the elevated wheelhouse. Near the rear on the main deck, two men in black jackets appeared to be fiddling with a rubber raft.

The camper was distracted by the sound of engines. He turned, looked up and saw a military helicopter with the Russian flag painted on the rear fuselage. It was fully loaded with weapons and flying up the river from the direction of Moscow.

When he returned his gaze to the boat, he saw the two men dressed in black jackets approach and shoot the businessman and the pilot. The two assassins undid the rubber raft, climbed into it and rowed toward the opposite shore.

Suddenly, the helicopter stopped, turned, pointed and fired a missile that destroyed the boat in a burst of fire and heat. The water around the boat hissed and snow in the trees near the shore melted. The camper stepped back further into the woods. The helicopter rose and flew away at a high speed.

It was quiet now. The boat was gone. The helicopter was gone. Two men rowed silently toward the far shore. Quiet waves washed small chunks of wood mixed with blocks of ice onto the shore.

※

"Sir, you have a phone call on line one. Sir? Are you there?" Galina's voice screeched over the intercom.

Mikhail sighed. "Yes, I'm here. Who is it Galina?"

"It's Boris Pyotrovich. He sounds excited. Do you want to take the call?"

"OK Galina, I'll get it on one. Thank you."

He lifted the receiver. *"Privet Boris. Kak dela?"*

Boris's voice was high pitched with excitement and burst into his ear. "Mikhail Nikolaivich, I've been trying to reach you all morning. Have you heard the news? Pavel is dead. My God, a helicopter blew his boat apart. No one is safe if they can get Pavel on the river."

"Are you sure it was Pavel? I can't believe this. How do you know? When did this happen?"

"It happened about eight-thirty this morning outside Moscow. Only pieces of the bodies were found."

Mikhail spoke deliberately, "Calm down. We need to contact Ivona and give her our sympathy. Try to find out when and where she plans to hold the funeral. I imagine it will be in Poland."

He hung up the telephone. His face was still flushed with excitement. The die is cast you bastard Jonah. I'm all you have.

He leaned back in his chair, shut his eyes and imagined his future with Pavel out of the way. He saw Jenia coming toward him with her arms out. She would need someone to take care of her. She was coming toward him faster now. Suddenly, she turned and walked toward the skinny guy in the wrinkled coat.

He reached for the intercom. "Galina, contact Yuri Sergeevich Usenko and arrange a lunch for today." He leaned back in his chair again and closed his eyes. A smile came across his face. Buddy settled softly onto his shoes.

❦

Alex hated Mondays. It was the start of another week and the day when he had to accompany Carl Weber all morning. Every Monday morning Alex gathered papers to be signed, arranged for a driver and had a meeting with a notary. For the last month he and Carl had been going to the landlord also. Carl was negotiating a new lease. Today was more difficult than usual, because Carl kept asking him questions about the project and he wasn't able to answer most of them.

The dirty slush from the snow on Sunday was still on the streets, and today's new snow made them slippery. The driver had to maneuver the car through traffic and it took forever to reach their destinations. Because of the traffic problems, Alex was forced to take a late lunch. It was three in the afternoon and he hadn't eaten anything. He was sitting in the La Gastronome Restaurant nursing a cup of coffee.

He liked this restaurant, with its marble columns, dazzling chandeliers and fine oak wood trim. He had come here a few times with Jenia. The La Gastronome was located on the ground floor of the former landmark Stalinist food shop. It was impressively decorated and impeccably clean. He wondered if the foreign patrons realized that a few years ago this fancy restaurant was a mere grocery store. What a difference a market economy can make, he mused.

Many of the patrons had finished their meals and left. The hot coffee filled his nose with its refreshing aroma. He stared at the steam for a short time. When he thought it was safe, he put the cup to his lips and took a short sip. It was still too hot and burned his mouth. He set the cup down and stared into the distance without seeing.

Why doesn't she believe I love her? It is love. I know it. It isn't infatuation. He recalled the weekend, the basket of flowers and pillows. Why did she have to go to Pavel? Why didn't she stay with me last night?

Finally, he managed to drink some of the bitter liquid. The hot coffee made its way to his stomach and he felt the warmth.

After a few sips, he leaned back and surveyed the room. Tanya? She was standing near the front of the restaurant scanning the room. He wanted to duck under his table, but it was too late. She saw him and marched, almost ran, toward him.

Nervously, he scratched the back of his hand. He took another sip of coffee, but now it was cold, bitter.

She arrived at his table and took a seat opposite. "Big lunch, huh?"

He didn't want to talk to her now. Half a day with Carl was a full day's work. He deserved some private time before going home. He had no energy left for the project.

"Tough weekend," he said and grinned. "I feel like somebody kicked me in the head, but the fun was worth the pain."

He didn't get the reaction he expected. She didn't point her finger or pout or show any anger. He thought he saw a mild look of disdain, but he couldn't be sure. She moved to the chair next to him and in a conspiratorial voice said, "Have you heard about Pavel Melninski?"

Alex tensed. A cold shudder rolled like a wave through his body. "What happened?"

"He was assassinated on his boat this morning."

Jenia, oh my God she was with him. He remembered her saying she would be with Pavel on the boat. He felt like he was going to throw up. He couldn't move. He wanted to cry.

"Did you know him personally?"

Of course he knew him, and she knew it. Why did Jenia have to go? Why was this woman sitting next to him giving him this bad news? She didn't care about Pavel or Jenia. They were statistics to her. God damn it Jenia, why did you leave me?

He had to answer. "I know someone who was close to him. She may have been on the boat."

"Jenia wasn't with him."

Sunrise! His spirit recovered. A moment ago she was dead. Now she is alive. With Pavel gone, she is his. He kicked himself for even thinking this way.

Did Jenia know something? Didn't she say Pavel wasn't going to live long? If she wasn't with Pavel or him, where was she? Who was she with? She must have lied to him. God, I hope she wasn't with Mikhail.

"A military helicopter destroyed the boat with a rocket."

"How do you know all of this?"

"I have a source at the police. A man was camping in the woods along the river and saw the whole thing."

Pavel was on the wrong side of Mikhail. Jenia had said so herself. He remembered now. She told him to be careful also. Why the hell did I have to pick a fight with some power-hungry creep like Mikhail? He's insane.

"Mikhail must have done it," He said as if speaking to himself. "Why would he use such an extreme measure? I don't get it."

He quickly scanned the big room looking for anyone suspicious. God, I wonder if the bastard is coming after me next? He continued to scratch the back of his hand.

"Mikhail? Why do you think he did this, huh?"

"There was some bad blood between Pavel and Mikhail. I think Pavel was in charge of a group of businessmen that included Mikhail and they had a disagreement."

"It could be some kind of coup. Maybe that's it. Maybe Mikhail used the helicopter to show his bosses he has influence with the Army."

Alex realized for all her faults she was good, real good. She knew how to take facts and make quick connections to cause and effect. She is much better at this than I, he thought.

She said, "I'm sorry. I didn't mean to scare you." Then she grinned, "After all, we fellow revolutionaries should watch out for each other."

"You know Jenia?"

"I know of her. I know a lot of things, Alex. It's just that you don't listen to me when I tell them to you."

"Were you really there in ninety-one?"

"Yes, and I knew before you told me that you were there also. That's one of the reasons I picked you to help me."

"You picked me?"

"Yes."

"Why?"

"Alex, we are not doing this for Yeltsin. We're doing it for Russia, for the same dream you and I had in ninety-one."

"Do you really think we can make a difference? All the power is in their hands."

"No it isn't. The power will be in our hands once we have the truth and can prove it."

"If we get close, do you really think they'll let us tell the truth? If they are willing to slaughter one of their own so spectacularly, they'll not hesitate to squash us like bugs under their shoe."

"Are you afraid?"

"Yes. Aren't you?"

"Yes. I'm afraid too. But look what we did in ninety-one, when we put our hands together. Join with me now. Let's make a chain so strong they can't break it."

Alex sighed and said, "You've been right all along. They control the Army already, maybe even the whole government. I've been an ass about this whole project. It's probably too late to save Russia, to save me."

"It's never too late," she said in her typically confident manner.

"What's our next move?"

"Let's go to the office and discuss our options, huh? Besides, you have a funeral to attend."

Alex motioned for the bill. The waitress came showing a big smile. He threw down an extra five Rubles and stood to leave.

Suddenly, he felt naked. He scanned the room again. He wanted to crawl into a hole and hide.

Tanya grabbed his hand and marched in front of him toward the exit on the other side of the bar. Alex saw her studying faces. Suddenly, she squeezed his hand, a small squeeze, but he felt it.

He also saw the man with a goatee. He was sitting on the other side of the bar near the entrance. His head was down as he prepared to drink his beer. Alex saw his gaunt, pale face with pinched nostrils and thin lips. His hair was black, curly. Alex knew the man watched without looking.

She pulled Alex by his arm. He liked her hand in his. He felt safe with her. What was it about this woman?

They hurried through the door and she quickly glanced back to the restaurant. He wanted to look back too, but she jerked his hand and said, "Let's hurry, huh?" He had to jog to stay with her.

8

Jerusalem, Solomon's Office – Wednesday, April 15

Jonah and Solomon sat in silence while the secretary set a full cup of coffee and some sweet biscuits in front of each of them. When she left the room, Solomon looked closely at Jonah and said, "You look tired my friend."

Jonah nodded, "I'm sixty seven and I don't travel well anymore." He grinned.

Jonah noticed a twinkle in the old man's eye as he responded, "Well, I'm eighty two and I don't travel at all. I don't miss it either." He pulled down the gray beard on his chin and lifted the cup to his lips. Jonah tasted his coffee also.

Solomon set his cup down and continued, "I guess it's not just that you look tired, you look sad also. I suppose it's Pavel's death, terrible, terrible."

"After eight years of working with the him, we had become close. I never met his family, but I can imagine what they are going through right now. He had a nine-year-old son. I don't envy anyone who loses a loved one suddenly. It's devastating."

Solomon reached for Jonah's hand and held it in his. "I remember. Does it still hurt?"

"I think of Sarah and Miriam every day, every single day; and it's been eighteen years."

"They wouldn't want you to suffer. The mourning should have stopped long ago."

"It's not mourning. I remember the good times we had and I sometimes think about what Miriam would be doing today. She was very bright you know."

Solomon smiled and sat back on the sofa they shared. "That's her Jewish blood. She got that from you."

Jonah's eyes clouded for just a moment. "Her mother was bright also. I met her through her father, a professor at the University of Chicago. They were Catholic, wouldn't convert."

"I was surprised that you didn't marry a Jew. There certainly are plenty of them in America, especially Chicago."

"God put her in my path. My heart did the rest."

Solomon looked at the ceiling, "God rewards; God punishes."

Jonah took a sharp breath, but remembered he was dealing with an old man set in his ways; so he let the comment pass. Instead, he returned to his business problems. "Pavel's death created some serious problems, and we have to move quickly. There's a lot of legal work needed, not to mention we have to select someone to lead the business operatives group. Our government operatives have sealed his offices, but he probably has papers elsewhere."

"Did you check with his wife?"

"She wasn't home when we looked for her in Russia. I'm afraid someone had already been to her home and messed up the place a bit. I think it was Mikhail."

Solomon face twisted in anger, "God, the body's not even cold yet. Couldn't he wait?"

"He did it on his own. He must believe that possession of Pavel's papers will put him in a stronger position with us. There's no doubt we have a rebellion on our hands."

Solomon nodded, "We need to get any other papers Pavel had before Mikhail or someone else gets their hands on them. Have you contacted his wife in Poland?"

"Let's wait for a few days after the funeral before we barge in on her. She has enough on her mind right now. Besides, Mikhail's break in has probably scared her to death."

"The funeral is tomorrow isn't it?"

"Yes, but I think it best I don't make an appearance. I don't know his family, and it might raise some questions. Besides, all the business operatives will be there. I'll have to find someone to contact her."

Solomon shook his head, "Don't worry about that. I have the perfect person to contact her."

Jonah opened his eyes wide, surprised. "You do?"

Solomon spoke as if he had not heard, "Mikhail is going to be a big problem, but I'm afraid he has us over a barrel for now."

Now, Jonah was stunned, and concerned. "The man has snapped. He's threatening our whole operation. I know we need to replace Pavel, but it can't be Mikhail. We'll lose all control. We have to take him out. We'll lose everything."

Solomon shook his head. "I know how much you want to get him. So do I. But we need patience. We need to establish a plan for someone to take over his empire before we can get rid of him. Our immediate concern is to get someone to take over Pavel's empire."

"Mikhail's trying to do that already."

"Don't kill him. Let's throw him a bone or two to keep him in line until we're ready to take him out. Make him the chairman of the group and throw him a small piece or two of Pavel's empire. Have you anyone in place to take over for Pavel?"

Jonah was too tired to argue. Besides he was relieved that Solomon didn't remind him that it was he, Jonah, who had wanted to hire Mikhail. Jonah knew in his heart that Solomon was right. Too many changes at once and the project will disintegrate. He said quickly, "Yes, I anticipated we might lose one or two key operatives."

Why hadn't he anticipated this revolt? He had considered Mikhail a player, not the leader type; Pavel was the leader. I would not have let this happen five years ago. I would have seen it coming and taken out Mikhail when I had the chance. Sixty-seven, I'm getting too old. Solomon should probably be planning my replacement. I wonder? "Have you given any thought to my replacement? I don't know how much longer I can do this. Every man should have a rest before the end."

Solomon laughed. "Replace you? I'm more worried about replacing me. I'm eighty-two. I should have been gone long ago."

Jonah felt the depression, and it showed. He was getting old and out of shape, physically and mentally. The business situation was bad, out of control. He dreaded more years alone, without Sarah or Miriam or grandchildren to cheer him. He noticed that Solomon was staring at him.

Solomon said, "Don't take it so hard. So, we've lost a bishop. The game is far from over."

Jonah's frustration showed. He snapped, "Pavel was a human being, not a chess piece."

Solomon was taken back, "I'm sorry. I wasn't thinking of Pavel. I was thinking in terms of our strategy. Please forgive me."

Jonah put up his hand and smiled. "I know you didn't mean it that way. I think I'm just reacting to pressure and this bad situation. The nice thing about chess is that your own pieces don't turn on you."

Solomon nodded. "Jonah, my good friend. Let's not focus on a short-term problem. Don't lose sight of our mission. Think of our dream back in eighty-eight. We have accomplished so much using your plan, not only on the income side, which you've handled so admirably, but also on the expenditure side."

Solomon got up, walked to his desk and returned with a file folder and a cigar. "Please my friend, have a cigar and I'll cheer you up." He sat next to Jonah, opened the folder and began to read.

Jonah leaned back, sniffed the cigar, wet it and lit it. He took a long drag and let the smoke flow back out his mouth and nose. The taste was incredible. Every man deserves at least one vice.

After a few moments Solomon looked up and said, "Let's review. We wanted to increase the settlements in the Palestinian territories. Since 1990 we've provided secret grants to settlers totaling over 200 million U.S. dollars. We've increased the settlement population in the West Bank and Gaza from about 80,000 in 1990 to almost 175,000 today. They're housed in 150 settlements in 45,000 homes. Our grants have made it possible for a settler to have a 150 square meter detached home for the price of a two-room flat in Tel Aviv.

We've had even more success in East Jerusalem. There are 180,000 Israeli settlers there. We're creating a chain of settlements surrounding Jerusalem, including Ma'ale Adumim, Beitar, Efrat, and Givat Ze'ev, which will help us successfully determine Jerusalem's future. Furthermore, these settlements will drive a wedge between the northern and southern Palestinian territories in the event world opinion forces us to allow them to have a State."

Jonah asked, "I thought all settlements, at least since ninety six, needed the approval of Yitzhak Mordechai; and, as far as I know he has approved less than 2,500 new units."

"Ah, but we have a nice way around that. His approval is for public consumption only. Many of the units begun during 1997 were approved as long ago as Shamir, but were frozen after 1992 by Rabin. All we had to do was unfreeze them. Furthermore, most of these unfrozen settlements are in small communities. We've kept them out of the official statistics. That's where most of the money has gone. Money you helped us raise, Jonah."

Solomon reviewed his file again. "We've also succeeded with our second goal, to expand our base of support. Our fifty million dollar propaganda campaign in Russia, carried out by our agency, Sochnut, has presented Israel as a rich and democratic western country where every Jew could find their place. We even emphasized our socialist traditions.

We've provided immigration grants of almost three hundred million to help immigrants get here with their families. The Russian population in Israel is almost one million, 600,000 voters, almost twenty-five percent of the voting population. Almost seventy percent of those immigrants are voting with the right. They've put us into power, and we're going to stay there for a long time.

We began, thanks to your plan, to take over the Russian economy. With our . . . your financial success, we're poised to take over Israel too."

Jonah said, "We're still doomed in the long run. If the Arabs become part of a democratic Israel, we're going to be the minority."

Solomon smiled. "We are working on that. There are two solutions. The first is we create a Palestinian state bordering Israel with a buffer in between. Then we close our borders to immigration allowing only Jews to enter. Since the Palestinians have their own state, they can't condemn us for telling Arabs to live in Palestine not Israel. The second solution is don't allow non-Jews to vote."

"Why not just build a fence around Israel?"

Solomon's eyes widened and a large smile pushed his long white beard toward his ears. "What a great idea! I'll bring it up at the next meeting of the Inner Circle."

Middle Game

9

Warsaw, Poland – Thursday, April 16

Massive old trees stood over the small group praying in the light rain. The mechanical wheels complained and the machine lowered the remains of Pavel into the dark hole. The wheels stopped. He was home, gone. Only sadness and memories remained.

Across the small space past the coffin Alex saw Mikhail and other businessmen standing with folded hands and bowed heads. Most were wearing skullcaps. Alex tightened his raincoat against the wet chill and pulled Jenia closer. She leaned hard against him and put her arm around his waist.

Ivona wept and accepted condolences from the mourners as they left the gravesite. Each, in turn, whispered to her, hugged her, and kissed her on the cheek.

Alex felt Jenia tense. Mikhail stepped forward and took Ivona's hand, kissed it and said, "My condolences. Pavel was such a good friend to all of us. We'll miss him." He leaned forward, toward her. Ivona leaned away from him, glared and tightened her lips. He dropped her hand and it fell to her side. Briefly, his eyebrows came together and quickly returned to their station. He bowed, turned and left to join Oleg and Ivan who had stayed by his Mercedes.

Alex and Jenia were last to leave. He wondered what would happen when Pavel's mistress met his wife. Jenia took her arm from around his waist and walked to Ivona. He followed her but stopped a few steps away, a stranger. She and Ivona stood a meter apart and stared at each other for what seemed to Alex a long time. Neither spoke. As if on cue, they fell into each other's arms and cried. Alex stared and shifted his weight.

Jenia kissed Ivona on the cheek, whispered something in her ear and turned her toward Alex. "Ivona, this is Alexander Ivanovich, who I've mentioned to you before. Alex, this is Ivona."

He moved forward to meet this stranger. For some unknown reason he felt a comradeship with her. He kissed her offered hand. "Ivona please accept my sympathy."

"Thank you. Thank you for coming."

Awkwardly, he leaned forward to hug Ivona and kiss her on the cheek. He wanted to do it. He didn't want to drop her hand like Mikhail.

Jenia led Ivona to the small Fiat where her sister and Lenya were waiting. Alex followed, but stopped a few meters away.

Ivona glanced toward Mikhail's vehicle, turned to Jenia and said, "He went with them to save us. They executed him, and now they come here and expect me to accept them as friends."

Alex was surprised Ivona not only knew who "they" were, but she assumed Jenia knew them also. Who are these two women and how are they connected?

Jenia opened the car door. Before Ivona entered she said, "I'm worried for our safety."

"Why?"

"Someone broke in and searched the dacha."

"Do you know what they wanted?"

Ivona looked around to make sure no one was too close. She stopped her gaze on Alex for a moment. "Pavel had some business papers in a bank here in Warsaw. What else is there to take?" She cried again. "They've taken my Pavel." Ivona's legs failed and Jenia steadied her. She pulled her close. The two women who had shared the same man held each other sharing the pain.

When Ivona regained her composure, Jenia suggested, "Give them the papers. What can they mean to you now?"

Ivona nodded toward Mikhail's car. "They must be important to him. Maybe there is something in those papers to make him suffer. He's an animal."

Jenia glanced at Alex and then hugged Ivona again. "You and Lenya should stay with your sister tonight. You need the support. Alex is a lawyer with a large consulting company. Get the papers and he can go through them with you tomorrow."

Ivona's face brightened. "Do you think he'll mind?"

"On the contrary. I think he'll be pleased to help you." They glanced at Alex, and he nodded.

Ivona kissed her and entered the rear door of the car. Slowly, the car pulled away from the side of the road and left the cemetery. Lenya waved to Jenia from the rear window. She returned the wave. In the background, Alex thought he saw a man with a goatee enter Mikhail's car. Was he the same man as in the restaurant? What would he be doing here? He wasn't at the gravesite. Is it possible he knew Pavel also?

"She must have no morals. God, she was Pavel's mistress," Mikhail said to no one in particular. He heard Yuri enter the car, but he kept his gaze on Jenia. She walked over to Alex, took his arm and headed toward their rented limousine.

Yuri said, "They're sharing a room at the Sobieski Hotel. They're scheduled to fly back to Moscow on a Lot flight late tomorrow evening."

The words tore at Mikhail. He pictured the little man thrusting into her. He hated him. He would kill him with his bare hands if he caught them in bed together. He hated her for letting that little bastard enter her. He wanted to punish her arrogant body, to attack her. I'll have her, even if I have to rape her, he told himself. Alex is getting in my way.

He turned to look at Yuri sitting next to him in the back seat. "Keep your eye on them. I'm going back to Moscow. Let me know if they meet with Pavel's wife again. Okay?"

Yuri nodded. On its way out of the cemetery the limousine carrying Jenia and Alex passed Mikhail's car. Yuri watched it go by, got out of Mikhail's car and made his way to a white Polonez waiting nearby.

Alex didn't realize the pressure he felt until he was safely sitting in the limousine. At the gravesite, he felt like an intruder. His only relationship to anyone was his affair with Pavel's mistress. Now, alone with Jenia and out of sight, he relaxed. As their car passed Mikhail's Mercedes, Alex turned his head to hide his face. I wonder if Mikhail or Oleg recognized me? I hope not.

What is Jenia's relationship to Ivona? They seem to know each other so well. Jenia's so confident, so in control, like Tanya. He glanced at her. She was looking out of the rear window. He followed her gaze, but saw only an old white Polonez slowly pulling away from the side of the road.

He had to ask, "Does she know you were Pavel's mistress?"

"Yes."

He waited, but she said no more. He said, sharply, "And?"

She looked at him with that impish look he loved, and hated. "I was orphaned in Irkutsk when I was ten. Ivona was one of the caretakers there." She paused, trying to decide whether to continue. "For six years we were together and became best friends. She went back to Poland a year before I left the orphanage."

He realized he knew nothing of her past. He was wondering whether he knew anything about her at all. His mind was cluttered with thousands of questions. He said sarcastically, "How did you became Pavel's — her husband's mistress?"

"I was living in Moscow in 1990, when Ivona and Pavel moved there. He had come into a lot of money, and had to move to Moscow as part of his work."

He growled, "So you renewed old acquaintances?"

She answered curtly, "So it seems."

He waited for more, but it wasn't coming. His jaws began to tighten. He snapped, "Are you enjoying this game?"

She sighed. "Pavel was having problems growing old. So, he bought the Knight Klub to recapture his youth. Ivona worried about his being around so many young women. She discussed it with me. I suggested a solution that would keep girls away from him. She accepted. He never knew."

He whispered, "Jesus."

She continued, ignoring his comment. "He loved her you know. Sometimes we would sit for hours and he would talk about her and Lenya. My affection, hugs and kisses on his cheek were the only youthful reassurances he needed."

She saw him staring and her mouth fell open in surprise. She poked him on the upper arm. "Before you saw me as a mistress to a rich man, a woman out for money. Now you know the truth and you look at me like I'm some strange creature."

He slowly shook his head. "I love you. You lead an unusual life. You always surprise me." He was happy to see a smile return to her face. It felt so comforting when she kissed him on the cheek. He put his head on her shoulder and she ran her fingers through his hair. He put his arms around her and hugged her tightly. He didn't see her look through the rear window to check on the white Polonez following them.

10

Warsaw – Friday, April 17

Alex had slept well. He woke up feeling great, rested. Everything seemed to be falling into place for him. His relationship with Tanya had improved immensely. She even admitted his Knight Klub connection was important. He told her everything he knew about the Klub, although he left Jenia out of his comments. At Tanya's suggestion, he had asked and received information from Konstantin about the men who met there, especially Mikhail. Alex had Jenia to himself for the last two days and nights and he kept dreaming about how much time they would spend together in the future. He didn't have a hangover.

On the other hand, Jenia was nervous, tense. Alex knew she hadn't slept well, if at all. She was already dressed and drinking coffee. Pavel's death is affecting her mood, he told himself.

When they exited the Sobieski Hotel, she stopped him from waving for a taxi. "I need to clear my head. Let's take a short walk." He was surprised. It was raining hard and the wind was gusty enough to threaten an umbrella.

He liked Warsaw. It was much smaller than Moscow and the pace was relaxed. He decided to revisit in more pleasant circumstances. They strolled along Jerozolimskie; he nudged her and pointed to the Palace of Culture sitting like a fat pyramid in the center of the City. It screamed for attention.

He said, "Stalin gave the building to the Poles as a gift."

She glanced behind them. Then she grinned at him and responded; "Don't say that to the Poles. They had a contest among architects to find out how to hide the monster. All it does is remind them of over forty years under the Soviet boot."

"Speaking of boots, my shoes are soaked. This rain is getting worse. How far do you want to walk?"

"We'll catch a taxi at the central railway station. It's only a few more blocks."

They walked the rest of the way in silence. At the station they stopped for a croissant. Alex wanted to have coffee with it, but she said they didn't have the time. While he was still chewing the croissant, they left the station and caught a taxi from the lineup. She gave the driver instructions, "*Witkorska Ulica.*"

After twenty minutes, the taxi pulled to the curb by a three-story brown brick house surrounded by a metal fence. Jenia searched the street before they left the taxi. She took his hand and quickly led him to the gate. The yard was small and covered with grass and a few beds of flowers mixed with bushes.

Alex was surprised when she reached behind the gate and pushed a button to open it. They entered and walked around the house through a carport to a side door. She knocked loudly. He asked her, "What's wrong? You act as if you are searching the area for Chechens."

She shook her head. Her face was drawn tight. When they heard someone come to the other side of the door, she said, "Ivona, *eta* Jenia."

He heard the bolts snap back from the door, it opened, and Ivona met them with a smile. "Welcome. Lenya is still with my sister. You were right. I needed both of them last night." She held out her arms and Jenia hugged her. Ivona hugged Alex too and said, "Please come into the parlor and I'll make some tea or coffee. Which would you like Alex? I know Jenia hates tea."

"I'll have coffee too, thank you," he said. They walked through the entryway into the parlor. He was ready to relax for a few minutes and drink some coffee. Jenia's tense mood had affected him, exhausted him. Jenia waved her hand and said, "I'll pass on the coffee. I need a short nap. I didn't sleep well last night."

"Alex and I can handle this ourselves, dear. Why don't you go lay down now?"

Jenia kissed him on the cheek, turned and climbed the stairs to the next level. She was comfortable with the place. Apparently, she had been there before.

Files and papers covered a table in the parlor. He sat down and scanned the lot. Many of the papers were in Hebrew, the rest in English,

Russian or Polish. When Ivona brought him his coffee, he said, "I'm sorry. I don't read Hebrew."

"Some papers may be of no interest and we can forget about them. I'll translate the interesting ones and you can take notes. Okay?"

He nodded and said, "I'll start by looking at those written in Russian and English. The one in Polish appears to be a last will and testament."

"Yes, I'll file that with my papers," she said and took it from the pile. "I'll be right back if you want to start on the others," she said and left the room.

He assessed the stack of papers. I should be able to get through this in a few hours, he decided. He noted most of the Russian and English documents related to company formations and bank accounts in Russia, Cyprus, Switzerland, Liechtenstein and Austria. "Hum," he said to himself, "nothing in the Bahamas or Bermuda. I'd have at least one account in the Caribbean so I'd have an excuse to visit there."

He roughed out an organization chart on a pad of paper. From the bank accounts and company formations, he easily put together a list of Pavel's companies and how they all fit together. Once he prepared the chart, he examined the dates on the bank authorizations to determine when they were opened.

Ivona came back into the room. "Excuse me, Ivona. Do you know where Pavel kept the bank statements relating to these accounts?"

"I think they are all at the office, except for this one." She selected a file folder containing three years of bank statements for an account in Liechtenstein. The documents were in English, but contained many handwritten notes and schedules written in Hebrew. Ivona read the notes and then told him, "This is one of our personal accounts. The money came from a Swiss company called Financial Management Associates." She pointed to a list of amounts. "There. You can see it is a monthly payment of one hundred thousand dollars for the last two years. Earlier it was fifty thousand."

"When did the payments begin?"

"It looks like they began in June of 1990."

"Well, Ivona. You won't go without food and clothing."

"Now, there is only one-hundred thousand left in the account," she responded. She picked out a letter written to her and read through it. "Pavel sent me this letter. Apparently, all of the money has been invested with money managers. He has given me a contact list. I didn't know Pavel had all this money put away for us. He said he was going to go to Zurich to tell a man named Jonah he was resigning. Then he . . ." Her voice broke. She cried.

※

When Mikhail sat on the leather sofa next to his dog, Buddy, it rolled onto its back and held its paws in the air. Mikhail scratched Buddy's stomach, and the dog folded its front legs over its chest and closed its eyes. Buddy's mood helped Mikhail to relax, to think. He had to put Jenia and that skinny little bastard out of his mind. He had other things to work on now.

I need to meet soon with Jonah. Now he knows. I have influence in Russia, even with the army. With Pavel gone, Jonah will have to rethink his organization. Who else does he have? The rest don't have my power and connections. I'm too important and powerful for him to write me off.

His thoughts were interrupted by the telephone ringing, once, twice, three times. "Mr. Kolodkin, you have a call," came Galina's screech over the intercom. He got off of the couch and walked across the room to his desk. Buddy rolled onto his stomach and watched him go. Mikhail grabbed the receiver and spoke, "This is Mikhail."

It was Yuri making his report. "They went to the hotel and stayed the night. One room shared." Mikhail's face reddened. Yuri continued, "At ten forty five this morning they left the hotel and walked to the Central Railroad Station where they caught a taxi. I arranged a taxi for them at the hotel, but for some reason they went to the station instead. The taxi took them to visit Pavel's wife. They're still there. They haven't checked out of the hotel. Earlier today, Pavel's wife went to a bank and removed some papers from a private box."

Mikhail was seething. Alex spent the night with her, the bastard. Now they were probably getting Pavel's private papers from Ivona. Why would they do that? He works for a consulting company. Maybe Pavel's a client? I wonder is it possible? I'll have someone look into it. Jenia certainly can't have any interest in the papers.

"Okay. If he tries to leave with papers, kill him." He remembered the bar scene, Alex at the gravesite, Alex staying in a room with Jenia. "On second thought, just kill him."

Yuri responded, "It should be no problem. Neither seems to be armed. I've arranged for a taxi to be conveniently available when they leave the house. I have a back-up plan in case they don't take the taxi."

"Don't hurt the woman! I'll take care of her when she returns to Moscow. Make sure she doesn't take any papers with her."

"Okay. As you wish. It'll make things more difficult. I'll take out the man, grab the papers and leave the woman unhurt. Bye."

Mikhail hung up the telephone, glanced down and saw Buddy lying at his feet. He reached down and petted his head. He picked a cigarette from the case on his desk and lit it. He sat in his chair, leaned back and blew smoke at the ceiling. Buddy was pushing a ball against his leg. He took the ball from Buddy's mouth and threw it across the room. Buddy ran after it, his feet slipping on the wood floor.

The ball bounced off a wall and Buddy leaped into the air to grab it with his mouth. He stood on the other side of the room with the ball hanging out the side of his mouth and looking back at Mikhail. Slowly he settled his body onto the floor and put his paws over the ball.

Mikhail shook his head and said, "Life is so simple for you. For this moment in time, your whole world, your entire reason for existing is to capture that particular ball. You care about nothing else. I envy you."

✻

Ivona translated the Hebrew documents for Alex. He took copious notes and the time passed quickly. It was late afternoon when they took a break. Still, they had many documents left to examine. It was clear to him the whole story of Pavel's financial empire was here in these papers.

"Maybe we can stay over another day and make copies of these documents. Would that be okay?"

Alex hoped to share a room with Jenia again. Last night he was unsuccessful. She was tired and irritated. Something was bothering her. Maybe after a rest she would be a better companion. As he was pondering this, she entered the room and answered his question, "No need for copies. We can take the originals with us. It's okay isn't it Ivona?"

"Of course. I only need the personal papers. You are welcome to take the rest. I don't want them anymore."

Alex leaned back in his chair. "Well, my job is a lot easier. I can have the Hebrew documents translated in Moscow." He asked Ivona, "You've mentioned a man named Jonah a few times, but I don't see his name in any of the papers here. Have you seen the name or any information about him in the Hebrew documents?"

"No. His name doesn't appear anywhere. But I know he's important. Pavel, like the others, reported to him. He lives in Zurich that's all I know."

As he talked with Ivona he glanced in a mirror and saw Jenia reading the Hebrew documents on the table. He asked, "Have you ever seen him, met him?"

Ivona responded, "No. I've never met him. Pavel met him at the synagogue here in Warsaw in late 1989. A few weeks later we took a trip to Israel and Pavel met him there also."

Alex glanced at Jenia. She looked irritated. She turned to him and said, "I think we should gather the papers and leave now. It's been a long day." She winked at Alex. "We can go back to the hotel and rest for a few hours before we return to Moscow. Okay?"

He was pleased. He was tired of reading papers and taking notes. He wished Tanya had reviewed the papers, because he was sure he missed some important matters. In any event, Tanya would get her chance. She'll be pleased with me. For some reason it was important to him. He fancied her smiling and patting his shoulder to congratulate him.

He put the papers into his briefcase. Soon it was bulging, but more papers were still on the table. "I'll have to leave a few behind. Ivona, would you send them to me in Moscow?"

"Of course."

"Here is my address." He began to write the PHD address, but then thought better of it. Instead, he wrote his name and home address and gave it to her. He stood and stretched his arms. He hadn't realized how stiff he had become hunched over the papers for so long.

Ivona said, "I've made some soup and sandwiches. You haven't eaten all day."

Alex responded. "I'm starved."

Jenia said, "We should be leaving . . . well, ok. We'll grab a quick bite and go."

Alex ate two sandwiches with his soup. Ivona beamed as she watched him wolf down the food. Jenia sipped her soup, but didn't take a sandwich. Alex leaned back in his chair and took a deep breath. He was quick to accept another cup of coffee with some small chocolates. It was dark outside when Jenia said, "Come on Alex, it's time to go."

He turned to Ivona, "Thank you for all your help." He saw hope in her face.

"Do you think there is anything in the papers to cause problems for Mikhail?"

"I think so. His name was on some of the charts."

She grinned, "His name appears in some of the notes also."

He said, "I'm sure we'll find something in here that will embarrass him and many others too."

He lifted his now heavy briefcase and he and Jenia walked through the foyer to the side door. They both kissed Ivona and gave her a final hug. Jenia said, "Don't turn on the lights."

The door closed behind them and they stood for a few moments in the dark letting their eyes adjust. Jenia took his hand and walked slowly through the carport to the front yard. It was still raining. She released his hand, walked through the front gate and turned right toward the corner nearest the main street. When he passed through the gate, Alex looked to the left and saw a taxicab. He shouted, "We're in luck," and ran to the taxi only twenty meters down the street.

"I'd rather walk," She shouted back at him.

It was too late. He was at the door of the taxi and had opened it. "Come on. It's raining." He shouted back. "We can take a walk after we get to the hotel and I get rid of this heavy briefcase. Besides it's better to walk in the center of town than in a neighborhood we know nothing about."

She hesitated and glanced up and down the street. She studied the driver carefully and in English ordered, "Sobieski Hotel." She motioned for Alex to slide over and she sat behind the driver.

The driver took the taxi to the end of the street, turned right onto a main street and increased speed. She was sitting straight backed, watching the road and the driver carefully. Her hand was in her purse, apparently searching for a tissue. Alex wondered if she was crying again thinking about Pavel. The rain had lessened to a mere drizzle by the time they approached the city proper. He was pleased with his decision to delay their walk. Now he wouldn't get wet.

They had been riding for twenty minutes when suddenly the driver spun the wheel to the left and drove down an alley. "Shortcut," he said. Jenia was on the edge of her seat, straining to see through the windshield. He followed her gaze. There were two men midway down the alley. One was the man with the goatee. Alex found it difficult to breathe. His chest was tight. His heart pounded.

"It's a trap," he heard her say. His stomach churned. He jumped when he heard a shot and smelled the powder. He was thrown to the left into Jenia when the taxi veered quickly to the right and hit the wall of a building.

He straightened himself and saw the gun in Jenia's hand. It was still smoking, as was the hole in the back of the seat. The driver had fallen sideways over the center gearshift.

"Run, Alex, run," she ordered. She opened her door and leapt out of the taxi. He quickly did the same out of the other side. The big man was running toward her. The man with the goatee was closing on him. Both had guns in their hands.

Alex turned and ran back toward the entrance of the alley. He slipped on the wet pavement and regained his balance, but lost valuable distance. He was afraid to look. He was sure the man would shoot any second. He weaved as he ran down the narrow alley and instinctively ducked his head, but he had to look. The man slowly raised his gun and pointed it at him. Alex ducked and weaved quickly, too quickly for the slippery pavement. He heard a shot and fell, but no bullet came past him or hit him. The briefcase flew out of his hand and went sliding away down the alley.

When he rolled over to get up, he saw Jenia on the ground and the big man on top of her. God, she's dead. The man with the goatee was walking slowly toward Alex, but looking back toward Jenia and holding the gun at his side, as if trying to make up his mind what to do. Alex leaped to his feet and ran toward Jenia. Suddenly, he heard another shot and his leg gave out. He stumbled to the pavement and felt a terrible burning in his calf. I've been shot. He was surprised it didn't hurt as much as he thought it would. As he skidded along the pavement, Alex rolled to the side and looked at the man with the goatee still walking slowly toward him. Alex saw the man's unblinking eyes, his face twisted from the tension, the smoke still seeping from the barrel of the gun. He was only a few meters away and couldn't miss. I'm going to die in this damn alley, Alex decided. It surprised him that he was so calm, everything seemed in slow motion. It's over.

The man stopped to steady his aim. Alex expected to see fire come from the barrel. Will I see the bullet coming? Instead, he saw the man's shoulder jerk upward and he heard a shot. The gun fell out of the man's hand, bounced onto the pavement and rolled away. The man grabbed his shoulder and spun around. Alex saw Jenia crouching and pointing her gun. The man ran past him, grabbed the briefcase and continued running to the end of the alley. Alex stared after him until he rounded the corner and disappeared.

Alex lay back on the pavement, exhausted. His leg was beginning to throb, now that all the excitement was over. He sat up and reached to pull the pant leg away to look at the wound. He was sick to his stomach and shivered when he saw the blood and the two holes in his calf. He felt a hand on his arm.

"Are you okay?"

It was like waking from a dream. "I thought you were dead."

"No. I pulled the big lug on top of me for protection. I guess the other guy thought I was dead too."

Alex looked past her down the alley. The big man was sprawled on the ground near the wrecked taxi. In his mind he saw the dead driver slumped over the gearshift. His throbbing leg reminded him someone had asked him a question.

"He shot me in the leg. Damn he got the briefcase."

Jenia examined his wound. "He didn't hit a bone. Come on. We have to get out of here. I don't want to explain two dead bodies to the police."

Alex was amazed. She was so calm, so in control. Who is this woman? He took out his handkerchief, but she pulled him up. "You can put it on when we get out of here. You won't bleed to death. Let's go."

God she's strong, he thought. She pulled him to his feet and dragged him along as she ran down the alley. Pain shot through his leg with every step. He was limping badly and had trouble staying with her. They rounded the corner at the end of the alley and slowed to a fast walk. He was panting.

She slowed to a comfortable pace and took his arm in hers. They crossed the main street and entered a large park on the other side walking like two lovers, except for his limp. He was tired and wanted to lie down to rest, but at least his leg didn't hurt so much anymore. He wondered if he'd get gangrene or something because he hadn't covered the wound.

She led him to a clump of trees near a small pond and helped him to sit down on a bench. His hands and legs were beginning to shake. He pulled away his pant leg. The bleeding had almost stopped. When he tried to tie his handkerchief around the wound, his hands shook so much he kept punching the wound. It was bleeding heavily again. He felt like a child.

He looked at her. She was watching, but not helping. She was calm, unusually so, alert and in control. He decided she enjoyed this. Who is this woman?

She spoke. "We need to get to the train station. It's only a kilometer from here. There's a train leaving for Gdansk in about an hour. Can you walk?"

"Train?"

"I've arranged for a car in Gdansk. We'll drive to Kaliningrad. I'll treat your wound on the train. It isn't bad, thank God. We'll catch a plane in Kaliningrad and be back in Moscow by tomorrow evening."

He was getting sick to his stomach. Sweat ran down the side of his face. It tickled. "I'm freezing to death," he said, still shivering. His mind was racing. I'm going to be arrested and probably charged with murder. I'm inadequate. Imagine. I was going to protect her. Hell, she doesn't need my protection. I wonder if she's been laughing at me the whole time, if the guys at the Klub, Tanya have been laughing at me.

She was staring at him, a worried look on her face. He felt more and more inadequate, even unmanly.

Softly, she said, "Can you walk?"

"Who are you really? How do you fit into all of this? Who were those men? Why were they trying to kill us?"

So many things became clear now. She expected this to happen. She knew this was going to happen, like she knew Pavel would be killed. Maybe that's why she didn't go to Pavel's house on Sunday. "Be careful," she had said. Fear began crawling around in his mind. He was going to die soon, if not in Warsaw then surely in Moscow. Mikhail wanted them dead, and Mikhail's money and power could get anything done. Hadn't Valodya said that?

He suddenly realized he was limping toward the edge of the park. Where am I going? What am I doing here? He stopped and stared at the ground. I don't know what to do. He turned, limped in another direction, this time deeper into the park. He didn't know where to go, except he wanted to get away from her, away from this situation. He wanted to get away from sweet Jenia who manages strippers, who makes deals with wives to become their husband's mistress, who reads Hebrew, carries a gun in her purse and kills without remorse.

"Alex, Alex are you ok?"

He turned to face her. He shouted. "You act like it never happened. You killed two men a few minutes ago and you act like we're out for a stroll in the park." He tried to escape from her, but every step was pain and he didn't know where to go. In the distance he heard a siren and felt his stomach turn. I don't want to be arrested. I don't like Warsaw. I want to be home in Moscow. He knew he was trapped. He turned and looked at her again.

"It's like . . . like you had this whole thing planned. Where did you get a gun?"

"From Ivona. I suspected something like this might happen. I told you Mikhail is dangerous. I saw him looking at us at the gravesite. Let's get out of here. We have a train to catch."

She reached out her hand, but Alex stepped back.

"I'm not going anywhere until I get some answers."

She scowled. "You have two choices. Come with me or explain two dead bodies to the Polish Police. They love Russians you know."

"I don't know which is more dangerous for me."

Her face softened and presented the impish grin he'd seen so often in the Knight Klub. Pointing toward the entrance to the park she said, "Why don't you crawl into the trunk of that Mercedes over there? Some Russian will steal it and you'll be in Moscow by morning."

Alex gave in. It was no use; she wasn't going to tell him anything and he had no alternatives. She would get him out of this mess.

"That would be different, a stolen car that comes with a driver in the trunk. With my luck, for the first time the Polish police will catch the thief and I'll end up in a Polish jail anyway. Come on, I miss the safety of Moscow." With those words he started to limp out of the park.

11

Moscow – Saturday, April 18

"I manage a string of Knight Klub dancers. I am the mistress of a dead man. What more do you want to know?" Alex had asked her over and over, but her answer, when he got one, was always evasive. Sometimes she would try to add humor. "I am the wild woman you bedded in Moscow and Warsaw. I'm the woman you say you love, although you don't know what you're talking about."

None of the answers satisfied him, but he eventually quit asking. He wanted her to say she wasn't involved with the conspiracy, to confess she was a secret agent working for the Russian government, or admit she was an orphan from Irkutsk who needed a man to protect and care for her. But he knew better.

"I don't know who you are really, but I know I love you. I want to be around you all the time. When I'm not with you I feel empty. You don't need me. You've never needed me."

"Stop it Alex. Why do you think I became involved with you? You're not a rich man. You're not an especially handsome man. You're simply Alex, and for that I love you, I need you."

Their conversation went back and forth all the way to Gdansk. On the way, she examined and dressed his wound. When they arrived in Gdansk, she led him from the station to a nearby parking lot. She reached under the front bumper of a Burgundy Audi 100 and found a small box containing a key.

He quit asking questions. He knew he was with someone who had excellent connections and was used to such intrigue. Besides, he was tired. He was asleep before they reached the road to Kaliningrad. He awoke in Kaliningrad and asked how he got over the border without someone checking his papers.

"They checked our papers. You were sleeping; so I vouched for you." She grinned like a young child with a secret. He always kept his passport in his jacket pocket wrapped in large rubber bands. He did this in case anyone tried to pick his pocket. The rubber bands would catch and warn him. His passport was still in his pocket. He was sure it hadn't been removed. He said nothing. He knew he wouldn't get an answer anyway.

The plane trip to Moscow was uneventful. When they neared the city she again became tense and alert. As far as he knew, she hadn't slept at all. He was convinced now she had special training, a professional. He no longer wondered how she fit in to all of what had happened. He was more concerned with how he fit in.

They landed at Sheremetyevo One. When they left the airplane, Jenia said, "We're vulnerable now. Stay close behind me. There's a car waiting for us."

"Why are we doing all of this? Do you think they'll try to kill us again?"

She stared at him bewildered. "Kill us? No one is trying to kill us Alex. They're trying to kill you. Hadn't you realized?"

He was stunned. "Only me?"

"Yes, you. You can't go back to your flat. It's not safe. Probably, someone has broken in and searched the place. If you go back there, he will be waiting to kill you."

His stomach was churning. My God, he thought, can this be true? He stopped walking and stared at her. He was scratching the back of his left hand. He opened his mouth to say something, but she grabbed his hand and pulled him after her. She was unusually impatient. "Come on. We can't stand out in the open like this. I have to get you to a safe flat. We both need some sleep."

They rode in a green Lada driven by a man in his mid forties. Alex didn't get a good look at his face, but he noticed the man was in good shape. He drove straight into Moscow until the Garden Ring where he turned right and drove toward Novy Arbat. The car passed Smolenskaya Metro Station and turned down a side street. A few blocks later the driver parked it in front of a large apartment building. He handed Jenia a set of keys. She got out of the car. Alex followed. She hurried down a side alley to the entrance. He glanced back and saw the green Lada pull away from the curb and speed away.

They stopped at a flat on the eighth floor. She unlocked the door and they stepped into a hallway running about five meters to a bathroom. To the immediate right was an archway leading into a reception room. The room contained a leather loveseat and chair, some tables, lamps and a television. All of the furniture looked and smelled new. Another archway led from the reception room to a bedroom containing a large wardrobe, a dresser and a new bed with an oak headboard. A double-headed Russian eagle was carved into the headboard. A menorah stood on the dresser.

"Who owns this place?"

"A friend of mine is visiting in Europe now. He said I could use it if necessary."

"He?"

She glared at him like she was going to slap him. Then she smiled. "Come on Alex. Don't make something out of nothing. At least I've found you a place to stay."

He challenged her. "I'll bet nothing has happened at my old flat. Why would Mikhail be after me? I may have smarted off to him once, but is that enough to kill me?"

"For Mikhail it's enough. Believe me, the man is dangerous. But he doesn't want to kill you because of your confrontation at the Klub."

"Then why?"

"Because we've been lovers. He wants me and you're in his way. You've had me and he knows it."

"Jesus. Does he think you love me?"

She grinned and put his face in her hands. "He knows I love you." He grabbed her and pulled her tight against his body. All the excitement, the tension had hit him and he needed someone to hold. He needed a safe haven. She was it.

"Do you love me? I mean like married having children love?"

She didn't answer. Instead she lifted the telephone receiver and made a call. He heard her say something about being safe and needing a driver. As she turned around he said, "You're not leaving are you?"

"No, but I need the keys to your flat. We need to get your clothes and whatever else you may want brought here."

"Come on. I'm a big boy. I can go get my own clothes. It's only a few kilometers. We can flag down a car and be there in ten minutes. Let's go together."

"Call a neighbor. Do you have the number of a neighbor you trust?"

"I can call Elzbieta. She and I talk often and she's given me her phone number."

Jenia laughed. "You were accusing me? You devil you."

"It's not like that. We're merely acquaintances."

"I believe you. But I'll bet Elzbieta has higher hopes. Give her a call. Go ahead. Call her."

He found Elzbieta's number in his address book and dialed. He waited for three rings and then heard the click.

"Hello?"

"*Privet* Elzbieta. It's Alex. How are things?"

"Alex? My God I'm glad you're safe. Where are you? I told you a wooden door is worthless in Moscow."

"What happened?"

"Yesterday, in the evening. I didn't see them, but I heard them burst through the door. I called the police immediately. I thought you were in there. I'm so happy you're safe. I was so worried about you." She began to cry.

"Don't worry Elzbieta. I'm okay. I owe you a dinner when I return."

He saw Jenia turn from the window and scowl at him. He stuck his chin out at her and made a face to show he was only joking.

He continued, "Elzbieta, tonight someone will be coming to my flat to gather some of my things. Don't worry when you hear them. Ok?"

"Ok. Do they need any help?"

"No. It is best you don't get involved or even let them see you. It's government business." He saw Jenia roll her eyes and he grinned.

Elzbieta gushed, "Oh this is so exciting."

"I'll tell you all about it when we have a dinner, but only if you don't get involved. I have to go now. Don't want to stay on the phone too long. *Poka.*"

Jenia was laughing when she came to him and wrapped her hands around his neck. She kissed him on the cheek and ran her hand through his hair. She took the telephone from his hand and made a call. It was short only a few words. "It's ok. See you in a few hours." She turned to face him. "We have a few hours before they come to get the keys." She unbuttoned her blouse.

He grinned and undid the buttons on his shirt. "Well, I suppose we can figure out a way to pass the time. I hope the traffic's heavy."

12

Zurich – Monday, April 20

Zurichbergstrasse is an impressive street. It runs from the Limmat River to the top of the hill, a small mountain really. It is a quiet street, with only an occasional car. Most people find it too steep for a casual stroll. Huge old mansions on large estates line the street. Stately trees, witnesses to more than one hundred years of Swiss history, guard each estate. The grass, the trees and the hedges provide a refreshing green background to the multicolored flowers everywhere.

It was exactly the kind of street Jonah was looking for in 1990 when he began operations in Zurich. The house was a seven hundred meter, three-story mansion about three quarters of the way up the hill. He loved it as soon as he set eyes on it. It had a red slate roof and spires on each corner. With its limestone exterior and arched doorways, it looked like a castle.

The house stood on a high patch of ground almost in the center of the property, which was well shaded by more than fifteen large oak and chestnut trees reaching over sixty feet. Tall spruce and other evergreen trees and hedges lined the driveway and the property's perimeter, which was also protected by high concrete walls or iron fencing.

Jonah made the purchase after difficult negotiations and paying what some considered a foolishly high price. The owner didn't want to sell at any price. Fortunately, Jonah had some friendly Jews in the local banking community who helped him with his talks and pressured the previous owner, who was deeply in debt.

A well-respected Swiss architect redesigned the interior, and a local company did all of the renovations. An Israeli company designed and installed the security system. One of the members of Solomon's inner circle had recommended the company.

He made only minor changes to the outside. He hired a service to clean the property and trim the bushes. That same company provided major cleaning service for the inside of the house, which it performed on the same day. He also hired a maid to come twice a week to perform normal cleaning services, such as dusting, washing, and ironing.

Jonah liked to climb Zurichbergstrasse. Most mornings, especially in spring, he would put on his sweater and walking boots and stroll down the hill to a café on Ramisstrasse. There he would eat a doughnut and have a cup of coffee before he would trudge back to his house, a climb of almost two kilometers.

Winded he stopped at the corner of Pestalozzistrasse. He gazed at his house 100 meters further. I've got to quit smoking cigars, he thought to himself as he did almost every time he made this walk. However, the thought of sitting in his library, reading philosophy and smoking a fresh Cuban cigar gave him new energy. He resumed his climb.

After a quick shower and a bite to eat, he was ready for his coffee and his first cigar of the day. He carried his cup into the library, which also served as his office, and took a seat in one of the two high-back leather chairs separated by an antique walnut table made from a tree trunk. Sarah was so proud of that table. She had purchased it in Amana, Iowa when they traveled there to see how the Amish lived. He kept the table and shipped it to Israel when he returned there in 1984. He brought it with him to Zurich after he bought the house.

From the humidor Jonah selected a cigar and held it before his eyes. It was thick and so perfectly round. Slowly, he rolled it in his fingers and heard the tobacco cracking. He ran it under his nose and sniffed the sweet yet pungent musky odor of the leaf. Ah Cuba, wonderful Cuba. When I'm through here I'll go there to live. I'll lie in tobacco leaves. I'll roll my own cigars.

He put the cigar in his mouth and rolled it over his tongue. When he pushed it in and out to moisten the outer leaves, he felt a slight burning sensation. The rough texture lightly massaged his lips. Again, he held it in front of his face and stared at it lovingly. He snapped his lighter and held it at the end of the cigar, which he twisted back and forth through the flame. Waves of heat rose above the flame and the cigar glowed. He put it in his mouth and took short puffs and continued to torture the other end with the flame.

Soon, he felt the hot smoke in his mouth. He let it drift back out and rise to his nose. He shut his eyes and inhaled to taste the wonderful aroma. Another long drag and he pulled the cigar from his mouth. He inhaled the warm smoke deep down his throat and into his chest. He felt the same slight dizziness as when he took a long quaff of a fine wine. The smoke engulfed his senses and removed all cares from his world.

He let his mind play, as he often did. I wonder if there is a heaven and a hell. I wonder if there's a cigar store in heaven. What a foolish thought. Surely there's one in hell. What convenience. No need for a lighter there, he laughed to himself. Turn left or right and the cigar is charged, ready to go.

He opened his eyes and scanned the long wall of shelves filled with hundreds of books in nine different languages. He couldn't read the titles from his seat, but he could almost recite them by heart. They were his darlings and only real source of pleasure. From the table, he picked up the Latin translation of Plutarch's *Parallel Lives* and placed it onto his lap.

It had been a few hours and Jonah had dozed off twice before the telephone rang. The reassuring voice of Benjamin, his head of security, was on the other end. "Mikhail and his bodyguard Oleg arrived a few minutes ago. No checked luggage. Ivan met them in a black Mercedes limousine. They are pulling away from the curb as we speak. They should be there in twenty to thirty minutes."

Jonah tensed. He wasn't looking forward to this day. It was going to be contentious. He wished Solomon had given him permission to kill all three of them. He'd dump their bodies in the lake. He glanced again at the book. Plutarch's heroes, like me, loved philosophy but killed when necessary. Somehow, it made him feel better.

He responded, "Thanks. Follow them here and go around back to the bungalow. I'll leave the intercom on so you can hear if anything gets out of hand. Don't let them see you arrive."

He returned to his chair and took a long soothing drag from his cigar. But he couldn't relax. He had loved Pavel; he hated Mikhail. In some ways he felt responsible for Pavel's death.

I can't believe Mikhail has the balls to come here and meet me in my own home. If it weren't for Solomon, this would be your last day on earth Mikhail. The thought made Jonah smile.

In spite of Jonah's recommendation, Solomon had been adamant that they should not eliminate Mikhail. More than once Solomon had said, "There is nothing in our plan for killing. Let's stick with the plan." Jonah wondered why Solomon was against killing. After all, he was quick to kill back in the days of the Stern Gang. Maybe when a man gets older he puts more value on life. Killing is easy when you're twenty. It becomes much more difficult after fifty.

True, there was nothing in the plan for assassinations, but some of their agents had been quick to kill in order to get rid of competition or to make a necessary acquisition. Quick success demanded it. Okay, he hadn't ordered them to do it, but they did it and they were in his employ.

He mentioned this once to Solomon, whose response was, "They're Russians. They have their own code. We're businessmen."

Jonah decided it was a bad time to remind Solomon his agents were also Jews. It would have served no purpose. Besides, Jonah had hired Mikhail against Solomon's strong objections. "Don't hire that Mikhail Kolodkin. He's nothing but a history professor. Any Jew with no more ambition than that will steal from you if he gets a chance." Solomon was right. Mikhail was stealing from them, their whole Russian operation. Surely they'd find a replacement; Mikhail is worse than no one.

One thought kept coming forward and it bothered Jonah. His revelations about Mikhail were old news to Solomon, who was unusually well informed. Solomon was too calm about the situation. *He must have someone in Russia I don't know about. Maybe I'll find out from my conversation today.*

Jonah glanced at his watch. It had been fifteen minutes since the call. *So, Mikhail is coming to my lair with only his two bodyguards. Well, he has balls.*

Jonah rose from his seat and walked to his desk. He opened the drawer and lifted out a 9mm automatic pistol. He switched off the safety and cocked the gun. The familiar clicking told him the bullet was now in the chamber ready to do its duty. The gun felt heavy in his hand, exactly as it had back in 1948. He wondered if he was still a good shot. He was then, although as it turned out he was too close to miss.

He placed the pistol back into the drawer; so he could draw and fire easily. He left the drawer partly open. The whole scenario reminded him of the old American cowboy movies. Each man walked into the street with a pistol hanging from his side. A quick draw, an accurate shot, and some poor fool went to meet his maker.

How fast can I draw and fire from this drawer. He decided he would prefer to carry the gun at his side and fire from the hip. When shooting from the hip, look at the knees or the bullet will go over the head. Look at the knees and hit him in the chest.

Jonah walked to the window and gazed across his large yard, past the front gate to the street. It was a bright day and the neighborhood was so peaceful. He heard birds singing in the trees. An old couple was walking on the sidewalk across the street. They swerved to avoid a limb from a large oak tree that hung over the sidewalk. Life here was so quiet, like a dream. Violence never happened on Zurichbergstrasse. It won't be long now, he thought. When Mikhail killed Pavel, he crossed the Rubicon.

✤

Mikhail got into the back seat of the limousine and Oleg joined Ivan in the front. I must be crazy. That bastard Jonah might have an army of Mossad agents waiting for me. No one would ever find out. They'd shoot me and throw my body into some cave in the mountains. When I'm missed, everyone will decide the Russian Mafia got to me. I wonder if Jenia will miss me? Of course she won't. Mikhail had heard from Yuri about the botched assassination attempt. He had apologized, but it didn't help matters. That skinny bastard Alexander was still alive, still pawing his Jenia. Goddamn thief.

Mikhail shook his head, angry with himself. Think Mikhail! You have important business today. It's possibly your last day alive. With the thought of death he let his mind drift for a moment to Marina and Stephan in London. They would miss him, surely. However, the moment passed and he concentrated on the task at hand.

If I live through this I've won. Russia is mine. I'll have shown the bastard I have no fear of him. I'll have dared him to kill me and he'll have backed down, probably on orders from his bosses.

Well, if I die today, you bastard, you'll be signing your own death warrant. He had arranged a series of assassinations and made the down payments on the contracts. If he didn't cancel, Jonah and everyone in his Russian operations would be dead within a week. I wish I knew who he reports to, I'd get him too. I need to make him understand I'm the most powerful person in Russia. There is nothing he can do but play my game. Otherwise, his whole scheme will come tumbling down. He and his bosses can conquer the rest of the world for all I care. I'll be czar.

Mikhail reached in his suit pocket and pulled out his gold cigarette case. He pulled one out, shut the case and tamped the cigarette on the case lid. The tobacco sifted down into the cigarette leaving a hole at one end. Goddamn tobacco companies, they pack these things so loosely I don't even get a full cigarette.

Mikhail lit the cigarette with the console lighter. He let the smoke cool his nerves. He took a long drag and inhaled. Tonight, if I'm still alive I'm going to get drunk. No, better, I'm going to get laid, then smashed.

He leaned back in the seat and tried to keep his nerves calm. They were passing through an auto tunnel. He remembered the trip. He, Pavel and the others had made many trips to Jonah's mansion. In about fifteen minutes the next game will begin. Who will be the winner, who the loser? Mikhail was getting excited. He felt himself getting hard. Yes, tonight will be a good time to get laid. I'm going to have a lot of tension to release.

※

Jonah saw the limousine arrive at his gate. He pressed the button and the gate swung open slowly. He scratched his chest. "Well, here we go," he muttered to himself. He made his way through the office and the foyer to the front door. He opened the door as Mikhail exited the limousine.

"*Shalom.* Welcome Mikhail Ivanovich," he said in Hebrew.

Mikhail answered in the same language. "Shalom. I'm pleased to be here my good friend. Thank you for the kind invitation."

The two men approached each other and shook hands. Jonah invited, "Please, your bodyguard and driver are welcome to wait in my house."

Mikhail, suspicious, replied, "No. No thank you. If you don't mind they can stay outside. I think they'll enjoy the fresh air in Switzerland."

"As you wish," Jonah responded and took Mikhail's arm. "Come, let's go into my office and have something to drink." Mikhail didn't want Jonah to take his arm, but it was too late. He knew Jonah did it to sense any fear or tenseness in him. He tried to stay calm and not think of what might happen when he walked through the door.

When they entered the office, Jonah released Mikhail's arm and pointed at the credenza containing liquor and mixers. "Please, select your poison."

Mikhail selected vodka and Jonah chose a single malt scotch. Each poured about three fingers of the liquor in their glass. They turned to each other and Mikhail said, "*Za Zdrovya.*" Jonah repeated the phrase and they drained their glasses. Each refilled and carried his glass to the walnut table between the two high-backed chairs.

Mikhail sat, pulled the cigarette case from his pocket and selected one. Jonah had a lit cigar resting in the ashtray. Both men sat facing each other, smoke trailing from their mouths. Each was waiting for the other to end the pleasantries and open the conversation. Mikhail began in Russian, "I understand you've influenced the government to stop the sale of the refinery. I want that refinery."

Jonah answered in Hebrew. "I've some power in Russia too. I told you the refinery was to go to Pavel."

Anger flashed in Mikhail's eyes. "Pavel's dead. Do you want to get someone else killed?" He said, still using Russian.

Jonah was scratching his chest. "Are you threatening me?"

Mikhail disregarded the opportunity to escalate. "The refinery fits better into my group. It would be wasted anywhere else."

"Yours isn't the only agenda. I have to make decisions based on the big picture, based on what's best for our whole group not one member."

Mikhail prodded. "You made a bad decision and I intend to overrule it by buying or taking over the refinery."

Jonah flicked an ash from his cigar. He glared at Mikhail and said, "Do you actually expect me to take this lying down?"

"There isn't much you can do. I'm the key to the project now."

Jonah challenged, "Without me you have no access to Israel."

Mikhail said, "You can't remove me without destroying the project. There's no one else with my power or my understanding of the Russian situation. Ask your Israeli bosses."

Jonah leaned forward ready to pounce on Mikhail. "I'm not going to stand by while you destroy all we've built up."

Mikhail leaned back in his chair, away from Jonah. He took a long drag of his cigarette and blew smoke into the air. "I'm not asking you to abandon your role as boss of the overall operation. You can run the whole world for all I care." He quickly leaned forward and stubbed his cigarette into the ashtray with finality. "I'll be in charge of all Russian strategy and operations."

Now it was Jonah who relaxed back into his chair. He tried to stay calm. He knew his hands were tied for now. Better to reduce the tension, he decided. "We have strategies and goals for all of our operations, including Russia. We've been successful so far and you're the proof."

Mikhail recognized Jonah's tone was conciliatory and he took it as a weak position. Clearly Jonah's bosses had restricted his actions. Mikhail responded, "None of us in Russia is privy to your world conquest plans. We followed orders and invested money as instructed. For the last few years, however, we've become so large and complicated we can't be directed from afar. We must be able to quickly respond to the problems that arise. The billions in cash flow coming to Switzerland is the result of our actions, not your grand strategies."

He stopped speaking and stared, challenging Jonah whose response was silence. I've got him, Mikhail decided. He threw down another card. "You have no idea of the day-to-day decisions that make the difference between success and disaster. You and your bosses are too far removed, too out of touch. I'm in charge of Russia now."

Jonah held his temper. The anger was building inside and he didn't want to lose face. He took a sip of his drink. I can't stand this bastard. How did I ever get fooled this badly? He took a comforting pull on his cigar. He felt the smoke burning its way into his lungs. This man is a liar and a murderer. Why do I have to meet with him, talk to him? He was nothing when I rescued him from the meaningless life he'd created for himself. God damn it Solomon, let me rid us of this cancer in our group. Calm, Jonah, stay calm, he told himself.

Jonah let the cigar smoke flow from his mouth and then responded, "You're welcome to make written suggestions of strategies. I'll review them and tell you if I approve."

Mikhail growled, "How can you possibly make any assessments of my strategies? You know nothing of the business situation in Russia. It's time to move more quickly, to grow faster. In a few years, we can have it all if we move with courage now. You've won, Jonah. All you have to do is get out of the way."

Jonah realized he was losing. Mikhail was not going to change. He planned to take over the Russian operations or die trying. What was Solomon thinking? This man will destroy all they had built. Jonah wondered if he should take matters into his own hands in spite of instructions from Solomon. Jonah stood and pointed to the credenza, inviting Mikhail to get another drink. Mikhail agreed. The two combatants refilled their glasses. Jonah suggested, "If you wish we can take a short break for a walk around the grounds. We can get some fresh Swiss air."

Mikhail shook his head. "No, I think it better we continue with our discussion. I want to get back to Moscow tonight. I have plans for this evening."

The two men returned to their seats. Mikhail squinted through the lingering cigarette and cigar smoke. "The flow of cash to Switzerland will be going down for some time. I need cash for some acquisitions to diversify my currency risk." Then he drove the knife deeper. "I'll let you know when the cash flow will resume again."

Jonah tried to hide his emotions, but Mikhail saw the anger in his eyes. He purposefully lit another cigarette to show Jonah his hand did not tremble. He blew smoke toward the ceiling. Jonah got out of his seat and walked to the window behind the desk. He saw Oleg and Ivan sitting in the limousine. He wondered. Can I take out Mikhail and get them also? Or, I could try to get a message to Benjamin and have him help me. He decided if he had to he would get all of them. The shot itself would bring everyone running to his office, a real mess.

Jonah turned to face Mikhail, who was now standing and staring at him. The two men faced each other for a moment. Jonah wondered if Mikhail would be so smug if he knew about Serot.

Jonah walked to his desk and pulled open the drawer. He reached in and wrapped his hand around the pistol. He felt the excitement building. The gun felt heavy and the steel was cold. He imagined the surprise on Mikhail's face when the bullet penetrated deep into his brain. Jonah raised his head to look at his prey. Mikhail showed no surprise, no fear. He's pushed me hard to see if I'll try to kill him. The man is psychotic. He wouldn't have come here if he weren't willing to die.

Jonah knew in his gut he should kill Mikhail to protect the project. He knew having Mikhail running the Russian operation without control from Israel would be a disaster. Yet, Solomon was not concerned. Why? Does Solomon have another plan? Maybe there's a plan to which I'm not privy.

He released the gun and pulled a file from the drawer. He opened it and examined a few of the papers pretending to read.

Jonah gave his concession speech. It was necessary to give it, but it almost made him throw up. "I'll relay our conversation and your planned actions to my board of directors. They'll decide what action we'll take, and I'll be contacting you with our decision."

Mikhail slowly exhaled. Imagine, a minute ago I was staring at a man who was thinking of killing me. I didn't flinch. I was ready. He backed down. I've won! He felt like he was standing on Jonah's chest. He was a Roman gladiator looking down at a vanquished foe. Yes, Vestal Virgins, let me plunge the sword into his chest. He sneered, "I think it's better if I address your board directly. It's inefficient to funnel this through you."

*

Moscow – Late evening

Mikhail pushed the key into the slot in the door and heard Buddy barking on the other side. He turned to Oleg and said, "Good guard dog." They both laughed at the thought. Buddy was friendly with everyone, even strangers. He opened the door and the little white bundle of excitement ran in circles, stopped and wagged his tail so hard his entire body was bending back and forth at the waist like some exotic dancer.

Mikhail lifted Buddy and hugged him to his chest. "Isn't he great. What a dog. He has unequivocal love. No conditions. No judgments. Everyone should have a dog. No wife, no son, no friend can love you like a dog, especially this dog."

Oleg reached out and patted Buddy on the head. The dog licked his wrist. "How did you happen to name him Buddy?"

"After Clinton's dog. Clinton and I have much in common. I decided our dogs should have the same name."

Oleg's face clouded. He didn't like any Americans, especially the President. "What do you have in common with Clinton?"

"When I'm president we'll both have the same title. Now we have dogs with the same name." They both laughed at his joke.

He put Buddy back on the floor. He and Oleg entered the reception room with the dog running around their feet. Oleg selected two glasses from the bar at one end of the room and poured vodka into each.

Mikhail put his arm around Oleg's shoulder and said, "We've had a long day, my friend, but a triumphant one. You're looking at the future czar of Russia."

Oleg clinked his glass with Mikhail's and said, "To the future czar." They drained their glasses and set them back on the bar.

With his arm still around Oleg, they walked to the bedroom door. Mikhail took a deep breath, looked at Oleg and said, "You were crucial to my success today. I won't forget it. I know it's been a long day, but I need you and Ivan to do one more favor for me before you go home."

Oleg responded, "No problem. Whatever you ask."

Mikhail opened the bedroom door and pointed at the triangular metal apparatus. It had two rings attached to an adjustable bar and two more rings at the bottom.

"I want a young one, thin, with black hair and dark skin."

Oleg stared at him. "We've been awake since four in the morning. We've been to Switzerland and back. It's now almost midnight. Are you sure?"

"I told you I was ready for a release. Today I put my life on the line and won the contest. I deserve a reward. I need a release or I'll burst." Mikhail was getting angry. *My bodyguard has no position to question me. Maybe I've been too familiar with him.*

Oleg said, "It's late, but we'll try. Most of the ladies are off the streets by now. It's too cold and wet out there."

"I'm sure you'll find me someone. You always have."

Oleg left the flat. Mikhail studied Buddy sitting on the couch. "Why can't Oleg be like you? Why can't Jenia be like you?" *I'll shave and take a warm shower so I'll be ready when they return.*

※

Mikhail had put on his dark blue silk robe, which was tied shut with a cotton belt of the same color. He loved the feel of silk against his naked body. It had been more than an hour and three vodkas since Oleg had left. Mikhail sat on his couch and rubbed Buddy, who was lying on his back, his paws in the air.

What's taking so long? All they have to do is drive down Tverskaya. There should be plenty of opportunities there. Maybe they're having trouble finding the right one. He wondered if Oleg had failed. Not likely. Oleg knew that failure was unacceptable.

Buddy suddenly jumped from the couch and ran barking toward the door. His nails clicked on the hardwood floor. Mikhail heard a soft knock. He opened the door and Oleg dragged a blindfolded girl into the room. She ducked afraid she would be hit. The skin on her hands and face, at least the part Mikhail spotted, was light. He glared at Oleg who shrugged.

He motioned for Oleg to remove her coat. She was wearing a white blouse and black pants with black boots that went halfway to her knees. She had small breasts. He imagined unbuttoning the blouse and pulling the pants down to her ankles. A rush of excitement shot from his groin through his stomach.

Buddy was at her feet sniffing her boots. Mikhail pointed to her hat and Oleg removed it. She had short curly blond hair. Anger surged through his body. He growled in a loud whisper, "I said black hair and dark skin." He reached out and removed the blindfold. She had blue eyes now puffy and red from the blindfold and crying. She was about sixteen or a young looking eighteen and had a dark bruise on her cheek. He touched the bruise and she winced in pain and leaned away from him. She continued to whimper like an injured dog.

He took her by the arm. Her face showed her terror, as though afraid he was going to kill her. He patted her shoulder and pointed to the couch. "You'll be okay now. Come, sit." Buddy ran ahead of them and leaped onto the couch. She sat down and Buddy cuddled next to her. She petted his head and continued to sniffle. Buddy tried to lick her bruise.

Mikhail said, "I'll get you a cup of tea. You'll soon feel better." She looked at him with wide eyes and nodded her head yes. She pulled Buddy onto her lap and continued to pet him. Mikhail took Oleg by the arm and led him to the kitchen. Oleg made some tea. Mikhail asked, "Where did you find her?"

"We didn't find anyone on Tverskaya or any of the other hot spots. Like I said, it's cold and rainy outside and the women are taken or have gone home. She was hitchhiking and Ivan pulled over to give her a ride."

"She's not a prostitute?"

Oleg shook his head no. "What difference does it make? I couldn't find a prostitute. I couldn't find anyone with black hair. Hell, how could I tell? They're all wearing hats. It's raining."

At first Mikhail was shocked. Then he felt warm, excited. She's not a prostitute. No wonder she looks so innocent.

"Why does she have a bruise on her face?"

"She gave me some trouble when I offered her money for services. She screamed and tried to hit me. I had to put her in her place. I only hit her a few times, but it was enough. She hasn't done anything but cry and sniffle since."

"Do you think she'll give me a lot of trouble?"

"If I were you I'd put a gag in her mouth or she'll wake all the neighbors."

"No. It would ruin the effect. I have no neighbors on this floor. The flat below is empty." He motioned for Oleg to stay in the kitchen and returned to the girl.

"Here. Have some tea," he said and put a cup in front of her. He touched her bruise again, lightly. "Does it hurt? I'll punish the man who did this to you."

"Thank you," she managed to squeak in a weak voice too young to be a woman. "It doesn't hurt much anymore."

He moved her curly blond hair from the edge of her face to behind her ear. With her eyes still wide with fright she looked first at his face and then the protruding front of his robe.

"What do you want from me? I want to go home to my mama." She cried and pushed Buddy away. She tried to get up. He put his hands on her shoulders and shouted, "Oleg. Come here."

The girl screamed and struggled to get up. Oleg came quickly into the room and grabbed her hair. He pulled her head back and held his hand in the air ready to strike her. Terrified, she stopped struggling.

Mikhail said, "Get her ready."

Oleg jerked her to her feet and took her to the bedroom. He tied her to the rings and removed her blouse. He glanced back at Mikhail who was now rubbing himself vigorously. Mikhail nodded and Oleg pushed her pants and underclothes down to her ankles. It was all he had imagined. He was so hard it hurt.

He nodded again and Oleg removed her bra. She was naked from her head to her ankles, except for her boots and a leather band holding a wood crucifix around her neck. She had a small rounded butt and was extremely thin. Oleg spun her around to give him a frontal view. The girl had her eyes shut, terrified.

He motioned with his hand and Oleg turned her to face the wall again. She shrieked and Buddy ran by Mikhail and stood behind the girl barking. Mikhail motioned for Oleg to take Buddy away. Oleg gathered the dog and returned to the reception room leaving the girl dangling from the rings. She was crying uncontrollably and her whole body was shaking.

"Will she be able to identify us?"

"She doesn't know where she is, but she has to know who you are. You've been seen on the television too many times".

"I don't want any trouble from her. Will she accept money?"

"I doubt it. Don't worry. There'll be no problem. I'm sorry I didn't find a dark one."

"Why don't you and Ivan take Buddy for a walk. Come back in a few hours. I should be done by then. You can take her away."

"Okay." Oleg patted Buddy on the head and left the flat. The young girl, her hair now matted with sweat, was slumped down, hanging from her hands tied to the rings.

He shut the bedroom door and stared at the defenseless child before him. He studied her thin arms leading from the rings to her small shaking shoulders. She was sobbing. He noticed the bones on her shoulder blades sticking out like wings on an angel. He gazed at her small rounded butt and thin legs. They were too thin even for her. Her skin was fresh like a baby with almost no blemishes. He noticed she had no tattoos or rings attached to her body. He was proud of her.

Mikhail was flushed. His whole body felt hot. He was shaking as he opened his robe and let it drop to the floor. He removed a small leather whip from his closet and returned to the girl. He stood behind her and sniffed to smell her odor, her fear. He untied the leather band and let the crucifix drop to the floor. For some reason, he didn't want her to wear it. He put his arm around the girl and put his hand on her small breast. It was firm. His fingers found the nipple and he rolled it back and forth. She yelped and tried to escape or to kick him. He smirked and raised the whip high above his head.

13

Moscow – Tuesday, April 21

"Where have you been? You drag me to this flat and then disappear. I haven't heard from you, not even a simple telephone call. You could have at least called me. I've been caged here for three days and nights." Alex knew he was being unreasonable, but the frustration of no contact was more than he could control. He saw the surprise on Jenia's face. Suddenly he realized he had not offered to let her enter the flat. He spun sideways and held the door for her. As she walked into foyer he attacked again. "Where have you been all this time? I've been sitting here going crazy."

She stopped and glared at him. Through clenched teeth she said, "I have work to do. So do you."

He pointed his finger at her. "Where were you? You weren't at the Klub last night or the night before."

She was livid. Her eyes flashed. "You fool, did you call the Klub? Damn it, I told you not to."

He wished he hadn't said anything. "I wanted to ask you to come here to see me. People are trying to kill me and I'm completely in the dark. What the hell's going on?"

Her voice softened. "I had to go see someone. Let's leave it at that. Alex I'm trying to save your life." She turned to walk into the reception room.

He said. "That reminds me. Where is our friend Mikhail?"

She stopped again and jerked her head to look at him. If her eyes were lasers, he'd have had two holes in his forehead. "Are you accusing me of something?"

He saw she was angry and hurt, and immediately regretted his jealous accusation. "No. No I'm not accusing you of anything. I'm sorry."

She calmed down. "I have to be out of the country for a week or so. But you'll have work to do with Tanya."

Alex complained, "You told me not to contact her or anyone else from PHD. How is she going to find me if I can't call her?"

"I don't want you calling any of them. I'll take care of it."

"What am I supposed to do? How long must I stay here?"

"Only until I return. When I come back, maybe everything will be settled and the danger will be over."

"Will you marry me then?"

"You don't love me Alex. You only think you do. Someday you'll look back on our relationship and realize it wasn't the love you thought it was."

"Is that a no?"

"Yes."

He walked over to the easy chair and sat down. She must be seeing someone else while I'm imprisoned in this damn flat, rejected and helpless. "If I don't love you why does it hurt so much when you're not with me?"

She crossed the room, leaned over the chair and kissed him on the cheek. She ran her hand through his hair. He pushed her away. "Damn it. I'm not your puppy."

She backed off, stunned. "I'll be back at the end of the month."

He stared out the window, refusing to look in her direction. He put on his best pout.

"Will you come here?"

"Do you want me to?"

Alex turned from the window to look at her. "Yes."

The concerned look left her face. "It's a date then."

He didn't know why, but he wanted to hurt her. He wanted her to know the pain he was feeling. "Was anything real or was it all an act?"

Her face fell. A single tear worked its way down her cheek and she tried to hide it. She walked out of the room into the hall. He made no effort to follow. She stopped at the entrance and looked back at him. The tear was gone.

"I went to see Ivona. She was in hospital. I should have told you but I didn't want to cause you more concern."

Alex felt sick to his stomach and barely whispered, "Is she okay?"

"She'll be fine. They broke her nose and arm. She has quite a few bruises on her face. I took her to her sister's home."

Alex felt the cold shudder start at his spine and work its way up to the back of his neck. He felt goose bumps on his arms. "They?"

Two men came to her home shortly after we were attacked. One was that man I shot in the alley. He had his arm in a sling. Ivona said the other man called him 'Yuri'."

"The other man?"

"Oleg. That son-of-a-bitch went to her home and beat her."

Alex stared at her without seeing her. He saw only the immense man beating the defenseless woman. He was too embarrassed, ashamed to speak. He had been with Jenia for less than thirty minutes and all he did was make matters worse.

"Please Alex. Please stay here and don't go to work or the Klub. If you go either of those places, someone will kill you. I'm sure of it." She opened and closed the door.

14

Moscow – Wednesday, April 22

Tanya entered Carl's office with a concerned look on her face.
"I'm worried about Alex."
"Why?"
"I haven't heard from him since last Wednesday. He went to Poland to attend the funeral for Pavel Melninski."
"Pavel Melninski, wasn't he one of the big shots?"
"Yes. Next to Mikhail Kolodkin the most powerful, huh?"
"Alex knew him?"
She grinned in spite of her concern. "I told you he was important to the project."
"Maybe he's sick or staying with a friend."
"He hasn't telephoned. No one answers at his flat."
"I'll send security to check out his flat and talk with his neighbors. Maybe they know something."
"Thanks. I'll be in the war room."
"Making any progress?"
"We've a lot of circumstantial indicators. No real evidence. We need to get a break or help from someone on the inside."
"Any ideas?"
"I'm working on it. If we can find Alex and I can debrief him on his trip —."
"Alex? What does he know?"
"Alex is the key to the magic door. You'll see. You judge him too harshly."
"You like him don't you?"
She disregarded his question, waved good-bye and left his office.
Tanya sat in the war room studying the many charts, schedules and articles pasted on the walls and attached to flip charts throughout the

room. She knew them by heart. They told her the story, but they didn't prove it. She knew who was involved in Russia and what role they played in the conspiracy. What she didn't know was who was involved outside of Russia and where the money went.

It was difficult for her to concentrate. *I wish Alex were here. I hope he's okay.*

The telephone rang. It was Carl. "Bad news I'm afraid."

Her heart sank. She didn't want to hear the rest. She knew Alex was dead. She had made him a target.

Carl continued. "Security said the police have been to his flat. Someone broke the door and trashed the place. All of his clothes are gone."

"Did they talk to any neighbors?"

"They tried to talk to the woman who reported the break in. She wouldn't talk to them. No one else would talk with them either. I guess they're afraid to get involved."

"Thanks for checking it out for me."

"Maybe we should give his picture to the militia. They can compare it to any unidentified bodies."

"No. Don't give them anything. It hasn't been that long yet. I have people I can contact who may know where he went. Let me look into it and I'll get back to you."

I'll have to try to contact Jenia. She went with him to Poland. She pulled out a telephone book and searched the pages for the number of the Knight Klub. She was interrupted by the arrival of the day's mail. She glanced at the pile and was surprised to see a brown envelope with the indication "hand delivered" written on it by reception. She wrapped her hand around it; it contained something hard. She tore it open. It was a key taped to a card on which was written a coded message.

"9a28i5o8o7iy 9. m/vn : nmgbsvk"

The note was in Latin letters and was in a woman's hand. In her heart she knew this involved Alex. She studied it with increasing interest and hope. *Since it's attached to a flat key, it must be an address. The building and flat number are separated by a slash. The letters after the colon are the right length to be a local telephone number. If so, the code substitutes letters for numbers and vise versa. However, there is no substitution for vowels, only consonants.*

She felt better, much better. *This has to be the address where I can reach Alex. Jenia must have sent it . . . or one of the dancers at the Klub.*

The telephone rang again. It was Carl; he'd received a hand delivered envelope and inside was another envelope addressed to her.

She was ecstatic. *Alex, you did it. I know it's from Jenia. I knew you would do it. Where are you? God I want to hug you. We're going to win this little game. We're going to win.*

As she expected the package contained a note. A scan showed her Jenia signed it. Yes! She almost jumped from her chair. *Alex you devil you did it. We've captured their queen.* The note was also in English.

"Dear Tanya,

"Alex is in trouble. I am sure he told you that someone ordered the assassination of Pavel Melninski. That same person has hired an assassin to kill Alex. I thwarted one attempt in Poland, but he was injured. A small thin man with a goatee shot him in the leg. I don't know the assassin's full name, but I think his first name is Yuri.

"I have to leave the country until the end of the month. I will contact you by phone when I return. I'm afraid that protection of Alex defaults to you. It's only fair we share this burden. We share the blame.

"You should also have received a separate envelope with a key to his flat and his address and telephone number. You probably have decoded it already, as it is a simple substitution. It will be harder for those who don't speak English well. The real key is that the substitutions are based on phonetic sounds. The telephone number is 236-9087.

"Jenia."

Tanya quickly decoded the card, filled her briefcase with some files and marched out of the war room. On her way out she stopped by Carl's office, stuck her head in and shouted, "Alex is alive. I'm going to see him now. The project is back on track."

She ran to the Metro, rode three different lines, exited at four stations and then reentered after satisfying herself no one followed. Finally, she came to Smolenskaya and exited.

After another search to ensure no one was following she hurried north along Smolenskiy Pereulok until she crossed Protochny. She turned left along Protochny and then right onto Panfilovskiy to building three. Alex would be on the eighth floor flat two.

One final check of the area and she darted down the alley leading to the building's entrance. This won't last long, she thought to herself. Sooner or later whoever wants him is going to find him by following me or someone else. We've got to find a better way. Poor guy. I've put him on the front lines.

She entered the building and took the elevator to the ninth floor. She walked down one flight to the eighth and stopped outside his flat. He would have a heart attack if I used my key and barged in unannounced. She beamed at the thought and recalled their first meeting in his office. I guess I've caused him enough trouble. She pushed the buzzer.

"Tanya. God it's good to see you," he gushed when he opened the door without even asking who was there.

"I never thought I'd hear you say that, huh?"

"Come on. I know I was an ass. Don't rub it in, please."

She felt sorry for him. His quiet, carefree life was gone. He was a prisoner in this flat. "I'm sorry. I was trying to make a joke. It was silly of me, huh?"

She glanced through the archway leading to the reception room. "What a nice flat. Are you going to give me the grand tour?"

She saw him blush and he responded, "Sure. But please don't take note of the mess and the unmade bed."

He walked her through the reception room and showed her the view of Kalininskiy Most and the White House.

She said, "Hey, with binoculars you can see the office from here." They walked down the hall past the open bedroom door. The bed was unmade and dirty clothes were piled on a chair. She saw his face flush when she looked into the room. She tried to put him at ease. "You men are all alike. Didn't your mother teach you to pick up your clothes and make your bed?" She grinned to make sure he knew she was joking. He looked uncomfortable in spite of her light remark.

They sat in the reception room and he recounted his trip to Poland. He told her about the man with the goatee and what it felt like to be shot.

She interrupted him. "I can't imagine what it would be like to have someone trying to kill me. I'm afraid I wouldn't do well."

He grinned and responded, "When that man was running toward me with a gun, all I thought was if I lose the papers Tanya will kill me."

She winced. Maybe I've been too hard on him. He presented it as a joke, but she decided there was more truth than he let on.

She tried her best to show surprise when he told her in great detail how Jenia had been nervous, how she had saved his life. He told about the escape to the park and the trip back to Moscow. She was amazed. Alex was clueless. He had accepted Jenia's actions as those of an unusual woman who managed the Knight Klub.

"It's lucky she was with you."

She made a mental note to bring him some decent food and some water. His kitchen was empty, no bread, no cheese, and no tea. She forced down another mouthful of the lukewarm bitter coffee.

Their meeting lasted for almost three hours, and he told her what he remembered about the papers and names, but he continually apologized about losing the documents. This only made her feel worse. The man was almost killed by an assassin and he was more worried about her reaction to losing some ridiculous papers.

My God, he's more afraid of me than death. Another legacy from my father, she decided, as she remembered him ruling over their family like a squad leader. The colonel kept his thumb on her mother, stifled her, frightened her, and broke her spirit. She swore she would not do that to Dmitry, but all it had got her was a drunken cheat with no backbone.

"Never surrender," the colonel had told her. From him she learned to fight on, not give up. From chess she learned to plan ahead. Dmitry gave up, surrendered.

She looked at Alex sitting on the edge of his chair, his mouth moving telling her about his adventure, his big eyes wide open, his face exploding with excitement.

When she left, she promised to return every day at ten to discuss the investigation. She would bring him some of the papers and files she had accumulated. She was looking forward to their meetings.

Moscow - Wednesday, April 29

Moscow was preparing for the big weekend beginning on May 1, the first day of spring and Labor Day, before 1991 known as International Workers Solidarity Day. Three days with no work. Three days to get the dacha ready for summer. The holiday would begin Thursday night and go through Sunday evening. This weekend signaled the coming of summer and holidays abroad.

Kolya was home. His school let the children out two days in advance of the official holiday. Tanya stayed with him in the morning playing backgammon and showing him how to beat her. He learned well, and she decided to intensify his chess lessons.

For over a week Tanya had taken papers and documents to Alex. He read them all. Since Pavel's death, Alex had shown more interest in the project. Since the attempt on his own life, he had shown keen interest in completing the investigation and nailing the conspirators. No longer did they have arguments about boring documents or wasted time. However, she was beginning to repeat the documentation. The investigation had stalled and they needed a breakthrough. So, she'd surprise him today; it would not be a day of work.

Her mother arrived shortly before noon and Tanya explained she had to visit her office in the afternoon. Her mother agreed to watch Kolya and make him some lunch. The telephone rang. Tanya answered it and heard Dmitry's pleading voice, "I've stopped drinking. I want to meet with you. I want to see my son."

She squeezed the receiver tightly and growled into the phone, "It's not only the drinking, huh? You beat our son with a horsewhip. I can't believe any man would do that to his son. You brought a strange woman, or maybe more, to our flat."

He responded, but she wasn't listening to him anymore. Her mind kept imagining another woman sweating and moaning on her bed. She felt ill, violated. She didn't want to ask him how many, how often. After he had left, she immediately discarded the bed and all the coverings. It was one of the few times she let herself go. She made a promise to herself, no one but she would sleep in the new bed.

Dmitry was still pleading when she hung up. How could he have done it? She had stood by him through all his troubles, his drinking, and his hardship. She had supported him and tried to make him feel like a man. She had not criticized his decision to waste money on riding lessons. She was sure his affairs began at the riding academy. She could find out, but she didn't want to know. That was in the past. She and Kolya had a new life. Dmitry would not be part of it.

Her mother asked, "Who was on the phone, dear. You look angry."

"It was Dmitry. He wants to meet with me and to see Kolya."

"What are you going to do?"

"Right now? Nothing. It's too early. I'm not sure I ever want to see him again. I'm not sure I want Kolya to see him either. What can he do for us? He gave up. Pants don't make the man. He's not a man."

"Men drink. Men love with their eyes. They're always chasing. It's normal, but to beat your own child with a horsewhip is unforgivable."

"I'm not an ugly woman. Am I?" She examined herself in the mirror. Why would Dmitry look elsewhere? Why don't other men make a play for me? I'm only thirty-two. I've had only one child. My face is clear. My eyes are a pretty green. I'm in great shape. If men love with their eyes, what do they want to see? Why don't they see me?

In her mind she saw Alex going into the Knight Klub. She saw him leering and throwing dollars at young naked girls. His words haunted her, "When that man was running toward me with a gun, all I thought was if I lose the papers Tanya will kill me."

She looked in the mirror again and saw the reflection of a woman. But I don't act like a woman, at least in the eyes of men. She caught herself picking out the Colonel's features in her face, the sharp eyes, the high cheekbones and stern look. Her doubts, previously kept under control in the background, were free and roaming through her thoughts now. A dress doesn't make the woman, but then I seldom wear a dress. Am I a good mother? Is my son afraid of me too? I tried to let Dmitry rule the home; he wasn't strong enough. Who is? Who could be?

"You should find an older man dear. They're more mature. Find one with money."

Her mother wasn't helping. Or was she? Maybe she was right. I need an older man, like Carl. He would see the girls in the Knight Klub as little more than children. He would see someone thirty-two, like me, as a young woman in the prime of her life, with classic beauty. It would never be Carl, not for the colonel's daughter.

She kissed Kolya and rubbed his head. "Tomorrow night begins the holiday. You can stay up later if you want to watch fireworks, huh?"

"Really, Mama, really?" His face beamed at the thought.

"Really," she responded and gave him another kiss.

She turned to her mother. "I have to go to work. I'll see you tonight, huh? Thanks for coming today. I hope you'll stay with us for a few weeks. I need your help, and company."

"It's my pleasure dear. I love the boy too you know. I'll be here as long as you need me."

※

Tanya entered the office and saw the electronic chess set on his desk. She scanned the pieces on the board and decided white could mate black in six moves. I said I'd teach him how to play. Maybe this will help. After she prepared a paper showing the positions of all pieces, she opened her briefcase and put the game inside.

She lifted Jenia's picture from the desk to study it closely, to compare it with what she had seen in the mirror only an hour before. She put the picture inside the briefcase. She walked to the door, stopped and returned to the desk. She took the picture out of her briefcase and placed it back on the desk. Satisfied, she turned and left the office.

When Alex opened the door, she had a big smile on her face and a box in her hand. His eyes widened and his mouth fell open. "A present? For me?"

"I thought you'd enjoy practicing, huh?"

He tore open the box and yanked out the chess game. She gave him the paper showing all the positions. "You can assemble the pieces and finish your last game."

"It was almost over anyway. I figured another five or six moves and the damn machine would mate me again."

"You were playing black?"

"No. I was playing white."

She laughed uncontrollably. "Ok. Maybe I'll teach you a few things about chess, huh?"

His face brightened again. "That would be wonderful." He lifted his finger, "wait," and ran down the hall. In a few minutes he returned with a tray containing a teapot under a cozy, two cups and saucers, some biscuits and milk. "It's tea. I know you don't like coffee."

Before she could stop herself she said, "You know it's dangerous to go out."

He beamed, "I don't care. The risk was worth the look on your face. Besides, I covered my head and part of my face with a woolen cap and turned the collar up on my coat. I only went to Arbat. Everybody's a tourist there."

"Well, I guess we're both full of surprises today, huh?" She was overjoyed. It was a good idea to bring the chess game.

"Maybe we can finish the work early today and you can show me some moves," he said and stuffed a biscuit into his mouth. He placed the pieces according to the paper she gave him.

"I didn't bring any work today. Today is devoted only to chess."

"You're an angel of mercy. I love you," he said flippantly. Together they finished the game. She explained each move and why it was a good one. "My God. I've beat it," he said full of pride. "That's the first time. Now it'll be easy." He stared at her for what seemed a long time. "You sure are good at chess. You're good at quite a few things actually."

"Thank you. It was nice of you to say that." They stared at each other through an awkward silence. Then she continued the lesson. "Remember. The most powerful pieces on the board are the black and white queens. Capture or neutralize the black queen and attack strongly with the white."

"It's easy to say, but not so easy to do. I usually lose my queen early in the game."

"By attack I don't mean you rush headlong into the center of the board with your queen. You design your strategy around her abilities. You can even use a pawn as your weapon, but you must use it as part of a plan centered around your queen and her offensive and defensive powers."

She was having such fun. Alex was fully attentive. He wanted so much to be a grand master, but he would never be an exceptional player. She was proud of him anyway. She had an urge to touch him, and for a moment only he and she existed.

"Tanya."

"Yes."

"When you picked up the game, did you see a picture on my desk?"

"Yes. It's a picture of Jenia isn't it?"

"Tomorrow, would you get it for me?"

"Sure." Her shoulders drooped. "I'm sorry. I have to go now. Kolya is expecting a special supper tonight and my mama's visiting. I'll bring the picture to you tomorrow morning at ten."

"Jenia is supposed to come back tomorrow from wherever she's been. I can't wait to see her."

Tanya left quickly. She hurried down the stairs and out the door into the late afternoon darkness. The wind was blowing dust and dirt left over from winter. Some of it blew into her eyes causing them to tear.

15

Moscow – Thursday, April 30

Tanya stifled a yawn. She was watching Carl read one of her memos in the war room. He put the memo down. She saw his mouth moving, but it took a second before she realized he was talking.

"So. Tell me. Where did Pavel put the cash, Cyprus?"

"He placed the cash into a Swiss investment fund called 'Vision.' It was created in 1990, but I don't know who owns or runs it. The owner might be a man named Jonah."

"Oh?"

"According to Pavel's wife, he was planning to go to Zurich to see a man named Jonah. Pavel and the others apparently reported to him, but Alex said his name didn't appear on any of the papers that were lost."

"How is Alex?"

"I'm worried about him. He's getting stir crazy after almost two weeks in that flat. I don't think he's been out at all."

"We need to find another, safer, place for our war room. Maybe we'll find a dacha outside Moscow."

"That would be great."

He went back to his questions. "How did Pavel get the cash out of Russia?"

She pointed to a chart lying on the table in front of him. "The usual way, transfer pricing. He formed a marketing subsidiary in Cyprus. His Russian company sold product at a low profit to the marketing subsidiary. It, in turn, sold the product at a high profit to companies in Europe and America."

Carl shook his head back and forth. "I can't believe the government doesn't stop this. Everybody is doing this."

She wondered whether Carl, like Alex, didn't realize the extent of the conspiracy. "They control the government. They allow their taxes to go uncollected and laws restricting their activities are left off the books."

"You're right'" he said, nodding his agreement. He examined his watch, got out of his chair and stretched. "I have to get an early start. I'm going to a friend's dacha this weekend. I hope you and your family enjoy your holidays."

"Thanks. Same to you."

Solomon was sitting behind his desk holding a telephone. In front of him a large notebook was open displaying an organization chart titled "Russia."

He spoke into the phone. "You can't take him out. You'll destroy the project. We've no one to replace him yet. As soon as we can, we'll replace him. I'm working on our alternatives." Solomon listened for a few more seconds. He spoke again. "We need to put a scare into him. Maybe that'll slow him down. In the meantime we'll find a replacement. I think that's the best way to handle this."

He put down the telephone and sat for a moment staring at his desk letting the situation play through his mind. He raised his head and gazed at Jenia. She was sitting at the table that held his ever-present chess game. She was drumming her fingers on the table.

"I'm sorry. I know you had your heart set on returning to Moscow this afternoon. I need to discuss this situation with you. I want to get your perspective on this Mikhail Kolodkin . . . and Jonah."

She responded, "I'd like to discuss a man named Oleg with you also."

He nodded.

The flat was somber as a tomb. Alex hadn't bothered to turn on the lights. For two hours he had been pacing back and forth. His bottle of vodka was running low.

Suddenly, many bright colors from an early fireworks display splashed through the window and onto the wall of the reception room. A few seconds later, he heard the familiar "Booms." Why doesn't she call? She was supposed to be here long ago. What happened?

His pacing took him near the telephone. He lifted the receiver and listened to find out if it was working. For the fifth time in the last hour he heard the familiar drone and replaced the receiver.

He started to sit down, but he was too restless. Another splash of color and a mooted boom attracted him to the window. He threw it open as far as it would go; and a flood of cool air, harsh street sounds and acrid smells washed over him. He stuck his head out and looked down the eight flights to the ground. It made him dizzy to look straight down; so he turned his head to the White House on the other side of Kalininskiy Bridge, which was strung with multicolored lights for the holiday. He watched the many headlights moving along Novy Arbat and across the bridge. He knew the cars were filled with husbands, wives and excited chattering children rushing to get to their country dachas. He tried to imagine driving one of those cars with his wife giving him directions and his children screaming, "Papa, Papa," to get his attention.

It was a life he had never known, probably never would. His father was gone before he learned to say papa. He and his mother had never had a dacha, only a seventy-meter communal flat they shared with another family, strangers thrown together by a system that rewarded the few who lived off the many. With the new capitalism system, only the owners of the money had changed.

He pulled his head back into the room and turned around to stare at the vacant furniture. I'm thirty-five, it's a holiday weekend and I'm stuck here in this damn flat like a child sent to his room for punishment. Where is Jenia? His chest tightened and he needed air; so he turned back toward the window and took a deep breath.

A large red and white flash lit the sky and reflected off the Moscow River and the windows of the White House, now just another government administration building.

But something has changed in Russia. There's a new feeling, a feeling of freedom. I can see it on faces; hear it in rock music; and feel it in my own fast footsteps. Now everyone is in a hurry to live rather than waiting to die. It wasn't the oligarchs, it was my brave friends and I outside the White House who saved Yeltsin and brought freedom to Russia.

He saw another flash and listened to another boom. *I wish I'd gone to the fireworks display with Tanya and her family. What's her husband like? I envy him.* He smiled. *It's hard to believe that only a few weeks ago I could not imagine anyone envying her husband.*

As he reflected, he realized that the good feeling, the freedom, did not disappear with Yeltsin's betrayal. Yeltsin didn't worry him, but the oligarchs did. Yeltsin would be gone with the next election; the oligarchs would stay, feeding off the country like insatiable Russian wolves. They had accumulated money and with it power. They were not capitalists in the true sense of the word. They were like a family, a mafia, above the law and insensitive to public opinion.

He was getting that same feeling he had when he locked arms outside the White House in ninety-one, *but how can Tanya and I possibly stop them? It's a dream. But then, hope is the last to die.*

Another round of fireworks lit the sky. He counted silently to himself, one, two, three, and four. He heard the missile's retort. His mood changed, and he left the window open and returned to pacing the room.

Why am I stuck in this damn depressing flat? Why isn't Jenia here with me? We'd be alone, together and in bed. Why couldn't I be playing chess with Tanya?

He sat down on his couch, took another drink from the bottle of vodka he had purchased when he bought tea for Tanya. He swished the bitter liquid around in his mouth; it burned his tongue. He swallowed and felt the fire scorch his throat on the way to his stomach. He examined the bottle. The vodka was almost gone. *I thought I had it whipped, no drinks for almost three weeks. It's all her fault.*

He struggled to his feet and returned to the window. This time he looked in the direction of the Smolenskaya Metro Station. *Maybe I'll see her walking along the street on her way to the building.* He gazed at the lights and crowds. He heard people talking, laughing, and shouting, but couldn't discern what they were saying. He was a spectator, far off, not part of their world.

The telephone rang. He ran across the room, snatched the receiver from its cradle. "Jenia?"

"Sasha. How are you? I'm sorry I took so long to call you. I've been in business meetings all day until a few minutes ago."

"That's ok. When will you be here?"

"Oh Sasha. I'm so sorry. I can't make it tonight. It's impossible for me to get there."

"But you promised. It was a date you said. I need you tonight. I can wait. Will you be an hour, two hours, even more? When can you be here?"

"I can't be there. I'm not even in the country."

"Where are you?" He was suspicious. Was she with another man?

"That's not important. I thought we'd talk together on the phone. I've wanted so much to hear your voice. I miss you."

"I don't want to talk on the phone. I want to hold you, kiss you, touch you." He wanted her there to be sure she wasn't with another. Was the other man listening, laughing? Were they touching while she talked to him? Maybe it's the same man who owns this flat.

They talked for an hour, but it made him miss her more. She finished her conversation. "I'm so sorry. I'll make it up to you. Haven't I always done so when I had to break a promise? I have to go now. I love you and miss you."

"I love you too," he said and dropped the receiver on the couch. He stood, stretched, and sat down again. What can I do? I have no control over anything. I have to accept whatever happens to me. Why can't I cause things to happen? Why am I always pushed this way and that way. What a shitty way to spend a holiday weekend. I don't give a damn if some bastard wants me dead. Surely assassins must rest, especially on the holidays. Don't they have families too?

He tried to remember if anyone had been assassinated in Moscow on a weekend or a holiday. He couldn't remember any. Even that psycho Mikhail waited until Monday to have Pavel killed. It makes sense. Everyone is at his dacha, except for those people having a good time by the metro station.

He stared at the vodka bottle sitting on the table next to the chess game. He snatched it with his left hand and with the other he swiped the game onto the floor. "To hell with chess. To hell with Jenia, to hell with Mikhail Kolodkin," he shouted as loud as he was able. He put the bottle to his lips and waited for the familiar warmth. Nothing.

Alex woke. The empty bottle was on the floor next to his feet. He looked at his watch. It was almost midnight. He had slept for almost an hour. He mumbled, "I need another bottle."

He pushed himself out of the chair, stumbled down the hall to the bathroom and splashed cold water on his face. The cold hurt, but cleared his head. He had a terrible taste in his mouth and realized he hadn't eaten anything. Well, a few biscuits he shared with Tanya when she brought him the picture of Jenia.

Strange, yesterday she was in a great mood, excited about showing me how to play chess. Today, she couldn't wait to leave.

"I can only stay a short time. I have a meeting with Carl to bring him up-to-date. Then I have to get home early. Tonight the city is setting off some fireworks. I promised to take Kolya to see them."

He struggled to put on his shoes. He tried to do it standing, but he kept falling to one side or the other. Finally, he sat on the floor and put them on. He grabbed his leather jacket, and without bothering to lock the door he left the flat and took the elevator to the first floor. When he stepped out into the night, the cool air refreshed him.

I love spring. Nights are not too hot, not too cold.

He walked briskly to the Metro looking for a liquor kiosk and found one near the station. It was a small trailer-like building with a counter and a rack of bottles. He asked for Smirnoff and the old woman put it into a paper sack. He thanked her and returned to the noise outside.

Everyone was happy, but the joy around him only served to remind him he was sad, alone. He opened the bottle and took a long drink. It tasted much better outside than it did in the flat. He threw his head back to let the fresh air wash over his face and took another gulp.

He stood in front of the Metro and watched people going in and out. Every man appeared to have a goatee.

After another swallow of vodka, he shouted to the crowd, "Come on you bastard. Here I am. Come and get me. Put me out of my misery." No one paid him any heed so he sat down on the curb and continued to work on his bottle.

Flashes of light and rapid loud booms told him the fireworks were ending. He stood and glanced around. He was dizzy and the vodka was almost gone.

Men and women were kissing. Alex focused his attention on a young couple standing between two kiosks by the station. They were locked in a long passionate kiss. He felt like someone had kicked him in the stomach. He put his bottle to his lips, took a long drink and finished it. He coughed when he tried to swallow and had to sit again to recover.

I'm tired. I'm going to go home and go to bed. Tomorrow I'm going to move out and I won't tell anyone where I've gone. I'll be free from all of them. Let both of them suffer like I'm suffering now.

He stumbled slowly through the crowd along Smolenskiy Pereulok, occasionally bumping into people hurrying along the congested sidewalk to or from the Metro. "Eezvineetye," he mumbled with each bump.

The crowd thinned out considerably when he turned onto Protochny Street, allowing more room for people to avoid the staggering disheveled drunk. He tripped over a curb when he turned onto the almost deserted Panfilovskiy Street. He pitched forward onto his knees and rolled onto his back clutching the bottle to his chest. He shouted, "God damn, why can't they clean the sidewalks." A young couple shook their heads, stepped around the prostrate Alex and continued down the dimly lit street. A man wearing an indigo cap and a worn black full-length military coat stepped around Alex and crossed the street. His head was bowed and his hands were thrust deep into his coat pockets. After crossing the street, he turned onto Panfilovskiy, walked about twenty meters, looked discretely up and down the street and stepped into a murky doorway. He stood in the shadow watching Alex intently.

Across the street, hidden in the shadow of the doorway nearest to the alley, two eyes watched the man and Alex. Tanya was wearing a black shawl over her head and had her hands stuffed into a black jogging outfit. She had been loitering in the shadows since Alex had left his flat. She had pressed her body hard against the back wall so that the man across the street didn't see her. Come on Alex, it's time, go home. Let's finish this.

Alex slowly wobbled to his feet and stood weaving in the middle of the street. He stayed in the middle of the street and began dragging one foot forward and then the other making his way toward the alley leading to the entrance to building number three. Two young men went by, pointed at him and laughed.

Tanya's hands and feet were stiff with cold. She wanted to shake them, make them ready for action, but she couldn't move or the man across the street would see her. "Please Alex," she urged under her breath, "Get into the alley." She was worried the man would shoot him in the street. Alex fell to his knees and the bottle rolled toward the doorway where the man was hiding. Alex crawled after it.

Tanya was poised. If that drunken fool starts to crawl farther toward the bottle, there is no way I can save him, except to call out his name and run out there. He'll get both of us killed. She concentrated on looking to the side of the other doorway so her peripheral vision would detect any movement.

The man stepped out of the doorway, but stepped back again when Alex found another empty bottle and managed to get back on his feet. He was slowly weaving his way into the alley. She heard him mumbling. He was trying to sing, but mumbled the words and bungled the tune.

She turned her attention back to the man in the doorway. He slowly stepped out of the shadow and searched the street to see if anyone else was in the area. Carefully, he crept across the street to the entrance of the alley. He checked out the street again, reached into his coat pocket and pulled out a small pistol. When his eyes stopped on her hiding place, she stood solid as a wall. Any movement would bring disaster. He screwed a silencer onto the end of the pistol. When he turned to follow Alex into the alley, she moved.

The man's full attention was on Alex. She shook her hands and quickly but silently rushed into the alley. The man was only twenty feet away watching Alex and moving slowly toward him. Think like a cat. You're a cat. Keep moving Alex. Don't fall.

She had ten feet to go, five, four, three. The man raised his pistol. He sensed her coming, turned and pointed the pistol toward her. She was too quick. She slapped the pistol from his hand and drove her fist into the front of his throat just below his goatee. She heard the bones snap. He fell to his knees choking and gasping.

It was quick, professional. She felt the rush come through her body. To stare at death and win is a thrill like no other. Her muscles relaxed and she exhaled. A funny thought crossed her mind. If it's going to be your last breath, make it a good one.

The man was clutching his throat, gasping, wheezing. She grabbed the gun and pointed it at his head, but kept out of his reach. From the corner of her eye she saw Alex strolling nonchalantly toward them.

"Come on Alex. Let's get this guy to your flat, huh? I want to ask him some questions." Alex stopped and weaved. He stood and stared at them. "Come on Alex. Move, huh?"

He shuffled to her. The man was wheezing, but he would live. "Get up," she ordered. He stood and she got a good look at his face. A sudden shudder went through her, just as it had in the restaurant. It was Yuri, but he didn't say anything, didn't seem to recognize her. His face was still blue from lack of air. She motioned for him to go toward the entrance to the building.

Before she could stop him, Alex pulled out his key and stepped in front of Yuri to open the door. She was out of position. Yuri reached into his coat, pulled out a knife and raised it. He arched the blade down toward Alex. She put the gun to Yuri's head and pulled the trigger. The gun jumped in her hand and she heard a muffled thump. The shell casing flew over her shoulder and Yuri's head snapped to the side. Bone, blood and flesh spewed out. He crumpled to the ground.

At first Alex didn't realize what had happened. Then he slumped forward and tried to reach his back to remove the knife. Thanks to the leather jacket and Yuri's inability to get his full force behind it, the knife had penetrated only a few centimeters. It wiggled every time Alex reached back. If it hadn't been such a serious situation, it would have been funny.

Tanya removed the knife. She hated herself for her error. Why didn't I search him? What's wrong with me lately? "Alex, are you all right? I should have shot him right away. Come on, we have to get away from here, huh?"

He didn't respond and dropped to his knees looking for his bottle. She saw blood dripping from his coat. She grabbed him by his left hand and helped him stand. "Come on Alex. We have to go."

She hated to leave Yuri lying there, but she had no time to dispose of the body. She had to get Alex away from this place and to a new safe flat. There might be more Yuri's in the area. "Come on," she said again, "I'll help you walk."

"Where are we going?"

"I've a place where you'll be safe, at least for a few days." She saw the painful expression on his face as the initial numbness from the wound wore off. Luckily, the pain sobered him and he did a fair job of walking with her to the end of the alley and another thirty meters to an old yellow

Moskvich. Tanya opened the door and pushed him inside. He mumbled, "I lost my bottle. What about my bottle, my things?"

She didn't respond. She pushed him forward in the seat and pulled off his coat. She examined the wound.

"Is it bad?"

"No. It's superficial. I'll dress it at the flat." She jumped into the car and started the engine. He had a confused look on his face.

"God damn it. I'm tired of living like a hermit. I need a drink."

"I'll get you another bottle. Happy holiday, huh?" She turned away and drove the car into the street. It took her thirty minutes to find a pint of vodka and reach the new flat. It was located on Prosvirin Pereulok, halfway between the Sukharevskaya Metro and Chistiye Prudy Metro, but a good walk from either.

Alex sat on a kitchen chair and she dressed his wound. He was drinking his pint of vodka to ease the pain, but he didn't finish much during the time she was there. Twice he said, "Thank you Jenia." She didn't bother to comment.

Moscow – Friday, May 1

Tanya opened the door to the flat. It was a small flat, with a combination bedroom/living room, a kitchen, and a combination toilet/bath. She didn't want to wake Alex. It was eight in the morning, but she was sure he would be sleeping. She carried a bottle of water, a carton of orange juice, bread, ham, cheese and a few eggs. She went to the kitchen and deposited the food and drinks. An empty pint bottle sat on the table. His shirt was hanging on the back of a chair. A pair of pants lay in a heap on the floor.

She crossed the hall and knocked on the door to the bedroom. He didn't answer. She tried for a minute knocking every few seconds, but he never answered. She considered leaving, but she had to check his wound and put on new dressing. So, she opened the door and peered inside the room. Alex was lying on his back on the bed. His underclothes were on the floor. He was naked. What to do? Frustrated, and embarrassed, she entered the room, walked to the bed and placed a sheet over him. She rolled him over in the bed.

He woke, surprised. "What's going on?"

"I'm here to dress your wound, huh?"

"Where am I?"

"You're in a new flat. Quite comfortable I would say." He lay in the bed with a sheet pulled down to his waist. She ripped the bandage off his back and he yelped. The wound was clean with no indication of infection. She said, "Don't move. I need to wash it and apply a new bandage." She washed the wound and he screamed when she applied the antiseptic. Sometimes it helps to be angry and aggressive, she decided. She reapplied a bandage. "There. You're fixed again."

She left the room and returned a few moments later carrying a glass of orange juice. He rolled over and sat to take the orange juice. The cover slipped lower and he glanced down. His face flushed. So did hers. He apparently hadn't realized he was naked under the sheet.

She said, "You get some rest now and I'll come back later and cook you a bite to eat."

His voice cracked from dryness, "Thanks."

"Alex?"

"Yes?"

"I think you should stop drinking."

16

Moscow – Monday, May 4

Park Pobedy (Victory Park) is located along Kutuzovsky Prospect on Poklonnaya Gora (Prostration Hill). In ancient times, travelers entering or leaving the city would stop on this hill, turn toward the city and prostate themselves in reverence to Holy Moscow and its saints.

The park is a memorial complex that spreads over 135 hectares and includes open-air exhibits of tanks, armored vehicles, fighter airplanes, helicopters, submarines and warships used by the Soviet Army during World War II. Its main segment is laid out around a grand fountain-lined axis culminating in the Central Museum of the Great Patriotic War (WW2), a vast concave structure, raised on stilts and crowned by a spiked bronze dome. Sculptures of equestrian Amazons blowing trumpets stand on both of its flanks.

At the front of the museum, on top of the hill, is a metal obelisk in the form of a three-sided Russian bayonet 141.8 meters high, one tenth of a meter for each day of the war. A collage containing several hundred bronze reliefs depicting famous military events covers the surface of the obelisk. Nike, the goddess of victory, flies close to its top.

A path runs from the park entrance to the obelisk past five large pools with towering fountains. In the evening, red lights illuminate these fountains making the water look like blood.

Tanya sat on the granite steps near the obelisk watching small groups of people pushing baby carriages and walking hand in hand. Some teenagers ran and roller-bladed on the mall often forcing people to jump out of their way. She thought they should be in school. She glanced again at her watch. Where is Jenia, she's twenty minutes late? Tanya was always punctual and didn't like it when others were late.

She often brought Kolya to the park. He and she would roller-blade on the mall, see the outdoor exhibits, walk among the trees. The museum was their favorite place. A true grandson of the colonel, Kolya especially liked the Hall of Glory with its huge golden soldier in the center and the names of decorated soldiers printed in gold on its circular wall. Tanya's favorite was the Hall of Memory and Sorrow containing threads strung with thousands of glass beads representing tears and a white marble pieta in the center symbolizing Mother Russia with her dead son on her knees. She cried every time she went there, but was drawn to it on almost every visit.

They had been here in the park on Saturday, with Dmitry. He begged her to take him back, but she remained strong. She wouldn't forgive him beating his son or his infidelity.

There she is, finally. Jenia entered the park mall from Kutuzovskiy Prospekt. She was wearing expensive sunglasses, a white silk jacket and jet-black pants, which broke over patent leather shoes. The bright red collar of her shirt rested outside her jacket. Her picture doesn't do her justice, thought Tanya. She looks like she just stepped off a runway.

Tanya studied her own brown wool business suit, shiny from too many rough Russian dry cleanings. There is no way I can compete if men truly love with their eyes, she thought.

She raised her hand to signal hello, but not so much as to attract attention. Jenia nodded recognition and weaved her way through the crowds while dodging the teenagers. The two women stood a meter apart. Jenia's face brightened with a professional smile and she held out her hand. "So, we meet at last. I've been looking forward to this. I'm sorry I'm late."

Tanya returned her smile. "Me too. I've seen your picture, but it doesn't do you justice."

"Well, thank you." Jenia's face showed her surprise at the comment. She recovered and said, "Alex has moved out of the flat I found for him."

Tanya responded, "Yuri tried to kill him Thursday evening."

"Yuri, short, thin, goatee?"

"Yes."

Jenia's face twisted in anger. "Damn. I should have killed the bastard when I had a chance."

"You won't have to. I did it for you."

"I know he worked for Mikhail, do you know who he was?"

"Yuri Usenko. He was an FSB agent, moonlighting I guess."

"Let's hope so."

"I moved Alex to a another flat. He was going stir-crazy anyway. He won't last long in the new one, it's about half the size."

The slight breeze lifted Jenia's short black hair and made it wave like wheat in a field. Tanya wore a forest-green, wool beret. Tanya extended arm. "Let's walk a bit. I don't like standing in the open like this."

"Good idea."

The two women walked away from the monument toward the Minskaya side of the park. They walked in silence, arm in arm, until they left the mall and took a path winding among the trees, which were beginning to bud.

Jenia broke the silence. "You picked a good day to meet. What made you pick this park?"

"I told you I saw the picture."

"God, I'd forgotten. That's right. My picture by the monument." She cocked her head and grinned. "I don't believe you. That's not the reason you picked it."

"I guess it's because I feel comfortable here. It's a new park built by the new spirit in Russia, and this hill represents many fateful moments in a succession of Western assaults on Russia, the Poles in 1610, the French in 1812 and most recently the Germans."

Jenia's face showed interest; so Tanya continued. "In 1812, Napoleon stood on this hill and saw Moscow for the first time. He waited here for the city fathers to surrender Moscow. Instead, they abandoned the city and continued fighting. Napoleon stood here and watched the City of Moscow burn along with his dreams of conquering Russia."

Jenia grinned, "You tell me this as if I didn't know it already."

"Did you?"

"No."

"I bring my son here often. He loves the exhibits and the museum. This Saturday is Victory Day, the best time to come here. The park will be full of flowers, processions of old women with medals and old soldiers in old uniforms, as well as field kitchens where you can try some *Kasha*." She saw a quizzical look on Jenia's face. "*Kasha* is buckwheat porridge, about all there was to eat during the war."

"You have a son, that's nice. I don't think I'll ever have children."

Jenia stopped walking, dropped her arm and turned to face Tanya. "How is Alex?"

"He's in love with you."

Jenia shook her head. "No. No he isn't. He thinks he is, but its only infatuation."

"Why do you say that?"

Jenia shrugged, hooked her arm with Tanya's again and they resumed their stroll. Jenia said, "What do you want me to do?"

"I'm not sure. Alex is in danger. I feel responsible. He won't be safe as long as Mikhail is around."

"Unfortunately, I'm not authorized to kill Mikhail."

Tanya responded, "Neither am I."

Jenia stopped, faced Tanya and whispered, "Mikhail and some others are involved in a secret project, 'Superpower'."

Tanya was suspicious of her candor, "Interesting name. Why are you telling me this?"

"You don't trust me. I don't blame you. Let's just say that I have a good reason."

Tanya stared into Jenia's eyes, searching for any sign of deception.

Jenia stared back as she continued, "You know who I am. I know who you are. We both benefit by working together on this."

"Okay. I'm listening."

"The project involves the acquisition and control of most large state-owned enterprises, especially infrastructure businesses." The two women locked arms and resumed walking.

Tanya waited for more. This only confirmed what she already knew, or suspected. I'll have to be careful. Jenia is dangerous and cunning. She's been trained for this type of diplomatic wrangling. I'm a research analyst.

Tanya said, "There must be some papers . . . something outlining or detailing the project."

Jenia didn't respond. Tanya assumed her silence meant yes; so she pushed on, "Does Mikhail have some papers about Superpower?" She felt Jenia's arm jerk involuntarily.

Jenia stopped walking and looked hard into Tanya's eyes. She was searching, trying to read her mind. "I hate the man."

Tanya backed off quickly. "I wasn't implying anything, but there have been rumors."

Jenia continued to look at Tanya suspiciously. "I'm sure, instigated by Mikhail. Has Alex heard them?"

"Alex is caged in a box waiting to be killed by that beast."

Jenia seemed satisfied. Her face relaxed, and she resumed walking. "If Mikhail has anything, it's probably in his office." She shrugged again, pulled a set of keys from her jacket pocket and discreetly gave them to Tanya.

Tanya put the keys in her pocket without looking at them and smiled, friendly. "*Spaseeba*." Without thinking, Tanya said, "If the papers aren't in his office, maybe they're in his flat. Do you have keys to his flat also?" As soon as she said the words she regretted it.

Jenia stopped and scowled at her.

Tanya quickly added, "I'm sorry, it was a poorly worded question. I know you're not his mistress. I'm sure you can make this easier for us."

"I'm not a traitor to Israel or to Russia. There is only so much that I can do directly. As it is, I am risking more than I want."

"I can count on your cooperation?"

Jenia nodded.

They continued their stroll. Jenia said, "You say Saturday is Victory Day. Will there be speeches, a lot of politicians?"

"Yes, all the key politicians will be here."

"That means Mikhail will be here also. I'll get him to invite me."

"It's too dangerous to break into his office during the day."

"I agree, but I know the man. He'll want to take me to dinner and his flat afterwards. I can keep him occupied until . . . say . . . midnight."

"So, he's in love with you?"

"Mikhail loves only Mikhail. No, he's not in love with me, more like an obsession. In his mind, I'm like a country to be conquered, plundered and trophied. No, getting into his flat will not be a problem, searching for documents and getting out, that will be a problem."

"You mean getting out without killing him."

"Exactly."

They turned around and headed back toward the monument and the busy mall. Jenia said, "Konstantin told me that Mikhail wants to see me when I return to the Klub. I'm sure he wants to continue the meetings there. I'll get Mikhail to commit to dinner on Sunday."

"Sunday. Why not Saturday?"

"He'll think he's done me a favor by taking me to the celebration on Saturday. He'll see his reward as dinner and the chance to take me to his flat. I want him to suffer through a wait. Is Sunday okay for you and Alex"?

"Sunday is fine. Who is Konstantin?"

"Alex hasn't mentioned him? They are best friends. Konstantin is the bartender at the Klub."

"What about the Klub, who owns it now that Pavel is gone? By the way, my condolences; I know you were close to Pavel."

"Thank you. Yes we were close," Jenia hesitated, "but we weren't lovers." She waited a few moments and added, "Pavel transferred the ownership to me some time ago. No one knew, other than those involved in the project. He didn't want his name legally associated with the Klub."

As they approached the mall, Tanya said, "Please be careful. The man is capable of anything. One little mistake and. . . ."

"You be careful too. Anything can happen. We won't necessarily control all events."

Tanya stopped and turned to face Jenia. She studied her beauty, her strength. She tried to see her as a man would see her. "Do you really think it's infatuation?"

Jenia nodded. "We have a good time together, but we'll never be married or have children."

Tanya looked at the ground. "I have a son, but my husband and I are separated."

"God, I'm sorry I didn't know. Hell, what do I know about marriage, love, children. I don't even have parents."

Tanya felt her heart go out to Jenia. She was in love with a man who wasn't her match, couldn't properly return her love. Tanya reached into the frayed pocket of her suit coat, which had become much too hot for the day. She pulled out a piece of paper, took a pen from her other pocket, and wrote a phone number. She handed it to Jenia and said, "Here's a number you can call." She grinned, "Don't be surprised if a man answers."

Jenia studied the number. A few tears slowly rolled down her cheeks toward the corners of her mouth. She said, "You can't imagine what it means to me to have your trust, to have you understand the difficult role I play."

She glanced again at the number and put it into her coat pocket. "I love the little bugger, you know. He's so completely irresponsible and innocent. He could have any of the girls at the Klub. Konstantin says that they dote on him. He's a friend to all the girls, but won't touch any of them. He says that Alex is a one-woman man."

Tanya felt a rush as she thought about Dmitry and his infidelity.

Jenia continued, "He's like a puppy that can talk. I wonder what he would do if I threw a ball across the room."

Tanya said, "He'd chase it but —."

Jenia finished, "He'd never bring it back."

They both laughed.

Tanya said, "He worships that picture you gave him. He's always thinking of you, talking about you." She said the words and then realized she had let her guard down. She blushed.

Jenia was too well trained to miss it. "You too?"

Tanya looked away. "Yes. We had a rough start. It's . . . I can't help liking him. He's so transparent."

Jenia returned to business. "I assume you picked him?"

"Yes." She reached in her pocket again, wrote an address on another piece of paper and gave it to Jenia. "The more I think about it, you should surprise him."

Jenia wrapped her arms around Tanya and kissed her cheek. The two then stepped back from each other, spun around and walked in opposite directions.

※

Mikhail stood by his office window and gazed across the Moscow River at St Basil's Cathedral. He put the cigarette to his mouth and took a long, slow drag. He inhaled deeply then let the smoke drift from his mouth and nose. *I'm a rich man, probably the richest in Russia. I've won my contest with Jonah. I have my little parties in my flat. Something's missing. I can't seem to get satisfied. It seems the more I have the less I have.* He moved his gaze to the cars passing the Kremlin walls. *I must be President of Russia. I must have Jenia.*

The telephone rang and interrupted his thoughts. In a few moments he heard Galina over the intercom. "It's Konstantin sir. Line one."

Mikhail lifted the receiver "Hello Konstantin."

"Mikhail, she's back. She's in her office right now."

It must be an omen. It's like the universe knew what I was thinking and responded. "Give her a few minutes to get settled and then go to her office. Talk to her about anything, inventory, business, anything but keep her there until I get there. I won't forget this Kostya. I'm leaving now. I'll be there soon."

✤

It was too early in the afternoon for the Klub to open, but Mikhail had a key. He and Oleg slowly, quietly, made their way among the tables, chairs and dance stages in the dark. When they neared the rear of the Klub, Mikhail saw light coming from under Jenia's door, and motioned for Oleg to be quiet as he stood near the door to hear.

Konstantin was saying, "I didn't know that Pavel had sold you the Klub."

"Yes. Well . . . with Pavel gone, the situation . . . has changed. I mean . . . well, it's just not what I want to do anymore."

"Are you planning to stay in Moscow?"

After a long nervous silence, Mikhail heard Jenia respond, "Who knows? I doubt it, too many bad memories and not much to keep me here anymore."

"Not even Alex?"

Mikhail almost burst through the door to say "No. No."

Konstantin spoke before Mikhail moved. "You don't have to spend all your time here. I've shown you I can run the place without your being here. Maybe we can work together and I'll buy it from you over time, say a year or so."

The silence taxed Mikhail's patience.

She responded, "I think I would like the glass of wine you offered earlier."

Mikhail waited until he heard Konstantin pouring the wine. He pushed open the door and stepped into the light. Jenia was sitting in one of two chairs along the wall; Konstantin was in the other. Two glasses of wine and a bottle sat on the table between them. Oleg stepped into the room, but Mikhail nodded to him and he left closing the door behind.

Jenia spoke, "Good afternoon Mikhail, what a pleasant surprise. We were reminiscing about Pavel and how much I'll miss him."

To Mikhail, her surprise didn't seem genuine, but he let it pass. "I guess Pavel's passing has created some problems for you."

There was a long embarrassing silence. She turned her head to look at Konstantin. Mikhail did the same. Konstantin excused himself. She said to Konstantin, "We'll finish our discussion later."

Jenia turned back to Mikhail and nodded toward the now vacant chair. He strolled across the room and sat. She said, "I ran into a minor problem in Poland."

Mikhail tried to act surprised, "Oh?"

"I stayed there after the funeral to help Ivona settle into her new flat in Warsaw." Mikhail realized she was not only lying to him, but she also wanted him to know it.

She continued, "Alexander offered help. You remember Alexander don't you?"

She was rubbing it in. He pictured Alex and her in bed together and wanted to choke them both. *I'll take her to my flat and make her beg for mercy like the little blond with the crucifix.*

"Yes, I think I remember him. Isn't he the drunk who was bothering you and the rest of us at the club?"

Jenia didn't take the bait. "When we finished, Ivona asked me to bring you some papers."

She hates me, thought Mikhail. *I can't decide whether I hate her or I love her. I know I want her.* "That was nice of her."

"Someone attacked us. Of course, I wasn't much help — Alex was so brave."

Mikhail fought to control his temper. *She wants me to get jealous. She knows Yuri reported back on what happened in the alley. He was right. There's more to this woman than anyone suspects. I'd better watch my back or I'll end up like Yuri.*

When Mikhail didn't respond, she leaned forward, cocked her head, grinned and gazed at him. "I'm sorry Mikhail. I hope the papers weren't important."

He lost control, and his face flushed with anger. His eyebrows gave him away. He snapped, "Don't worry. The robbers probably wanted the briefcase Alex was carrying. I hope your friend wasn't injured."

He saw her raise her left eyebrow and smile. She enjoyed this game.

"They were more like thugs than professionals." She paused to give him a chance to speak. He held his comments so he wouldn't say something he'd regret. He wanted her more than ever. She resumed. "You don't think Pavel was into something criminal?"

Mikhail was frustrated, losing control of the conversation. He wanted to scare her, let her know he was in charge. "Where is Alexander? He seems to have disappeared?"

She ignored his question and mused, "Pavel would never do anything crooked."

Mikhail decided she blamed him for an attempt on her life. He wanted to tell her Yuri had specific instructions not to hurt her. He wanted to explain, but he knew it was best not to say anything. They stared at each other through a long uncomfortable silence.

Suddenly Jenia stood leaving the still-full wine glass on the table. "Well. I should get back to work. The girls will need a good pep talk tonight before they begin taking their clothes off." As she spoke, she walked proudly, in control, past Mikhail to her desk.

He was seething. She's perfect for me, would have dealt with Jonah the same as I did. I wonder how she handles the whip? He wanted to make his offer. It embarrassed him to do it this way, but her control of the conversation forced him into it. "Before I leave . . . I know Pavel's death has been difficult for you. I want you to know I'm always ready to help you."

Jenia sat behind her desk and turned toward him. Her face told him she knew she had won. "Thank you Mikhail. It was kind of you to say." She glanced down at her calendar and then turned to look at him again. "As a matter of fact, you can. I'm going to Victory Park this Saturday. I've never been on Victory Day and I understand the flowers, the people and the food are worth it, though I've heard the speeches are boring. It would be nice to have an escort."

Mikhail's heart jumped. I've got to have her. I've got to get her to my flat. She'll lose her attitude when I get her there. He stood and walked to the door. "I'll take you if you agree to have dinner with me."

She got up from her desk, walked to the door and put her hand on the handle. "I suggest the La Gastronome, Sunday night, late." She opened the door.

"It's not my favorite, and why not Saturday night?" He saw her frown. "But, if that's what you want."

"That's what I want," she said with finality.

Mikhail left the room. She's perfect for me; I'll have her. She needs a master not some puppy that follows her around licking her shoes. I'll have her and I'll have Russia.

※

Alex was tired, even though it was only seven in the evening. He was lying on top of his bed, looking at the ceiling and daydreaming. There are too many flats in my life, he decided. My back hurts. My leg hurts. I wish I were back in my own flat. I don't like this life. How did I get involved in all this mess?

Every time he went to sleep, there would be a large group of men with goatees chasing him waving pistols. Sometimes in his dream he saw all the way down the barrels of the guns and big smiling bullets.

He wanted companionship, fresh air, sunshine, visitors, and meals in restaurants with friends. He wanted to talk to Konstantin. He wanted to be with Jenia.

He was only partly awake, but he thought he heard a knock at his door. His heart jumped. Who, at this hour? Surely Tanya was home with Kolya. No one else came here. He hurried to the door. His socks slipped on the hardwood floor and he almost fell. He tried to be quiet. The door had no peephole; so he would have to open it to find out who was there. Damn. I can't believe there's no peephole.

What to do? If I call out, whoever it is will know I'm here. I know a wood door will be no help. The flat's too high to escape out the window. What the hell, if I'm going to die why not now? He swung open the door and stared wide-eyed. For a moment she stood staring at him, then she showed that famous grin he knew so well. She rushed in and threw her arms around him. She kissed him on the neck and cheek. Finally, she kissed him passionately on the mouth.

He was shaking. He didn't know whether from fear or excitement. He felt little tingles everywhere. She held him tightly then leaned back, winked and said, "Tired?"

"Not any more."

Her eyes flashed. She stepped back, reached forward and took his hands in hers. "Let's go to bed. Do you think Tanya put in cameras?"

Alex grinned at the thought. "I hope not. She laughed and removed her shoes. Like children, she and Alex ran and slid across the floor.

She stopped at the entrance to the bedroom. She scanned the room. "Cozy isn't it?" She stood in the middle of the room taking off her clothes. Alex threw his shirt at her. She ran across the room and tackled him onto his bed. He was lying on his back and she straddled him. She looked down on him and grinned. "If there are pictures, send them to me will you?"

Alex scanned the ceiling and walls, pretending to look for cameras. "Where should I send them?"

"I don't know, maybe advertise in the *Financial Times* and say, 'Jenia I've got the pictures you ordered'."

For a moment she straddled his stomach and looked at him. Her smile disappeared and she said, "Alex, you've got to stop drinking. You have a lot of work to do, and I want to be proud of you."

He stared at her, unable to think of anything to say. Suddenly, her smile returned, She leaned forward, kissed him and rocked back and forth on top of him.

17

Moscow – Friday, May 8

Alex fought the steering wheel. A gusty wind was trying to blow the white GAZ van from the highway. He glanced in the rearview mirror at the load of files and equipment to see if anything had shifted or fallen.

"Tough wind, huh?"

"Yes, but at least the road's in good shape."

"We'll be turning soon. I'm sure that road will be a challenge, huh?" Tanya was studying Carl's handwritten map. To Alex, the map looked like a child's scribbling. The road straightened and he was now heading into the wind. The steering became easier and he relaxed.

It had been a marvelous three days, all he had dreamed. He had Jenia to himself twenty-four hours a day. They even joined forces playing chess against the computer Tanya had retrieved when she picked up his clothes. They won every match. She had been impressed with his new knowledge of chess strategy. He admitted he'd learned most of it from Tanya. She was pleased. He wasn't prepared for it to end. Neither was she.

On Thursday he received the call from Tanya. "You're going to move to the dacha."

"What dacha?"

"We're moving the war room to a dacha and you'll be staying there. It's safer."

"When?"

"Tomorrow afternoon. I'll collect you at your flat. Pack everything you have. You won't be going back."

"But I like it here. Jenia and I . . ."

Tanya interrupted. "Trust me, you'll love the dacha."

He told Jenia, but she already knew. He was the last to know, when it came to something affecting his life and happiness.

On Thursday evening, Jenia had been in a strange, almost melancholy mood. She hugged him more than usual. She wanted to be in contact with him all the time. When she said goodbye, she had tears in her eyes.

"There it is."

He jumped out of his daydream and almost lost control of the van. His foot automatically pushed on the brake when he heard her shout. The van slowed quickly.

"Alex. Were you sleeping?"

"No. I guess I was daydreaming."

"It was a nice few days wasn't it?"

"Yes."

She pointed at the turnoff. The opening was hidden by brush and trees, which had grown to the edge of the highway. He slowed the van almost to a stop.

"If you didn't know this road was here, you'd never see it," he said and turned the wheel. It was a close fit. He heard crunching when the tires left the pavement and rolled onto the gravel. He drove slowly, as the ruts in the road were deep and made the load shift precariously.

"Careful, huh," she said. "We don't want to smash the equipment."

He took his eyes off the road long enough to scowl at her. "You may be better at chess, but I'm the better driver."

At the top of a hill they had a nice view of the terrain. He had to fight the wheel to stay on the road, because the wind was much stronger. Both opened their windows and inhaled the fresh country air. She said, "I should have brought Kolya. He needs some time in the country."

"Why didn't you? We'd have played football. There must be a lawn near the dacha. We'd hunt for wild mushrooms in the forest."

She gazed at him, studying him. She smiled and said, "If I get a chance I'll bring him. I'm sure he'd enjoy meeting you."

He let the van roll down the other side of the hill and was forced to fight it around the next corner. He almost hit a tree and had to stop and back up. He shrugged. She opened her mouth to say something, but thought better of it. Instead, she turned her head and looked out the side window. "I love all the trees and fresh air. I wish I lived in these woods."

"Me too," he responded.

"It would be a long way to the Knight Klub," she commented and turned to face him.

"It's a phase I went through. Sometimes I think I never wanted to leave my twenties. Lately, I've been thinking I should get more out of life and less out of a bottle." He grinned, "Maybe it's a mood that comes with playing better chess."

She laughed. "Getting shot and stabbed will make anyone rethink his life."

He nodded and maneuvered the van around another narrow bend and increased speed along a straight stretch of road.

She checked the map again. "Careful, we're coming to a turnoff soon. We'll be making a left onto a short dirt road and then a quick right onto a gravel driveway. It's not far now."

A few moments later he drove onto the gravel driveway between two huge fir trees. Spring flowers bloomed on both sides. The dacha was fifty meters ahead.

He pulled to a stop next to the dacha and cheered, "We're here!" His arms were sore from fighting the steering wheel. He could barely move his fingers when he pulled them from the wheel. He flexed them back and forth to get the blood moving again. It was painful, but felt good.

Tanya jumped from the van and was talking to Carl, who was by the door of the dacha. Alex searched around, but he didn't see a car. How did he get here? He walked to Carl who held out his hand, "Greetings. What do you think of our new war room . . . and your new home?"

Tanya answered first. "Nice. How did you find it?"

Alex finished her comment, "Even with a map it was a challenge."

Carl said, "I rented it for three months from a friend of a friend. It's tucked away in the woods, isn't it? I think you'll both enjoy working here, even though it's a long drive from Moscow for Tanya."

Alex entered the dacha to examine the place. The ground floor had a main room, a kitchen and a toilet. It was sparsely furnished with wooden tables and chairs. An iron stove was apparently the only source of heat. Two electric lights hung from the ceiling. The room had only three or four electric outlets.

He climbed a staircase leading to the second floor and found two small bedrooms and a bath. The windows in each bedroom provided an impressive view. He saw only forest, no other dachas, no twelve-story flats, no cars whizzing down the street, no people. When he opened one of the windows, cool air rushed into the room. He looked down at the yard. It was flat enough. Kolya and I will practice football on the lawn. We might kill a few flowers, but there are plenty of them.

When he returned to the ground floor, Tanya and Carl were talking about the electrical hookups. He ignored them and went to the kitchen. It was much larger than the kitchen in his flat near Oktyabraskaya, and it was new. Out the kitchen window, through the trees, he saw the road almost four hundred meters away. He studied it for a moment and then realized it was a part of the road he had driven. It was a section of road about six hundred meters before the turn onto the dirt road leading to the driveway.

He returned to the reception room. Tanya and Carl stopped talking. Carl turned to him and said, "Well, what do you think?"

"I like it. What a peaceful place. You should move the whole office down here and you'd never lose your people."

She said, "Speaking of PHD, our files and equipment are still in the van . . . men. If you two will bring the equipment, I'll set it up."

They managed to empty the van in less than thirty minutes. Tanya was busy connecting the equipment; so the two men stood by the van talking.

Alex asked, "How did you get here?"

"I wondered when you'd ask. Follow me."

He led Alex to an overgrown path that entered the woods near the back of the dacha, opposite the driveway entrance. They walked along it for five hundred meters and came to a clearing. On the opposite side, was a dark-green Volvo 850 parked behind some trees. Carl explained, "I took another road that connects to a separate part of the highway you were driving on today. It's actually a shorter route, but there's no connection to the driveway into the dacha."

Alex said, "Nice. It might come in handy. Do you have a map?"

Carl reached in his jacket pocket and gave him another hand written map and said, "I have to go now. I assume Tanya can find her way back to the city in the van."

"Probably better than me."

The two men shook hands. Carl got into his car and drove down a dense path toward the edge of the forest. Alex returned to the dacha to help Tanya. She had made some tea and was sitting at a table. "I took the liberty of making a bed for you in the front bedroom. I hope that's okay."

"Thank you. What about this weekend, are we going to work?"

"I'll be back tomorrow and we can get everything organized."

He interrupted, "Bring Kolya. It's Saturday. Surely he doesn't have school."

She beamed at the thought. "I'll do that. I'm sure he'll love to have you teach him some football tricks."

"Maybe you'll stay the night. There are two bedrooms."

She waited some time before she answered. "Okay. We will. I'd like that." Suddenly, she returned to the professional Tanya he knew so well. She showed him a set of keys. "Jenia gave me keys to Mikhail's office and files. We're going in Sunday night at 2100."

He was shocked. "Going in? What do you mean going in? Christ, you're going to get me arrested. What if we're caught?"

"We won't be caught. Jenia's arranged a diversion to help us. The guard checks the offices a few minutes before 2100 and not again until midnight. It'll be tight, but I think we can make it."

"You think?"

"I know we can make it."

He saw her looking at him and smiling with that same look he often received from Jenia.

He scratched the back of his hand. This is crazy and I shouldn't take part in it. "I'm a target. How will I hide from my assassins if I'm in prison? I want to stay here in this dacha, read papers and make analyses."

"Alex, you know what will happen if we don't stop these men. You risked your life to create a new Russia in ninety-one, do you want that effort wasted? Who will stop them, if not us? Where is the man who stood hand-to-hand with me at the White House? I need your help, your protection."

Alex shook his head. "Yes, we risked our lives, for what? Our leader turned on us in ninety-three."

"I don't know what would have happened if Yeltsin hadn't fired on the White House, but I do know what happened because he did. It's not all bad."

"I don't know whether history will condemn Yeltsin, or make him a hero or merely a footnote. He's a man who tried to change himself, or at least had the courage to try; but he wasn't always successful. The Soviet crust built up over half a century is difficult to break through in a few short years. It was the changed Yeltsin who took on his former Soviet allies; it was the Soviet Yeltsin who ordered the army to fire.

"If we don't want to lose what he tried to give us, we have to be as brave as we and he were in ninety-one. In a few years Yeltsin will be gone, but these oligarchs will continue bleeding Russia. These men are not elected leaders, they want to rule through the power of money, the kind of power Mikhail dreams about. We have to join hands and fight these monsters." She reached out and took his hand.

Alex didn't know what to say. He knew she was right. Hadn't his mother said almost the same thing in ninety-one? "Alex, I am so proud of you and your friends. You have given Russia a new birth, a new dream; but you can't rest now. Like the body fights off bacteria and virus every moment, you must be vigilant every day or the strong will try to take your freedom away."

Tanya was staring at him, "Have you been to the Hall of Memory and Sorrows? Have you seen the beads of tears and the pieta"?

"Yes, a few times; but I don't like to go there." His face reddened, "It makes me cry."

"That's because you care about Russia. You are her son, Alex; you must protect her. You can't let those men kill her, or me."

Alex nodded, and it made him feel good, like in ninety-one. "You're right. Let's do it."

She squeezed his hand, smiled and said, "I have to go now. I want to be back before Kolya goes to bed."

He raised his hand. "Wait a minute. I'll ride with you."

Now it was her turn to be surprised. "What are you talking about? How will you get back here?"

"Don't worry. I own a car, although I haven't driven it much. It's a red Lada I keep parked in a garage in Moscow. You can drop me there on your way home."

"Why do you want your car here?"

"It might come in handy. Besides, I want to buy a football."

18

Moscow – Sunday, May 10

Alex heard a loud click when Tanya turned the key in the door. She pushed the door open slowly, leaned inside, and directed her flashlight across the floor and the walls. The light settled on the secretary's desk. "Come on," she whispered and stepped into the room. He followed and quietly shut the door. Both were dressed in dark clothes. He was wearing a backpack and carrying a large, heavy bag.

She swiftly, stealthily crept across the room to the secretary's desk. She put her hand on the side of the desk, and when he heard a buzz he opened the door to Mikhail's office. She hurried to join him.

Alex sniffed. "It smells like a dog in here," he whispered.

She pointed her flashlight around the room, across a leather couch, some leather chairs, file cabinets and finally a large executive desk. She turned off her flashlight. They made their way across the room to the windows. She closed the blinds on one and he closed the other.

Tanya walked to the desk and turned on a lamp. Alex felt his heart beating fast and hard. He was warm. He took off his jacket and placed it on the couch. He stared at his shirt fully expecting to see it moving in and out with each heartbeat. Nothing. He put his bags on the couch, emptied them, took out a laptop computer and a scanner, and put them on a round meeting table not far from Mikhail's desk. Out of the corner of his eye he saw Tanya, all professional and efficient, searching Mikhail's desk.

"Aha," he said in a low voice when the equipment came to life. She stopped her search, stared at his equipment, shook her head and returned to her task.

Alex remembered her comment when he had proudly shown her his acquisitions. "If we have to run, I'd rather have a small camera in my pocket than all the equipment you'll have to carry."

He saw her glance back at him again and noticed the beginnings of a grin. "Hey, don't laugh. With this little feeder we can put in fifty pages at a time."

"I'll decide what we copy, huh?"

She turned back to the file cabinets to unlock them. He glanced at the clock on the wall. It was twenty-one fifteen. He leaned toward Tanya and in a loud whisper asked, "Are you sure no one will check this office until midnight?"

She turned and over her shoulder whispered back, "If anyone comes, we'll have to deal with him."

He felt a shudder go through his body. He thought about the bodies that had fallen to Jenia and Tanya. "What a pair," he mumbled to himself.

"What?"

"Never mind."

She unlocked a cabinet, turned to him and grinned.

Mikhail was excited. This was going to be his night. He looked across the table covered with plates, glasses and a bottle of Rothschild Cabernet Sauvignon. His gaze rested on the most sensual woman he had ever seen. Jenia was radiant. She was wearing a red ribbon in her short black hair, which gave her a look of innocence. It drove Mikhail crazy. Her only makeup was bright red lipstick that matched her ribbon. Her shell-white dress was cut low. At some angles he saw a whole breast, almost.

He glanced to his left and saw Oleg sitting three tables away. Jenia, surprisingly, had not protested when Oleg sat there and ordered a drink.

La Gastronome had more waiters than diners. She had said it was her favorite restaurant. He didn't like it much; it had been a grocery store. He considered it a spot for foreigners, not Russians. Near the entrance, a man dressed in white played classical music at a black grand piano. The music was quiet, but loud enough to keep their conversation private.

A waiter brought their salad dishes. Mikhail said to her. "I'm starved. Do you often eat this late?" He felt hunger pangs in his stomach. He leaned toward his plate and ate in big gulps.

She replied, "Not always. But I'm a night owl, as they say."

He noticed she was taking small bites and moving the food around on her plate. "I know we've had some differences in the past. I hope we can have a better relationship."

She smiled at him. It made his heart jump. "I think you see me as a trophy."

Why did she have to say that? Can't we have a pleasant dinner? I don't want to spar tonight. He tried again. "There's something about you, something that makes men want you." She continued to eat her food slowly. When it appeared she wasn't going to respond, he went back to his eating, flustered.

After a few minutes she said, "What makes you want me?"

He wanted to show her not tell her. He didn't know what to say without sounding foolish. She reached for her glass of wine, and smiled seductively. He challenged, "Did I say I wanted you?"

"Maybe I'm not available."

He visualized skinny Alexander sniffing after her. "You're a woman who needs a mature man, a man of financial substance. Alexander could never take care of you."

She held out her wine glass waiting for him to raise his. He felt a rush of adrenaline. He clinked his glass with hers, gulped down the wine and shattered his glass against a wall a few feet away from the table.

Mikhail motioned for a new glass. The busboy squatted by their table collecting pieces of broken glass.

※

Alex looked over the side of Mikhail's desk at the glass figurine he had accidentally knocked off of the desk. Pieces of it sprayed across the room. He heard Tanya growl, "Now he'll know someone's been here."

"I'm cleaning it up. He'll never miss it." He knelt and gathered the bigger pieces into a sack. He pushed the smaller ones under the desk.

When he finished, Tanya brought him another small stack of papers. He glanced at the clock, almost twenty-two thirty. I can't believe we've been at this for over an hour. She took the scanned pages and replaced them in the files. His heart was beating fast, and his face was flushed. He said, "These organization charts are interesting. Probably, we can sell this information to his competitors."

Tanya sounded frustrated. "In all these papers, I haven't seen the word 'Superpower', not in Hebrew, not in Russian, not in English."

Alex returned to his scanning. It was a more pleasant task than hers. As he scanned he daydreamed about his day with Kolya, and her. What a nice young man, and good at football. The kid sure laughed a lot. We had a great day. Alex gazed at Tanya. She was wrestling with a stuck drawer. He felt a warm glow and remembered holding her hand when they joined Kolya hunting for wild mushrooms. Together they watched him running in the yard. He was trying to get in all the fun he could before he had to go home. She was much different than the Tanya he knew at the office. She had said, "Thank you for playing football and spending so much time with Kolya. I couldn't get him to sleep last night. All he wanted to do was talk about how much fun he had with you."

He watched her working on the drawer and touched his cheek where she had kissed him earlier in the day. It was still warm.

※

Mikhail looked at his watch, almost eleven. This woman eats slower than anyone I've ever met. She drinks more too. His heart pounded with anticipation as he imagined the night ahead.

Jenia stood. "I have to go to the restroom." She spoke deliberately, unsuccessfully trying not to slur her words.

God. I don't want her too drunk, he decided. She walked unsteadily toward the toilets near the entrance. She walked by Oleg without noticing him. Mikhail began to follow, but she waved him away. He stopped at Oleg's table.

"Tell Ivan to go back to the office. I left a briefcase there and . . ." he winked, "I don't think I'll be returning there tonight."

Oleg grinned, stood and left the restaurant.

※

Alex was beginning to sweat. This was taking forever. It was eleven thirty. We'd better get out of here soon. He put the last paper through the scanner and gave the last small stack to Tanya.

She asked him, "Are we done with the desk and the briefcase?"

"Yes."

She locked the desk, closed the briefcase and carried the remaining papers to the file cabinets. Alex stuffed his equipment into his backpack and the large bag. They made a final check of the office to make sure they didn't leave any sign they were there, other than the missing figurine and some small glass fragments under the desk. Tanya turned out the light. They opened the blinds again and left the room. Alex sighed, "We'll be out of here before midnight."

She said, "I should check the secretary's desk, huh?"

"Jesus, why push it? Let's get out of here before the guard comes. I can't imagine she would have anything critical."

"I want the phone log."

※

Jenia drained her wine glass. It was almost midnight and Mikhail wanted to go, but he didn't want to say anything that would ruin his chance to get her to his flat. He pictured her hanging from the rings.

She held her glass in one hand and grabbed one of the empty wine bottles with the other. She acted like she was going to throw both, but didn't. She set them back on the table and held out her hand to Mikhail.

He took her arm to help her stand. She was unsteady and leaned hard against him. All down his side he felt her body against his. He saw the waiter and the busboy smiling knowingly. Eat your hearts out assholes. Go back to your fat wives; I'll bed this beauty. He felt a rush of power.

※

Tanya placed the key in the secretary's desk and turned it. They heard a small click followed by a much louder click at the door. Oh no, thought Alex, the guard is early. He was sick to his stomach. Tanya snapped off her flashlight and rushed to the side of the door. Alex froze, stood in the middle of the room wearing a backpack and holding the large bag.

The door swung open and light from the hallway rushed into the room followed by Ivan. He stopped, surprised when he saw Alex. He opened his mouth to speak and reached inside his jacket. Alex saw her arm and hand move so swiftly they were almost a blur. Ivan crumpled to the floor. He didn't fall forward, backward or sideways. He collapsed like a deflated hot air balloon.

Alex was frozen to the spot. He stared at Ivan. Then he recovered his voice. "That's Ivan, Mikhail's driver. I think he recognized me." He saw thousands of assassins searching every flat in Moscow looking to kill him.

He heard her stern order. "You have the materials. Get out of here. I'll take care of this mess and join you at your flat."

He wanted to stay, to help her. He wanted to be by her side. What if the guard, came? He'd help protect her. The thought of protecting her made him feel good. She looked at him sternly, motioned. "Go. Go."

✤

Mikhail studied Jenia slumped next to him in the back seat of his Mercedes. Her dress was high on her thighs exposing the top of her stockings. He glanced to the front seat and saw Oleg adjusting the rear-view mirror to look at her. You'll get your chance, he thought. This is my dream come true.

The top of her dress had become cockeyed when she leaned against him leaving the restaurant. One of her breasts was almost free. Mikhail found it difficult to avoid staring. He wanted to wrap his hand around it, to kiss it, to suck it. I'll bet it has a sweaty taste after such a long evening. The thought made him shake with excitement.

Jenia opened her eyes and for a minute didn't seem to know where she was. She straightened herself in the seat, pulled her dress back to her knees and tucked in her breast. Mikhail said, "Welcome back. I suggest we have a nightcap at my flat."

He saw her look at Oleg's face in the rear-view mirror. "I hope you have a large flat." She pointed her thumb toward Oleg, "Your watchdog takes a lot of room."

Mikhail wanted this woman, maybe more than the Presidency. His mouth and throat were dry with anticipation. His voice croaked when he spoke. "I'm a rich and powerful man. I need a bodyguard. After all, this is the land of opportunity. I don't want to be someone else's opportunity."

She leaned against him. He wanted to kiss her, to run his hands over her body, to hit her. She put her arms around his neck and nestled her head into his chest.

✤

Alex left Tanya without saying a word. He hurried down the hallway and took the exit steps to the first floor. When he opened the stairwell door, he saw the guard sitting at his desk. Alex looked at his watch. It was midnight. The guard got out of his chair, grabbed his flashlight and walked to the elevator. The guard pushed the button, the bell rang and he entered. Before the door had fully closed, Alex was out the side door into the alley.

I hope Tanya gets out of there soon. What will she do when Ivan wakes up? What if the guard is there? The two of them will capture her, probably worse. He wanted to go back, but he knew she had told him to go so he wouldn't lose the evidence, again.

19

Moscow – Sunday, May 10

Tanya had watched Alex scurry down the hall and through the door to the stairwell. She shut the door to the office again, crouched next to Ivan, and reached into his jacket for the gun he was carrying. He stirred. She quickly straddled him and snapped his neck.

Calmly, she walked back to the secretary's desk, collected the log and stuck it in her pocket. Meticulously, she scanned the room for anything out of place. As Jenia had directed, she placed the keys in the secretary's desk and shut the drawer.

She grabbed Ivan by the legs, pulled him out of the office and shut the door, which locked automatically. *Thank God this is his driver. I've seen his bodyguard. That elephant is too heavy to drag anywhere.* When she reached the elevator the indicator showed it was moving upward. Quickly, she dragged Ivan through the stairwell door. It closed as the bell rang and the elevator door opened. She cracked open the door and watched the guard saunter down the hall to Mikhail's office, unlock the door and enter.

She dragged Ivan back to the elevator and pushed the button. *I hope it's still on this floor.* The bell rang, the door opened, she dragged Ivan's body inside and pushed the button for the ground floor. The perspiration from under her arms was tickling down her sides.

On the ground floor she dragged the body across the foyer and through the same exit door Alex had used a few moments before. Once in the alley, she lifted Ivan's body, carrying much of it over her shoulder, and trudged toward the street at the end of the alley. She tried her best to look like a woman helping her drunken husband. She crossed the street, entered the next alley and trudged onward. She crossed one more street, entered a third alley and threw Ivan's body hard against a wall.

She stared at the body for a moment and then walked away. It'll be a long walk back to the flat, but the weather is beautiful and the breeze is refreshing. She was covered with sweat. "We did it," she said out loud to herself. "Alex and I did it." She pulled out a cellular phone and turned it on. Jenia, God help you.

※

Mikhail heard Buddy before he put the key into the door. With Jenia holding onto his arm for support, he swung the door open and entered the foyer. She stumbled in followed by Oleg.

Buddy, wagging his tail, ran to Mikhail, sniffed his shoes and then Jenia's. She gushed, "What a cute dog."

Mikhail stooped and lifted Buddy into his arms. "Hello Buddy. Did you miss me? Oh yes, yes, yes I'm home." He held the dog and she petted it. Buddy was squirming to get to her. She held her hand in front of Buddy's face. He sniffed it and then licked it.

She leaned over, almost stumbled, and kissed Buddy on the forehead. "You cute little thing. Mikhail, I didn't know you had such a beautiful, friendly puppy."

"It's a Shih Tzu. They were originally bred in China to be playmates for the royal family." He saw her eyebrows rise.

She grabbed his hand and led him from the foyer into the reception room. There she threw her coat across a chair and fell onto the couch letting her feet fly into the air.

Oleg checked out the flat. He came back shortly and said, "Everything's okay." She glared at Oleg and raised her middle finger. He glanced at Mikhail and then scowled back at her, but she had looked away and was rubbing Buddy, who had joined her on the couch.

"I like this watchdog much better," she said.

Mikhail accompanied Oleg to the door leading out of the flat. Oleg turned to glare at her again. His face was twisted and his eyes bulged. Mikhail tried to soothe him. "I don't think I'll have any trouble with her. Wait in the hallway and I'll get you when it's your turn." A grin formed on Oleg's face and Mikhail felt a touch of sympathy for Jenia.

He returned to the reception room. She was resting her head on the back of the couch and was slowly rubbing Buddy's stomach. Buddy had gotten onto her lap and in the process pulled her dress above her thighs.

Mikhail went to the liquor cabinet and mixed a vodka tonic. For her, he filled a glass with tonic only. He returned to the couch and held out the glass to her. "Will you join me for a vodka tonic to celebrate your first visit to my flat?"

She continued to stare at the ceiling and sighed, "I'd love a vodka tonic." He handed her the glass and sat next to her. She tried to clink his glass, but missed and slopped tonic onto the couch. Buddy immediately licked the spot. Mikhail steadied her wrist and clinked his glass against hers. She drained her glass and threw it into the foyer. It shattered and broken glass skidded across the floor. The door flew open and Oleg rushed in crunching the glass as he stomped across the floor.

Buddy leaped off the couch. "Get Buddy," Mikhail shouted to Oleg, "Don't let him eat any of the glass." Jenia was grinning like a fool. *She's too drunk. This won't be any fun if she's too drunk. I've got to get her some air to sober her.*

Oleg brought Buddy back to Mikhail and returned to remove the pieces of broken glass. She said, "I'm sorry I shouldn't have done that. I forgot about your dog."

"That's okay. Oleg will clean it up. I'll close the doors to the foyer to keep Buddy out. Oleg can finish cleaning it tomorrow."

Oleg came back from the kitchen where he had discarded the largest pieces of broken glass. He nodded to Mikhail, scowled again at her and left the flat. Mikhail handed Buddy to her and closed the sliding doors that led to the foyer. He returned, sat on the couch and put his arm around her. She looked down at her dress as though for the first time noticing it had lifted so high above her knees. She didn't push it back down. He leaned toward her and kissed her on the lips. Her mouth opened and he pushed his tongue inside. He ran his tongue between her teeth and lips and then deeper into her mouth. He sucked her upper lip.

She pulled away, because Buddy was between them. "Maybe we should put Buddy in another room."

Mikhail's head was spinning. He loved the taste of her lipstick, her mouth. Her lips were so soft. He wanted this woman more than he had wanted anything in his life. "I have a better idea. Why don't we leave the dog here and lock ourselves into another room. I have a nice balcony off my bedroom if you care for some fresh air, a beautiful view of Moscow at night."

She shrugged, "Why not?"

She struggled, but with his help she managed to stand. She walked to the chair and grabbed her coat. Was she leaving? Surely she didn't think she was going to get out of here now. No one teases Mikhail Kolodkin and walks away, especially this one. Tonight I'll get my satisfaction for all your smart remarks and teases.

"Where are you going?"

"To the bedroom."

"It's not cold in there. You can leave your coat here if you wish."

"I dearly love your dog, but I don't want him to ruin my coat."

He wondered why she had even brought the coat. It wasn't cold and she never put it on. "Yes, I guess you're right. He'd probably tear it up. Why don't you let me hang it in a closet for you?" Rather than answer, she walked into the bedroom and threw her coat onto the bed. Buddy was at her feet and followed her when she walked to the rings attached to the triangular apparatus. Slowly, she ran her hand over each ring. She walked across the room toward the balcony door. When she reached his dresser she stopped and examined a leather band and wood crucifix. She cocked her head at Mikhail and furrowed her brow with an unspoken question. He shrugged. "It's a souvenir, Catholic I think."

She examined the crucifix for a few moments and placed it back on the dresser. She pulled open the doors to the balcony and stepped out into the night air. He put Buddy back out of the room, shut the bedroom door, and joined her.

He put his arm around her and they stood on the balcony looking at the lights of Moscow. Mikhail's flat was high on the Lenin hills so they had a panorama of the entire city with all its spires. A strong wind blew the red ribbon from her hair.

He turned her so she was facing him. He wanted her lips again. He puckered his mouth and moved his head forward to kiss her. She turned away. Anger surged through him. Adrenalin charged into his brain and muscles. He was losing control, but so what. He jerked her head back so she was looking at him. She stared past him. He hated her attitude, the teases, the smart remarks, spilling her drink on his couch, breaking her glass in his foyer. He slapped her, slapped her hard. It felt good. He grabbed her hair and pulled back her head. Her face was now open for him. He pushed his face into hers and attacked her mouth with his. His tongue, hard, pushed at her lips trying to force them open. She held them tight.

He dragged her back into the bedroom and threw her on the bed. Her dress slipped down exposing one of her breasts. He slapped her face again. He saw her skin turning darker. She raised her hands to protect her face. He slapped her thighs, hard cracks mixed with her yelps. Her skin felt so smooth, warm. He wanted to enter her, to force her open, to tear her apart. I've got her. She's mine. "You bitch. Did you think I gave a damn about you? I'm going to have my fun. When I'm done Oleg will have his."

His heart raced. His groin hurt with excitement. "Did you hear me bitch? Oleg will have you next. He'll jam that finger of yours right up your own ass."

He grabbed her hair and twisted her head to the side. He studied the shape of her ass. He wanted to kiss her again. He saw the bare breast, the nipple, and leaned over to put it into his mouth. His tongue was ready to massage it. He would bite it, make it hurt. He saw her eyes flash. She didn't look drunk anymore. Her mouth and jaws were pulled tight.

Suddenly, he couldn't breathe. He tried to suck in air, but he felt like he had a rock caught in his throat. God it hurt worse than any pain he had ever felt. Where was she? She was no longer under him, only the bed. He tried to breathe, but it hurt too much. I'm getting dizzy. God, my whole body hurts, I can't move.

He was face down on the bed and watched her reach into her coat and pull out a needle. He couldn't move to stop her. He felt a sharp pain in his thigh. No more pain. He heard Buddy barking far away in another land in another time. I'm so tired, so ti . . . ."

Jenia stood over Mikhail's body. "Sleep you bastard."

She reached into her coat and pulled out a pair of tights and a shirt. She tore off the dress and draped it over him. She stood for a moment wearing only her panties and nylon stockings. She stared at her shaking hands. Quickly, she put on the tights and the shirt. Again she reached into the coat and pulled out a pistol and a silencer. She put the two pieces together, cocked the gun and put it against Mikhail's head. "I wish I could kill you," she growled and shook her head.

She threw her coat on the bed next to him and opened the bedroom door, slowly. Buddy came running into the room and stopped barking.

He was running in circles around her feet trying to get her to pick him up. She glanced into the reception room. It was empty. She shut the door, leaving Buddy in the bedroom with his master. He barked and scratched at the door. She opened one of the sliding doors to the foyer. Empty. She entered the foyer and slid the door closed behind her. In the confined space, she took a position behind the door. She knocked hard on the door leading out of the flat.

The door burst open and Oleg came charging into the foyer headed for the reception room. He stopped when he saw the closed doors. He spun around grinding broken glass into the varnished floor. He looked at her face, then the gun. His face showed surprise, then fear.

"Tell me Oleg. Did it feel good to shoot Pavel, to beat Ivona? Are you proud you left Lenya with no father? You bastard."

She took a deep breath and let it out slowly. "My orders do not let me kill your boss. For you, I have special permission." With those words, the gun jerked in her hand. Poof, a small hole formed between Oleg's eyes. Slowly, the blood oozed from the hole and the period turned into a comma. Blood ran into his staring eyes, down both sides of his nose and along the corners of his mouth.

Surprisingly, he didn't fall. He stood, balanced, with his legs apart and knees locked like some perverse statue. Slowly, the statue stiffly fell backward against the foyer doors and bounced to the floor. Oleg's head was twisted to one side. A bruise had formed a circle around the hole between his eyes.

She growled, "A gift to Ivona from Jenia." She stepped over the body, opened the doors to the reception room, walked to a telephone and dialed a number. "Hi. Can you come?" She listened for a few moments. "Really. Well, I recently took out the other one here. We have all night if we need it. I have plenty of juice for our friend. See you soon. Oh, how did he do?" She listened again. "That's great. I'm so proud of him. Hurry over here. I want to hear all about it." She returned to the bedroom. Buddy turned his body sideways to make it easier for her to lift him.

20

Moscow – Monday, May 11

Alex put the pillow over his face to block out the light coming through the bedroom window in the dacha. The early morning cool breeze was turning warm. He rolled over and looked at his watch on the dresser. It was almost noon. He had been sleeping for six hours. What a night it had been. Thank God Tanya had called him or he would have died from concern. She didn't arrive at the flat until almost four in the morning. She was carrying a big box full of papers, originals she had gotten from Mikhail's flat. Alex never asked her how she got them, and she never volunteered to tell him. Both were too tired.

They had left the flat as soon as Tanya arrived. She told him it was best to leave Moscow immediately, because the roads would be blocked by eight or nine o'clock. He didn't ask why. The break-in was exciting, but it left him feeling dirty, cheap. He didn't want to know if she had done something else to make him feel guilty.

Tanya and he had taken a big step. Before yesterday they had been reading and analyzing documents to make guesses about a conspiracy, except for a few dead bodies scattered over two countries. Yesterday they had broken the law. If they were found out, he would spend the rest of his few remaining days in a Russian prison in Siberia.

He was still tired, but he forced himself to get out of bed. It was time to get up, besides he had to pee so bad it hurt. He'd make some tea for Tanya. She had to be exhausted. He fought off the temptation to peek into her bedroom.

Cold water in the face does wonders for getting out the cobwebs, he decided. He rubbed the towel over his face and looked into the mirror. I can't believe it. I've looked better when I had a hangover.

At the head of the stairwell he smelled coffee. After he worked his way down the narrow steps to the first floor, he was surprised to see Carl holding a cup of coffee and going over some documents with Tanya, who was drinking tea. A laptop computer connected to a printer was spitting out page after page. Alex made his way to the kitchen and poured a cup of coffee. He stared out the open kitchen window and studied the forest. A cool breeze wrapped around him. He finished his coffee and returned to the reception room.

Carl and Tanya were still engrossed in their project. The printer, however, had stopped. The television was on, showing a program about the ballet in St. Petersburg. Alex stifled a yawn. "Tanya, do you ever sleep?"

She turned, smiled and waved to him. "Good morning. I'll grab a nap later." She returned to Carl. "I've found Jonah's name in the logs. It's a Zurich telephone number and address. His home, or office, is on a street named Zurichbergstrasse. His name appears often in the papers we got from Mikhail's flat."

Alex thought, we? The news came on the screen. He saw Jenia's face and shouted, "There's Jenia." Tanya increased the volume; they listened to the commentary.

"One million US Dollars is offered for information leading to the capture of Eugenia Stanoslavovna Tarelkina, wanted for the murder of Oleg Pavlovich Irugov and the attempted murder of Mikhail Nikolaivich Kolodkin."

Alex said, "Jesus Tanya. What happened last night?"

She glanced at him but didn't respond. He continued, "We, huh?" She raised her hand for quiet.

The news continued. "In a related matter. This morning the Moscow Militia discovered the body of Ivan Vladimirovich Osin, the driver for Mr. Kolodkin. His body, with a broken neck, was found a few short blocks from the office of Mr. Kolodkin. The Militia is investigating whether these terrible crimes against associates of one of Moscow's most respected businessmen, a Duma member, are related in any way."

Alex couldn't breathe, felt chilled, felt his stomach churn. He wanted to run away and hide in a corner of the world; no one would find him.

He whispered, "How did this turn into multiple killings?" He tried to picture how Tanya would break a neck, but he had no idea.

With an official tone, Carl said, "These things happen. Let's focus on saving Russia. We have a lot of work to do."

Alex gazed at Jenia's picture on the screen. Now he understood her mood on Thursday. This was not an accident. I'll never see her again, he convinced himself. Dazed, Alex sat down on one of the wooden chairs. He half listened to them talking.

Tanya said, "Some of Mikhail's papers discussed Superpower, but not many details, nothing more than I had gotten from Jenia in the park." She stopped for a moment, thinking, then continued, "One thing may be valuable for us."

Carl asked, "Oh?"

"Apparently each member of the group makes a report to Jonah every Friday early in the afternoon. There's a set time for each."

"It makes sense. Our friend Jonah would need weekly information to anticipate cash flow for investments. I assume he personally runs the investment company."

She continued, "As far as I can tell, yes."

"We need to get you and Alex to Switzerland immediately. You can leave today and go through Kiev. I'll make arrangements."

Alex saw Carl look in his direction. Through the fog surrounding his mind the word Switzerland came bursting through. Slowly he mouthed, "Switzerland?"

Tanya came over to Alex. She pulled a chair next to him, took a seat, and held his hand. "Jonah is our next step. He has the smoking gun." It was a poor metaphor. It made him jump. She continued, "Maybe we can find the name of Jonah's boss."

He was too stressed to answer. He knew he would go. He no longer controlled anything. He would only stumble from place to place as he was instructed. He would do this until they would decide where to move him next. Confused, he turned to her and said, "If I bring my game, will you teach me some more chess?"

Her face showed shock and then concern. She pulled his hand to her lips and kissed the back of it. "I won't let anything happen to you. Everything will be okay." She dropped his hand back in his lap and returned to the documents and her conversation with Carl.

Alex watched the television. A cartoon was playing. It showed a big chicken holding a small dog by its hind legs and smashing its head on the ground. He heard Carl say, "I have a friend in Zurich." For some reason

Alex wasn't surprised. He would no longer be surprised if he discovered Carl was the head of the CIA spying in Russia.

Tanya said, "Can he help us?"

"I'm not sure. He retired from the international department of a German bank a number of years ago. Judging from what I read about Jonah, their paths may have crossed."

"Do you think your friend can arrange some German passports? It'll be impossible to move around freely with Russian passports."

Alex was stunned by this conversation. Why would she assume Carl's friend, a former banker, would be able to supply false passports? *Am I the only person in the world who isn't criminally connected? Come to think of it, I guess I am a criminal, a thief.* He felt better, part of the group, a professional.

Ivan saw me. He'll turn me in. I'll be arrested before I reach the city limits of Moscow. I'm doomed. Prison here I come. He recalled the newscast, ". . . the Moscow Militia found the body of Ivan Vladimirovich Osin, the driver for Mr. Kolodkin. His body, with a broken neck, was discovered a few short blocks from the office of Mr. Kolodkin." He also recalled Tanya's comment, "I won't let anything happen to you."

Alex leaned forward and the coffee from his stomach exploded from his mouth. It splashed over his bare feet and onto the floor. His stomach kept trying to throw out more. He continued to wretch uncontrollably. *She killed Ivan because of me. If I hadn't stood there like a fool, if I'd hidden myself, he'd be alive today. I might as well have snapped his neck with my own hands.* He couldn't stop the spasms in his stomach.

Tanya ran to him with some wet cloths and towels. She knelt down in front of him and wiped the vomit off his feet. He stared, immobilized. He thought he saw some tears fall from her face.

"My poor Sasha. I'm so sorry. What have I done to you?"

She finished cleaning his feet and the floor around them and stood next to him. He wiped his mouth with a wet cloth and she took it and the rest of the materials to the kitchen. She returned with a glass of water and a few biscuits. "Eat these. They'll help your stomach."

He took the biscuits from her and munched them. He stared without seeing; chewed without tasting. She leaned over and kissed him on the forehead. "You'll feel better in a few minutes. Then we can talk, okay?"

"What happened to huh?" She didn't understand his question. She stared at him for a moment and then went back to Carl.

Carl said, "We'll have to drive you out of Russia to be safe. Every place will have security checks looking for anyone who might have known Jenia." They both looked at Alex.

Suddenly Alex thought of Jenia's safety. "God, what will they do if they catch her?"

Tanya put her arm around his shoulders. "Jenia was in another country before you woke today."

"What country?"

"Israel."

He remembered Jenia reading Hebrew in Ivona's flat. "She's a Jew?" No one answered. Tanya was going over a plan with Carl.

Kiev – Tuesday, May 12

It had been an uneventful trip. Tanya drove the Volvo 850 and Alex drove his Lada. They came south to Kiev to a farmhouse. Soon after they arrived, Tanya went into Kiev with the farmer and returned with two German passports. Alex had a new name, Dieter Hollenbeck. He was married to Olga Hollenbeck, Tanya's new passport.

"Hey Tanya, we're married. How nice."

She grinned at him. "Don't get your hopes up. Besides, my name is not Tanya, it's Olga. I guess I'd better start growing hair under my arms." She laughed at her own joke. Alex didn't get it.

He became concerned. "I don't speak German. At least not enough to pass myself off as a German."

"Good. Then keep quiet and let me do the talking, huh? I speak it fluently."

Alex mumbled, "Why am I not surprised?"

"What?"

"Nothing. I was simply practicing some German phrases."

Alex left the Lada at the farmhouse in Kiev and in the morning they drove the Volvo twenty-six hours to a farmhouse near Munich.

Munich – Wednesday, May 13

Using the map Tanya got in Kiev, they had avoided all checkpoints and never had to show their passports. In Warsaw, Alex had wanted to visit Ivona, but Tanya said they didn't have time and it was dangerous. Ivona would be under surveillance because she was a known friend of Jenia. Alex suggested they call, but Tanya forbade it. They arrived at the Munich farmhouse mid morning on Wednesday. They showered and slept.

At three, Gustav Reinhardt arrived. He was tall, early sixties, with a full head of snow-white hair and smooth skin with no age spots. His eyes were ice blue. He spoke perfect Russian in a soft voice accenting the words so well they sounded like music. He was dressed in a gray suit. His smooth white shirt had cuffs held together by two diamond links. In the center of his blue and red striped tie was a diamond tie clasp of at least two carats. He had a strong presence, but a jovial nature.

Alex shook his hand, firm grip, once up and once down. Yes, he's a true German, he thought, a gentleman of the first order. Later he joked with Tanya, "When I grow up I want to be just like Gustav." They both laughed so hard their stomachs hurt.

Gustav checked out their German and was impressed by Tanya's command of the language. He told Alex his German was good enough for most things, but to stay out of long conversations. "Use English as often as possible," he told him in perfect English.

To impress him, Alex tried some English. "My English is not for shit either."

Gustav, laughing, responded, "Bad English is not a problem. People will assume you are an American."

Tanya and Alex left their Volvo at the farmhouse. Someone would drive it back to Carl in Russia. Alex was amazed by the extensive, efficient organization surrounding these people. This isn't a bunch of amateurs like Tanya and me. How did I get into this mess? He didn't know whom to blame, but Jenia and Tanya were prime candidates.

They started late, about five thirty. It was a three hour thirty minute trip to Zurich. Alex sat in the back seat and Tanya in the front to discuss Jonah with Gustav. Alex tried counting trees to pass the time, but they were going by so fast he got dizzy. Soon, he fell asleep.

He awoke when they were entering Zurich at nine in the evening. He heard Gustav tell Tanya the flat would not be ready for another two days. His associate had arranged for rooms at the Hoffmanhaus Hotel near Zurichbergstrasse. "You can walk to Jonah's house from there if you like," he said.

He dropped them at the hotel and agreed to meet with them the next afternoon at his home in Griefensee, a forty-five minute train ride from the central rail station. The hotel was small, quaint with a counter two meters long. It served for check-in, checkout and information. Two young women were working behind the counter. In her perfect German Tanya said, "Reservations for Hollenbeck."

"Yes, Herr and Frau Hollenbeck. Your room is ready. We hope you have a pleasant stay."

Alex beamed when he heard they would share a room. He asked, "May I inquire, what kind of bed? Is it king size, queen size?"

Tanya glared as though she was going to slap him. Alex wondered if he had used bad German. He noticed the ladies wince when they saw the look she gave this poor henpecked man.

"I'm sorry Herr Hollenbeck. We have two single beds in the room. Maybe we can find you another room tomorrow. All other rooms are taken now."

Tanya growled, "This room will be fine. We do not need another one, thank you."

The elevator was not big enough for both of them and their baggage. She put him in the elevator with the bags and pushed the button for the third floor. She was waiting for him when the elevator arrived. Her fists were clenched. He considered pushing the down button, but decided to face the music.

When he stepped from the elevator, she snarled in Russian, "We're not here to play games. We have a job to do. Your German is not good."

He was embarrassed, angry. "Maybe I should try another hotel so we have separate rooms." She seemed not to hear and opened the door. The room was a nice size, about six meters by five meters. It contained a sofa, a chair, and two single beds separated by an inexpensive wooden nightstand. A glass coffee table sat in front of the sofa with another glass table at one end.

She unpacked her suitcase without looking at him. He did the same. This is going to be a long few days. I can't wait to get to the flat and separate rooms. I wonder why she got so upset? Surely, my little question wouldn't have caused this much of a problem.

In her professional voice she asked, "Do you mind if I use the bathroom first?"

He responded in the same manner. "Be my guest."

He sat on the sofa and read the hotel's guest book. We get a free breakfast every morning if we eat between seven and ten. The breakfast room is on the second floor. Oh, what's this? In the same room they have fruits, coffee and tea available all day until ten in the evening. He looked at his watch. It was nine forty five.

He was sitting on the sofa when she finally opened the bathroom door. He saw steam coming out into the room. She followed wearing a powder-blue robe over a nightgown that appeared to be the same color only faded. She was drying her hair with a towel. "I wonder if they have a hairdryer in this hotel?"

He grinned his most perfect smile and pointed to the crackers, peeled oranges, apples, tea and milk on the coffee table. "Peace offering," he said hopefully. He patted the sofa and she sat next to him.

"They were open until ten; so I ran downstairs and grabbed us something to finish off the day."

"I'm sorry. I shouldn't have gotten angry."

"It wasn't my German was it?"

"No."

"I won't be any trouble. I know you're married and have a wonderful son." He gave her his best smile.

She grinned back, but looked uncomfortable.

She studied the table and then moved her hand forward and selected a slice of the orange. She turned to face him and slid it slowly into her mouth. She stared directly into his eyes. Now, he was uncomfortable, couldn't look at her. She turned back to the table and selected an apple. Dreamily, again she gazed into his eyes. She put the apple to her mouth and licked the skin before taking a small bite. Her eyes bore right through him. She said, "It's delicious. Thank you."

His voiced cracked when he said, "My turn in the bath." He jumped from the sofa and went to the dresser by his bed. He grabbed his bath kit and robe and glanced into a mirror on the wall. He saw her take another small bite of the apple. She was still watching him. He shut the bathroom door and stared at his flushed face in the mirror. "She's not worried about me."

21

Zurich – Thursday, May 14

Alex woke when he heard a closet door close. Tanya was putting on a jacket. "Where are you going?"

"Thought I'd take a stroll along Zurichbergstrasse."

"Why didn't you wake me I'd go with you," he said annoyed she left him out of her plans.

"Really? Are you sure you want to go? It's a big hill."

He looked toward the window. It wasn't dawn yet, but it wasn't black night either. "I can be ready in ten minutes. Can you wait?"

"Okay ten minutes," she said and walked to the sofa and sat down. He didn't move. He lay under the covers on the bed and made no move to get up. "You'll never make it in ten minutes if you don't get out of bed, huh?"

"Turn your head."

"What?"

"Turn your head. I sleep in the nude."

She shook her head, stood and walked to the door. She turned back to him, grinned, and said softly, "I'll go downstairs to have a cup of tea. I'll meet you in reception in ten minutes."

✤

"Wow, that's some house," Alex wheezed.

They had finally stopped after a long climb up Zurichbergstrasse, and were standing on a corner looking at Jonah's mansion across the street. Alex was bent over at the waist and had his hands on his knees trying to catch his breath. Tanya made a few scribbles in her notebook, motioned for him to follow and continued her march to the top of the hill almost a kilometer farther.

"Where are you going? We've seen it. Let's go back down the hill and have a donut. I saw a coffee shop at the bottom."

"Come on, huh? I want to see where this street leads. This may be our escape route. If we stand here staring at his house he may come out and notice us, huh?"

If we passed him on the street I wouldn't know him. Do you know what he looks like?"

"I'm sure he's old. Come on. Or do you want me to carry you."

"Would you please?" He reluctantly trudged after her.

※

Alex was happy to sit down on the comfortable new seats. The train was spotless. He and Tanya had been riding for almost forty minutes on their way to Griefensee. For much of the trip, the train ran along the side of a large lake. The sun was high and he saw its reflection on the lake. The sky was a soft powder blue with few clouds.

I can't believe she wouldn't stop at the donut shop. Instead we dash back to the hotel and rush out to catch this train. Why can't she take it easy? Jonah's house isn't going anywhere. I hope I never have to climb that hill again. I'm out of shape.

He said over his shoulder, "Beautiful country isn't it."

She leaned over him to look out the window. "Yes it is. I've always loved Switzerland. It's like a fairytale."

He felt provincial, left out. "You've been here before?"

"I came here for an international chess tournament, a convention really."

"In Zurich?"

"Well, it was in Bern, but I came through Zurich."

Suddenly he felt adventurous. "Let's go there."

"Where?"

"Bern or some other Swiss city. I want an excuse to ride Swiss trains. Let's go somewhere you haven't been. We'll discover it together."

She interrupted, "Oops. This is our stop. Let's go, huh?"

He dragged himself out of the seat. Too bad this wasn't farther away. I suppose we'll have to walk ten kilometers to Gustav's home.

It was a small station, a commuter stop really. She led him down the steps and pointed along one of the streets. "His lives one kilometer from here. We take this street a stretch, make one turn and we're almost there."

Thank God it's not farther, he thought, and it's not on a long hill. He followed after her along the sidewalk like a baby duck. She was walking at least ten meters ahead. It was unusually quiet, almost too quiet like a dream. Everything was spotless. "I'll bet we could eat off of this street it's so clean," he half shouted so she would hear.

"What did you say? I didn't hear you."

"Stop," he bellowed.

She turned and watched him confused. He ambled to her and took her hand. "From now on, Mrs. Hollenbeck, we will walk hand-in-hand. I'll be damned if I'm going to shout in order to have a conversation with you."

"I'm sorry. I guess I'm excited to see Gustav's house and find out what he knows about Jonah."

Soon they were standing on a corner, holding hands, and looking at Gustav's home. The light breeze carried the scent of flowers and kept them comfortable even though the sun was at the top of the sky. They heard children shouting and playing in a schoolyard a few blocks away. He liked the feel of her warm hand in his. He turned to her and she faced him. She was beautiful with her blond hair blowing in the wind.

She said, "Well, we made it. There it is." She continued to look at him, staring deep into his eyes. He blushed and hoped she didn't read his mind.

He moved his gaze from her to the house across the street. It was a quaint brown brick home surrounded with an aging wood fence one meter high. The fence protected a lush, green lawn and colorful flowers. A small wooden bridge over a pond near the middle of the yard gave it a serene atmosphere.

He looked along the street and saw the lake was only a few hundred meters farther. He had a sudden urge to pull Tanya to the lake and jump in with her. Too late, she pulled him through the gate to the front door.

As expected, Gustav was a perfect host. He prepared a meal of baked chicken, mashed potatoes, carrots and corn. Tanya and Gustav washed the meal down with cold white wine. Alex declined and drank only water.

Alex was impressed when he learned Gustav had cooked everything himself. Gustav had never been married and said he never regretted it. Alex remembered Konstantin's warning against marriage. He decided, for real this time, when I grow up I want to be like Gustav.

After a desert of mixed berries, they carried their cups of tea to the reception room and sat in large comfortable chairs. The house smelled of fresh pine. "If you don't mind my asking," Alex said, "how do you know Carl Weber?"

"He was working on a consulting project for PHD in the eighties. I was in charge of international banking for Deutchlander Bundesbank at the time."

"So you kept in touch with him?"

"I left the bank about five years ago and became an independent consultant. Carl offered me a position, but I decided I would do better on my own. We correspond occasionally."

Alex waved his hand through the air, "You were right."

Gustav laughed. "Thank you. I was a consultant to the World Bank, the IMF and some corporations. Recently, I've been providing advice to the European Bank for Reconstruction and Development relating to its investments into Poland, Hungary and the Czech Republic. I stay away from Russia.

Alex asked, "How did you learn to speak Russian so well? It puts mine to shame and I'm Russian."

"I was born and raised in East Germany."

They sat through an uncomfortable silence until Tanya broke it. "What can you tell us about Jonah?"

"I knew him a number of years ago when he worked in Citibank. We shared some deals involving third-world government securities. Believe me that game will make you old before your time. He knew his stuff."

She continued with her questions. "Does he have a wife, children?"

"When I knew him he was married, happily as I recall. He suggested I should get married. They had a daughter. Odd though. He's an orthodox Jew, but his wife and his daughter were devout Catholics.

"Sometime in the early eighties both his wife and daughter, she would have been a teenager then, were killed in an automobile accident. He left Citibank shortly after they were buried. Went back to Israel as far as I can determine."

Alex asked, "Do you know when he came to Zurich?"

"He bought the house on Zurichbergstrasse in 1990."

Tanya's eyes widened. "Has he had work done on the house, huh?"

Gustav beamed at her. "That's a smart question. You're good at this aren't you?" The tone of his voice and the look he gave Tanya made Alex feel invisible.

She replied, "I'm a research analyst at PHD. We ask many questions and find a lot of answers. You know the type."

Gustav laughed. "Well, I'm actually ahead of you. You won't have to do a lot of research here." He stood and motioned for them to follow him back to the dining room. They helped him clear the dishes from the table. They returned to the dining room and Gustav opened a wide drawer normally used for tablecloths and serviettes. He pulled some large architect's drawings from the drawer and spread them on the table.

Tanya studied them with interest. "Jonah's house, huh?"

Gustav nodded, "He had some renovation on the house when he first arrived. These are the drawings used by the general contractor."

Alex said, "That's great. Where did you get them?"

"When Carl called and asked for help I did some checking. One of my good friends did the work and had the drawings. He gave me these copies. You can keep them."

She looked up from her study of the drawings and asked, "Any chance your friend will mention this to Jonah?"

Gustav replied, "Not a chance. He and Jonah had a falling out over the cost and some of the workmanship. They're not the best of friends."

She asked, "Did he install a security system? There's no indication on the drawing?"

"I asked him the same question. He said an Israeli company installed a security system."

She shook her head, irritated that she would not have schematics of the system.

"My friend doesn't think it works. He said it works if you test it with the test button, but his people should have set it off many times when they returned to do repair work. It never went off."

She cocked her head. "Interesting. Well, I guess we can test it too." She was making large red dots and circles on the page. "Alex. We need to get some battery operated electronic recording units placed outside the house where I've indicated with dots. I'll place the microphones inside. They'll send a radio signal to the recording units. We should be able to record all their conversations. Get digital and analogue devices. We'll use duplicates in case one of them doesn't work."

Alex made a note. "What about the circles?"

They show where we'll put miniature cameras connected via radio to battery operated video recording units hidden outside the house."

She pointed to a built-in safe in the corner of the office. She put a big circle around it. Alex pointed to a spot on the drawing. "Look here. There's another safe in the north wall about two meters above the floor."

She circled the spot. "I'll bet that's where we'll find the gold, huh? He probably has a picture or something in front of it."

It was late afternoon when they finished studying the drawings. Gustav said, "We should take a walk; let's stroll to the lake."

It was cooler now, but still comfortable. They stood on the edge of the lake under a large oak tree and stared at the well-kept green hills and homes on the other shore. They saw two rowboats with a fisherman at each end. Alex took Tanya's hand in his. She leaned against him and rested her head on his shoulder. He felt important, powerful, contented.

On the way back to Gustav's home, she asked, "Any ideas how we might get in Jonah's house?"

"I can get you in for a day, maybe only one-half day."

Alex was impressed with Gustav's advance planning. He was aware of everything they would need. He decided to check with him later as to the best places to buy the electronic equipment.

Tanya asked, "How?"

"Jonah has a service come in every few weeks. The same service cleans the yard and the inside of the house. I can get you on the crew. You'll have to do the rest."

She asked, "Won't the regular crew be suspicious, say something?"

"You'll have to work one or two other jobs before Jonah's. That will make you a regular and you'll have learned what they do."

Alex chimed in, "You have another friend I take it."

"Same guy. Jonah doesn't know my friend owns Zurich Landscape Service in addition to the construction company. My friend enjoys that he's still collecting money from Jonah, since he had to take Jonah to court to get the renovation fee."

Tanya asked, "When will they go to Jonah's home?"

"Next Thursday. You won't have much time to enjoy Switzerland."

Later, back at the house, Tanya was leaning over the table studying the drawings. She dropped her pencil and straightened. "So, we'll complete our plan, work a few jobs with the company, and go into Jonah's house. A tight schedule all things considered."

Gustav answered. "Tomorrow morning I'll collect you at the hotel. You should check out, because your flat will be available by evening."

They nodded.

He continued, "We'll go to Zurich Landscape Service, it's located on Mythenquai, near the lake. I've made arrangements to get you assigned to the crew that normally provides service to Jonah." He smiled deliberately, "There'll be no papers to sign. You'll go to jobs with the crew Saturday and Monday. You should be well prepared by Thursday."

Alex said. "When am I going to find time to buy all this electronic equipment? I don't even know where to start."

Tanya said. "I'm sure Gustav will be able to help you."

Gustav put his hand on Alex's shoulder. "Tomorrow afternoon I'll take you to meet Herr Schmidt. He has a small electronic supply shop on Rohrstrasse, near the airport. He specializes in security systems. He'll have everything you need."

Alex resigned himself to missing his chance to travel in Switzerland.

✤

On the train back to Zurich Tanya was lost in thought, even sad. Alex asked, "Are you okay? Is something wrong?"

"I don't like to be away from Kolya."

"Why don't you bring him here?"

"And, if we get caught, what would happen to him? This is not going to be easy."

Alex had forgotten they might get caught. They might end up in a Swiss jail, or worse. He said, "I feel sick. Maybe it's because I'm riding backward on this train. In the future I'm going to sit riding forward."

She laughed.

22

Zurich – Friday, May 15

It was late on Friday before Alex and Tanya entered their flat on Gartenstrasse. It was located on the other side of the Limmat River, but only a fifteen-minute walk from the hotel and Zurichbergstrasse.

The flat had a large reception room, two bedrooms a kitchen and a bathroom that separated the bedrooms with a door facing each. The kitchen was small, but it contained new equipment. Alex was happy to have his own bedroom. He slept in the nude without embarrassment.

Saturday, May 16

Tanya woke him at nine in the morning. She had been out for a walk and had showered. She cracked the door slightly and shouted, "Come on. Time to get up, huh?"

"I'm coming. I'm coming," he growled back at her. He was not looking forward to a day of manual labor with a bunch of strangers. *Something'll be too heavy to lift and they'll think I'm weak. God, I hope I don't do something stupid, like kill some flowers.*

He complained the entire way on the walk to the landscape company. She kept assuring him, "It'll be okay. You'll enjoy it."

He felt like a small boy on his first day of school. She was mothering him, but he didn't mind.

His nervousness disappeared quickly. The other five men were all welcoming and helpful. When he was introduced, he held out his hand and said in his best German, "My German is not so good. I come from the Ukraine. I want to go to America some day." Repeatedly, they assured him that he spoke German well. Their insistence proved Gustav had been right. His little lie about coming from the Ukraine made him feel like a spy in a novel. So, he pretended to be a foreign agent, which was good because it helped him keep his conversations to a minimum.

Tanya worked for the domestic division. On this first job, her group was going to the same site as the group with Alex. The site was not far from Zurichbergstrasse and Jonah's mansion.

Alex worked hard and loved it. He liked being outside in the fresh air. He helped the men cut the lawn, trim the hedges, weed the flowerbeds and clean the yard. During a break, Tanya complained of the stuffy house. He gloated, "It's so refreshing out in the yard. It's like when you move from a smoke filled room into the outside air." She said she envied him and returned to her work.

It was only an afternoon job, which suited Alex. During the day he saw Tanya washing windows. He stared at her. She was so different in her uniform with a rag wrapped around her head. He felt a warm glow. Maybe it was the uniform, maybe the rag, maybe because she was so different, so domestic. He wanted to hold her in his arms.

That night, she let him hold her hand without protest, and they walked through the old town looking for an Italian restaurant. She had suggested Italian.

The air was cool and the street was overcrowded. No matter which way they walked, people having fun and drinking beer bumped into them. They found a small place and sat in the middle of a large room surrounded by cigarette smoke and loud talk. But they both liked the food. When they returned to the flat she immediately went to her room. He sat in the reception room hoping she would reappear. For some reason he felt lonely, empty.

She reappeared to get a glass of water from the kitchen. She was in her robe and nightgown. His heart jumped. "Why don't you have a seat here and drink your water."

She walked back through the room and said, "It's been a long day and I have to rise early tomorrow. I want to take a walk before breakfast.

"I'm planning to get up early myself. You want me to go with you?"

"If you're up, I'd love it." She disappeared into her room.

He didn't get much sleep. He kept waking and checking his watch. He didn't want to miss the walk. I hope I can keep up. I wonder where she'll go?

Sunday, May 17

It was so embarrassing. What crazy timing. Fate was working against him. He opened his door at the same time she was opening hers. She was still wearing that pretty blue robe and nightgown. For a few seconds, until he saw her staring, he didn't realize he wasn't wearing a pretty blue anything.

"Oops. I'm sorry," was all he managed to mutter before he closed the door. It didn't help she never mentioned it when they took their walk. He wanted to apologize, but he didn't know how, or why.

After a full day of planning, they had a quiet dinner not far from the flat and returned early. He was surprised he had no craving for vodka. When she asked, he told her he had stopped drinking since his ordeal. She was pleased.

They stayed up later than usual, sitting on the sofa talking about childhood, school years, and hopes for a better life. She didn't mention her family and he didn't mention Jenia. In fact, he hadn't thought about Jenia for a few days. He fell asleep on Tanya's shoulder and dreamed she kissed him on the head.

Monday, May 18

"You're not going to the same place?"

They had received their job assignments and were taking a short walk among some trees and flowers along the lake until it was time to leave. About fifty geese and ducks were vying for food along the edge of the lake, and their honking and quacking drowned out the birds in the trees. Alex didn't enjoy the pretty morning, didn't hear the birds trying to get his attention. He never considered they wouldn't be working together. He felt empty when he heard.

"No. I'm going to the Gold Coast today. We're cleaning two homes there. I'll be finished later than you. So I'll see you back at the flat."

"Damn. I don't like this. I'm in a strange land doing physical labor with a bunch of foreigners."

"Don't be nervous. Besides, you're the foreigner, not them. You'll enjoy it. It's a nice day."

He continued to look depressed, nervous. She added, "Everything will be ok. Trust me."

He stopped walking, turned to her and rolled his eyes. "Trust you?" She laughed, a full laugh like a young girl. He felt better. He said, "You know what bothers me?"

Still grinning she responded, "No. What?"

"I've gotten used to being with you, looking at you. On the last job I couldn't stop watching you at the windows. I'm going to miss you today."

He saw it in her eyes. He had hit a nerve, a tender nerve. She stepped forward and wrapped her arms around him. She put her head on his shoulder with her hair next to his neck. She was squeezing him tightly like a child afraid of the dark. Her body was hard, but warm. He felt her shake. She was crying.

After a few seconds, he leaned back to look at her face. She didn't let go. He saw the wet lines where tears had rolled down her cheeks. For the first time, she looked vulnerable. Her body was tense.

He kissed her on the forehead. He smelled the shampoo odor in her freshly washed hair. He kissed her cheek, ever so gently, and tasted the salty tears. He kissed her mouth barely pressing his onto her soft lips. She kissed back, not a hard kiss, but a loving kiss. It wasn't passion. It was caring. It was a need to protect and to be protected in this strange place on this dangerous mission.

They stood by the lake embracing each other. The moist breeze chilled them, caused them to hold each other for warmth. He had never felt like this before. It was deep, warm comfortable.

They heard their fellow workers calling and walked back to the vans. He knew the day would be too long.

Tanya tried to concentrate on working, tried to keep busy. The other ladies commented she was working like someone possessed. She thought it was to keep her mind off of what had happened by the lake, but she knew better. She wanted to finish early, to get back early.

When the group returned to the office, Alex was waiting. The ladies teased her. "He's so handsome, so friendly, so loving. You are a lucky wife to have such a husband."

Then the doubts, the fear, began. I'm a married woman with a child. He's so irresponsible. He drinks too much. We have a job to do. But deep down she knew. The fire had begun and the flames were growing. All of her training, her willpower, hadn't prepared her for such a blaze.

He had a big grin on his face. He had a glow about him she had never seen before, not even when he spoke of Jenia. He held out his hand turned so she could rest hers on top. "Thought I'd walk you home. Had nothing else to do."

She heard herself respond, "That's nice of you. Thank you, I'm pleased." It felt good to put her hand on top of his. God it felt so good.

"While you've been working, I've been busy too. We finished a few hours ago and I had the van drop me at the train station." He showed her two tickets to Lucerne. "We've two days before the job at Jonah's. I want to take one of those days and think only about enjoying your company. I don't want to even discuss work."

She kept telling herself, this is wrong. I know it's wrong. We have work to do. Russia is depending on us. I'm married. She heard herself respond, "That will be nice." She listened to their steps on the sidewalk, felt his warm hand squeeze her own, saw the geese lounging by the side of the lake. She was afraid. The fire was burning out of control.

Lucerne – Tuesday, May 19

It was a dream for both of them, the train ride, the mountains, the lake, the painted buildings, and the monuments. It was all so beautiful, so peaceful. They let the happiness flow. They forgot Jonah, Russia, Kolya, Jenia. They were alone, strangers to everyone but each other. Now it was over. It was still mid afternoon when they boarded the train to Zurich. He took her hand to help her step into the car. She smiled like a young girl and thanked him. He saw the delight on her face.

She picked some seats near the end of the car. He sat across from her. The bright sunlight reflected off of her golden hair. Her face was pink, glowing. She was smiling, staring at him. He stared back at her.

The train moved. Smoothly it increased speed. The visit was over, but he didn't care. He was with her, riding on this train through the mountains and valleys of Switzerland. She cocked her head to one side.

Her smile changed into an impish grin. "I thought you didn't like to ride backwards?"

He hadn't realized it. He almost said he didn't mind, because across from her he could look at her. Before he spoke she continued, "You can sit next to me if you want. You don't have to ride backwards."

He nearly leaped across the short distance and sat next to her, close to her. His hip was touching hers. She turned her head to him. The smile was gone. The impish grin was gone.

She was on fire. She knew her face was flushed. She was afraid to touch him, to burn him, but she must. She wanted his arms around her again. She wanted his lips against hers. She wanted him to be lying next to her. She leaned toward him and he responded -- no sound, no train, no people, no sunlight, no mountains, lakes or valleys, only his lips pushing against hers. She tested him with her tongue and he opened. She felt his body respond against hers. In her mind she saw him standing in the bathroom doorway, so beautiful, so bashful.

She wanted so much to lie down on the seat, to pull him on top of her. She wanted to be back in the flat, sharing her love, hidden from the world and all its problems.

"Tickets please." The world was back. The two lovers separated and stared for a moment at the young conductor. He had a grin that ran across his whole face. He wasn't more than twenty. Alex stammered, "Sorry." He reached into his pocket for the tickets, gave them to the conductor and wished him gone.

When he left Alex returned to Tanya. He held her tightly the rest of the trip to make sure she was not torn away from him. He wanted to protect her, to make her proud of him.

He suggested they take a taxi from the station, but she said no that it was better to walk. It was late afternoon, but the sun was still bathing everything in light. They walked past the shops on Bahnhofstrasse to Paradeplatz. When they stopped to rest, he brought her close and kissed her. Her hard, thin body was touching him everywhere. He pulled her tighter and put his head on her shoulder. She did the same. Their bodies melted into one. Finally, he took her by the hand and led her toward the flat ten minutes away.

It happened when they turned the corner only a few blocks from the flat. A group of young boys was playing football in a fenced playground.

Alex and Tanya stopped to watch them playing. A young boy broke away and ran kicking the ball toward the goal. A quick fake, a fast shot, and the ball dove into the net.

Alex cheered. Tanya thought of her little colonel at home and felt her stomach twist. "An oath is sacred."

Alex saw the tears flowing fast down her face. She didn't make a sound, but the tears kept coming. She pulled a tissue from her pocket and wiped her cheeks and eyes. She stepped to him, held him in her arms and whispered, "I love you so much. I want you so much, more than I've ever wanted anyone. My whole body says now is the time, give yourself to him."

"But?"

"I love you. It is the most magnificent pain I've ever felt. I love you and I want to make you happy. But I cannot. Not now."

He wanted her, but it would not happen. He didn't know why, but he knew it was true. He also knew that despite his breaking heart, he should not push her, at least not now. He wanted to cry, but not for himself, for her. Hers was the greater pain, because she had to love many. He loved only one, and he would die for this one. Now, he knew love, real love.

23

Zurich – Thursday, May 21

It was a perfect day for landscaping. The sky was clear and the temperature would not go above twenty-three. The vans were ready. Alex glanced over his shoulder. Tanya was getting into the maid's van. She waved. He blew her a kiss. She caught it, put it in her pocket, and climbed into the van.

"Let's go," he heard someone say. It was time. He reluctantly crawled into the van. He was afraid for her. His task was easy, outside, hidden by bushes. Hers was difficult, inside, others watching.

"You must be newly married. You have that look. You can't take your eyes off of her." He heard them tease.

He wanted to shout, "No. I'm not married to her. I want to be, but she belongs to another."

He had wasted his chances. In the flat, in Moscow, she visited him every day. He remembered the look on her face when he said, "Would you bring me my picture of Jenia?" What a fool he'd been.

What if she's caught, prison, deportation? His face flushed in anger. She would be a nice package delivered into Mikhail's waiting arms. Alex knew he would die for her. She had killed to save him. Would he kill Mikhail for her?

The gates opened slowly. His hands shook. The van climbed the steep incline and continued around the house to a flat piece of ground in the back. He jumped out hoping to see her, touch her. He looked for her, saw her and started toward her. She shook her head to say, "no." She went into the house pulling her cleaning cart.

The men walked the grounds. The supervisor assigned tasks. Alex had earlier volunteered for the worst job. He would spend the afternoon bending over and crawling under bushes to gather leaves, twigs and trash from the beds.

Like her, he wore a small backpack. The others had seen the food, books, and clean clothes that came from the packs. Today, the packs held tiny electronic spies for Russia.

He had a map of his placements. He had his cart with tools and a trash barrel. He had his tiny spies. But he was missing his heart. It was inside the house sharing the danger with her.

Tanya moved quickly to the office. The door was open. She pulled her cart inside and unloaded her materials, dust rags on the desk and other strategic places, a bucket of water under one of the windows. She hurried back to the truck for a ladder and placed it near the chandelier.

She walked the perimeter of the office and checked the safe, locked, the desk drawers, locked. She looked behind the picture on the wall. The small safe door was there. She ran to the office door, closed it and placed the sweeper in front of it.

She returned to the picture by the safe. On the wall was a switch for the lights over the pictures. She removed the plate and put a transmitter inside. She did the same for the light switch by the door.

Now for the hard part, she thought. She climbed the ladder until she reached the ceiling by the chandelier. She took two cameras with transmitters from her pocket and placed them against the ceiling. She sighted one to the dial on the safe in the wall and the other to the safe on the floor. She climbed down the ladder, moved it a few feet closer to the chandelier and climbed it again. She placed two more tiny cameras and transmitters on the ceiling near the chandelier and sighted them as before.

"Bang," the door hit the sweeper. She jumped from the ladder and pushed the picture to the wall covering the safe. Someone pushed the door hard and slid the sweeper across the floor out of the way. She grabbed a dust rag. A young man, early thirties, handsome, with black curly hair, pushed his way into the room.

He glared at her. He studied the ladder, her cleaning cart, the rags and the bucket by the window. He tripped over the cord connecting the sweeper to the outlet in the wall and became angry.

"What are you doing in here?"

"I'm cleaning. I work for the service."

He was confused for a moment. "Leave this door open. Who told you to clean this room?"

"I was told to clean the house, to sweep, to dust and to wash the windows." She tried to look innocent, but her heart was racing. Don't make him angry, she decided.

"Why did you close the door?" He was still suspicious.

"I'm sorry sir. I was planning to sweep and it's very noisy. I didn't want to disturb anyone."

"Leave it open. You shouldn't be in this room unless someone from the household is present. Do you understand?"

"Yes sir."

He stood in the doorway next to the sweeper watching her. He wasn't going to leave. She walked to the picture covering the wall safe and turned the on the switch for the light above the picture. She dusted the top of the picture frame. Benjamin watched every move she made.

She climbed the ladder and dusted the chandelier. Once near the top of the ladder, she checked that the cameras were on. She climbed down and turned off the light over the picture. Suddenly, as if an afterthought, she said. "Sir. Where is the switch for the chandelier lights?"

The man walked to a switch near the door. He flipped the switch to on and the chandelier glowed. She looked at it and shook her head. She climbed the ladder again and rubbed some of the lights and the arms. The cameras were on.

"Thank you," she said and climbed down the ladder. She walked to the switch and turned the lights off again. She stood next to him and tried to look innocent. "Are you the owner of the house?" He laughed at the thought, but said nothing. She stared at him for a moment, then walked back to the ladder and folded it. She dragged it to the door and almost dropped it. He ran to help.

"Oh thank you. It is too heavy for me."

He took the ladder to the foyer and returned. She had taken the sweeper in her hand. "If you are in here with me, you can close the door and I won't bother anyone else in the house." For the first time he smiled. He pushed the door shut.

She finished sweeping and wrapped the electric cord around the sweeper. She pushed the sweeper toward the door, but he was in her way. He didn't move. He looked at her suspiciously. "I haven't seen you here before."

"I joined the company last week. I was so pleased to find this work. I'm from the Ukraine."

"You have relatives in Switzerland?"

"I'm a refugee, passing through." She tried to look afraid. "Please, I didn't mean to do anything wrong. I need the work to eat."

A friendly smile formed on his face. He likes me. She flushed in spite of herself.

"Maybe I can show you some sights in Zurich?"

"Oh no. Impossible. I don't know you."

"I'm the director of security here. I live in a nice bungalow on the grounds. My name is Benjamin."

"I must take this sweeper to another room so others can use it." She walked around him.

"Which room. I'll take it for you. You must finish in here quickly."

She tried to look pleased. "How nice. While you do that I'll take the ladder to the conference room."

"I'll get them both. You finish in here."

He left. She ran to the desk, pulled the cord from the phone, opened the receiver and installed a transmitting device. She replaced the receiver and reconnected the phone cord. She ran to the phone by the side chairs and did the same.

He returned and watched her. She dusted furniture, shelves, artifacts and pictures. He didn't see her placing a bug here and there. She knew the rest of the day would be easy.

※

When Alex saw her washing the window, he crawled behind the bushes to the receiver/storage device he had previously attached to the wall of the house. She sang an old Ukrainian love song. He saw the tiny red light on the audio receiver blinking. Everything was working fine.

She had stopped singing. He waited. He heard her ask, "Benjamin, will you please turn on the light so I can see if there is any dirt on the window." Alex gazed at the four video receivers. The red lights blinked.

They checked all their equipment over the course of the afternoon. It was always the same. She washed the window while singing, and he checked the receiver/storage devices. In the meantime, they completed their assigned cleaning and landscaping tasks.

The vans left Jonah's property and Alex turned to watch the gates close. He breathed a sigh of relief. He felt like he had been holding his breath the entire time.

They walked back to the flat, hand-in-hand. The sun was low in the sky. He said, "I hope he'll open his safes today or tomorrow."

"I think he will. Anyway, I'm sure he'll open them by Monday." She crossed her fingers behind her back.

He said, "We have to check the equipment every twenty-four hours to replace the tapes. I wonder if we can receive the signal from the street."

"Let's wait until tomorrow night. We can go in after midnight. The guard should be home by eleven. He'll probably be asleep by twelve."

"How do you know?"

She grinned, proudly. "He asked me for a date. I told him 'No.' I wouldn't tell him how to contact me. He gave me his number and said he's always in by eleven."

Alex grinned, "Well, I'd say he's a good judge of beauty."

Her eyes told him he had said the right thing. She leaned toward him and kissed him on the cheek. He stopped, pulled her close and kissed her gently on the mouth. She didn't resist.

He said, "I know this is difficult for you. It's not easy for me either. At least for now, while we are in Switzerland, Mrs. Hollenbeck, we should kiss each other on the mouth."

She hugged him tightly. "Thank you. I shall always love you. I will be so jealous of the woman who gets you for herself. I wish with all my heart it were me."

She saw the pain in his face, and the love. She saw two small tears forming in his eyes, but he pulled her to him and put his head on her shoulder before the tears fell. She held him tightly and let him release the pain. She was so happy someone loved her as a woman, a companion.

Zurich - Friday, May 22

A lone figure dressed in a dark, tight jogging outfit and a backpack ran across the Munster Bridge over the Limmat River and continued running along the steep Kirchgasse until the figure stood at the bottom of Zurichbergstrasse. Tanya caught her breath and then continued up the hill at a fast pace. It was after ten in the evening, after dusk but not yet black enough to be comfortable. She walked past Jonah's mansion and turned on the next side street. From there she observed the bungalow in the rear of the compound. It was unlit and, she hoped, empty.

She checked to see no one had observed her and ducked into some bushes along the road. From there she crawled through the underbrush to the back fence of Jonah's property about 10 meters from the road. She waited for fifteen minutes in case someone had seen her and reported an intruder.

She pulled a black stocking cap out of her backpack. Now she was covered well. She climbed the fence and jumped down on the other side. In a crouch she ran to the bungalow.

She tried each window and found one open. He said he liked the fresh air of Switzerland. She crawled inside the bungalow and searched for the security equipment. It was in his reception room. It was a simple affair, which surprised her. She would have suspected something much more sophisticated if an Israeli company had installed the system.

Now she knew why the alarm never went off. The system was merely a few outside cameras, which showed on the television set. Benjamin and these cameras were the only security. When Benjamin slept, the security slept.

She emptied one of two water bottles sitting on a shelf into the sink. She threw the empty bottle into the trash bin. She pulled a small vial from her pack and poured it into the remaining full bottle. I hope you're thirsty when you get home, she thought to herself. She knew this was an extra, probably unnecessary precaution.

She was surprised to find the door to the bungalow was unlocked. I'm not sure I would want Benjamin for my security. She wondered where Jonah found him. Sloppy, exceedingly sloppy she decided. She left the bungalow and ran to the house in a crouch. She dove under the bushes near the office. The house was dark, except for a light in Jonah's bedroom. He must be reading, she guessed. She removed the tapes from the storage receivers and replaced them with blanks.

From the bushes she gazed across the grounds to make sure no one was there. She returned the way she had come.

"Where have you been? God, I've been worried."

"I told you I was going for a run. Are you ready to go, huh?"

Alex looked at his watch. It was almost midnight. "What time do you want to leave?"

"Soon. I need to shower and get into some dry clothes. I'll be with you in fifteen minutes and we can go."

She hurried to her bedroom and removed her wet jogging outfit. She quickly put the tapes into a player and listened. She listened and fast-forwarded until she heard a pop. She had placed a thin wire over the edge of the door near the bottom of each safe. When the door opened, the circuit broke and the transmitter sent a pop signal to the receiver. She searched some more. Another pop told her the other safe was opened. Tonight is the night she told herself and she turned on the shower and jumped under the cold water.

24

Zurich – Saturday, May 23

Tanya dropped Alex near Jonah's mansion along with all of their equipment. As she had done for the three previous evenings, she parked the rented gray Volkswagen Passat on Nachtoldstrasse near the corner with Zurichbergstrasse. It was almost one in the morning. She, like Alex, was dressed in dark tight-fitting clothes, but nothing that might attract undue attention. Calmly, she strolled toward Jonah's mansion.

She found Alex crouched in the shadows at a section of the wall Alex had identified on Thursday. Instead of the steel pointed fence, this part of the wall was brick with a flat top. Some large trees near the wall gave them cover. Alex lifted Tanya, and she reached the top of the wall. She tied a rope to a tree limb and threw it to him on the other side. He joined her under the trees. They worked their way around the perimeter to the opposite side from the bungalow. They crouched low and ran across the open part of the yard to bushes near the house and quickly made their way to the rear of the mansion.

Alex positioned a small camera pointed at the bungalow. Tanya placed a small camera on the window to the main hall of the house. Then she pulled out an extendable pole from her bag and placed a miniature camera on the ledge by Jonah's bedroom window on the second floor. From each camera they ran wires, which Alex carried along the perimeter of the house until he was below the office window. He taped the wires to the window, extracted the tapes from the four video machines and placed them in his bag. He joined Tanya at the front door.

"The security is asleep," she grinned.

She finished working on the lock and the door swung open. She motioned for Alex to wait and she crossed the foyer and checked the office door. It was unlocked. She motioned for Alex to join her.

He nodded toward the office windows, "Why didn't we come in there?"

"They're locked, huh?"

Alex pulled a small receiver from his bag and put it near the window. He opened the window, reached outside and pulled in the wires. He hooked them to the receiver. He turned it on and saw Benjamin's bungalow. It was dark. He turned to another channel and saw Jonah's bedroom. It was quiet. Another channel showed the main hall. He fiddled with some knobs until he had a split screen showing the bungalow and Jonah's bedroom.

"Everything's working fine."

Tanya, meanwhile, loaded the videotapes into a player attached to a laptop computer. She turned on the first one. It showed the picture on the wall. She fast-forwarded the player until she saw a hand come into view. It turned the dial to the left until it stopped at forty-three. She quickly checked a list of numbers. She circled the number forty-three and whispered, "Wife's year of birth."

She saw the hand turn the dial again, this time to the right. It stopped somewhere below forty. The hand was in the way. She studied her list and circled thirty-one, Jonah's year of birth. She didn't wait for more. She rushed to the picture and pulled it away from the wall. She checked the number on the dial and wrote it in a notebook. She turned the dial left to forty-three, right to thirty-one and left again to sixty-six, daughter's year of birth. The door clicked and she opened it. Inside she saw a manila envelope, labeled with the name of the investment company, and a binder titled "Superpower." All were written in English.

Her heart raced. "Yes," she whispered loudly. She glanced at Alex, who was watching her as he often did lately. He gave her a thumbs-up.

She hurried to the desk where he was working on the microfilm equipment and put the materials on the desk. "We're going to copy all of it, huh?" She rushed over to the large safe standing in the corner. "Please be lazy," she said. She checked the dial and recorded the number in her notebook. She turned the dial left forty-three, right thirty-one and left sixty-six. She tried the handle, but the door was still locked. She tried again, only this time right, left, right. It worked. The door clicked and she opened it. She stared at a safe full of files containing people's names, company names and a set of accounting books.

She quickly grabbed the laptop and brought it to Alex at the desk. He hooked the camera to the laptop. He was using a special camera that made two films at once. It also had a port for connection to a computer. He would get not only microfilms of the documents, but also a digital image on the ten-gigabyte hard drive.

She warned him, "Check the screen to make sure you're getting the entire image, huh?"

He smiled to let her know he knew what he was doing. His camera was attached to a copy stand. The bottom was marked for placing pages to be copied. Once the document was placed, he would move the camera higher or lower along the mechanism to get a focused picture. Once set for a specific size, the camera was properly positioned for any other page of the same size.

They helped each other gather and copy the tremendous volume of information. The time went quickly. He continued to check the monitor to make sure no one was stirring. He glanced at his watch. It was almost three and it would be light before five. He had not yet begun to copy the personnel files.

Tanya was beside herself with joy. They had copies of everything they needed to prove her theory with hard evidence. She took a red pen out of her bag, opened the Superpower binder to page thirty-one and wrote in Russian the word "Chak" and the letter "T" at the bottom of the page in the margin. She did the same on pages forty-three and sixty-six. She closed the book and returned it to the wall safe along with the manila envelope. She spun the dial and then checked her notebook. She set the dial back to the same number it was on before she opened the safe in case Jonah had set the dial to a specific number to warn him if anyone had touched the dial. She swung the picture back into place.

Tanya replaced the batteries in all the electronic listening devices. She used the extendable pole to retrieve the video cameras from the ceiling. Once she had completed these tasks, she went to the desk and worked on the center drawer lock. The small click told her she was successful and she pulled the drawer open. Inside she found a set of keys for the other drawers. She unlocked and opened the top right drawer, and was surprised to find a nine-millimeter pistol inside. A larger drawer was below the drawer she just opened. She assumed it was for files. She pulled it open, but it wasn't a drawer at all. It was a door that swung down. She crouched to see what was inside. It was a telephone. Her heart sank.

She glanced at Alex. "I don't think we're going to get much off of our telephone bugs, huh?"

He saw the disappointment in her eyes. "Why?"

"He has a private phone he keeps locked in his desk. I'll bet all the reports are made through this private phone."

"We can bug it now."

"How will we get the tapes?"

Alex leaned over and kissed her on the forehead. "We'll have to come back to Switzerland."

She stood. "Mr. Hollenbeck, you know where you're supposed to kiss me." She pulled him to her and kissed him hard on the mouth.

He scowled and pointed to the telephone. "Bug it Mrs. Hollenbeck." She followed his order and closed the door to the desk.

"Now the hard part, huh?"

"What's that?"

"I'll lock all these other drawers with the keys, but to lock the center drawer I have to pick it." She laughed at the irony of it.

"Can you do that?"

"We'll see."

A few moments later she succeeded, just in time. Alex pointed to the screen on the receiver. Jonah was out of his bed. He was walking directly toward the video camera.

She turned toward Alex. "How much copying do we have left?"

"About ten minutes I would guess."

She glanced at her watch, three-thirty. "It's going to be light soon. I'll put back what we've done so far. Keep going. I want to get it all."

She watched the screen. Jonah's face was so close to the window she was surprised he didn't see the camera. Alex was watching too. She glared at him for stopping his work, but softened when she saw his excitement.

She said, "Fun, huh?"

He replied in a loud whisper. "Jesus. I can't believe I'm doing all of this."

She kissed him quickly and pointed to the camera.

He grinned. "If I do a good job do I get a reward?"

"Yes. If you do a good job you won't get caught and go to jail." She returned her attention to the receiver and Jonah.

She watched him walk away from the camera and into the bathroom. Alex whispered over his shoulder, "I hope the guard doesn't have to pee too. How are we going to get out of here with both of them up?"

"I don't think the guard will wake for some time," she said. Alex didn't know about the doped water or that it had been replaced with fresh water. He didn't know Benjamin was asleep when she put a needle into his thigh. He would sleep until noon.

Her concern was Jonah. She would easily overpower him. Besides, his gun was in the desk. That was not the solution she wanted. Instead, he should be unaware anyone had visited. Better to surprise him later, when it came time to get the money back.

Jonah came out of the bathroom, but he did not walk toward his bed. Instead, he walked out of the camera's view toward the door of the room. She quickly switched to the hall view, but he was not in the camera's view angle. If he came to the stairs she would see him. However, once down the stairs he would disappear from view again.

She went to the office door and locked it. She checked with Alex. He was finishing the last file. She scanned the room to make sure everything was in place.

Alex was finished. She grabbed the materials and ran to the big floor safe. She reviewed her notes to make sure everything was replaced exactly where it was before. She closed the door and spun the dial. Then, after checking her notebook again, she set it on the number fifty-seven. Given his level of security, I doubt if this is necessary she told herself, but why take a chance.

By now, Alex had packed everything except the video receiver. They were ready to go, but had to wait because Jonah was standing on the landing. At least they assumed he was standing on the landing.

"Did you see him come down the stairs, huh?"

"No. Did you?"

"Maybe we missed him."

"Christ, he might come walking through the door any second."

"For his sake, I hope not, huh?"

Alex cringed. He remembered Ivan. He decided to get out of the line of sight so Jonah wouldn't see him before she put him to sleep.

"There he is," he said when Jonah came into view. He was at the top of the stairs. He might come down. "We can't leave until he's back in his bedroom," Alex said seriously. Tanya stared at him as if he was crazy. He grinned and shrugged his shoulders. "Sorry. Excited I guess."

She stepped closer to him. "If he comes in here, we'll pretend to be lovers who got lost." She kissed him passionately. He forgot about Jonah. His mind imagined all manner of wonderful things. "I think he's coming down the stairs," she said. Alex turned to look at the monitor.

The telephone rang. It exploded into their ears. Alex felt like he could take a bite out of his heart. Even Tanya jumped and her eyes widened considerably. They both turned their attention back to the screen. The telephone blared again, seemingly louder than before.

Jonah disappeared from the screen. Tanya changed the channel and saw him enter his bedroom and pick up the receiver. She grabbed the monitor and Alex threw the wires outside, shut and locked the window.

They left the office and she made sure the door didn't automatically lock. When they reached the front door, they heard Jonah saying, "Hello. Hello . . . Hello."

Alex crouched and ran to the trees. Tanya gathered the wire and the video cameras. Fortunately, Jonah wasn't near the window when she yanked the cord and removed the camera. She had decided she would leave it if Jonah had been looking in her direction.

It was getting light when she joined Alex under the trees. They searched over the wall to make sure no one was in the street. She helped him to the top of the wall and he jumped down the other side. She sent him the backpacks and the large bag containing the monitor. She grabbed a tree limb to help her get to the top of the wall, and she too dropped down to the other side. "Still clear. Let's go, huh?"

They walked briskly up the hill toward the car. To be safe, she took both backpacks and gave him the monitor and car keys. "I'll meet you at the top of the hill. Drive carefully, huh?"

Tanya was exhausted by the time she reached the top of the hill. The sky was a mixture of red and yellow on the eastern horizon. It was like "white nights" in St. Petersburg near the end of June. The breeze that had cooled them before was now warm. When she got into the car. Alex handed her a small towel. "You sure are into exercise," he joked.

She grinned. "You're lucky I'm married. I'd likely kill you in bed."

He felt a sudden surge go through his body. He pictured her in bed, waiting for him. "For all your life you can know there is a man who loves you with all his heart. He loves you not only because you're beautiful, but also because you are such a joy to be with. He would die for you. You made him happy solely to know you and to look at you. He would gladly devote his entire life to your happiness."

His words and delivery stunned her. She felt the emotion in her throat. "I'm so sorry. I'll never tease you about sex again. But I want you to know you will never find someone who loves you more than I. If ever it happens I am free, I will come running to you with my heart in my hands begging you to take it."

He kissed her and she responded. He whispered in her ear, "You will never have to look far to find me."

"Let's go," she croaked.

As he drove toward the flat, he said, "I can't believe our luck."

"Luck? Why do you call it luck? It was well planned and executed, huh? That's not luck."

"The phone call. That was luck. He was going to come down the stairs. He was coming to the office for all we know."

"Lucky for him he didn't."

Alex snapped a quick look at her, but she was looking away, out the window. He said, "We were damn lucky for the call. Who would call him at that hour?"

"I wonder."

"Wonder what?"

"I wonder if it was luck."

25

Zurich – Saturday, May 23

Alex woke in the afternoon. Tanya sat in the reception room typing on her laptop.

"Did you sleep?"

"Some. I woke a few hours ago."

He stood behind her and massaged her shoulders. Her muscles were tense. He said, "What are you doing?"

"I'm preparing an index of all the documents we copied. Next, I'm going to make a transcript of the audiotapes. I don't expect them to have much on them, because we didn't bug the phone in his desk."

"At least we'll get his side of the conversation. Can I help?"

"Sure. Get the tapes and we'll play them, huh?"

He said, "Let me shave and take a quick shower. Then we'll relax and listen to Jonah."

"Okay. In the meantime, I'll make some tea and toast."

He sat on the sofa. She was in one of the easy chairs. The player was on a small table between them. Most of what they heard was boring, such as Jonah grunting when he took down information from his operatives in Russia.

Tanya was frustrated. "I wish I had known about the phone inside his desk."

"It's probably lucky you didn't. It would have taken you too long to pick the lock and tap the phone." Then he added with emphasis, "Especially with Benjamin staring at you."

She grinned, happy Alex had noticed Benjamin's attention. "I think he liked me."

Alex gave her an over emphasized evil look. Then he grinned and said, "I told you you're an attractive woman."

"Thank you," she said.

The tapes played on, and they continued making transcripts. He asked her, "How do you spell 'grunt'."

She laughed. Then the tape became interesting. They heard Jonah's voice rise in anger.

"Where have you been? I haven't heard from you since our meeting in April." The tape went silent. Jonah was waiting for a response. Then he continued, still angry. "This is unbelievable. Of course I had nothing to do with it. You're alive aren't you?"

Again, Jonah listened to the other speaker and then responded, "I didn't even know he had a mistress. What was she doing in your apartment?"

Their eyes met. They mouthed, "Jenia."

Jonah spoke again. "I know it's none of my business who you're screwing." Tanya saw Alex pale. She was tempted to say nothing and was surprised by her jealousy.

She paused the tape. "I can assure you Jenia was not Mikhail's lover. He tried to attack her. She immobilized him. It was all part of a plan to get to the papers in his flat."

"How do you know?"

"I was there later that evening. Remember? I brought the papers we found back to the dacha."

"I didn't hear anything about missing papers in the conversation." He was bitter. He clearly still had some strong feelings for Jenia, but they were turning into anger toward her.

"Of course not. Would you tell your boss if a woman immobilized you and stole some papers that implicated him in a conspiracy?"

He started the tape again. "Give me her name and description and I'll see what I can find out from our people." They heard Jonah replace the receiver. After a few moments he dialed a number.

"A few minutes ago, I received a telephone call from the man we discussed a few weeks ago. Apparently a woman about thirty-five killed his bodyguard and almost killed him, a professional." He paused, and then continued. "In fact, you and I both know who it is. She sat next to you during our meeting in Jerusalem, when you assigned me this project."

Tanya saw Alex look at her, but she avoided his eyes. She wished she had previewed the tapes. She heard Jonah speak again, angry this time.

"God damn it. Why wasn't I told? How long has she been operating there? He said she was Pavel's mistress." A pause. "Sorry. Well he's dead anyway. What's it matter if someone hears his name?" Another pause. "I didn't tell him anything."

Jonah was listening for a long time. They heard the click of his lighter when he lit a cigar. He spoke. "I know you said you were going to do something. I wish I had been consulted. I'm trying to run a business here. I'm not sure what you've accomplished. If it had been my decision, I'd have had her kill the bastard."

Alex shut off the tape. He was clearly shaken by the news. "She was working for them all along. I had no idea." Tanya felt sorry for him, but could do or say little to make him feel better. He spoke again. "I can't figure out how I fit into all of this. Why me?"

"You had nothing to do with her role in the conspiracy. She loves you, and I think I know why."

Monday, May 25

The plane left at ten thirty in the morning. Before leaving they put the microfilms and the laptop into a safe deposit box in Zurich. They flew from Zurich direct to Kiev. Tanya fell asleep on his shoulder. He smelled her hair. He kissed her forehead.

The farmer was waiting for them when they exited Kiev customs about fifteen thirty. He took them to the farm. It was too late to start for Moscow and the dacha; so they stayed the night and left about nine the next morning.

Dacha outside Moscow – Wednesday, May 27

It was early morning when the knock on his bedroom door woke Alex. "Time to get up, huh? I'm going to take a run. When I return I'll make you a nice breakfast."

He heard her running down the steps. His watch showed it was six. He was still tired. It had been almost midnight when they arrived last night. They were too tired to unpack. He barely remembered going to bed. A blown tire and an overheated engine added hours to the trip. Why do we have to get up so early?

He managed to get himself into a sitting position, bent over, put his hands between his legs dangling over the side of the bed, stretched his stiff back and reflected on his feelings for Jenia and Tanya.

I wonder if anything between Jenia and me was real. Was she acting? Was it part of her role? It is so different with Tanya. Why am I so unlucky? Why didn't I find her first? I don't know where she gets all her energy. He dragged his tired muscles from the bed.

He smiled as he remembered his first encounter with Tanya and realized that except for this project they would never have become friends, much less lovers. Now, the job was almost done. He would soon be able to get back to playing chess and his quiet life.

He searched through his bags to find his shaving kit. He stood and bent over to each side to get the kinks out of his muscles. God it's hard to get up, but I'd better get moving if I'm going to share a breakfast with her. The thought gave him new energy. He glanced out the window to look for her. God, it's going to be a beautiful day. I know I love her. She loves me too. He sang at the top of his lungs in the shower. He finished a cup of tea by the time she returned.

"How far did you go?"

"I don't know, probably about ten kilometers. It's not easy to run here because of all the ruts in the road and the forest is too dense. But it felt great. We did it Alex. We did it well, and I am ready to celebrate. We're going to enjoy this day. We can take a walk in the woods. Maybe even have a picnic."

"I need a walk."

Her face brightened, "Why don't we go now? It will give you a good appetite for breakfast."

"That's a great idea," he said and took her by the hand. "I'll show you Carl's parking lot."

They ran out of the dacha and he led her to the path. He squeezed her hand and guided her along the path knocking branches out of the way as he went. By the time they reached the clearing their shoes and clothes were wet from the dew. It was chilly and he hugged her for warmth. They stood in tall grass at the edge of the clearing and she rested her head on his shoulder. The trees surrounding the clearing spread long shadows across the ground. He led her to a fallen log bathed in early morning sunlight. They sat on the log, let the sun warm them and watched the mist rise from the grass and bushes.

Alex pointed to a squirrel running silently across the branch of a tree. She glanced at it, turned to him and whispered, "Thank you for showing this place to me. It's beautiful." She stared at him.

He squeezed her hand and said softly, "You know I — ."

"Don't say it," she whispered. "You don't have to say it. I know."

He stared at her. She reached out and touched his shoulder. She had a dreamy look in her eyes. He leaned to her and kissed her on the lips. She put her arms around his neck and returned the kiss. They rolled off of the log onto the ground, groping, kissing, and breathing hard. He lay next to her with his arm over her stomach. The kissing became more intense. He touched her breast. She didn't stop him. He placed his hand under her sweatshirt and cupped her breast. It was still moist from her run. He felt her respond, her breathing quickened. He kissed her neck and she moved his head across her shoulder to her breast. He bit her softly through the thick shirt and moved his hand to her stomach. His whole body began to shake with excitement. She hugged his head to her breast and wrapped her legs around one of his. He put his hand on her back and began to rock her back and forth.

"Let's go back to the dacha," he murmured. She nodded. He rose to his knees and pulled her up. They kissed long, hard and passionately. He rose to his feet and took her hand to help her stand. Again he pulled her close, felt her body pushing hard against his, heard her breathing next to his ear. She kissed his neck and he felt a chill race across his shoulders and down his back.

He led her to the path. They stopped and kissed every few meters until they reached the door. She turned to him; her breathing was slower, softer. She wrapped her arms around his back and pulled him closer. "I need to take a shower," she said. "Why don't you move the car to where Carl parked his. No one will know we are here."

"I'll hurry," he said, and jumped down the steps of the dacha. The Lada started immediately, which surprised him. He drove two kilometers until he saw the turnoff Carl had described on his map, an inconspicuous little dirt road. After driving only a few meters onto the road, he could no longer see the highway.

He followed the road for about a kilometer until he saw the two-wheel path leading further into the woods. He came to the edge of the clearing, and stared at the log and matted grass where a few moments ago they had held each other.

He opened the glove compartment on the dashboard. The passports, one for Dieter and one for Olga, were still in there. They had forgotten to remove them last night. I guess I'd better take these back to the dacha. He took them out and put them in his jacket pocket. His hands were shaking with excitement. He saw himself with her in the dacha, holding her, kissing her, loving her. This was it, what he had dreamed of, hoped for all his life. She loved him, wanted him. He wasn't her toy, a diversion for a weekend.

He knew now what Konstantin had meant. This was not infatuation. He wanted her, and only her, forever. He wanted to protect her, to give her a rich home, to share her life and children.

He got out of the car, ran across the clearing and stopped to examine the matted ground by the log. It all came back to him, her smell and her warm body, her soft lips, her breasts in the palm of his hand. He pictured their two wet bodies rolling across the grass, hungrily groping, trying to become one.

"Oh God, how I love you," he said as though she were standing there with him. He took a deep breath, turned and walked briskly to the path leading to the dacha.

※

Tanya showered and looked at her flushed face in the mirror. She wanted him, needed him. I must be strong. If we do this, it will change our relationship forever. What will it do to his life, my life? I made a commitment to Dmitry. If Dmitry and I will no longer be partners, then it will be time for Alex.

God, why did I go so far and raise his expectations? If I stop him now, he'll be so angry. I don't blame him. I wanted him. I couldn't make myself stop him. Will I be able to stop him now? He's going to come back here full of anticipation and energy. What will I do? I can't merely push him away. "Think, Tanya, think," she said to her face in the mirror.

She went to the kitchen and put a frying pan on the stove. I'll cook him some eggs so he'll have to eat as soon as he returns. That will give him time to calm down. I'll talk to him and make him understand.

She looked out the window to see if he was coming through the woods. The path was still empty. She scanned the area and saw movement near the road. She focused and saw men pull weapons from three cars parked at the edge of the road. They were about four hundred meters away when they entered the woods and began working their way toward the dacha. Her problem with Alex was solved. Her first hope was Alex would not return to the dacha too early. I've got to find a way to warn him. You have to get away, my love. It's too late for me.

She ran to the reception room. Alex had lit a fire in the small stove. She threw in papers, computer disks, and the audiotapes. The door to the dacha swung open and banged against a wall. A large man stood in the doorway with a kalashnikov pointed at her. She stared at him for a moment, hoping he was a professional. She turned as if to run into another room and he fired a short burst into the wall over her head. She smiled, stopped and raised her hands onto her head.

※

Alex dropped to the ground when he heard the shots and crawled along the path until he saw the men searching around the dacha.

What happened to Tanya? Was she shot? What would she do in this situation? He remembered what she said, "If something happens to me, don't get caught trying to help me. Russia's future is in your hands. Get back to Zurich and get control of the evidence we put in the bank."

For a moment he lay there trying to decide what to do. Why did he leave her in the dacha alone? Better to be a prisoner with her than a fool running around Europe. Damn Alex, do what she told you to do. God, I hope she's okay. I've got to get out of here.

He backed quickly until he no longer saw the men. He ran through the trees and across the clearing to the car. He jumped in and turned the key. He stared back across the clearing toward the path and begged for good luck when the engine protested too long. It finally started, and he spun the car around and drove toward the road. I've got to get back to Zurich.

Two men grabbed Tanya and tied her onto a chair. Two other men pointed guns at her face. She heard more men talking outside. They were searching the perimeter of the property. Oh God, Alex, stay away from here, she prayed.

Mikhail's large frame filled the doorway and cast a shadow across the room. He entered the room and walked toward Tanya. "You fools, somebody put out that fire."

Mikhail put his hip against the table. Part sitting, part standing he stared hard at his young prisoner. He felt power surging through his veins. One of the men brought him her passport. "So, I see your name is Tatyana Gunina, if this is your real passport."

She stared at the table, trying to play a game of chess in her mind. She recalled the first time she showed Alex how to beat the computer. Move by move she replayed the game.

Mikhail handed her passport to an associate. "Check this out. I think it's her, but we need to be sure." Mikhail walked away from the table and behind her. He grabbed her hair and pulled her head back. He put his face close to hers.

"I know you're working with Alexander and Jenia. I want answers to all my questions or I will hurt you. Where are they?"

She stared past him at the ceiling. In her mind, she watched as her pawn relentlessly marched across the board to the end of the enemy side and a new piece to replace the captured queen.

Unexpectedly, she felt Mikhail's lips on hers. For a second her mind went blank. In spite of herself, her eyes showed surprise. She saw his face, his sneer and his hand coming toward her cheek. To lessen the blow, she tried to roll with the slap.

Endgame

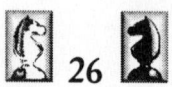

26

Kiev – Thursday, May 28

Alex drove the Lada for all it was worth. His stomach would not stop churning. He felt guilty he wasn't with her; he was impotent; he didn't save her.

Why did this happen now, just as my dream came true. My dream, what about her dreams, her family's dreams. He was embarrassed that he had even mourned the loss of his own dream. God, she might even be dead. He stopped the car and vomited along the side of the road.

He stood next to the car and tried to calm himself. On the distant horizon he saw the lights of Kiev. Think, Alex, think! They had talked about this situation, planned. In his mind he went over the list of actions she had made him repeat over and over during their trip to the dacha. Contact Gustav and arrange to meet him in Zurich. Contact Jenia and tell her I have the evidence about the Superpower scheme. Go to Zurich and get control of the films and computer. Give one film to Gustav and mail the other to my address at PHD. Find another bank in Zurich and store the computer in a safe deposit box. Return to Moscow and contact the FSB. Give them the film.

She had said, "You'll have only one or two days at most to save the evidence. I can last forever, but I've a family and they'll use them. I'll not sacrifice my little colonel."

He sat waiting for his flight to be called. He wished he could shave and wash. What will happen to Kolya? What will happen to Tanya? How did they find us? He saw it clearly now. Jenia had used him and Tanya.

She had her own agenda. Of course she didn't kill Mikhail, they were on the same side. She must have told Mikhail about the dacha.

But then, why did Tanya tell him to contact Jenia? Nothing seemed to make sense to him. He didn't know if he was doing the right thing, but then he had no one to ask for advice.

Carl, what about Carl? Tanya never mentioned him. Why? He can help me. Hell, this project is as much his as Tanya's, ours. He found the dacha for us, knows we have the evidence. Alex recalled the look of surprise on her face when he joked Weber might be part of the conspiracy. "You think Weber's involved?" Maybe she doesn't trust Carl. Maybe she had good reason.

He pulled his cell phone out of his bag, dialed a number and listened until Gustav answered. "This is Alex. Someone, I think it was Mikhail, raided the dacha yesterday. I was outside at the time. I heard shots."

He heard worry in Gustav's voice. "Is she dead?"

"I don't think so, but I can't be sure. I didn't see her, but the way the men were acting I think she's still alive. I thought it best to get out of there."

"Where are you?"

"I'm in Kiev. I'll see you in Zurich at eighteen hundred. I'll meet you by the Delta ticket desk. Okay?"

"I'll be there."

Alex pressed the button and broke the connection. He checked on his flight, the only one available to Zurich, Lufthansa thirty-two sixty-one. *I should arrive about sixteen hundred. It will give me enough time to clear passport control and customs.*

He walked to a newsstand and selected a *Financial Times*. In it he found the advertising telephone number. "Hello. I'd like to place an ad in your paper beginning tomorrow and running for one week."

Moscow – early afternoon

Tanya sat on a wooden straight-backed chair in the interrogation room and stared at the photograph Mikhail had thrown on the table. It was a picture of her mother, Dmitry and Kolya at the Moscow Zoo.

Mikhail said, "You have until tomorrow to think about it. If we're not going to get anything out of you, I want you to know you won't go to your grave alone."

Her stomach turned, because she knew he meant it. Something had snapped in Mikhail's brain. He was no longer rational. She was surprised the conspiracy hadn't done something about him. Maybe it was too late.

She was glad she couldn't see the puffiness in her face. She was numb from the slaps and punches. Occasionally, a trickle of blood ran down her chin.

Mikhail signaled and the men grabbed her again. One was pulling her hair to get her head back. The other was holding her shoulders. Mikhail leaned forward and put his face a few inches from hers. "You're going to die, Tatyana Nikolaevna. You're going to die by tomorrow night if you don't talk."

She struggled to speak. She wanted her voice to be strong not weak. She thought she was shouting, but her voice sounded normal. "You're too late. My information will destroy you and your whole operation. If I go public with the information, you'll never be President."

Mikhail backed away from her. "So, she can talk. That's better. Don't try to fool me. You don't have anything."

Again she struggled but made her voice strong. "My information will destroy you, Jonah and even Israel." Her words shocked him. She knew he was surprised. It was written all over his face.

He said, "We've taken possession of all the information you didn't manage to destroy."

She had him. He was unsure. He couldn't afford to disregard her. "I was destroying what I didn't need anymore. Do you think we're fools? The important information is safely tucked away outside of Russia."

He unconsciously reached for his cigarette case, pulled one out and tapped it on the table while staring at her and thinking. One of his men jumped forward to light the cigarette when Mikhail put it to his lips. He took a long pull on the cigarette and blew the smoke toward the ceiling. As an afterthought he nodded to his men to release her and offered her a cigarette. She shook her head and stared past him at the wall.

She thought about her first days with Alex, his drinking problem whenever he is alone and under pressure. No doubts, she told herself, he'll do fine. The Alex who saved Yeltsin will save Russia and me. He knows what he has to do. She imagined her pawn moving relentlessly another square toward the end of the board.

Mikhail smiled, friendly, "Tell me more. What is this information about — did you say his name was Jonah?"

Zurich – early evening

Alex stood by the Delta ticket counter and saw Gustav come through the entrance. He was alone, searching. Alex waved and walked to meet him. They exchanged hellos and Gustav led him back out the door to the black Audi waiting by the curb. Carl was sitting in the back seat. Gustav opened the door and motioned for Alex to get in. Gustav drove.

"We lost most of our work. It was with Tanya in the dacha. How did they find us?"

Carl responded, "I don't know. Did either of you go to Moscow?"

"No. We went straight to the dacha. Who else knew we were there?" Alex heard the irritation in his own voice.

Carl was irritated too. "Let's focus on what we have to do. Where are the microfilms? Surely you didn't have them with you?"

"They're in a bank deposit box."

"Well, they should be safe there."

"Not really. Tanya said if she got captured I had to get them out in a day or two, no later. She has a family."

"Let's get them first thing in the morning. I'd like to review them anyway."

Alex leaned back in his seat. Carl was more interested in the films than in Tanya. He hadn't so much as mentioned her. Alex decided he'd better be careful. He felt more alone than ever.

Zurich – same time

Jonah was looking at the Superpower binder on his desk and commanded into the phone, "Bring her here!"

Mikhail responded, "I don't think it's necessary. She has nothing. She's bluffing to save herself." He almost added "and her family," but he decided Jonah might not approve of his methods.

Jonah drummed his fingers on the desk and scratched his chest. Something had gone very wrong. A lot had gone wrong lately. Pavel killed, Mikhail revolted, Mikhail attacked by Solomon's agent, and now this. Too many bad things were happening and he didn't know why. He examined the binder. It was intact. Nothing was missing from the office and Benjamin had said there was no evidence anyone had broken in. "She's made statements to you about things only I know. We need to find out what else she knows."

Mikhail responded, "Give me another day with her and I'll get it out of her. We have ways in Russia you know."

"Damn it. Don't mess around with this. It affects both of us not only me. We'll both go down if we don't find out what's happening and get it stopped. Bring her here now."

"If you insist."

27

Zurich – Friday, May 29

It was almost ten in the morning when Alex walked through the bank doors wearing a business suit and carrying a briefcase. He approached the clerk who guarded the vault area and showed his identification. After he signed the log, she escorted him to the box. He opened it and took out the envelope and the laptop computer. He placed an identical envelope containing a blank microfilm back in the box.

He nodded "thank you" to the clerk when he passed out of the vault area and walked briskly to the front door. Before he opened it he saw Tanya, Mikhail, Jonah and two bodyguards crossing the street toward the bank.

Now's my chance, he thought. I'll run out there and make a scene. The police will help me save Tanya. What about Mikhail? He has no qualms about shooting both Tanya and me. I can't do this alone. Better to get Carl and Gustav to help.

Alex quickly moved to one side of the room and watched the group enter the bank with Tanya. When they walked to the vault area, he left the bank and ran toward the Audi.

Carl and Gustav stepped out of the car when they saw him running toward them. Carl asked, "Did you get the microfilms?"

Alex was panting when he arrived, but he managed to say, "Yes" and nodded at the bag. "She's in the bank. Mikhail, Jonah and two guards are with her."

They stared at him blankly. Finally, Gustav said, "Olga?"

"Yes Tanya. She's in the bank. We can save her now." He tried to leave but Carl and Gustav stopped him.

Carl commanded, "Wait. Wait in the car. You can't do anything. All you'll do is to get yourself arrested. You're in this country on an illegal passport. You'll both be deported and you'll be in a worse predicament. Better try it our way. She's safe enough."

"What do you mean she's safe enough? You don't know what that madman is capable of."

"There's not much you can do for her in jail. Now let's get out of here." They pushed him into the car. Once in the back seat, Carl nodded to Gustav. The car pulled away from the curb putting more and more distance between Alex and the woman he loved and wanted to save.

Gustav drove them to his home in Griefensee. Alex was crazy with worry. He was shouting, "We have to save her. I know Mikhail. He'll kill her eventually, no matter what kind of bargain we think we made with him. If he gets her back to Russia, she's dead."

Carl glared at him. "Calm down. We'll see what we can do. First we need to find out what we have to trade for her."

Alex volunteered, "There's an index of all the evidence we gathered. I saw Tanya enter it into the computer."

Carl said, "Good. When we get to the house, you can print it out for me. In the meantime, I want to review the film."

The three men entered, and Gustav led them to the reception room. He had placed a microfilm reader near a large comfortable chair. Carl took a film from Alex and began to review it. Gustav led Alex to a small room used as an office. After Alex printed the index, Gustav and he went back to the reception room.

Carl looked up from the reader. "You and Tanya did a great job. This is what we've been looking for, evidence of a conspiracy. Everything is here, names, dates, amounts, and procedures. If this ever became public there would be hell to pay."

"What are we going to do about Tanya?"

"Simple. We'll exchange one of the films for her release."

Alex was stunned. He hadn't told Carl about the two films. How did he know? Gustav told him, of course. He told Carl what equipment they'd been using. So what. It didn't matter. Carl had a good idea. "Okay. Let's contact them and I'll take them the second set of film."

Carl said, "Give me the other film. I'll review it to make sure everything is okay. Then we'll decide how to proceed with the exchange."

Alex was in a panic. The films were made at the same time and Carl knew it. There was no need to review it too. The situation was slipping out of his control. Now he had no film, only the computer. He turned to Gustav. "Call. Let's call. You have the number."

Carl said, "Not so fast. We have time. We have to plan these things. We'll have to convince them we actually have something of value."

Alex responded, "Tanya will have done that."

"How do you know?"

Alex answered, "She's here in Zurich isn't she?" The men stared at him but said nothing. They were waiting for his next move. Alex decided to get the computer to a safe place so he would have a bargaining chip. "Okay. You guys decide what you want to do. We have to do it soon. I'll go to the hotel and wait."

He walked from the room and packed his computer in the briefcase. He returned to the reception room to say goodbye. Carl looked at him and then at Gustav. "I'm afraid the computer has to stay here Alex. The information on it will create the biggest mess anyone has ever seen, and I can't let that happen."

Alex was angry now. "I don't think you plan to help Tanya at all. I'm taking my computer with me." He turned to leave the room, but Gustav was standing at the doorway with a gun in his hand.

Carl said, "You are free to go Alex, but the computer stays."

"There's nothing on here that will cause any problems. I need my computer. What sensitive material are you talking about?"

Carl was getting angry. "Shall we boot it up and see? Come on Alex. I know what's on the hard disk. Who do you think arranged the equipment for you?"

Gustav took the bag from Alex and gave the computer to Carl. He removed the hard disk and gave the computer back to Alex. "Now you can take it. I'll call you when we're ready to negotiate Tanya's release. By the way, I wouldn't mention anything about the two tapes and hard disk. Best the enemy doesn't know all we have."

Alex tried to look as mean as possible. He clenched his teeth and growled, "If you two botch this up and get her killed, I swear I'll spend the rest of my life hunting you down. I'll kill the both of you."

He saw the grins forming on their faces. He threw the computer onto a chair and left before he cried in frustration. No one followed, but he thought he heard Carl laughing in the background. He kept hearing the laugh even when he boarded the train for Zurich. I'll go to Jonah's and get Tanya myself. I wish I had a gun.

It was early afternoon. Alex had walked past Jonah's house twice, but found no way to get Tanya away from them. Guards were everywhere. He jogged to the top of Zurichbergstrasse and pulled out his cell phone.

He heard Gustav answer on the second ring, "Hello."

"Have you contacted Jonah yet?"

"Carl says we'll call first thing in the morning."

"You bastards. I'm declaring a state of war exists between us. I am going to kill the both of you, after I kill Jonah and Mikhail." He punched the button to end the transmission. Carl and Gustav had their own agenda and he wasn't part of it.

His phone rang. It must be Gustav; they've changed their minds.

"Hello."

Carl growled from the receiver. "Alex, if you step even one foot onto Jonah's property I'll destroy the film and Tanya will die. It will be your fault, you hear me, your fault. You will have killed her."

Alex shouted back, "You're a dead man Carl. I'll kill you and your whole family." He pushed the button again. That was foolish. No way am I going to hunt down Carl or anyone else. I'm Russian and can't go anywhere without a visa. I only want to get her back safely. He hated Carl, Gustav, Mikhail and Jonah, but he knew he was not able to kill them. He was ashamed of his own weakness.

The phone rang again. He answered, "Hello," and heard her voice.

"I read your advertisement in the *Financial Times*. So, you have some pictures for me?"

Alex wanted to choke her. He felt used, dirty. "Yes. I've got a bunch of pictures and I'm going to send them to every single paper in the world. Everyone will know what you've been doing."

"Calm down Alex," she said.

"Do you have a buyer?"

"I'm the buyer."

Her tone made him angry. "Don't play games with me or the pictures get posted on the Internet."

She chided him, "You can't be serious."

"Oh, I'm serious for sure. I've had an unpleasant spring. I feel like a punching bag that keeps popping back up to be hit again. I'm ready to do some punching of my own."

"Calm down. Let's talk about this. You sent the message so you must want something."

"I want Tanya released."

"Who has her?" Her voice betrayed her concern. He was glad she cared, because no one else did.

"Mikhail captured her. He and Jonah are holding her in Zurich. You know Mikhail. He'll kill her."

She whispered. "That's a dangerous situation."

A surge of anger pulsed through his body. "If she dies I'm going to release all this information immediately. You had better tell your bosses I'm serious. I have nothing else to lose."

"Okay. What do you want me to do?"

"I'm coming to Israel. I want to talk to your boss. In the meantime, tell him to instruct Jonah not to hurt Tanya and not to release her to Mikhail."

"When will you be here?"

For once Alex was ready. He had planned his move if she called him. "I'll meet you at Ben Gurion Airport tomorrow at fifteen hundred. I'll arrive on Lufthansa Flight Number six eight six."

"I'll meet you there. I'll see what I can do to help Tanya from here."

He hung up. Somehow he felt better. Somehow he knew she would do much more than Carl. Alex ran to the top of Zurichbergstrasse and waived for a taxicab. "Airport please."

※

Jonah asked Mikhail, "What are you going to do with her? We can't hold her forever."

"I'll take her back to Russia. She's committed a lot of crimes. I'll see to it that she spends the rest of her life in jail." He grinned at the joke. Tanya's life was destined to be a short one. It will be easy to keep her in jail for a few days, until he disposed of her.

Jonah was unable to do anything now. He had bigger problems to solve. "First we need to find out everything she knows. We need to find her associates."

Mikhail shook his head in disgust. "I don't think she found anything. I haven't seen any evidence she was even in your house."

"Oh, she was here. Benjamin recognized her. She was disguised as a cleaning lady. She was in my office with the door closed."

"Your Benjamin is a piece of shit. Why didn't he kill her when he found her in your office? The least he should have done was search her. She probably had the materials with her then."

"I have ways of knowing she didn't touch my safes. She didn't have anything with her then. That's why I want to talk with her some more."

Jonah knew it was probably useless to talk with her. The game had moved on; it was in the hands of her associates now. There would be some kind of trade, maybe her and money for the evidence and secrecy. *I need to protect her from this madman.*

But in his heart he knew another reason he wanted to talk with her more. She impressed him, pretty, clever. She reminded him of Miriam, was about the same age as Miriam would have been. He felt the guilt gnawing at him again. *I didn't protect my baby, my sweet Miriam.* He decided he would protect this Russian, this Tanya.

Mikhail prodded, "Maybe I should assign one of my bodyguards to you. Then we won't lose valuable information to some young woman disguised as a maid."

Jonah responded, "She's a professional and you know it."

Mikhail bragged, "Not so much of a professional that I didn't catch her."

Jonah said, "I've been meaning to ask. How did you find her?"

"I have my sources."

Jonah laughed. "I'll bet you do. I'm sure his name was anonymous. Has it ever occurred to you such a source is using you?"

Mikhail scowled, but didn't respond. He turned on his heel and walked the ten meters to the maid's room, where his men were guarding Tanya. She was tied to a bed with tape over her mouth. Her face was puffy and bruised. Mikhail took off the tape. He saw the pain in her eyes when he ripped it slowly from her mouth. It pulled her lips far away from her face before they popped back into place when the tape released them.

"I'm going to kill you Mrs. Gunina. I don't care if they offer me a million dollars for you. I don't need the money. I want the pleasure of killing you. It will be a painful death, for sure." He waited for her to say something, to beg, but she didn't make a sound. "I'm going to kill your friends Jenia and Alexander too. My police are looking for them."

He thought how magnificent it would be if Alexander watched him torture and kill Jenia and Tanya. Still she made no response. His face turned red and the adrenaline induced anger surged into his brain. "Where is your friend Alexander?" He slapped her face, which snapped her head to the side. Tell me or I'll kill you right here, right now." He had lost control. He wanted to see her die.

"Stop it!" Jonah was at the door with Benjamin. Jonah had a gun in his hand. "You're not going to kill anyone in my house."

Mikhail glanced at his bodyguards and shook his head. He returned his attention to Tanya. "If you're not going to talk, you won't need free movement of your mouth. He put a new piece of tape over her mouth. He pushed so hard he was gritting his teeth. Then he put another piece over her nose to pinch the nostrils shut. He squeezed her breast hard and walked from the room.

Benjamin ran to the bed and tore the tape off of her nose. He saw the nostrils flare out when she sucked in the lifesaving air. Her face was red from the effort. He took the tape from her mouth. Her eyes said, "Thank you."

28

Tel Aviv – Sunday, May 31

He was lucky. He had to do some fast-talking and fly out of the way, but he managed to arrive in Tel Aviv by four in the morning. Now, he was riding in the cab from the airport to a nearby cheap hotel trying to read the signs on the buildings and streets. What a crazy language, he thought. It looks like Chinese in a way. I think they even read it backwards. I'll ask Jenia. He tried to remember who invented writing. He didn't remember whether the first writing went right to left or left to right. The thought caused him to remember Tanya and the combinations that went in two different directions.

He felt the emotion and uncertainty growing. Tomorrow he would see Jenia for the first time since she left Moscow. It was a lifetime ago. Yet, it had been only a few weeks. He thought he was in love with her then. Now he knew he wasn't, at least not in the same way he was in love with Tanya. Yet, he knew he still had strong physical feelings for Jenia. The taxi pulled into the drive of the Shalom Hotel. He paid the driver and entered.

By five he was lying on his bed in his room. I have to get organized, he told himself. I have to anticipate and be ready to act. Jenia's hard to figure. She saved my life, but she was the one who insisted I take the originals instead of Ivona sending me copies. Did she do it as some part of a plan to get the papers away from Ivona and have me take the blame? Why did she help Tanya? Why give her the keys to Mikhail's office? Why did she kill Oleg? Maybe the whole thing was a hoax. Maybe Oleg is still wandering the streets of Moscow hoping to kill me.

This is all way above my head. I'm not a strategist. I merely march forward, trudge through the muck and try to enjoy my life. All of the sudden I am surrounded by assassins and strange women who kill almost without effort or care. I can't understand Tanya. Why get involved in this work? She has a family. Is she crazy? Jenia, on the other hand, seems well suited to this work.

He recalled the tape of Jonah's conversation again. "She works for my boss. She must be monitoring the Russian operation for him."

Sure, it makes sense. She works for the big boss in Israel. Anything she did to Mikhail or for Tanya was on his orders. No, that doesn't make sense either. Why would her boss let Tanya to get her hands on Mikhail's papers?

Why can't I talk to Tanya? I'll bet she's figured this out. Hell, maybe she's in on this too. She's probably sitting in a soft chair enjoying a glass of wine and having a good laugh about poor Alex who is running around in circles.

He set his alarm to wake him in six hours. Exhausted, he fell asleep.

Alex's taxi pulled to the curb at Ben Gurion Airport. He paid the driver and exited the car. He was wearing a silly false mustache. He walked through the entrance and to the nearest monitor. It said, "Flight Lufthansa 686 on time, Gate 10A."

His watch read 1:30. Plenty of time, he thought. I'd better get a roll and some tea. He passed through security and walked the concourse to a coffee shop not far from Gate 10A. Black metal stanchions that looked like chess pawns about one meter high supported a white heavy braided rope that separated the shop from the people walking. Alex sat at a table with a good view of both the concourse and the gate. He ordered a cup of tea and a Danish roll.

I have no idea what I'm going to do when Jenia arrives. I'm not good at this like Tanya and Jenia. I just can't seem to plan ahead very well. I'm better at reacting, he told himself to improve his confidence.

It was two thirty when he saw her. She was strolling toward the gate with a male companion, a bodyguard type. Alex left the coffee shop through an exit where they wouldn't see him. He sat at another gate with a good view of the shop. They entered the roped off area and took a seat.

He watched Jenia sip her coffee and remembered how important the first cup of coffee was for her in the morning. With some sadness of a lost time, he remembered he made a game of keeping her busy so she would forget her coffee. In spite of everything, he still cared for her.

After an announcement in Hebrew, Jenia stood. The announcement was repeated in English. "Lufthansa Flight six eighty six has landed and will proceed to Gate 10A." A crowd formed near the gate; she joined them. Her male companion stayed in the shop.

Alex noted that there was a broken leg on one of the chairs in the waiting area. It was a short piece of metal with a round end where the leg met the floor. He picked it up and put it into his pocket.

Alex returned to the shop and took a seat behind the man who had accompanied Jenia. Alex kept his gaze on her. She watched the people exiting the plane. Her companion was watching the passengers also.

Alex leaned forward and stuck the cold piece of metal against the man's neck and growled, "Put your hands flat on the table or you'll never see tomorrow. I'm serious. I have nothing to lose." The man did as he was told. Alex reached around him and took his pistol. "Stay sitting with your hands on the table and don't turn around."

He sat back and crossed his arms to hide the pistol. It felt heavy, cold. He didn't like it. The jet way emptied and Jenia asked a stewardess something. She shook her head and Jenia turned and walked toward the coffee shop. She shrugged to her companion but he didn't move. Alex knew she realized something was wrong; so he stood. A big smile formed on her face.

Alex had a full grin, so wide it loosened his fake mustache. Part of it fell over his lip. He waved and pointed under his arm at the pistol. She walked to his table and laughed. When he leaned forward and handed the gun back to her companion, the mustache fell further over his lip.

Jenia and he stood a meter apart from each other. She reached out and removed the fake mustache and threw it on a table. He wanted to hug her, because he had missed her. He knew she felt what was in his heart, his mind. She held out a hand and he took it. She turned to her companion and said, "It's okay. I can handle this alone." He left. She turned back to Alex and said, "I'm proud of you. You've come a long way." She locked her arm in his and they walked on the concourse toward the exit.

Alex said, "Let's go see your boss."

29

Tel Aviv – Sunday, May 31

The taxi came to a stop at the entrance of the Yamil Towers Hotel. Alex searched out all the windows checking for suspicious people that looked like security agents. He thought, I still want her, but I don't trust her. She works for them. He glanced at her. She was watching him. I'm an amateur, but I'm giving it my best. Anything less, Tanya will be dead.

The driver had turned around waiting to be paid. She said to Alex, "Relax. Everything will be okay. I won't let anything happen to you."

He had heard the same phrase before. Jenia had said it with the same inflection and caring in her voice as Tanya.

She paid the driver and opened the door. "Let's go."

She led him to a room on the third floor at the end of the corridor. She knocked three times, waited, then five more times. When the door opened, Alex faced an old man in his late seventies or early eighties. He was dressed like an orthodox rabbi, with a full gray beard and curls falling down the side of his face. He was of medium height and slender. Jenia said something to him in Hebrew and he stepped back. She led Alex into the room. In Russian, she said, "Alex, this is Solomon. Solomon, Alex."

The man nodded but didn't extend his hand or make other gestures of welcome. However, in perfect Russian he said, "*Ochin Priyatna.*"

Alex said nothing and scanned the suite. To his right was a small kitchenette. Fruits and breads as well as a coffee pot and a tea service were arranged on a table. He peered past Solomon into the reception room. He saw a sofa and two easy chairs with a low coffee table between the chairs and the sofa. A hallway led off of the reception room.

"*Ochin Priyatna.* Your Russian is excellent," he said.

Solomon responded without smiling, "I was born in Russia and lived there until I was twenty."

Alex glanced at Jenia and asked, "Near Irkutsk?"

Solomon frowned briefly but didn't answer. Instead, he pointed to the table and offered, "Please help yourself . . . coffee, tea, fruits, bread."

"Thank you." Alex poured a cup of coffee for himself and, after a nod from her, one for Jenia. He put a roll onto a small plate. They moved to the reception room. Alex took one of the easy chairs and placed his plate and cup on the table. She took the other, but held her cup on her lap. She sat back, relaxed, observing.

Alex leaned back and crossed his legs. Solomon was leaning forward, anticipating the conversation. Alex waited for him to speak first. "Jenia tells me you have some information I might find interesting."

Alex waited a long time before responding. The two men stared at each other like boxers before a fight. He said, "I have microfilms of documents from Jonah's safes. Some of the documents I filmed were from a binder titled 'Superpower'."

Solomon sat back. "Who is Jonah?"

Alex kept calm. He showed no emotion, although anger was surging through him. He spoke calmly, but with authority, "I didn't come all this way to play games. Let's agree to be straightforward."

Solomon spoke. "Okay. Okay. Why do you think these documents will interest me?"

Consciously, Alex kept a serious expression on his face. He wanted to show he was not in the mood for friendly conversation or nonsense. "The documents reveal the plan to take over the Russian economy. Other documents we filmed show the progress made, the monies accumulated, who was involved and the people who died in the process." He turned and looked directly at Jenia. "Including Pavel."

For what seemed to Alex a very long time, Solomon did not respond. Finally, he cocked his head to one side and looked askance at Alex. "You found my name in one or more of those documents? I don't think so."

Alex responded quickly, "Your name is irrelevant. The documents provide a clear path to Israel. That's enough." He glanced at Jenia. Her attention was focused on her coffee.

Solomon tried again, "No one will believe it. Most people will believe these are some more anti-Semitic lies coming out of Russia."

Alex leaned forward. He placed his arms across his knees. He stared hard directly into Solomon's eyes. "Russians will believe it. People in other countries, including some bordering Israel will want to believe it and will use it." Alex remained in his position waiting to see and hear Solomon's response.

Solomon had previously crossed his arms in front of his chest, but now he dropped them to his sides. "What do you propose?"

Alex leaned back and put his hands on the arms of the chair. "Jonah and a man named Mikhail Kolodkin are holding my associate captive. I want her released."

"Her? That's all?"

"No, that before anything. Now."

"And then?"

"The conspiracy must end immediately."

Solomon sat without making any change in his expression. Suddenly he stood and walked to the table in the kitchenette. He lifted the coffee pot and returned to the reception room. He refilled Jenia's cup and then filled Alex's. He set the pot on the table without filling his own cup. He sat down on the sofa, leaned back, and crossed his legs. "I see no reason why Jonah would want to hold your associate."

Alex nodded his agreement. Solomon crossed his arms.

"As for the conspiracy you refer to, I don't see any reason to stop what we are doing. Based on what I know about our plans, whatever we have done or are doing is business. It's capitalism in action. You Russians probably don't understand that yet."

Alex kept his expression neutral. He leaned forward, picked up the coffee pot and refilled Solomon's cup. He returned the pot to the table, picked up his own cup and sat back in his chair. He took a sip of coffee. "So, you think the Loans For Shares Program, the political bribes, and an assassination here and there are normal business?"

Solomon remained silent and crossed his arms in front of his chest. Alex continued, "If you've broken no laws, you won't mind if I publish the story and make the documents available to the public."

Solomon dropped his arms to his side, leaned forward and glared into Alex's eyes. "I'm not convinced you have anything to publish."

Alex knew it would eventually come to this. He had to put up or shut up as the saying went. But, he had nothing to put up. Carl had taken all of it and Mikhail had captured the rest along with Tanya. Stay calm. Stay calm. He doesn't know about Carl. I have to bluff my way through. Don't show anything on your face. Stay calm. "I have another associate who is guarding the films. Tell Jonah to open his Superpower binder to pages thirty-one, forty-three and sixty-six. He will find the word 'Chak' written in Russian along with the Russian initial for 'T'. They are written in red ink on each of those pages."

Solomon seemed to be in deep thought. Suddenly, he sat back, crossed his arms and said, "Even if the marks are in the binder, it doesn't prove you've made films of it."

"My proof will come with publication."

Solomon grinned and dropped his arms. His face clearly showed he was convinced. Solomon said, "I'm curious. Why the word 'Chak' and the initial? Why on those pages?"

Alex shrugged his shoulders. "I'm not sure. My associate wrote the word and the initial. She's good at chess, a master I would guess. The initial is from the first letter of her name, Tatyana."

Solomon eyes widened. He shifted uncomfortably in his seat. "I'll have your associate released." He nodded to Jenia who dialed the phone and handed it to him. When someone answered at the other end he said, "This is Solomon. Are you holding a woman named Tatyana?" He listened for a few seconds and continued, "Release her, immediately." Again he waited, longer this time. He spoke, "A man named Alexander is sitting in front of me at this moment. He says he has microfilms of all the documents in your safes. Can this be true?"

Solomon waited for a few seconds and said, "Wait a minute." He turned to Alex. "Is your associate named Carl?"

"Yes."

"Apparently, earlier today your associate offered to deliver a set of microfilms to Jonah for five million United States dollars." Solomon turned his attention to the phone.

Alex knew his face showed surprise. Had Solomon been looking at him, he would have seen it and the rest of the conversation would have been a waste of time. Alex glanced at Jenia. She was looking at him with a worried expression on her face. She had seen his surprise. She knew Alex had a problem. Think Alex think, he challenged himself. He doesn't know anything, yet. "My associate did that to get Jonah's attention. We would be crazy to sell our information for such a small sum."

Solomon stared at Alex for a moment. Alex had regained his serious facial expression. Inside, his heart was racing so fast he thought he heard it beating. How is it possible Solomon didn't hear it also? Alex glanced at Jenia. She was smiling, proudly.

Solomon decided. He spoke into the phone again. "Is it possible they have gotten into your safes? What security do you have there that would allow someone to get into your safe without your knowing about it?"

Alex heard the voice coming loud through the receiver. Jonah was angry and almost shouting. Solomon turned to Jenia. "Jonah says that we recommended the company that installed the security system. As I recall it was your suggestion."

She responded with her usual confidence, "Their security is excellent if they use it properly."

Solomon returned his attention to the phone. "Alexander says there are some identifying marks on pages in a Superpower binder they found in your safe. The marks are on pages thirty-one, forty-three and sixty-six." He listened and frowned. Alex saw his neck redden.

He smiled at Alex. "That's good. We both know he's going to find the marks. So does he." He turned to Jenia, "The pages correspond to the numbers needed to open the safes. Creative, I like it." She looked at Alex. When Solomon looked away, she winked.

Zurich – same time

Tanya turned her head to look at Benjamin. He was sitting in a chair staring at her with a worried look on his face. He stood, walked to the door and looked down the hall. Slowly, he shut the door and hurried across the room to her bedside. He stood there for a moment staring at her. "You are a beautiful woman," he murmured and put his fingers onto her cheek. Softly, he ran his fingers across her cheek to the end of the tape. Quickly, he yanked the tape from her face.

She whispered, "Thank you. I would have died if not for you. I won't forget your help."

He smiled and quickly cut the plastic cuffs that held her hands to the bed. He leaned over her to cut the cuffs from her ankles. He paused to look at her leg. His hand lingered ever so slightly on her calf. He took her hands and helped her to her feet. "Can you walk?"

"I think so." She willed the blood to move, to renew her muscles. She shook her head trying to get the drugs out of her brain.

He said, "I'll help you out the window. There's no other way."

"I can make it," she said and limped toward the window and her freedom. She was still too weak, too drugged to open the window by herself. He stood behind her, reached around her to help. She felt his warm breath on her neck.

Meanwhile, a few rooms away, Jonah walked into the conference room where Mikhail was sitting with his two bodyguards. Jonah said, "Mikhail, release the lady. I'll have Benjamin take her to her friends."

Mikhail's face reddened and his eyebrows narrowed harshly. "What? I'm not releasing her. She's wanted for crimes, treason in Russia. She's returning with me."

Jonah insisted, "We've been ordered to release her. Do it now."

Mikhail glared at Jonah. He glanced at his bodyguards and nodded toward the bedroom. The men left the room. He turned his attention back to Jonah. "I don't think your Benjamin will be taking the lady anywhere." They heard a shot. Jonah felt as if his heart leaped into his throat, and he felt the sickness forming in his stomach. It was the same feeling he had when he saw the blood running down the side of Serot's face and Cohen shouted it was a mistake. He jumped from his chair and ran toward the bedroom. Mikhail followed.

Jonah ran into the room and saw the bed was empty. One of the bodyguards had a smoking gun in his hand and was looking at a body on the floor on the other side of the bed. Tanya was sitting on a chair with the other guard pointing a gun at her. Jonah ran to the other side of the room and saw it was Benjamin on the floor. He had a bullet through his back. Jonah knelt beside him. He felt like he had to throw up. When Mikhail entered the room, one of the guards spoke. "He was trying to release her when we came into the room. He was going to help her out a window. He tried to stop us from taking her."

Jonah vowed that somehow, someday he would balance the accounts with Mikhail. He swore to himself he would avenge Benjamin's death.

Then he realized they might all be killed. He growled at Mikhail, "This is murder. He wasn't armed."

Mikhail grinned. "It doesn't matter. We're leaving and she's coming with us." One of the guards put a gun to Jonah's head. Jonah prayed to his God he would live to avenge Benjamin. If not, he prayed Solomon would avenge the death. It was written, an eye for an eye. But he wanted more than an eye. He wanted Mikhail to suffer, to know he was going to die.

The guard asked, "What do you want to do with him?"

"Cuff him to something solid in the bathroom so he can't raise an alarm until we're out of Switzerland. It's time to take our little lady back to Russia."

Tel Aviv – same time

Alex spoke, "My last requirement is the money stolen from Russia is returned."

Solomon broke out laughing. "Young man, you have balls, but no sense. I've released your friend, but you will get no more concessions from me. It was business. We earned that money. We're keeping it. It will make us the most powerful party in Israel. We'll rule this country and kick the Palestinian bastards out."

Alex was stumped. His only weapon was to make the information public. Solomon didn't seem to mind. Solomon stood and glared down at Alex. "Go ahead and publish. Israel will be isolated, but it is isolated now. Israel will be blamed, not me. They'll throw out the party in power. It will make it easier for me. Yes, there will be war with the Palestinians and the Arabs; bring it on. Better to die quickly on a battlefield than rot away strapped to a bed."

Jenia saw Alex trying to find an answer to this situation. Alex hadn't considered what to do in the event Solomon didn't care if he published. The only weapon he had, was a weapon Solomon wanted him to use. She stood and motioned for Solomon to follow her to one of the bedrooms. Alex wanted to shoot himself. *I'm no good at this game. The only benefit of his meeting was that Tanya was released, or was she.* Something in his heart told him all was not good with Tanya's situation.

It was less than five minutes when Solomon returned with Jenia. Alex stood, thinking he would be thrown out. She had seen him fail. She had told Solomon he had won and they were deciding what to do with him. Solomon said, "I accept your offer. We will stop the conspiracy as you call it, although I think it is fair business under any capitalism rules I know. However, we cannot return the money, unless you find a way to do it without exposing what has taken place."

Alex was dumbfounded. What had happened in the room? Surely Solomon knew he had won. Surely he had no reason to capitulate now.

In spite of his victory, Alex wasn't happy. He scratched his left hand and said, "I'm worried about Tanya. I know you told Jonah to release her, and I believe he would follow your orders. Mikhail is there and I don't trust him. Can you call again and make sure she was released?"

Jenia said, "Let me check." She dialed. After a few moments she got a worried look on her face. She said nothing. She placed the phone back on its holder and walked briskly into a bedroom. Alex and Solomon followed her. She walked to a desk in the corner of the room. Alex realized this was her operations center. She typed onto a computer and connected to the Internet. The screen showed an outside view of Jonah's home.

Alex said, "Where's Mikhail's car? He always rides in a Mercedes. I saw it when I was in Zurich."

She pushed a key and the view changed to the inside of the house. It was empty; at least it seemed so. She hit some more keys and they saw the office, the conference room and each room in turn. When she reached the bedroom on the first floor, they saw a body on the floor. Alex felt sick to his stomach. He heard Jenia say, "Benjamin." She increased the volume. They heard a voice shouting in the background. She turned to Solomon, "It sounds like Jonah. I think they put him in the bathroom." She said sheepishly, "I didn't cover the bathrooms."

Alex was losing control. "Mikhail's taken her. I'm sure of it. He'll kill her."

Jenia added, "Not until he gets her back to Russia. I know where he's going to take her. He's too sick to only kill someone. He needs to see them suffer first."

Alex was turning to his left then his right. His hands moved up and down like a puppet out of control. "God, how can I get there?" He wanted to cry, imagined her pain. "So help me God, I'm going to kill him." He ran back into the reception room and grabbed the telephone book.

Jenia said, "What are you doing?"

"I've got to stop him. I've got to get there before it's too late. Tears of frustration ran down his cheeks. He pleaded out loud and searched through the book. "Please God, take me. She has a family. I've nothing."

He found the airline page and reached for the phone. Jenia was standing in the doorway talking on a cell phone in Hebrew. She spoke quickly, with authority. As she talked, she packed a small case.

Alex assumed she was calling someone to rescue Jonah from the bathroom. She clicked off her phone, ran to Alex, grabbed his arm and pulled him toward the door. "Come on. I've arranged a flight for us."

30

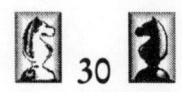

En-route to Moscow – Sunday, May 31

Mikhail stared at Tanya sitting across from him in the chartered plane. Her hands and feet were cuffed to the seat. The two bodyguards were sitting in another row near the rear of the plane. Mikhail removed her gag. "In only a few hours we'll be back on mother Russia's soil, where I am king."

She sneered at him, "You panicked, Mikhail. You're not thinking straight anymore. The Jews will kill you for what you did to Benjamin. They always get their revenge."

"They're a bunch of bastards. Maybe when I'm elected President I'll make Israel part of Russia."

She shook her head. "What makes you think you can get elected President?"

"Money, my dear Tatyana, money. Money gets people elected all over the world. The poor never rule unless they revolt, like in seventeen. Even then, the Germans financed Lenin. He had money or he would have lost."

"You're a sick man," she said.

Mikhail saw from the expression on her face that she knew he was right. He was going to enjoy her tonight. She was a feisty one. She would be much more fun than those who merely suffered and cried. He felt the muscles in his forearm tensing with anticipation. "I'm going to enjoy my evening with you. You have nothing to bargain with. I don't care what information you have about Israel. It doesn't concern me. I'm not a queasy old man like Jonah." He felt his face flush and his heart pump faster.

She looked away from him, out the window. He realized she was preparing herself for the ordeal ahead. He wondered if she could make her mind control her body. A wonderful test was ahead for him, and her.

Alex had never flown in such a plane. It was small, but it was going fast. It had markings on its side indicating it was an overnight delivery plane. However, the pilots saluted when Jenia got on the plane.

He asked her, "Who are you really?"

"I can't tell you, but you can probably guess."

"Did you enjoy watching Tanya and me filming the documents?"

"I was proud of you. Look how far you've come. You're much braver and smarter than you give yourself credit. I was . . . I am impressed."

"I wondered why the security system didn't detect our bugs. I thought for sure Benjamin would find them."

"He did. I told him they were mine. Benjamin works for . . . worked for me. I've been watching Jonah's home since the beginning."

"Why didn't you stop us?"

Jenia beamed. "I tried to call Jonah to warn him. But by the time he answered the phone you were leaving."

Alex looked at his watch. "They must have a head start on us. Can we get there in time? I don't want to think about what he'll do to her."

"Would you kill him?"

"Why do you ask?"

"Curious."

"Can we go any faster?"

"Yes, but we'd have every Russian MIG from here to Moscow scrambling. Package delivery planes don't go Mach one."

"Why did you help us? You work for Solomon?"

"I don't work only for Solomon. You might say I was an independent observer for another party."

"The Mossad?"

She disregarded the question. "After Pavel was assassinated, my employer agreed the situation was out of control. Israel had everything to lose and nothing to gain."

"Why not stop it yourselves? Why use us?"

"There is danger in any action we might take. If the government tried to stop it, we would make a martyr out of Solomon and his group. There are some in my employer's group who think Solomon's was a great idea." She grinned. "Your independent discoveries showed the danger we face."

"And me? How do I fit into all of this?"

She turned to face him. "You were my inspiration. You captured my heart, truly. I've been cheering for you all along, even when I learned you were working with Tanya to uncover the project."

She leaned toward him and kissed him on the lips. In spite of himself and all his doubts, her kissed her back.

"Tanya," he said. "We have to save her."

A voice came over the speaker system. "We can't get permission to land at Sheremetyevo. They're backed up there. A strong thunderstorm is going through."

Jenia's face tightened and became serious. The smile disappeared. "We don't have time to mess around. Find another airport fast. Try Domodedovo."

She pulled out her cell phone. "This is Spartan. I need a helicopter to meet us at . . . just a moment." She turned toward the cockpit. "Can you get us to Domodedovo?"

The voice returned, "Yes, we'll be there in about fifteen minutes. We have permission to land immediately upon arrival. Customs is waiting to check out the plane."

She returned to her cell phone. "Send the helicopter immediately to Domodedovo."

Alex interrupted. "Get a medical helicopter. No one will question where we're going."

She finished her first call and turned to face him. "I know Alex. I'm impressed. You should become a member of my team." She made another call. "This is Spartan. Get somebody to make sure passport control or customs doesn't delay us at Domodedovo. This is code blue."

31

Moscow – Monday, June 1

Mikhail heard Buddy barking. He put the key into the door. Tanya was groggy from an injection they had given her shortly before they landed. She was gagged again, although no one was around to hear her other than the guards. It was well after midnight. The guards stood on either side of her and held her arms. Her clothes were wet and sticking to her body. Her legs were tied with a short rope passed up her back and around her neck. If she kicked out or tried to run, all they had to do was grab the rope and choke her.

Mikhail swung open the door. Buddy was jumping, waiting on the other side. He ran to sniff her legs when the guards pushed her inside the flat. One of the guards said, "We can take her downtown and put her in a cell. Why bring her here. It's unnecessary."

Mikhail frowned. "I have no intention of explaining my reasons to you. Follow orders. That's what your paid to do. Follow orders." Mikhail squatted and lifted Buddy. Buddy licked his face and Mikhail said, "Did you miss your papa? Are you happy to have me home?" He lifted the dog and held it close to her. Buddy licked the water from her face. "See, he likes you. He likes everybody."

He turned to one of the guards. "I'll keep her here tonight. I have a secure place for her. There are some rings in the bedroom attached to a large metal frame. Put her there and tie her legs to the frame also." The guard took her into the bedroom. When he returned he had a disgusted look on his face. Mikhail felt compelled to make excuses. "I plan to interrogate her through the night. She's tired. She'll talk. I'm sure of it."

The guard responded, "We can help you with the interrogation."

Mikhail said, "I've taken you away from your families long enough. I find it strange you don't appreciate that I'm trying to give you a chance to go home to visit your wives and children."

Both guards shook their heads, turned and left. When the door swung shut, Mikhail said, "You little angel. I'm so glad to be home with you. Let's go see our guest, shall we?"

He walked into the bedroom. Tanya was handcuffed to the rings and her legs were cuffed to the metal stanchions. When he put Buddy on the floor, he ran immediately to Tanya and circled in front of her. He turned his body sideways so she could lift him.

Mikhail was flushed and felt desire pulsing through his veins. She was fully clothed, but he noticed her tight muscles through the wet clothes. She was in excellent shape. She was pretty. Unfortunately, she had light skin and hair, like the young one with the cross. He wondered if she had wings on her back also.

He removed his wet shirt. She was facing away from him and didn't see him, although she knew he was in the room. He made a mental note to put a mirror on the wall so the next time he would be able to see the entire body at once. His victims would also be able to see him and anticipate what was coming. He would watch the fear on their faces when he prepared to strike. He was surprised and disappointed he hadn't thought of it before. He removed his belt and swished it through the air. He let his pants fall to the floor. He shut the door.

Inexplicably, Buddy whimpered and ran under Mikhail's bed, afraid. Mikhail paid him no heed. His mind was on the coming pleasure. He put one hand on her shoulder and the other around her waist. Slowly, he undid the bottom button on her blouse, then the next and the next.

※

The rescue helicopter slowly, too slowly for Alex, worked its way through the strong wind-whipped rain to the flat roof of the building. It was turbulent and they had already made three passes. Lightning filled the sky everywhere, above, below and next to them. The quick flashes and thunder reminded him of the fireworks on the night Yuri tried to kill him. He jumped every time.

In spite of his own fear, Alex insisted they try again and try harder. He wanted them to go faster. Every second counted, they were wasting precious time.

Jenia said, "We won't be able to help her at all if we hit the side of the building."

That didn't appease Alex. "Hover over the roof and I'll jump down."

Jenia told the pilot if the next pass didn't work, they should land on the lawn near the building. On the fourth pass, the pilot managed to land.

Jenia, carrying a pistol in her hand, led an unarmed Alex out of the helicopter and through the heavy rain to the stairwell. They were lucky. The door was unlocked. They ran down one flight to Mikhail's floor. She opened the door slowly and was surprised. The hall was empty. She led Alex down the short hall to Mikhail's door. It was locked. Alex was surprised when she pulled out a key, inserted it into the lock and opened the door. She looked inside and nodded for him to follow. He ran into the room behind her.

The apartment was dark, but they saw light under the bedroom door. Loud music with a fast beat was playing. Jenia pushed Alex behind her and slowly turned the knob on the door. It was unlocked. Slowly she pushed it open and peeked through the crack.

Alex was looking over her shoulder. The dog ran to the door barking. Jenia pushed the door open further and Alex felt sick to his stomach. He saw Tanya, naked, hanging from rings attached to a metal stand. Her clothes were ripped and lying at her ankles, which were attached to the metal also. Behind her stood Mikhail. He was naked and holding a belt in his hand. Alex noticed red marks on Tanya's back. He pushed past Jenia and raced toward Mikhail, who still didn't realize they were there. Alex hit him and drove him to the floor. Alex was punching, punching with all his might. Mikhail was sturdy, but Alex was inspired. He subdued him quickly. He tore the belt from his hand and wrapped it around his neck. He pulled it tight.

Jenia arrived with the gun and gave it to Alex. He was surprised. It was much heavier than he had imagined. Mikhail lay on the floor and Alex pointed the gun at him.

He heard Tanya shouting above the music. "The keys are on the dresser, huh? Get me down from here. Turn off that horrible music."

Jenia pulled the plug on the CD Player and grabbed the keys from the dresser. She released Tanya's arms. Tanya immediately turned to look at Mikhail. When she saw Alex she blushed. He looked away.

Alex pulled on the belt and dragged Mikhail to the reception room. When he left, he saw Jenia covering Tanya with a robe.

Jenia helped Tanya into the reception room. Mikhail tried to get off of the floor and Alex tightened the belt. He heard Jenia say, "I'm sorry it took us so long to get here. I should have killed him before."

Tanya was still shaking. "He's . . . he's insane. He was laughing and touching me. I was too sick to even throw up. God, I feel so dirty."

Alex felt a surge of anger, even hate. He heard a buzzing in his head. He pulled hard on the belt and heard Mikhail cough as he choked, "At least let me put on a robe or something." He tried to rise and Alex kicked him back to the floor. Mikhail tried to cover himself with his hands.

Tanya, her eyes bulging in anger said to Mikhail, "You need to be put away."

Alex studied Tanya, who had some black and blue marks on her face. They reminded him of the many marks on her back and buttocks. He felt his control slipping away. He squeezed the gun involuntarily. Fortunately, he didn't have his finger on the trigger.

Mikhail was defiant. "No one is going to do anything to me. I'm a member of the Duma, immune from prosecution. Can I get some clothes on now?"

Alex said, "Okay. Get up." He dragged Mikhail into the bedroom and the dog followed, barking. Alex shut the door.

Tanya wrapped her arms around Jenia and cried, deep sobs of relief and shame. She needed someone to hold her now. She needed Alex to hold her. Suddenly, she heard a shot from the bedroom, then another shot. She was horrified. She glanced at Jenia who stared back at her wide-eyed. "What have we done to him? Oh God, we destroyed him," Tanya said.

Jenia responded, "Poor Alex. It's our fault. We used him and now it has come to this." She opened the bedroom door and Tanya followed her into the room. The sharp smell of cordite was overpowering. Alex was standing near the apparatus with a smoking gun in one hand, holding Buddy with the other. Mikhail was dangling from the rings, his arms stretched to their limit, his head forward on his chest. Alex was facing Mikhail and hadn't realized they had entered the room. He threw the gun on the bed and wrapped both his arms around Buddy. "You're mine now, Buddy. I'm going to take you home with me."

Tanya said, "Sasha, what have you done?" He spun around looked at two women staring at him with their mouths open. Suddenly, he realized what they were thinking and shook his head.

He murmured, "Surely you don't think. . . ." but it was clear they did. He glanced at the gun on the bed and then to Mikhail dangling from the rings. "After I got him hanging, I put the gun to his head and told him I was going to shoot him. When I turned and fired into the bed, he passed out. Strange, the gun went off a second time and I didn't even pull the trigger."

Tanya saw tears pool in his eyes and then run down his cheeks. He put Buddy on the floor and rushed to her. He wrapped his arms around her and they both stood there crying. He kissed her on the forehead. She put her head on his shoulder and continued to cry.

Then she pulled back and said, "Mr. Hollenbeck, I expect you to kiss Mrs. Hollenbeck on the mouth." For the next few minutes they stood there kissing. Suddenly, Tanya remembered Jenia was still in the room. She blushed and said, "It's a private joke."

Jenia responded, "Yes I know."

Tanya was bewildered and looked to Alex for an explanation. He said, "I'll tell you later."

Jenia joined them and the three formed a small circle with their arms around each other. Buddy was in the middle jumping. Occasionally, he would turn sideways.

Finally, Alex broke the circle and lifted Buddy. He held him in front of Tanya, and Buddy licked her face. She said, "I've wanted to do this since I arrived, but didn't have the chance." She took Buddy away from him and hugged him to her bosom. She rocked him back and forth and kissed his head. Buddy rested his chin on her shoulder.

Jenia petted his back. Alex moved around behind Tanya and rubbed Buddy's head. Buddy licked his wrist. Alex said, "I'm going to take this one home with me. I need a companion. We have a lot in common." The two women laughed and nodded their heads in agreement.

Jenia used her cell phone. "This is Spartan, I have a package to ship."

Alex asked, "Where are you going to take him?"

She answered, "We'll take him to a warmer climate for a short visit. I have some friends who will want to talk to him. We'll make sure that he doesn't bother you anymore."

"Are you going to kill him?"

"We have ways to control him. A few compromising pictures, a few threats, a taste of what's to come if he doesn't cooperate."

Alex shuddered and tried to imagine the ordeal Mikhail was about to experience. "What pictures would bother Mikhail? He seems to have no morals, no humanity."

Jenia shook her head. "The man is obsessed with power and control. There are certain things such men would not do. We'll have pictures he will never want seen. He'll be happy to do our bidding."

Tanya was lying on the sofa, exhausted. He went to the guest bedroom and pulled down the covers. He returned, lifted Tanya and carried her to the bed, she was smiling. Her robe came open when he laid her down. He pulled it back over her body and lay down next to her. She rolled to him and fell asleep in his arms.

It was five in the morning when Jenia returned. She brought some clothes for Tanya. When Tanya left the room to dress, Jenia said to Alex, "I have a car waiting to take her home." She gave him an impish grin. "I have to leave in a few hours to return to Israel. Maybe we can spend them together in your flat, or even here?"

Alex stared at the floor. "I think I had better take her home."

Jenia kissed him on the cheek. "You're right. She needs you now." She turned and left the room. Alex didn't see her tears.

32

Moscow – Monday, June 1

Some of the neighbors going to work paused to stare at the large Mercedes that stopped in their neighborhood. No one who lived here could afford such a car. They naturally assumed it was Russian Mafia.

Tanya had fallen asleep again. He had put a small pillow in his lap, and she was lying on her side with her head on the pillow. Alex put his hand on Tanya's shoulder and shook it. "Time to wake up my love. You are home."

He helped her from the car and hugged her close as they entered the building. They were lucky that the elevator was working. It was cramped, big enough for two people only. It smelled of urine. He helped her inside, closed the door and pushed the button. The small space and smell of urine made him dizzy. He listened to the machinery complain of the load and the box rose slowly. He was gasping for air and feared he would panic or pass out. At the moment he felt he was going to explode, she hugged him and said, "I love you. Thank you for helping me." He pulled her close and put his cheek against hers, which was wet with tears. He forgot about the confined box crawling up the shaft. He knew only that he was with her and it would end too soon.

The box protested and halted on the tenth floor. Alex quickly opened the elevator; afraid the box would move again. He knocked on her door.

Tanya had rallied. Her face showed a few bruises, but she was more alert as the drugs had worn off. Fortunately, her family would not be able to see the welts and bruises on her back. He wished he was the one to apply a soothing salve. The door opened and before them stood her mother, Kolya and Dmitry.

Kolya was first. He leaped in front of his Nana, wrapped his arms around Tanya, and buried his face in her waist. Her mother followed. She wrapped her arms around Tanya's neck. They sandwiched Kolya between them. For a few moments, no one spoke other than the muffled sounds of Kolya saying "Mama, Mama."

Then her mother stepped back and took her face in her hands. "Oh, my baby, my baby what happened to you?"

"I'm okay Mama. The bruises will go away in a few days."

Alex on one side and Dmitry on the other stood silently watching the small group between them. Alex felt awkward and out of place and questioned whether it had been wise for him to accompany her home. He hadn't realized her husband would be here to take possession. He couldn't help being jealous. He didn't know what to say, but consciously tried to keep a pleasant smile on his face. He felt the same feelings he had on his trip to Kiev.

Tanya was surprised to see Dmitry in her flat. Her mother had said nothing. She wondered how long he had been staying there, but now was not the time to inquire about it. As Kolya clung to her, she glanced at Dmitry, who was looking alternately at her and then Alex. She knew she would have to do something, but she wasn't sure what. It may be that her time with Mikhail was the easier of her tasks.

As Tanya straightened, Kolya saw Alex and ran to him. "Alexander, I am so happy you have come to visit me. Maybe we can play some football today. I don't have school anymore." Alex was uncomfortable and wondered what Kolya had told Dmitry about the day and night at the dacha. Then he realized he had done nothing wrong, except fall in love with Dmitry's wife.

Tanya introduced him. "Mama, this is Alexander Ivanovich. Alexander this is my mother, Lyudmila Andreevna."

Alex took her hand when offered and kissed it. "*Ochin priyatna.*"

"*Ochin priyatna,*" was her reply. "I've heard much about you from Kolya. Ever since he visited your beautiful dacha and played football with you he has decided to become a great player." Alex was surprised. He didn't realize Kolya thought it was his dacha. He wondered what her Mama would think if she saw the Mercedes and driver waiting outside.

"Alexander, this is my husband, Dmitry Egorovich. Dmitry, this is Alexander Ivanovich." Alex reached for Dmitry's hand and made it a point to look directly into his eyes. I have nothing to be ashamed about he kept telling himself, but he wondered whether his face showed how much he loved the man's wife. Dmitry's response was cold enough to let

Alex know no amount of innocent looks would convince Dmitry that Alex was not Tanya's lover. Strange, thought Alex, after all these years I would think he would know she was faithful to him. Alex felt guilty; he knew in his heart he would not have had her strength. He had not gone to bed with her, because she wouldn't allow it. It was not any moral decision on his part.

Alex had been in her apartment for over an hour when he finally managed to pull himself away from Kolya and return to the Mercedes. He wished Dmitry had come outside and seen the driver open the door.

The Mercedes pulled away from the curb and raced down the street. Alex waved his hand to the building through the rear window. She was gone, and he felt the emptiness only she could fill. He let his head rest on the back of the seat and shut his eyes. He dreamt of her again, hair wrapped in a maid's scarf, washing windows.

✣

Shortly after Alex left, Tanya excused herself and prepared a hot bath. The hot water filled the tub and she added a half bottle of lilac bath oil and some lilac bubble crystals. By the time the tub was filled with hot water and bubbles, the room was fogged with a warm mist, almost dreamlike. She slowly pushed her body through the bubbles and into the still too hot water. She noticed her skin turning pink, felt the healing warmth. A large folded towel served as a pillow on the end of the tub. She closed her eyes and the aches and shame were washed away. She remembered Alex watching her from Jonah's yard. She had washed the same window three times and Alex had never noticed.

It was late evening by the time Kolya was asleep in Tanya's bed. Her mother had been on the edge of her seat all day waiting to find out what would happen between her daughter and Dmitry. She was also curious about Alex and asked Tanya if Alexander was a rich banker. Tanya didn't answer. She had growled at her mother in the kitchen. "Why didn't you tell me he was here?" Her mother said nothing. "Who's been sleeping in my bed?"

Her mother responded, "Only I. He slept on the couch."

Dmitry had been uncomfortable all day. She knew because he avoided her eyes and said almost nothing to her. He focused most of his attention on Kolya. However, a number of times she caught him staring at her when he thought she wasn't looking. "Let's take a walk," she said. An afternoon shower had cleaned and cooled the late spring air. They stayed away from the main streets to avoid the automobile noise and exhaust. She let him hold her hand. They looked like many of the other couples escaping the stale air of their too crowded flats.

"I'm sorry," he said, but she didn't respond. They walked in silence for another ten minutes and the darkness settled over them. "I'm ashamed," he tried, but she said nothing. Finally, he stopped to face her. "I can't reverse what I did. I can only promise not to drink, not to fail you and Kolya again. I have found a job."

Still, she could not push Alex from her mind. She loved him now; she couldn't help herself. It had happened as if dictated by the gods. She thought too of Pushkin's Tatyana in his epic poem "Yevgeny Onegin" and how proud she was that Tatyana remained loyal to her husband and true to her vows. I am Tatyana not Anna Karenina she told herself.

She studied Dmitry, afraid to say anything. She saw Kolya in him and remembered the early days, holding hands, kissing, testing their self-control. She remembered her wedding vows, "I promise you love, honor, and respect; to be faithful to you, and not to forsake you until death do us part."

He went on, "I can only pray you'll let me prove I love you."

She put her arms around him and pulled him close. He put his head on her shoulder and his body shook and tears of relief flowed. She was crying too, for him, and for herself.

33

Langley, Virginia – Thursday, June 4

The blue Ford Taurus pulled next to the gate at CIA headquarters. The guard looked through the window and checked the identification badge. He motioned for the driver to proceed. A few minutes later, the car pulled into an employee-reserved parking lot. The door swung open and Carl Weber, carrying a briefcase, stepped into the southern sunshine. As always, he was impeccably dressed.

Carl entered the building, showed his badge to the guard and passed through the metal detectors. He took the elevator to the third floor and walked down the hall to a door marked "Director Israeli Affairs." The secretary looked up when he stepped into the room. "Good morning Mr. Hanson. He's expecting you." She motioned for him to enter the office.

Benjamin Rosenthal rose from his desk when Carl entered. His hand was out ready to shake. "Great to see you Bob. I had a call from Israel yesterday. They're pleased. Good job."

Carl said. "Yes, I gave the film to Jenia as we had agreed."

Benjamin stared at him expectantly, "And the second copy?"

Carl grinned, reached into his briefcase, and pulled out an envelope. He held it in the air, wiggled it back and forth and handed it to Benjamin.

"There are no other copies?"

"Gustav said they tried to make a digital copy on a laptop computer. I took the hard disk, but it was a waste of time."

"Why?"

"The disk was corrupted. They are amateurs and had bungled the connection. I couldn't open it, but our boys managed to get the bits sorted out. We could read a few documents, but most were gibberish."

"Excellent job. Excellent job. I'll contact PHD and thank them for their patriotism, again. I think you've a few weeks vacation coming?"

Moscow – Friday, June 5

Tanya was sitting at the table in the war room. She heard rain on the window and an occasional clap of thunder. She gazed around the room at the charts, news articles and other material she had gathered over the course of her research. Don't need this anymore, she thought.

Back in December, the corporate finance group had asked her to gather basic data about the large financial/industrial groups operating in Russia. In particular, they wanted to know who the key people were and what businesses activities were involved.

Her research into Pavel led her to the Knight Klub. For an entire week she had an assistant photograph everyone entering or leaving the Klub. She lifted a picture from the table. It showed Jenia standing in front of the Klub talking to Alex. She was surprised when she discovered he worked for PHD. She suspected him also, but her background checks revealed nothing incriminating.

God has been on our side, she decided. It's amazing how such small incidents can have such important results. She had gone to Switzerland for a chess conference in January. She saw them, Carl and Jenia, lunching outside the Neu Klosterli restaurant in Zurich. Tanya happened to be walking by on her way to the Zurich Zoo. She was going to introduce herself, until she recognized Jenia.

In February, Carl had taken her to dinner. "I understand you're doing a study for Greg in corporate finance. Tell me about it." His request was so innocent. "I'm intrigued," he had said. "Check into the backgrounds of the owners and let me know if you find anything unusual. I wouldn't be surprised if there is something funny going on."

It hadn't taken her long to put it together, and to discover Carl's real employer. She was surprised, and disappointed. I suppose I could have used him, she thought. The man wanted me, or did he? She remembered the dacha.

Alex and his relationship with Jenia were presents from heaven. She was pleased on that first day when she realized he was clueless about Jenia. He was floating through life, happy, ignorant, chasing balls. She kissed his picture and put it back into the folder.

The door burst open and Alex came charging through. "We won. We won." His face was flush with excitement.

He reached the table. She grinned and said, "You've been hanging around too much with those Israeli agents. Do you always charge into someone's office uninvited?"

For a moment he stopped, confused. Then he remembered and laughed. "Hey, I have good news. I met Jenia this morning. She says Solomon has begun to wind down the conspiracy."

"What about Mikhail? Did she say anything about Mikhail?"

"He's back in Moscow. It's almost as if he didn't leave. But she said we'd have no problems with him. He's under control."

"Whose control?"

"I don't know. I hadn't thought about it. What a good question."

"What about the five billion dollars. Are they going to give it back?"

"She didn't say anything about it. She wants to meet you this afternoon. Maybe she'll discuss it then. I'll bring her by about three."

"No you won't."

His smile disappeared. "Why?"

"I need you to make a trip for me, huh? I've arranged for a visa to Switzerland."

"What? Switzerland?"

"Yes. I need you to go to there and get something for me. Is it a problem for you?"

"No. Who do I see?"

"Gustav will meet you when you get off the plane." Alex pushed his head forward and stared at her. She continued, "He's going to give you a hard disk and some tapes. You get back on another plane and return to Moscow tomorrow. In the meantime, you can have dinner in Switzerland. Gustav will buy."

Alex opened his mouth to speak but stopped. Finally, he got his thoughts together. "Gustav held a gun in my face. I don't ever want to see him again. He was working with Carl. If it hadn't been for Gustav and Carl, we'd have the Israelis by the balls right now."

"Don't worry. Gustav likes you. He has some great stories. You'll have a wonderful time, trust me." She grinned at him, but he was still uncomfortable. "Tell Jenia I'll see her at three, in your office. I might as well make use of it." She looked at him and her face softened.

Alex said. "You and I made a good team, didn't we?"

She rose and walked to him, hugged him and said, "We sure did. We still do." They looked into each other's eyes for an awkward moment. The fire was there; they both knew it would never go out. She pulled herself away from him, kissed him on the cheek and said, "Have a nice trip. I look forward to your return."

Jenia arrived at three twenty. Tanya went to reception and led her to Alex's office. She showed her the picture Alex kept on his desk. They exchanged small talk for a few minutes and then Tanya asked, "Alex says Solomon is shutting down the conspiracy, huh?"

"Well, in a way. Jonah will no longer be in charge. There'll be no co-ordinated effort, but there seems no way anyone could prove they've broken a law. What used to belong to Solomon and Jonah now belongs to the men in Russia."

Tanya nodded her head. "Including Mikhail?"

"Yes, much as I hate the bastard, that was part of the deal. They'll all keep whatever money wasn't transferred to Switzerland. They're on their own now. No more financing or coordination."

"Well, I suppose in a few months they'll all be at each other's throats for real this time. What about the money that went to Switzerland?"

"There's no way the government can let Solomon have so much money. It would make him too powerful. We're trying to find a way to return it, but it seems impossible without exposing what happened. None of us wants that, do we?" Jenia stared into Tanya's eyes.

Tanya was calm. She perceived the Israeli plan as if it were written in front of her. Mikhail would be President of Russia, controlled by Jenia and her government. She thought for a minute and responded, "No. None of us wants this whole mess to become public, huh? I think the Russian silence is worth five billion, don't you?"

For a while Jenia did not respond, as if she wanted to be sure to say the right thing. "I remember our meeting in the park. I consider you a friend, not a foe."

Tanya smiled back at her. "You and I should not be on opposite sides."

"I would like to help in any way I can. But my employer has all the pictures you took. It will be hard to persuade them you have any proof for any accusations."

"Does your employer know I made two films?"

"Can you produce the second one?"

"No. Your Carl was not as good a friend as you thought. He's taken one home with him."

"That still leaves you without proof."

"If Carl can have a copy, I might have a copy too."

Jenia thought for a minute. "I can get into some trouble if I go along with this."

"You're both Russian and Israeli. You have two loves. I know how painful it can be. Let's assume," she smiled, "I have the proof I need. Can you convince them to cooperate if I can find a way to get back the money without exposing the conspiracy?"

"I'll work on it."

Tanya leaned back in her chair, as did Jenia. The tough part was over. It was time for other matters.

Tanya asked, "About Mikhail, how did it go?"

Jenia shook her head in disgust. "The man is a beast. He bragged about a teenaged girl Oleg kidnapped for him. She was wearing a small crucifix...."

Moscow – Monday, June 8

Alex, Tanya and Gustav sat at a table in the PHD conference room. Gustav had decided to come to Moscow with Alex, because he wanted to discuss some ideas for getting the money returned.

Alex turned to Tanya and said, "I asked Gustav why he held the gun on me, but he said you'd have to tell me."

Tanya glanced at Gustav, "Is it okay to tell him?"

"He'll burst if you don't. He was testy with me in Switzerland."

She said, "Gustav and I go back a way. He was with the Stasi in East Germany, even after he left the bank. We had worked together before. He was also being paid by the CIA."

Alex shook his head in amazement. "I am sure out of my league here."

Gustav said, "No you're not. You did a great job. If it hadn't been for you and your trip to Israel, we'd have lost Tanya."

Alex said, "You could've saved her by giving Jonah the film."

Tanya answered. "No, he couldn't. Mikhail controlled the whole situation. He didn't care about the film."

Alex shook his head, unconvinced.

Tanya continued, "I told Gustav about Carl. That's when I found out he knew him. We arranged to have Gustav contact Carl at exactly the right time to get involved. Once that happened, I was in control of the game."

Alex rolled his eyes. "You fooled me. I never felt we were in control of anything. Well, at least I never felt in control. I still don't." Gustav and Tanya laughed. Alex made a sourpuss face at Tanya and then broke into a big grin. Alex asked, "What are we going to do about the money? How can we possibly get it back without letting everyone else know what happened?"

Gustav said, "I've been studying the situation. I know how we can get the money back and no one will be the wiser. Alex, you'll deliver the instructions. Okay?"

Alex grinned from ear to ear, "I'd love to."

Jerusalem – Wednesday, June 10

Solomon was finishing his conversation with Jonah. "Yes, that's the agreement. Beginning today, start liquidating your positions at a rate that will avoid undue losses." He listened for a moment and then responded, "We don't have two or three months. We have one month, no longer." He waited again then added, "I knew you could do it. Take the proceeds and invest in Russian long-term government bonds payable in Rubles."

Even across the room, Alex heard Jonah's voice coming through the phone, "That's crazy."

Solomon kept calm. "Remember what you said when we embarked on this. If what we are doing ever becomes public we'll destroy the country we love? Well, that's our choice. Invest in Russia or make your fear come true." Solomon put down the phone and looked at Alex sitting in a chair across the room. "I'm no fool, and neither is Jonah. We're throwing money down a hole, aren't we?"

Alex responded, "Sometimes one has to make sacrifices to avoid a bigger disaster. Besides, these bonds pay a high interest rate. You'll be better off." Alex grinned.

Solomon laughed. "If I didn't know you were joking, I'd worry about you. Too bad you're not getting a commission on the sale of those government bonds."

Alex stood and bowed. "I am."

Solomon slowly pushed his aging frame out of his chair, came around his desk and shook hands with Alex. "I need a good man like you. Why don't you immigrate to Israel?"

"I'll give it some thought. I have to admit, there's no other country in the world that would have had the balls to try this."

Solomon's face became serious. "Few countries find themselves in our situation. We have to take drastic measures to survive. Survival is the strongest motivator, I think. Jenia, please buy a nice dinner for Alexander this evening."

Jenia took Alex by the arm and led him to the door. He stopped and turned to Solomon. "I beg to differ with you sir. The strongest emotion is love."

They left Solomon's office and Jenia said, "Are you hungry?"

He responded, not really. I'd rather go for a walk or get a cup of tea," he grinned, "or coffee."

"It sounds good to me. You know I'm always ready for coffee."

They sat at a small table for two in the corner of the almost empty shop. Alex raised his steaming cup and she touched it with hers. He said, "To a good friend and a fabulous lover."

She responded, "My words exactly." She took a sip, put her cup on the table and sat back. She gave him the Jenia look he knew so well. "Tell me. Will you actually get a commission on the sale of those bonds?"

He grinned sheepishly. "Yes, but it's not as great as it sounds. Gustav established a small company in Switzerland to handle the deal, and it will receive one percent in five-year, Russian-Ruble Government Bonds."

"God, Alex. That's about fifty million dollars for a commission. You're rich."

"Not so fast. Let's not divide the hide before the bear's caught. Remember, it's payable in rubles. Gustav says, and Jonah agrees by the way, by this time next year the Ruble will devalue by as much as five times. In dollar terms, we will have lost eighty percent of the face value on the bonds."

"Can't you hedge it?"

"I leave all of that to Gustav, but I doubt if we can hedge all of it at a reasonable price. Everyone expects a devaluation."

"So, Jonah's five billion will be worth about one billion when everything shakes out. It's not so bad, huh?"

His eyes widened. "Jesus, I hope you didn't pick up her habit."

She responded, "What do you mean?"

"Never mind. As to Jonah's billion, it's not as great as it sounds at first. According to the records, Genesis invested almost three hundred million, including expenses, into Russia to finance its operatives. After eight years they finish with a paltry billion. That's an annual return of only sixteen percent. They would have done better on the U.S. stock market with less risk and without endangering Israel."

"You seem to know a lot of details. You read those records quickly."

Alex blushed. "I get all my information from Tanya and Gustav. I haven't seen any records since Carl took away my microfilm."

She frowned, but let it pass. "What will you do with the money?"

"Well, it's not all mine. I own only twenty-five percent. Tanya owns twenty-five percent and Gustav fifteen. The other ten percent is for one-time administrative costs, including some nice directors' fees. Of course the stockholders are also directors."

"There seems to be twenty-five percent missing?"

"The remaining twenty-five percent is owned by a blind trust, with Gustav as nominee."

"Who's the beneficiary?"

He reached into his briefcase and handed her a small stack of papers. He said, "Please read these and sign them if you agree with the terms.

34

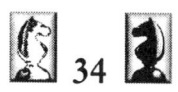

Moscow – Monday, August 17

Tanya was in the war room packing all the materials into boxes. The charts were gone from the walls and the flip charts had been removed. The door opened and Alex came rushing into the room holding a newspaper in front of his chest. The headline read, "Ruble Tumbles." He said, "Gustav was right about the coming devaluation. It's here. I'm surprised it came so fast."

She responded, "It's only the beginning. I'm sure the government will soon announce a default on government bonds. It won't be long and most banks in Russia are going to collapse, huh?"

He said, "I think the country is committing economic suicide. Those oligarchs and their cronies have ruined this country. I'm embarrassed."

She said, "We're not committing suicide. It's painful, but we'll be better off in the long run. It will be a fresh start. Who knows, maybe this time the companies will be owned by people interested in working for Russia rather than a foreign country."

Alex dropped the paper on the table. "I feel sorry for the babushkas and others who will lose their savings."

Tanya motioned for him to follow her and walked across the room to a television set. She turned it on until she found a business news channel. They listened to the commentators explain the devaluation and its effects for Russia and investors. In the background they saw pictures of long lines of people at banks and currency exchanges.

Alex said, "I feel sick." The broadcast switched to a reporter interviewing a small group of people standing in a currency exchange line. The reporter asked a man about his thoughts on possible bank closings.

The man responded, "I don't own any banks. I don't care if they all close down. I've never trusted them, never put my money in them. Never trust a bank." Others in the group nodded.

A woman said, "It's the foreigners. They come here with their money and fancy ideas. They give us all hope about freedom and capitalism. It doesn't work any better than the system we had before. I'm still standing in lines. I have no food. In fact maybe I'm worse off. Now I can't even afford the Bolshoi."

Another leaned toward the microphone and hollered, "It's the Jews."

Jerusalem – Monday, September 7

Jonah pushed open the door to Solomon's office. Solomon held a small letter in his hand and was concentrating on his chess game. He laid the letter on his table and reached for the white queen to take the black bishop.

Jonah tried not to disturb him. He walked quietly to the chair next to him and sat down. When Solomon looked up, Jonah spoke, "We've lost most of the dollar value on our Russian assets because of the devaluation."

Solomon shrugged his shoulders. He stood and walked to his desk. He opened a drawer and pulled out a large Cuban cigar. He walked back to Jonah and handed it to him.

"Have a cigar. It's not the end of the world. I know you Jonah. I'm sure we managed to squirrel away a few dollars someplace."

"We kept a little over a billion. Here are the documents and investment statements. I'm glad it's over." Jonah handed the files to Solomon and lit his cigar. He pointed to the chessboard. "How's the game coming along?"

Solomon shrugged again. "I was doing well until one of her pawns captured my queen. I captured hers in turn, but that same pawn made it to my end of the board and I had to promote it. She just took my rook and put me into check."

"Do you have any escape?"

"Yes, but I'll lose another piece. I thought I had her beat, but she managed to get a draw."

"I thought you said a draw wasn't so bad?"

"If you come back from certain defeat and get a draw it's not so bad. If you thought you were going to win, it's tough to swallow."

"You say she, who is she?"

"A Russian woman I met at a chess convention last January."

He handed Jonah the letter.

"Dear Solomon,

"I have received your latest move "!?" and my response of Nxa5+ is my only alternative. I assume you know the next move. I await your acceptance of a draw. It has been my pleasure to play you again. You are a worthy opponent. I look forward to more games in the future.

"Your friend,

"Tanya."

Moscow – Sunday, December 13

Tanya was sitting in her reception room with Kolya. They were playing a game of chess. Dmitry was sitting in a chair watching television. He rose from his chair and turned off the set. He came over to Tanya and massaged her shoulders.

He said to Kolya. "How's it going? Are you going to beat your mama again?" Kolya grinned and lifted Tanya's bishop from the board.

Dmitry said, "I was watching a political speech on the television."

Tanya said, "A speech. I'd be bored to death."

"I don't think so. It was Mikhail Kolodkin. He's dynamic. He'd make a good president. Women seem to like him. They say over sixty percent of women will vote for him. Imagine, from a professor to a multimillionaire. We need a good businessman to run the country. Look what a mess Yeltsin made of it."

She sat back in her chair and put her hands on his. "I'm going to Switzerland in a few days. I hope you don't mind. I'll be there for a day."

Zurich – Tuesday, December 15

Jonah was sitting in his chair. He took a long drag of his cigar and blew the smoke toward the ceiling. Two glasses of sherry were sitting on the table. The second glass belonged to Tanya.

He said, "I'm happy we had this chance to meet under more pleasant circumstances. I'm afraid I wasn't the best host the last time you were here."

She said, "We all have our roles to play. You played yours well. I'm sure if it hadn't been for you and Benjamin, I wouldn't be sitting here now."

He bowed his head. She saw tears forming in his eyes. He mumbled, "I swore to get even, but my hands are tied."

"He may become president you know."

"I know, but my hands are tied. I'm sure I don't have to spell it out for you."

"You seem bitter?"

"I loved Benjamin like a son. I lost my daughter years ago."

"Yes, I know. I'm sorry. I'm sure your daughter would have been a great success no matter what field she chose. Sometimes it's hard to understand the ways of fate."

"Or God."

"Speaking of God, I think there's something else you should know about Mikhail. It's a story Jenia told me. When they held him in Israel, Mikhail was bragging about how he came to own a crucifix...."

Moscow – Sunday, December 21

Alex felt Buddy's cold nose pushing against his own. He opened his eyes and saw two large brown ovals staring at him. "*Dobraye ootra*," he said as best his dry throat would allow. "How's my Buddy doing today?" Alex rolled to his side and scratched Buddy's head. The dog immediately rolled to its back and held its legs into the air. Alex spent the next five minutes rubbing and scratching its stomach. This had become a daily ritual at six in the morning. A thirty-minute walk always followed.

"I've got a new trip for you today Buddy. We're going to ride the Metro and visit Konstantin at the Knight Klub." The Klub was closed until mid afternoon, but Konstantin had suggested Alex visit and bring Buddy.

It was ten o'clock when Alex knocked on the door at the Knight Klub. A few moments later, Lidiya opened it. Alex broke into a big grin, "What are you doing here? I can't believe it."

She paid no attention to him. She reached for Buddy and lifted him away from Alex. "What a lovely puppy. Hello Buddy. I've heard all about you. You're beautiful." She kissed Buddy's head and squeezed him.

Alex stood at the door staring. Finally, she looked at him and said, "Sasha, it's nice to see you too. I'm a waitress here." Still carrying Buddy, she turned and led Alex into the Klub toward the bar where Konstantin was waiting.

He was pouring tea into two cups.

She shouted, "It's Alex and he brought Buddy." She pranced up to the bar and held Buddy for Konstantin to see. Then she continued to the doors in the back of the Klub.

Konstantin looked at Alex and said, "I heard you've eliminated at least one of your bad habits. I guess Buddy is a good influence on you."

Alex nodded. "I don't have time for anything anymore. Early in the morning I take him for a walk. When I get home at night, exhausted from playing chess at work, I feed him and take him for another walk."

Alex shook hands with Konstantin and took a seat. "How does it feel to be a business owner?"

Konstantin patted him on the shoulder, "Not bad. Not bad at all. Jenia told me you put in the good word for me. Thanks, I owe you."

"No you don't. You said you always wanted to run a sports bar. How's business?"

"It's great. I kept most of the old customers, and I've added many new ones."

"Do you miss the girls?"

"I hired some of them as waitresses. But I can't pay enough to keep most of them. They made too much with their dancing. I feel guilty in a way. For some of them, the ones from outside Moscow, it was a good living and better than prostitution."

Alex looked above the bar and grinned. "You kept the birdcage."

Konstantin laughed. "When I switched to a sports bar my customers told me if I removed the cage they wouldn't come back. Some of the guys drink at the bar and stare at the empty cage. Like a trophy, I guess. How is life with you?"

"I've only one complaint. I'm in love, but she belongs to another man."

Konstantin laughed, "Some things never change."

"I know you think it's funny, but it's painful. I never knew I could love somebody so much. This isn't like Jenia. Why do I have to be so unlucky?"

Konstantin said, "I'm sorry Sasha. I know it's not funny to you, and I know it's not infatuation. I told you that someday you would know what love is. Well, how do you like it?"

"It hurts. It hurts a lot."

"Someday you'll learn. Women are like fine works of art. They are best viewed from a distance."

Konstantin poured another cup of tea for each of them. They lifted their cups and clinked them over the table. Alex said, "Do you think it will happen again?"

"What? That you and Tanya will be together again? Hope is the last to die, Alex."

"No. Do you think we'll ever be a superpower?"

Epilogue

Moscow – Wednesday, January 6, 1999

The cold swirling wind blew the heavy snow into narrowing circles. It was seven in the evening on the eve of Russian Orthodox Christmas, and Tverskaya was decorated everywhere with colorful lights and banners. The rush hour was almost over. Most people on the street were walking quickly to the safety of the Okhotny Metro entrance near the National Hotel.

A man wearing a large fur coat exited the Ministry of Economics. He headed north along Tverskaya. His hat was pulled low. During a break in the traffic, he jogged across the street toward a line of women standing near the Intourist Hotel. One of the women had caught his attention.

Her coat was pulled tight around her. She wore no cap. Her short black curly hair was decorated with snow. Her skin was dark, Middle Eastern. She wore short boots edged with fur. She was stomping her feet to keep them warm. When he approached her, she was putting a shawl over her head.

He spoke to her for a few minutes. She followed him to a large black Mercedes parked along the street. The driver jumped from the car and held the rear door for them. Soon, the big car pulled into the street and was gone. No one paid any attention.

Mikhail pushed open the door to his flat, which was dimly lit and empty. The woman entered. She was young, maybe twenty-five. He offered to take her coat. She declined. Instead, she walked through the double sliding doors into the reception room. She threw her coat on a chair and fell onto the sofa. Her dress was short and Mikhail saw to the top of her legs when she sat down. She leaned back her head to rest it on the sofa.

He followed her into the room. She was perfect, exactly what he had been seeking for so long. His heart was beating quickly. His mind was racing with anticipation. "Can I get you anything?"

"Maybe a glass of tonic."

"No vodka?"

"No. I want only tonic, please."

He filled her glass, poured three fingers of vodka into his own glass and filled it with tonic. He took her the drink and handed her a towel to dry her hair. It was the blackest hair he had ever seen. It was short, but curly. Her skin was beautiful, so swarthy, blemish free.

She held her glass high in a salute before she drained it. He leaned toward her and kissed her. She responded. He heard his heart roaring in his ears. "We can see the whole city from my balcony."

"I'd love that," she whispered and attacked his mouth again. He stood, took her hand. She followed him into the bedroom, looked briefly at the rings and stopped at his credenza. She picked up the leather band attached to a wood crucifix and examined it. "Are you a Christian?"

"I'm not. It's a souvenir."

She replaced it on the credenza and followed him to the balcony. He swept his hand across the horizon. "In a few months, I'll rule the largest country in the world. Did you know I was so important?"

"Yes. I've seen your pictures."

Mikhail felt the power surging through his body. Sure there had been some problems. That was in the past now. He still had his money. He would soon be president. Jonah was gone. The past was forgotten. He deserved this one. She was so much like Jenia. This would be his final time. He'd need no more after this one. This was the end of his search.

Mikhail gazed at the girl. She was taking in the view. It was cold on the balcony, but still she stood there in her short dress. He offered, "It's cold out here. Let's go inside where it's warm. I am chilled and you are wearing so little."

She nodded. He turned to lead her into the room. Suddenly he was on his knees. She was behind him with her hand under his chin pulling his head back. He tried to struggle, but he was in an awkward position and couldn't get any leverage. She held him tight. He felt something cold against his neck, then a slight burning sensation. He was getting dizzy weak. She pushed him forward. Oh it felt so good to rest on the floor. He rolled over on his back and held his hands up to reach to her.

He thought he heard her say, "This from Jonah." His ears were ringing and he was tired. He felt better now, on his back. She was standing over him. He stared up her dress. He could see everything. She lifted her leg and stepped over him. He moved his eyes and watched her take the leather band with the crucifix. He noticed a large pool of blood on the floor, and he knew he would never be President of Russia.